Copycat

Copycat

A NOVEL

BETSY BRANNON GREEN

Covenant

Covenant Communications, Inc.

Cover illustration © Thinkstock/Getty Images, Inc.

Cover design copyrighted 2005 by Covenant Communications, Inc.

Published by Covenant Communications, Inc.
American Fork, Utah

Printed in Canada
First Printing: June 2005

11 10 09 08 07 06 05   10 9 8 7 6 5 4 3 2 1

ISBN 1-59156-920-6

To Tommy—who demands little and deserves much.
May the Lord grant you the righteous desires of your heart.

Acknowledgments

I owe the largest debt of gratitude to Butch and our children. They provide me with encouragement and support and inspiration. But mostly they give me the eternal incentive to strive to be all that I should be. I can't imagine what I ever did to deserve my association with all the wonderful people at Covenant. I am continually amazed by their patience, insight, and professionalism. I appreciate their efforts on my behalf. And last, but certainly not least, thanks to my readers, who take a chance on me every time they buy a book. I'm trying hard to live up to the confidence they show in me!

CHAPTER 1

Mark Iverson, resident agent for the FBI in Albany, Georgia, was shutting down his computer for the day when his secretary, Marla, knocked on the open door to his office. "Call on line one," she told him.

Mark raised his eyebrows. "I was supposed to be home thirty minutes ago. Can you take a message?"

"I could, but it's the warden of the Georgia Diagnostic and Classification Prison."

Knowing this call could not be ignored even though it was likely bad news, Mark reached for the phone. "Agent Iverson," he said into the receiver.

"Warden Slezak," a voice announced through the phone lines. "Sorry to call so late, but I have a death-row prisoner requesting an immediate audience with you."

In Mark's experience, wardens were rarely anxious to fulfill a prisoner's request, so it was with mild curiosity that he asked, "Does your prisoner want to see me as an agent of the FBI or as a bishop of the LDS Church?"

There was a brief pause, then the warden said, "I'm not sure. Can you be here at nine o'clock this evening?"

Mark stifled a groan as he checked his watch. It was a solid three-hour drive to Jackson, and in order to make it to the prison by nine, he'd have to leave immediately. "Can't we set it up for tomorrow?"

"That will be too late," the warden replied. "My prisoner is scheduled for execution at midnight."

Well, that explained the urgency and gave Mark a good idea why the prisoner wanted to see him—a last-minute confession. "Then I guess that settles it." As an afterthought he asked, "What's the prisoner's name?"

"Lyle Tweedy," the warden answered. "You may have heard of him. He's a serial killer who murdered five women."

Mark, like everyone else in the country, *had* heard of Lyle Tweedy. He had never been personally involved in the case, since Tweedy had tortured then murdered all his victims outside of Mark's jurisdiction. However, Mark had seen some of the documentation and couldn't think of anything much worse than having to listen to the man recount his many sins. But it was all a part of his job.

"I'll see you at nine," he told the warden, then disconnected the call and dialed his home number.

* * *

Eugenia Atkins stepped out of her enclosed back porch and into her kitchen. Then she flipped on the light before glancing through her mail. "*Occupant* gets more letters than I do," she muttered to herself. She spotted a purple envelope postmarked Honolulu, Hawaii, and a big smile spread across her face. "Well, I declare. What do we have here?"

"Talking to yourself again, Eugenia?" her sister Annabelle asked as she walked in without knocking. "You know that's one of the first signs of insanity."

"If I'm still in the early stages, I won't let it worry me too much," Eugenia returned absently. "Mila Edwards sent me a note all the way from Hawaii."

"That's Daphne Roper's daughter?" Annabelle clarified.

"Yes, the former policewoman who found a kidnap victim in the old gristmill while you and Derrick were tromping around the Holy Land."

Annabelle read the note over her sister's shoulder. "I hate that I didn't get to see her all grown up, but our trip to Jerusalem was fabulous."

"You know how Mama hated to hear you brag."

Annabelle looked offended. "I'm not bragging."

"Humph," Eugenia responded. She returned her attention to the letter. "Mila says the surfboard business is going well and . . . they're getting married!"

"Who?" Kate Iverson asked as she walked into the kitchen. Her children, Emily and Charles, followed closely behind their mother, both dressed in pajamas. Eugenia noted that Kate had circles under her eyes and her hair needed to be trimmed.

"Mila and Quin!" Eugenia explained, handing the note to Annabelle so she could kiss both children soundly. "How are my precious little darlings?"

"We're fine," Emily spoke for herself and her brother. "But it's bedtime, so we're coming to say good night."

"And I'm mighty glad you did," Eugenia replied. "How about a cookie?" She lifted the foil covering off a plate of homemade tea cakes. "These are fresh."

"They've already brushed their teeth," Kate complained as the children reached for a treat.

"And they can brush them again," Eugenia told Kate, then she turned and spoke directly to Charles and Emily. "Help yourselves."

While Eugenia settled the children at the table and poured them milk to go with their bedtime snack, Annabelle continued to read from Mila's note. "It says that they're planning a wedding in September at the Mormon temple in Hawaii."

"Well, good for them," Kate said with a weary smile as she took a seat beside Emily. "I'll have a glass of milk too," she told Eugenia, then reached for a tea cake.

"And all thanks to me!" Eugenia took the credit for successful matchmaking. "Well, I guess I did have a little help from O. Henry."

"O who?" Kate asked around a mouthful of cookie.

"O. Henry. He wrote a short story called 'The Gift of the Magi.'" Eugenia saw Kate's blank stare and waved a hand in dismissal. "Never mind." She took Mila's note back from Annabelle. "But I sure do wish I could go to that wedding."

"A trip to Hawaii does sound nice," Kate acknowledged, her tone wistful.

"Your wedding anniversary is coming up," Annabelle reminded Kate. "Why don't you ask Mark if you can celebrate it in Hawaii?"

Kate polished off her cookie and reached for another. "I'll be sure to tell him you suggested that."

Eugenia studied Kate through narrowed eyes, then said, "And speaking of Mark, where is he anyway?"

Kate shrugged. "Working late."

"Again?" Eugenia demanded. "I thought he promised to be home early tonight."

"He did," Kate said. "But something came up."

The sisters exchanged a knowing look. "Yes indeed," Eugenia said thoughtfully. "It sounds like a trip to Hawaii is what you need to rejuvenate your marriage."

"My marriage doesn't need rejuvenation," Kate told them. "And I don't mind when Mark has to work late."

"Humph," Eugenia responded. Then she quoted from a book she had been reading written by David O. McKay. "'No amount of success can compensate for failure in the home.'"

Kate seemed irritated by this. "Mark's not failing in his home. He's just fulfilling his other responsibilities."

Before further comment could be made on the subject, Emily asked, "Why are you all dressed up, Miss Eugenia?"

Eugenia smoothed the polyester fabric of her Sunday dress. "I just got home from a meeting of the Haggerty Garden Club," she explained. "And a mighty big waste of time it was too. I would have much rather been here playing with you and little Charles. If I'd known your daddy was working late *again,* I'd have come over to entertain you instead of going and listening to all those old biddies boast about their roses."

"Your roses are very pretty," Emily assured Eugenia.

"Why thank you, Emily," Eugenia said approvingly. "What beautiful manners you have. I guess we'll attribute that to your mother since your daddy is gone so much."

Kate's expression went from irritated to angry. "There will be no more criticism of Mark." She lowered her voice. "Especially in front of his children."

"Maybe we could *all* go to Hawaii for the wedding," Annabelle interrupted in an obvious attempt to steer the conversation to a safer subject.

"I would love to be there when Quin and Mila get married!" Eugenia exclaimed, then the excitement left her face. "But I'll bet that would cost a fortune!"

"It might not be as much as you might think," Annabelle mused.

"Widows like myself, who are all alone in the world, can't spend money foolishly," Eugenia told her sister. "We have to prepare for the days when we are aged and infirm and unable to care for ourselves."

Annabelle looked at Kate. "Is she saying that's a point in her *future?*"

Some of the anger left Kate's face as she smiled. "Well, she is still basically able to function."

"Make fun if you will," Eugenia told them. "But I cannot with good conscience spend money on nonessentials."

"A trip to Hawaii probably wouldn't cost much more than the ones we used to take to Florida every summer before The Arms closed down," Annabelle speculated. "Especially if several of us went together and split the expenses."

"How many people would we include?" Kate asked.

Annabelle shrugged. "The more people we have, the less the cost will be per person."

"Let's make a list of possibilities," Kate suggested.

"Well, there's you and Mark," Annabelle itemized. "And Eugenia, Derrick, and me. Then we could ask Miss Polly."

"That's six so far!" Eugenia calculated aloud.

"We could invite George Ann," Annabelle said with a smile. "She's got plenty of money."

"And she's mighty stingy about parting with any of it," Eugenia reminded them. "Besides, if George Ann comes on the trip, none of the rest of us will want to go."

Annabelle nodded in a rare moment of agreement with her sister. "That would sort of defeat the purpose."

"I'm volunteering at the library tomorrow," Eugenia told them. "Maybe I can look on the Internet and see how much it would cost to take a trip to Hawaii."

Kate picked up another cookie. "That's a good idea."

The phone started ringing, and Eugenia answered it. "Hello."

"Eugenia, this is Whit Owens," a familiar voice said from the other end of the line. Whit was an attorney, like his father before him, and had graduated from high school with Eugenia.

"Hey, Whit," she replied, then covered the receiver and whispered to her guests, "It's Whit Owens." Returning her attention to the caller, she asked, "What can I do for you?"

"We read Geneva Mackey's will this evening," Whit told her.

Eugenia frowned. "Well, it's about time. The funeral was almost a week ago."

"I know," Whit acknowledged. "Her grandnephew was out of the country and couldn't get here until today."

"I thought it was scandalous that he didn't attend the funeral," she told Whit, then whispered to her audience, "Geneva Mackey's grandnephew."

"He said it was something that couldn't be helped," Whit said, making a halfhearted effort to defend the young man.

Eugenia was disdainful of such a lame excuse. "Humph!"

Whit cleared his throat. "Anyway, Miss Geneva left you a bequest. Can you be in my office first thing in the morning to pick it up?"

Eugenia was stunned but pleased. "Well, certainly I can."

"I'll see you in the morning then," Whit said, and then he disconnected the call.

"What?" Annabelle demanded when Eugenia hung up the phone.

"Whit says they read Miss Geneva's will this evening and she left me a bequest."

Annabelle looked mystified by this announcement. "Why would Miss Geneva leave *you* anything?"

Eugenia shrugged. "I don't know. We were in the church choir together for years, and I brought her dinner a few times after she fell and broke her collarbone. It's probably just a doily or a photograph—something like that."

"Maybe it's money," Annabelle said, her eyes shining with mischief. "Enough to pay for all of us to go to Hawaii!"

Eugenia had to laugh. "I promise if Miss Geneva left me a bunch of money, my first stop when I leave Whit's office will be a travel agency in Albany."

Kate was smiling as she stood. "We've got to get home. It's past bedtime."

"And we have to brush our teeth again," Charles reminded them.

"He has such good dental hygiene," Eugenia praised as she covered up the surviving tea cakes. Then she lifted the little boy from his chair. "I'll carry Charles to keep him from getting his pajamas wet with the evening dew."

"That's a good idea," Kate acknowledged and held out her arms to Emily.

After they got the children home, rebrushed their teeth, and tucked them into bed, Kate invited Eugenia down to the kitchen for a cup of hot chocolate. Chocolate was the last thing Eugenia needed at this time of night, but she suspected that Kate was lonely, so she accepted. After all, she'd have plenty of time to sleep when she was in the grave.

Once they were settled around the kitchen table sipping hot chocolate, Kate asked, "How long has it been since you've had a cup of coffee?"

Eugenia shrugged. "Months."

Kate raised an eyebrow. "Is that all?"

"I haven't been keeping track, but somewhere along the way I kind of lost my taste for it."

Kate laughed softly. "When are you going to give in and admit that you want to be a Mormon?"

Eugenia winced. "I don't *want* to be a Mormon," she corrected. "I *want* to be a Methodist."

"But . . ."

Eugenia sighed. "But, I believe the Book of Mormon is scripture, just like the Bible."

"Mark says it's been his experience that dedicated Baptists and Methodists make some of the best Mormons."

Eugenia looked up. "He said that?"

Kate nodded. "He thinks it's because they were taught to love the Lord so thoroughly in their youth."

Eugenia stood and took her mug to the sink, hoping that Kate hadn't seen the sudden moisture in her eyes. "I don't want to rush into anything."

"Just don't take too long," Kate advised as Eugenia tore off a paper towel and dabbed her eyes. "Or you'll leave your fate in my hands."

Eugenia laughed. "That's an old threat."

Kate resumed her seat at the table. "But not an empty one." She pushed a lock of hair behind her ear. "I guess Brother Stoops is in Houston by now," she said, referring to their elderly home teacher.

"Yes, his daughter picked him up last Friday."

"I know. Mark and I took the kids over to say good-bye on Thursday afternoon. Not that he recognized us."

Eugenia sighed. "No, he rarely recognizes anyone now. But he's not in pain, and he's fortunate to have a daughter willing to assume responsibility for his care."

Kate nodded. "That's true. I just wish she lived closer. We're really going to miss him."

"Me too. It's a shame he has to spend his final days in confusion. He had such a wonderful mind."

"And a kind heart," Kate added, tears slipping over onto her cheeks.

"We shouldn't grieve. We should be giving thanks to the Lord that we had the privilege to know Elmer Stoops!"

Kate grabbed the paper towel from Eugenia's hand and pressed it against her face. "You're right." She returned the paper towel to Eugenia, who used it to staunch the flow of tears from her own eyes.

"I declare, I'm turning into Polly, crying like a baby. I haven't shed this many tears since I completed the change of life!"

Kate laughed. "And what's my excuse?"

Eugenia shook her head in mock disgust. "You've always been a crybaby."

Kate raised an eyebrow. "At least I'm not a coward."

Eugenia stood. "Well, after that ungracious remark, I think I'll see myself out."

* * *

Mark Iverson controlled a shudder as the prison guard ushered him into the interview room of the GDCP. He'd been uneasy since his phone call with the warden, and the feeling intensified during the drive north. Now, after passing through three metal detectors and being frisked twice, his nerves were taut with anxiety.

The guard directed him to a chair near the thick Plexiglas divider, and Mark sat down. He had to wait for several minutes before an inmate, clad in a bright orange jumpsuit, emerged through a door on the other side of the glass wall.

Lyle Tweedy was a small man, unimposing and seemingly harmless. It was hard to imagine he'd killed five women. Then he sat down, and Mark found himself staring into the coldest pair of eyes he'd ever seen. Instinctively he moved his chair back a couple of inches. Tweedy smiled, detecting the agent's discomfort.

"Thanks for coming on short notice," Tweedy said, although his tone was more mocking than appreciative. "At times like this a fellow really needs someone to talk to."

Mark studied the killer and wondered what the man wanted of him. "Are you a member of the LDS Church?"

Tweedy shook his head. "Naw, but studying religions is sort of a hobby of mine, one I've had plenty of time to indulge in lately." He waved his hand to encompass the prison. "I find the Mormons particularly intriguing. I was looking for someone to share my last night with, and when I found out that you're a Mormon bishop *and* an agent for the FBI . . . well, that made you irresistible."

"If you've studied my church then you know I can't offer you absolution for your sins," Mark told him.

"I don't want forgiveness," Tweedy assured him.

"And I doubt that anything I can tell you about the next life will be of much comfort to you."

Tweedy laughed, and the sound, amplified through the speaker, made a chill run down Mark's spine. "I don't want comfort either. I want you to help me set the record straight."

"The record?" Mark questioned.

"You know that I'm convicted of killing five women?"

Mark nodded.

Tweedy let his eyelids fall shut and smiled. "Such sweet memories," he crooned, then opened his eyes and stared at Mark. "Unfortunately, the number is a little off."

Mark felt helpless fury build within him. "You really killed more than five innocent women?" he demanded through clenched teeth.

Tweedy laughed again, and Mark clutched the sticky counter in front of him to keep from pounding on the glass.

"Actually, that's true. I had eight special *friends,* not five."

Mark reached into his coat pocket and removed a small notebook and pen. "Give me their names and the location of the bodies."

Tweedy shook his head. "I've already prepared a list for my lawyer so their next of kin can have some closure. Don't you think that's nice of me?"

There was nothing *nice* about Lyle Tweedy. "I think you must have another reason for admitting to the additional murders besides concern for their families."

"I like things neat and tidy. Inaccuracies drive me *crazy!*" Tweedy widened his eyes in an exaggerated maniacal expression.

Mark put his notebook away. "And why am I here?"

"Because I didn't murder one of the women I am convicted of killing."

Mark blinked, his tired brain assimilating the information. "You killed eight women," he repeated and Tweedy nodded. "But one of the five women you were convicted of killing was not one of your victims."

Tweedy looked pleased with Mark's shocked reaction. "Very good, Agent Iverson. You're obviously a quick study."

Mark ignored the sarcasm in Tweedy's voice. "So why didn't you say something sooner—like while you were on trial?"

Tweedy shrugged. "One more death sentence wasn't going to make any difference, and I preferred spending my days in the court-room to sitting in my cell—so I played along."

"And now that you've decided to set the record straight, why didn't you just tell your lawyer about that too?"

"I felt that it was my duty as a citizen to let someone in *law enforcement* know—personally," Tweedy said, his evil grin returning. "Now *you* get to decide what to do with the information."

Mark considered this. Apparently, Tweedy wanted to continue his lifetime of torture from the grave. So he was giving Mark a moral dilemma. The woman was dead, her family had grieved and moved on. If he reopened the case, they would suffer more. But if he didn't, someone would get away with murder.

"What was her name?" Mark demanded as he pulled the little notebook back out.

"Erica Helms." Tweedy's lips turned up in an evil smile again. "Isn't that a beautiful name? I wish I *had* gotten a chance to meet her."

Mark pushed his chair away from the glass wall and stood.

"Leaving so soon?" Tweedy asked.

"You've played with me long enough."

"But I still have almost an hour before my final meal," Tweedy whined. "I thought you might want to hear about all my special friends."

Mark turned and hurried to the door. "That's the last thing I want to do," he replied, then knocked for the guard to let him out.

"I'll see you in your dreams!" Tweedy called after him.

Mark shuddered and hurried down the hall—very much afraid that Lyle Tweedy was right. He'd probably be haunted by this experience for many months to come.

By the time Mark pulled into his driveway in Haggerty, it was almost midnight. Kate had left a light on in the kitchen and dinner in the microwave, but he couldn't eat. He scraped the food into the garbage can and rinsed his plate, then headed upstairs. After kissing both his children, he tiptoed through the master bedroom, where Kate was sleeping soundly, and into the bathroom. He stripped off his clothes and put them in the hamper, then took a long, hot shower— trying to rinse away the odor of the prison and the unclean feeling that came from proximity to Lyle Tweedy.

When he finally climbed into bed, Kate rolled over and put her arms around him.

"You're home," she murmured drowsily.

"Yes." He pulled her close, savoring her warm softness.

"Love you," she said, then burrowed her face into the hollow of his neck and fell back asleep.

As Mark held his wife, he stared into the darkness and tried not to think about Lyle Tweedy or the women he murdered or the one that he said he didn't kill.

* * *

On Wednesday morning Eugenia left her house at seven fifteen and walked briskly into town. Although she had no reason to suspect that Geneva had left her anything more than a worthless keepsake, throughout the night her imagination had run wild. What if Geneva had been secretly rich? Maybe she'd hoarded proceeds from playing the stock market or from the covert purchase of a winning lottery ticket.

Eugenia was shaking her head in self-disgust as she leaned down to pull a dandelion out of Polly Kirby's yard.

"Morning, Eugenia," Polly called from the front porch. Eugenia looked up in surprise.

"You're up mighty early," she remarked.

Polly giggled, causing her several chins to ripple. She had always been chubby, but a recent hip replacement surgery and the requisite bed rest combined with Haggerty hospitality had resulted in several unneeded pounds. "My friend Lucy is coming to visit me today. You remember, the cook from The Arms."

Eugenia nodded. "I remember. I guess the two of you will be exchanging recipes and cooking up a storm." *And eating yourselves into the next larger dress size,* she thought to herself.

Polly pulled a handkerchief from the neck of her floral print dress and dabbed perspiration from her flushed face. "Lucy wants to try a low-carbohydrate diet and thinks if she had a partner, she'd be more likely to stick to it. So she asked me to help her."

Eugenia raised her eyebrows, pleased with Lucy's tact and wisdom. "That was mighty nice of you to volunteer to support her."

Polly blushed. "Well, what are friends for?"

Eugenia frowned. "I hope it's not one of those fad diets where you only eat oranges for a day, then pineapple the next. Those things can be dangerous."

Polly laughed. "No, nothing like that. It's a special diet Lucy's doctor gave her for women who have passed the first bloom of youth."

Eugenia examined her friend. Polly was well past several blooms of youth. "How long will she be staying?"

"For a week or two. Lucy's son Tyrone is driving her up in his new Cadillac. I've never ridden in a Cadillac before. Have you?"

Eugenia gave this some consideration. "I rode in a Lincoln Town Car once but never in a Cadillac." She looked down the empty street.

"You want me to wait here with you till Lucy arrives?"

"Oh no!" Polly declined. "I'm sure you've got better things to do."

"I do have an appointment this morning," Eugenia admitted. "So I guess I'll go on. Good luck with your diet." With a wave, Eugenia left Polly and hurried into town. She didn't realize she was still holding the dandelion until she pushed open the door to Whit Owens's law office. She saw Idella Babcox, Whit's receptionist, sitting behind a nice desk with a tissue pressed against her nose. Eugenia extended the hand that held the dandelion. "Is there a garbage can where I can put this?"

Idella pointed toward the door. "Throw it outside. My allergies are in an uproar as it is. All I need is weed pollen floating around in here."

Eugenia reopened the door and deposited the wildflower on the sidewalk. Then she returned to the receptionist's desk and said, "I didn't think you'd be in this early, Idella."

"I've been basically working around the clock for the past week and a half." Idella blew her nose violently, then stood. "Whit is waiting for you."

Idella led the way down a hall and through a small conference room. As they walked, Eugenia mused that life was strange. Whit, Eugenia, and her husband, Charles, had been the best of friends in high school. She and Charles had often double-dated with Whit and whatever girlfriend he'd had at the time. But in all the years since graduation, she hadn't had much contact with Whit.

"This is it." Idella gestured toward the room at the end of the hall with her soggy tissue.

Idella paused by the door, allowing Eugenia to pass inside. "Morning, Whit," Eugenia greeted her old classmate.

Whit stood and came around his desk to give her a little hug. "You're looking wonderful, Eugenia!" he said.

"Why thank you," she returned demurely, noting that Whit wasn't looking half-bad himself. Tall and athletic in his youth, he was still tall, trim, and had most of his hair—which for a man in his seventies was equivalent to gorgeous.

"Thank you so much for coming," he said.

"I came first thing, just like you told me," Eugenia replied, hoping this would prompt him to get to the point of her visit immediately without the usual small talk.

"Have a seat," Whit invited. "Can we get you some coffee?"

So she wasn't going to be able to avoid the small talk. Eugenia sat in the chair Whit offered. "No, thank you very much."

"Well, I believe I'll have some," he said to Idella, who was still hovering by the door. "And some doughnuts if we have any." Whit pulled a chair up beside Eugenia's. "How have you been?"

"Just fine," she assured him, then searched for a safe question. Whit had been married several times, and she wasn't sure about his current marital status, so she didn't dare ask about his wife. And she couldn't remember the total number of offspring his various spouses had produced, so she kept her polite inquiry general. "How are your children?"

"Good, very good. Thanks for asking. Your garden looks particularly bountiful this year."

She nodded in gracious acknowledgment. "That late freeze last spring scared me to death, but everything came through it just fine."

Idella returned and handed her boss a coffee mug. "No doughnuts," she reported. "I can run and get some if you want."

Whit shook his head. "Don't bother."

The suspense was building, and only years of good Southern etiquette training kept Eugenia from screaming *What did Geneva leave me?* Then she heard a little scratching noise from behind Whit's desk. Afraid the lawyer might have an undetected rodent problem, she asked, "Did you hear that?"

Whit smiled. "I did indeed."

"It's Miss Geneva's miniature dachshund." Idella pointed to the far side of the room. "It was a gift from her grandnephew."

Eugenia squinted enough to see a little basket shoved into a corner. Peeking over the wicker edge was the smallest, most pitiful canine specimen her eyes had ever beheld.

Eugenia looked down at the small heap of matted fur. "Why? As some kind of cruel joke?"

"Oh, no," Whit assured her. "He gave Miss Geneva the dog so she wouldn't be alone."

Eugenia stood and walked closer and studied the poor thing. "We had a dachshund when I was a child, but it didn't look anything like that."

Whit came to join her by the basket. "She's of the fairly rare wire-haired variety."

The dog was roughly the size of a malnourished, elongated rat and not quite as appealing.

"Is it a puppy?" Eugenia asked, still trying to make conversation.

"Oh, no," Whit said. "It's full grown."

Eugenia wasn't sure she believed him. "Humph."

"And now she belongs to you!" the lawyer announced cheerfully.

"Me?" Eugenia cried, aghast.

"Miss Geneva left you the dog in her will," Idella said from the doorway.

"Her name is Lady von Beanie Weenie Mackey," Whit provided helpfully.

The dog looked up at Eugenia with woeful eyes.

"She's not much to look at, but the grandnephew said she cost a small fortune," Whit commented.

"And maybe she'd look better if you had her groomed or shaved or something," Idella suggested.

"I don't want a pet," Eugenia said, then regretted her words as the little dog lowered her scruffy head. "I mean, I'm sure we can find it a nice home."

"You can sell it or give it away or take it to the animal shelter, but please just get it out of here," Idella begged. "I've been taking care of it since Miss Geneva died, and all that hair is playing havoc with my allergies."

Eugenia had no plans to take the poor animal anywhere. Whit was Miss Geneva's lawyer, and she figured he could find a home for it. She opened her mouth to tell him so, but Whit spoke first.

"Geneva wanted *you* to have the dog, Eugenia. She told me so personally."

Eugenia didn't try to hide her confusion. "Did Geneva say why in the world she would want me to have her dog?"

Whit put a finger to his chin and considered this. "Let's see. She said the dog was an excellent companion and she thought you needed company."

Eugenia did not appreciate this remark. "The very idea!"

"She also said that you were the ultimate champion of the underdog," Whit told her. "And if anyone ever needed a champion— that poor dog does."

Eugenia couldn't help but be a little pleased by Geneva's favorable evaluation of her character, and she had to agree that the dog needed support. But she had no intention of taking responsibility for a pet, ugly or otherwise. "It sounds to me like Geneva got senile at the end," she told Whit.

"No," he assured her. "Geneva was just as clearheaded as ever, right up to her last breath."

"She left her nest egg to the Albany Humane Society," Idella contributed. "If you call *that* clear headed."

Whit frowned. "Maybe you *could* go and get some doughnuts," he said to Idella. The receptionist looked abashed and headed down the hall, sneezing as she went. After she was gone, Whit cleared his throat. "I handle a lot of final requests, Eugenia, and I've come to consider them almost sacred. The person making them usually puts a lot of thought into what they ask, and, well, I think you'll regret it if you don't at least give the poor dog a try."

With a sigh of resignation, Eugenia leaned down and picked up the little basket. "Geneva left her money to the Humane Society and you to me," she said, and the scraggly dog bent its head in apparent apology. "All right, Whit, but this is just a trial period. Chances are I'll be making a trip to the pound within a week."

He bestowed a beaming smile of approval on her. "I knew you would honor Geneva's wishes." He picked up an envelope from his desk. "Here are the registration papers and veterinarian records," he said. Eugenia accepted the paperwork, and as they walked toward the front door, Whit added, "You won't regret this."

"That shows how much you know," she told the lawyer. "I already do."

* * *

After a largely sleepless night, Mark finally dozed off at dawn. The kids woke him an hour later. "Mama's got pancakes and sausage and orange juice," Emily informed him. "And she said you'd better hurry and get up or you'll be late for work."

Mark forced himself onto an elbow. "And what if I don't mind being late for work?"

Emily gave this some consideration then said, "You still better hurry before Charles eats it all!"

He examined Charles, who had a generous smear of syrup on his left cheek. "I guess waiting would be dangerous." He stood and swung his son up into his arms, leaving a safe distance between the child's sticky cheek and the bedsheets.

When they reached the kitchen, Kate wiped the little boy's face with a damp paper towel, then sent the children into the family room to watch cartoons. Mark helped himself to the stack of pancakes.

"Miss Polly's starting a diet today," Kate informed him.

"That's good."

"Well, for her maybe. I don't think its right for us to let her cook dinner on Sunday if she can't eat it."

"I guess that's true. So, what will we do?"

"I *can* cook," Kate reminded him as she sat in a chair beside him, tapping the front page of the paper. "They finally executed that horrible Lyle Tweedy," she said.

Mark glanced at the large picture of Tweedy smiling at the camera and felt the pancakes in his mouth turn to sawdust. Averting his eyes, he picked up his glass and took a big swig of orange juice. Before he could tell Kate about his meeting with the convicted murderer, the phone rang and Kate jumped up to answer it.

"It's my mother!" she told him.

He nodded and turned the newspaper over so he didn't have to look at Lyle Tweedy while he ate. Then he concentrated on the pancakes until Kate ended her phone conversation.

"So, what did your mother have to say?" he asked.

Kate frowned. "Kelsey is on her way here," she said, referring to her twenty-four-year-old sister.

Mark put down his fork. "Now?"

Kate nodded. "Mother said her plane leaves Salt Lake at noon."

"Is her husband coming with her?"

"No."

Mark gave Kate his full attention. "And to what do we owe this unexpected visit?"

"I don't know," Kate replied, chewing her bottom lip. "Mother was vague, which either means she doesn't know or she wants Kelsey to explain it to me personally."

"Maybe she thinks it's not any of our business," Mark suggested as he stabbed the last piece of sausage and transferred it to his plate.

Kate laughed. "Yeah, right." She squeezed his shoulder then headed for the doorway. "I've got to get the guest room ready for Kelsey. Her plane arrives in Albany at seven fifteen tonight. Can you pick her up on the way home from work?"

"I get off at five o'clock," he reminded her.

She glanced back over her shoulder. "You haven't made it home before seven in weeks."

He acknowledged this with a wry smile. "I'll pick her up."

"Let me know if you get involved in something important," Kate requested. "I'm sure Miss Eugenia can watch the kids long enough for me to run into Albany."

He promised, then watched her disappear into the hallway, intent upon unexpected housework. It wasn't until she was gone that he remembered Lyle Tweedy and the fact that he'd forgotten to mention his brief contact with the dead man to Kate. Glad that she didn't have to share even a portion of that awful experience, he finished his breakfast, then went upstairs to dress for work.

CHAPTER 2

Eugenia had no idea what was required to keep Geneva's little dog alive, much less healthy, while she decided what to do with it. So on the way home from Whit's office, she stopped by Donaldson's Feed and Seed. The owner, an unkempt man in his forties, was behind the counter.

"What you got there, Miss Eugenia?" Roscoe Donaldson asked with a curious glance into the basket.

"It's Geneva Mackey's dog," she told him, at which point he promptly threw his head back and laughed.

"I wondered who'd end up with that little runt." He leaned down and spoke directly into the basket. "Hey Miss von Beanie Weenie Mackey."

Eugenia shuddered at the unwieldy name. "Lady," Eugenia corrected him.

Roscoe scratched his head. "You changed her name?"

"No," Eugenia told him in exasperation. "She's not *Miss* von Beanie Weenie Mackey, she's *Lady* von Beanie Weenie Mackey." Eugenia frowned. "Although that's just as bad."

"If she's your dog now, I guess you can call her whatever you want," Roscoe pointed out.

"You are absolutely right, Roscoe." *For once in your life,* she thought to herself. "And I think that from now on she's going to be called just plain Lady."

Roscoe looked disappointed. "The other name is more fun to say."

"Since that catchy name is now available, feel free to get yourself a dog and use it." Eugenia pointed to the rows of pet food. "Tell me what to feed Lady."

"Can't help you there," Roscoe replied as he pulled out a pocketknife and began cleaning his fingernails. "Miss Geneva bought birdseed here, but she got that little thing special food from a vet's office in Albany. You'll have to check with them."

Eugenia frowned. "Well, what if she's hungry now?"

"Get some of that canned stuff at the Piggly Wiggly," Roscoe suggested. "That should tide her over until you can get to the vet."

* * *

When she got home, Eugenia checked through the papers Whit had given her and found the name of Lady's veterinarian in Albany. She called, and they graciously arranged an emergency appointment for the following day. "There's no telling how much an emergency appointment at the veterinarian costs," Eugenia muttered as she opened a can of Piggly Wiggly–brand dog food. Lady sniffed it and whimpered. "I know it's not what you're used to," Eugenia apologized. "But it's the best I can do for now."

The little dog ate a few quick bites, in an obvious effort to please, then looked up at Eugenia.

"That's a good girl," Eugenia said with a smile.

Lady barked once, then walked over to her basket and climbed inside.

The back door opened then slammed, and seconds later Annabelle appeared in the kitchen. "I can't stay!" she said breathlessly. "But I had to stop by and find out what Geneva left you in her will!"

Eugenia gestured toward the basket. "Annabelle, meet Lady, my inheritance."

Annabelle seemed speechless for a few pleasant seconds.

"She's a rare kind of dachshund—very expensive," Eugenia informed her sister. "I just made an appointment for her with a veterinarian in Albany where I can buy her special food."

Annabelle regained her composure and said, "But you hate dogs. *Especially* weenie dogs."

"Don't mind Annabelle," Eugenia told the dog. "She is often mistaken, like now. I do not hate dogs."

"That weenie dog we had when we were kids bit you," Annabelle reminded her.

"That was your fault," Eugenia returned. "You did everything you could to make that dog like you better than me."

"Ridiculous," Annabelle scoffed.

"Well, now I have my own dog, and she likes *me* best." Eugenia picked up the dog basket. "It's too bad you can't stay," she added without sincerity as they walked together toward the back door.

"While you're at the vet's you should get her dipped," Annabelle advised. "She looks like she has fleas!"

Lady stood in the basket and turned circles in agitation.

Eugenia said to the dog soothingly, "Annabelle's just jealous that she doesn't have a fine dog like you."

Lady seemed to consider this, then sat down and rested her head on her tiny paws.

"I've never been jealous of you a day in my life!" Annabelle said. "And if I was going to start it wouldn't be over that hideous little dog!"

"Good-bye!" Eugenia called out. Then she watched Annabelle walk across the yard, climb into her car, and drive away. Then Eugenia headed across the lawn toward the Iversons' house. "Come on, Lady," she told the dog. "I'll introduce you to some *nice* people."

* * *

As soon as Mark got to his office, he placed a phone call to the state capitol in Atlanta. He was sorting his mail a few minutes later when the call was returned.

"You need me, Bishop?" Jack Gamble, a recently appointed Georgia state senator and part-time resident of Haggerty, asked through the phone line. Before his foray into politics, Jack had been a very successful criminal lawyer.

"I'm not sure what or who I need, so I decided to start with you," Mark replied.

Jack laughed. "Good. You know how I love a challenge."

"Speaking of challenges, how are Beth and the kids?"

"They're all great," Jack reported. "The baby's teething so we're not getting a lot of sleep, but otherwise I can't complain."

"Sleepless nights are a huge part of parenthood."

Jack laughed. "That's true."

"When do you come home?"

He heard Jack sigh. "If they don't extend this special congressional session, we should be back by the end of the month. Although that's a big *if.*" There was a slight pause, then Jack added, "I know you didn't call me on FBI time to chat about Beth and my children."

"No," Mark conceded. "I need an opinion. With your legal background and membership in the Church, I felt like you could help me the most."

"So what's the problem?"

Mark briefly outlined his visit with Lyle Tweedy and the information the dead man had left in his hands. When he finished, Jack murmured, "So based on what Tweedy told you, this other woman's death could have been a copycat murder."

"That's what I'm thinking. If you want to kill someone but don't want to draw any attention to yourself, you set it up to look like a serial killer was responsible."

"And now you have to decide whether to even report this unsubstantiated and possibly confidential hearsay."

"I'm obligated to report it," Mark told him.

"Even though reporting it might ruin your career?"

Mark was surprised. "How?"

"Because people don't like being told they were wrong, and you'd be telling a *lot* of important people that they made *big* mistakes. Law enforcement personnel on the local and federal level, judges, a jury . . ."

"I understand that," Mark interrupted. "But I can't suppress evidence."

"What you have isn't evidence," Jack objected. "It's the word of a killer. If Tweedy murdered eight women, I don't have any trouble believing that he might have also been a liar."

Mark rubbed the back of his neck in frustration. "That's for someone else to decide. The fact is he did tell me and I have to report it."

"Then file your report quietly and forget about it," Jack advised.

"If I don't press the issue, it will never be investigated."

"Exactly," Jack agreed.

"And someone will get away with murder."

"People get away with murder all the time. You've been with the FBI long enough to know that."

"People may get away with murder," Mark conceded. "But never because I looked the other way."

Mark heard Jack sigh. "You're still wearing those rose-colored glasses. Take it from someone who used to be one of the bad guys. Leave this alone, Mark. It's nothing but trouble."

"I can't."

"Of course not." Jack didn't sound pleased or surprised. "So here's some more advice. File your report and then if you must investigate, do so discreetly. Hopefully, when the press gets wind of this story— which they will—you'll have a nice, tidy solution to give them. Then, if you're really lucky, they'll focus on the sensational new case instead of trying to crucify everyone involved in the false conviction."

"And if they don't . . ."

"Then you will become Tweedy's final victim."

There was a brief pause, then Mark asked, "Do you think Tweedy was telling me the truth, or is this just a sick game he's playing from the grave?"

"The man was insane," Jack returned. "I don't know what went on in his mind and I don't care. I just want you to play this *smart*."

"I'll do my best."

"If I can help in any way . . ."

Mark laughed. "Without sacrificing *your* career? I don't think so."

"Well, at least keep me posted."

"Once I file my report it would be unwise for us to discuss the case," Mark told him.

"Then I guess you'll have to fill me in on the details when it's all over."

"Unless you see it on the ten o'clock news first," Mark muttered. "Thanks for listening."

"Anytime." After a short pause, Jack added, "Be careful."

"I will," Mark promised, then ended the call.

* * *

When Eugenia arrived at the Iversons' house, she knocked once on the back door, then stepped into the laundry room. "Helloooo!"

she called. No one answered, so she continued through the kitchen and into the family room, where she found Emily and Charles watching *Sesame Street* while Kate folded clothes.

"What do you have there?" Kate asked, looking up from her basket of towels and sheets.

"Kate, meet Lady. Lady, Kate," Eugenia introduced.

The children abandoned the television and came over to see the dog.

"She's very little," Charles said after further introductions had been made.

"And I think you need to comb her hair," Emily pointed out.

"Where did you get her?" Kate asked.

"Lady is my inheritance from Miss Geneva Mackey," Eugenia explained.

Kate laughed. "This is what Mr. Owens called about last night?"

Eugenia nodded. "Yes."

"Can I hold her?" Emily asked.

Eugenia sensed some anxiety from Lady. "She's a little nervous, so I think it would be best if you just hold the basket for now."

Kate watched as Eugenia settled the basket into her daughter's lap. "I don't guess it has fleas or anything like that?"

"Of course Lady doesn't have fleas! The very idea." Eugenia reached over and rubbed the dog's wiry pelt. "So what brought on this flurry of house cleaning?"

"My sister Kelsey is coming to stay with us for a while," Kate replied, the happiness obvious in her voice. "So I'm getting the guest room ready for her."

Eugenia narrowed her eyes in Kate's direction. "I don't remember you mentioning that she was planning a visit."

"I didn't mention it because I didn't know," Kate replied.

"Ahhh," Eugenia said with sudden understanding.

"What?" Kate demanded.

"She must be having marriage troubles."

Kate seemed annoyed by this observation. "Why do you say that?"

"Because you didn't mention the husband coming with her and you said she's staying for 'a while,'" Eugenia replied. "That sounds like marital discord to me."

Kate shrugged. "I won't know until I get a chance to talk to Kelsey. But you're right—it doesn't sound good."

"Well, there's no point in borrowing trouble. Wait until you know for sure before you start worrying." Eugenia glanced over at Charles and Emily, who were admiring Lady. Charles stuck his finger in front of the dog, and Lady licked him, causing both children to giggle. "I'll bet your sister is anxious to see the children."

Kate smiled. "I hope she is, because I plan to take advantage of having a built-in babysitter."

Eugenia felt a little pang of misgiving. "You know I'm always glad to babysit."

"But now we won't have to bother you," Kate replied.

Eugenia nodded reluctantly. "I guess having Kelsey here will be convenient."

"Very," Kate agreed. "Miss Polly's got company."

"I know. I saw her waiting for Lucy to arrive in a Cadillac."

Kate smiled. "Tyrone gave them a ride around town in his car, then Lucy convinced Miss Polly to walk to the grocery store."

"Polly walked?" Eugenia confirmed. "All the way to the grocery store?"

"Just to the Piggly Wiggly," Kate replied. "It's part of their weight-loss program. To help with that, Lucy brought Miss Polly a nice pair of walking shoes as a gift."

"That Lucy is even smarter than I realized," Eugenia murmured. Polly was much too polite to refuse a gift and would feel obligated to use the shoes as a way of showing appreciation.

"That does pose one little problem for us, though," Kate added. "It doesn't seem fair to let Miss Polly cook for us on Sunday when she has to eat dietetic foods." Kate lifted an armload of sheets. "With Kelsey we'll be quite a crowd, so I was thinking that I could just cook my own Sunday dinner here. That will take most of the work out of the meal for Miss Polly."

Eugenia was not about to give up her Sunday afternoons with Emily and Charles just because Polly was pretending to be on a diet. "That will be too much trouble for you. We'll eat at my house," she said firmly.

"That will be a lot of trouble for *you*," Kate pointed out.

Eugenia smiled. "I've been needing to clear off my dining room table for a decade. Now I have an excuse."

"I'll be glad to bake a pie or something," Kate offered. "It won't be as good as one of Miss Polly's, but then no one's is."

"I'm a decent cook myself," Eugenia told Kate. "I've been in retirement too long. It's time I show you what I can do."

Kate laughed. "I'll be looking forward to that. But right now I've got to get clean sheets on the bed for Kelsey." Kate lifted her clean laundry and moved toward the stairs. "Good luck with your pet."

"Lady's so wonderful I don't need luck," Eugenia said to Kate's back. Then she kissed the kids, collected Lady, and headed home.

* * *

Mark typed his report on Lyle Tweedy three times before he was satisfied with the wording, then he put it in an interoffice envelope and addressed it to Dan Davis, the field agent supervisor in Atlanta. As he relinquished the envelope to the mail bin, he had a feeling that Jack Gamble was right. Nothing more would come of his visit with Lyle Tweedy unless he pressed the issue. So he dialed Dan's number.

When Dan answered, Mark explained his meeting with Lyle Tweedy and the concerns Jack had raised, although he didn't attribute them to the state senator by name.

"Yeah, I can see how this is a real sticky problem," Dan said once Mark was finished. "What do you plan to do?"

"I'd like to carry on a low-key investigation and see what I can find out about Erica Helms and her death."

There was a pause, then Dan said, "Keep it very low-key and be prepared to drop it if you step on the wrong set of toes."

Mark wasn't exactly pleased with this response, but knew he could have been ordered off the case completely. "I'll be careful," he promised.

Dan said good-bye. Mark noticed as he hung up that Dan didn't offer any assistance or ask for updates. Before starting the monthly reports that he knew would take him most of the day to complete, he asked Marla to request an in-depth background check on Erica Helms.

"Are you looking for anything special?" Marla wanted to know.

"Whatever you can come up with will be helpful," Mark replied. "How long will it take?"

"Depends on how busy the system is," she replied.

He turned to his office. "Well, please bring it to me when you get it."

He spent the rest of the morning on the reports, and when Marla returned from lunch, Mark asked about the information on Erica Helms.

"Nothing yet," she told him.

Disappointed, Mark returned to his paperwork, but his mind kept straying to Erica. Finally he pushed aside the monthly mileage statement and ran Erica's name through an Internet search engine.

Most of the information that printed out related to Lyle Tweedy and his trial for her murder, but there was a little bit of personal information on Erica herself. She was from Patton Chapel, a small town seventy miles south of Albany. At the time of her murder she was thirty-four years old and a widow. Her husband and both her children had been killed in a car accident two years before her death. Her strangled body was found in the pond behind her house four months after she had disappeared. As Mark read about Erica Helms and her sad life, he was consumed with sympathy for her. He became determined to find out who killed her and to bring the guilty party to justice.

Then he scanned the newspaper articles that detailed Tweedy's various trials. He found no new information, but when he finished, he felt like he knew Lyle Tweedy better. The man was a heartless psychopath who argued the case for capital punishment better than any lawyer could.

Mark was staring at his computer screen when Marla walked in and put a printout on his desk. "Here's the information you requested on Erica Helms."

"Thanks," Mark said, reaching for it.

She nodded and returned to her desk while Mark started reading the report. According to a summary of the autopsy, Mrs. Helms's body was badly decomposed and had been further damaged by wildlife in and near the pond. Her face was essentially gone, so she was identified with dental records and prints from two fingers that had partially survived four months in the warm pond full of catfish.

Mark had to force himself to read the distasteful details and was relieved when he got to the bank statements. This was his area of expertise. A quick review told him that before tragedy struck, the Helms family had been financially secure, if not rich. Erica was a part-time dental hygienist, and her husband managed the local Honda plant. The most recent appraisal, which was almost three years old, valued the house and surrounding property at over $300,000. After the accident, Erica quit her job and became something of a recluse. The insurance proceeds increased her liquid assets to over a million dollars, which she left dormant in a money market account for two years. Then, the week before her death, she cashed out all her personal accounts.

"What were you planning to do with all that money?" Mark whispered to himself.

"Did you call me?" Marla asked from the door.

Mark looked up, startled. "No, oh, sorry. I was just thinking out loud."

"You'd better be leaving for the airport if you plan to get there on time," Marla reminded him.

"Is it that late already?" Mark was surprised, but a quick glance out the window confirmed that night had fallen.

"It's six thirty," Marla told him. "I'm headed home."

"See you tomorrow," Mark said. He quickly put the information on Erica Helms into his briefcase and left for the airport.

* * *

As Kate changed the sheets and dusted the guest room, she hummed to herself. Starting with a move to Chicago from Utah over six years before, Kate had lived away from her mother and sisters. She missed them all, but her relationship with Kelsey had suffered the most during the separation. So Kate was especially anxious to spend time with her and was surprised, but pleased, that Kelsey had turned to her in a time of need.

As she cleaned, she thought about all the things they could do together. Shopping trips to Albany, lunches at her favorite restaurant by the river, pampering, and pedicures. She sighed with pleasure at the prospects.

When Kate was satisfied with the condition of the guest room, she recruited Emily and Charles to help with the rest of the house. She fixed Kelsey's favorite dinner and set the dining room table with her best china. Finally, everything she could do had been done, and she paced anxiously back and forth across the entryway, waiting for Mark and Kelsey to arrive.

"When are they going to be here?" Emily asked.

"Soon," Kate assured her as they heard a car pull up into the gravel driveway.

"Daddy's home!" Charles announced.

Kate glanced out one of the long glass panels that flanked the front door. "Yes, he is."

Kelsey came in first, followed closely by Mark, who was carrying her luggage. He put the bags to the side, then closed the door while Kate gave her sister a thorough, yet stealthy, inspection. Kelsey was pale and had dark circles under her eyes. She was wearing baggy clothes and seemed to have gained a little weight.

Kelsey submitted to Kate's welcoming embrace with characteristic reserve then greeted the children with more enthusiasm.

"You're tired," Kate guessed.

"I'm exhausted," Kelsey admitted.

"Well, dinner's ready," Kate said as she pressed a quick kiss to Mark's cheek. "Let's eat so you can get to bed early."

Kelsey nodded, and Mark reached down to pick up the suitcases.

"Just leave them here for now," Kate suggested. "You can take them up after we eat."

Mark swung Charles up onto his shoulders. "That's fine with me."

"We're eating roast and mash potatoes and pink Jell-O," Charles said from his lofty perch. "And it's not even Sunday!"

"It *is* a special occasion," Kate reminded them with a warm glance at Kelsey.

Emily moved up beside her aunt. "Because Aunt Kelsey came to visit."

Kelsey smiled, but Kate could tell she was anxious to get the family gathering over with so she could go to bed. Kate tried not to be disappointed. It was unreasonable to expect that she could rekindle a close relationship with Kelsey in just a few seconds.

While everyone settled at the table, Kate distributed the food. Mark and the children ate heartily, but Kelsey just picked at her meal.

"Don't you like the roast?" Kate asked finally.

Kelsey looked up as if she was surprised to find other people at the table. "Oh, it's fine. I'm just not all that hungry."

Kelsey had always loved to eat, and she was never distracted. Kate's anxiety level jumped higher. Things must be worse than she had anticipated. Once the meal was over, Mark carried Kelsey's suitcases upstairs, then offered to put the children to bed.

"That would be nice," Kate accepted gratefully. "Be sure Charles doesn't brush his teeth too long. I'm afraid he's going to rub the enamel off." She turned to Kelsey. "Wouldn't you know I'd have the only child in the world who considers brushing his teeth a hobby."

Kelsey gave her a wan smile as Mark and the children left. Kate stood up and started to clear the table. Kelsey assisted her automatically.

"So," Kate said after a few minutes of silence. "How was your flight?"

"Fine," Kelsey responded.

Kate handed her sister a dishcloth. "If you'll wash off the table, I'll finish loading the dishwasher."

Kelsey walked over and wiped the wooden surface of the table as requested.

Determined to be patient, but anxious to keep a conversation going, Kate said, "I put you in the guest room that's the farthest from the rest of us, hoping to give you some peace and quiet. But if you don't like it, we do have another one."

"I'm sure it will be fine." Kelsey clutched the dishcloth and faced her sister. "I guess you're wondering why I'm here."

Kate abandoned the dishes and joined her sister at the table. "Why don't we sit down?" she suggested. They had just taken their seats when Mark walked in. He opened the refrigerator and removed what was left of the blackberry cobbler Kate had made for dessert.

"The kids are in bed—we'll see if they go to sleep." He took a saucer from the cupboard and a spoon from the drawer then walked over to the table. He held up the casserole dish. "Anybody want some?"

"No," the sisters said in unison.

Mark smiled. "Good. More for me." He sat beside Kate and dished the cobbler onto his plate. Then he seemed to notice that all conversation had ended with his arrival. "Did I interrupt something?"

"Kelsey was just about to tell me the reason for her visit," Kate explained with a meaningful look in his direction.

Mark glanced at his sister-in-law. "Would you like me to leave?"

Kelsey shook her head. "No. I'd rather you stay. That will keep me from having to say this twice." She took a deep breath. "I'm not sure how to explain it. Everything's wrong and nothing's wrong. It's very confusing."

"We're talking about your marriage, I presume?" Kate asked.

Kelsey nodded.

Mark remained silent, but Kate noticed that he was frowning at his cobbler. Leaning toward her sister, she said, "Nothing is wrong."

"It's true," Kelsey replied. "Travis is righteous and hardworking, and I have absolutely no reason to complain."

"And yet you also say everything is wrong," Kate probed gently. "So even though Travis is righteous and hardworking, you're not happy together?"

Kelsey sprung up from her chair and started to pace around the room. "I'm not even sure it's fair to say that! I'm just . . . uncomfortable with Travis and with some things he's introduced into our lives."

Mark put down his spoon and studied Kelsey with deep concern. "What kind of things, and how do they make you uncomfortable?"

Kelsey sighed. "When I met Travis he was an undernourished, shaggy-haired computer nerd."

"And what is he now?" Kate asked.

"He's . . . different," Kelsey said. "He changed jobs and made new friends."

Kate braced herself for Kelsey to add a *girlfriend* to this list, but she didn't.

"Travis used to cut his own hair with a pair of clippers—now he has a *stylist*," Kelsey continued. "He used to be content to sit around in the evenings and watch television or play computer games. Now he wants to spend his spare time bicycling or hiking or working out at the gym."

That didn't sound so bad. Kate and Mark exchanged a mutually confused glance, then Kate addressed her sister. "You used to love bicycling."

"That was a long time ago, and I was *never* a fitness fanatic. Besides, that's not the point," Kelsey insisted stubbornly.

Kate frowned. "There must be something else."

Kelsey sat back down and told them, "He's also started cooking. Mostly low-fat, healthy stuff."

"And you don't like what he prepares?" Kate ventured.

"I don't like the fact that he's taken over the kitchen!" Kelsey cried with vehemence. "I used to enjoy cooking, but now I wouldn't dare prepare anything. I can't begin to compete with Chef Travis, and whatever I make is sure to have too many fat grams or preservatives or carbohydrates!"

"If Travis wants to prepare the meals, it seems like that would give you a lot more free time for your business," Kate pointed out.

"It does," Kelsey admitted. "But you can't imagine what it's like to be exiled from your own kitchen." Kelsey looked down at her hands, which were clasped tightly in her lap. "And to be intimidated by your husband's knowledge of cooking gadgets." She glanced up. "He exchanges recipes with my friends, so they all know Travis does the cooking in our family." Kelsey shook her head. "It's humiliating."

"You should tell him . . ." Kate tried, but Kelsey interrupted her.

"What? That I don't care enough about my body to protect it from all the horrible stuff in regular food? That I like sitting around in the evenings and being lazy? That I prefer my old, comfortable clothes to the 'hip' outfits he keeps trying to get me to buy?" Kelsey reached up to wipe a tear from her cheek. "I know it sounds crazy to complain about things that most people would consider improvements, but I like the *old* Travis. I feel like I'm married to a stranger."

Kate glanced at Mark for direction, but he seemed as much at a loss as she was.

"I thought if I gave it some time I'd get used to the new Travis. I hoped I'd get comfortable in our relationship again. But I haven't. I'm miserable." She looked up at her sister. "So what do you think?"

"I think that people change," Kate began carefully. "Have you tried talking to Travis about the things he's doing that bother you?"

Kelsey signed heavily. "Of course."

"What did he say?" Kate asked.

"He offered to stop bicycling and exercising and cooking."

"But . . ." Kate prompted.

"That won't work!" Kelsey said, frustration obvious in her voice. "I'll know he still wants to! He'd still be different—just *pretending*."

Kate felt a sense of dread swell within her. "Are you getting a divorce?"

Kelsey laughed, but it wasn't a happy sound. "That's not an option for a good Mormon like me, is it?" Her voice was heavy with bitterness. "The Lord never intended marriage to be temporary."

Kate shook her head. "You don't want to divorce Travis," she stated positively. "That would just make you more miserable."

Kelsey sighed. "I don't know what to do." She glanced up. "And please don't start telling me everything that's wrong with your marriage."

Mark looked startled. "Why would we tell you the things that are wrong with our marriage?"

Now Kate was surprised. "What *is* wrong with our marriage?" she asked her husband.

Kelsey spoke before Mark could. "The first thing most people do when they find out that I'm unhappy in my marriage is to tell me what's wrong with theirs—as if that's going to make me feel better." Kelsey spread her hands in bewilderment. "All that does is make me think that there are no happy marriages—everyone is just enduring to the end."

Mark smiled. "Marriage, like life, does involve a certain amount of endurance, and happiness *is* relative. Take your sister, here."

Kate looked at him with narrowed eyes.

Mark continued, apparently unconcerned. "She thinks she's ecstatically happy married to me, but who knows how much happier she *could* have been if she'd chosen to marry someone else?"

"Or how much *more* unhappy," Kate pointed out.

Mark nodded, either missing or choosing to ignore her sarcastic tone.

"True," he agreed. "There's no way to compare what could have been with what is."

"Nothing could be worse than my reality," Kelsey assured them sadly.

"I think you made the right decision in coming here," Kate said and saw some of the tension drain from Kelsey's shoulders.

"I was afraid you'd think I was just running away from the problem," Kelsey said.

Kate gave her sister a hug. "You just need a little space to make a good decision."

Kelsey actually smiled as she disengaged herself from Kate's embrace and stood. "Thanks. Well, I guess I'll go unpack."

"What about your business?" Kate asked. "Are you just closing it down for a while?"

"I communicate with clients almost exclusively over the Internet," Kelsey explained. "So I can run For Your Information from anywhere. I shipped my computer equipment overnight, and it should arrive tomorrow."

Kate pulled Mark to his feet, and they followed Kelsey from the kitchen. "That's good, then."

After walking Kelsey to the guest room, Kate and Mark checked on their children. Emily's room was right across the hall from theirs and she was still awake, so they read her a bedtime story before kissing her good night. Then they walked through their bedroom to the adjoining room where Charles slept. Kate reached into the crib and straightened his quilt, trying to ignore the pang of guilt she felt each time she saw him still in the baby bed. He had turned three in April, but she was clinging to his baby status as long as possible.

Once they were back in their own room, Kate closed the door and asked, "So what do you think?"

Mark shrugged. "It's hard to say. On the surface, Kelsey's marital problems don't sound too bad, but she seems very unhappy."

"I'm so glad she's here so that we can help her," Kate said. When Mark didn't respond, she asked, "Don't you think that coming to us was a good decision?"

"You don't bail out on any relationship, Kate—especially marriage."

"If you feel that way, why didn't you say anything to Kelsey?"

"Because she wasn't asking me," he pointed out. He sat on the edge of the bed and untied his shoes.

Kate turned to remove a nightgown from her dresser drawer. "So," she said, unable to resist teasing him a little, "marriage is all about endurance?"

"I said all marriages involve a certain amount of endurance."

She glanced over her shoulder, intending to continue her harassment, but the words caught in her throat. Mark had loosened his tie and unbuttoned the top button of his dress shirt. His dark eyes were circled with fatigue, and they regarded her earnestly.

"And every night I beg the Lord to let me endure your company forever," he added softly.

She was overwhelmed with tenderness toward him. She crossed the room to embrace him. "I love you."

"I know," he whispered into her hair as he drew her close. "Sometimes I forget just how lucky we are."

She tilted her head so she could look up at his face. "Because we're happy?"

He nodded.

She pursed her lips and said, "I can only think of one thing that would make me happier at this moment."

He raised an eyebrow. "And what's that?"

She smiled. "A big kiss."

"Okay," he said with feigned disinterest. "But just one."

"Liar," she accused him as his lips claimed hers.

CHAPTER 3

On Thursday morning Eugenia woke up early, dressed in a pair of her deceased husband's old overalls, and went out to work in her garden. She had been ambitious in her planting, and as the fruits of her labors approached the ripening stages, she was beginning to feel a little panic. Lady explored the yard while Eugenia worked, coming back frequently to check on her new master.

"I'm still here," Eugenia said with a smile. "And I don't plan to go anywhere, so you can relax."

The little dog looked relieved and continued her inspection until lunchtime, when Eugenia insisted they go inside. Eugenia opened a can of dog food for Lady and made a grilled cheese sandwich for herself. Lady ate a couple of bites of dog food, but seemed more interested in the cheese sandwich, so Eugenia gave the dog half of hers. After their meal, Eugenia changed clothes, loaded Lady into her basket, and they drove to Albany.

Their visit to the veterinarian's office took considerably longer than Eugenia had anticipated. The waiting room was crowded and all the strangers—especially the groomer—terrified Lady. So Eugenia had to hold the little dog throughout the combing, clipping, and bathing process. Then the vet convinced Eugenia to buy a huge bag of designer dog food, which Eugenia figured would last Lady a lifetime. Encouraged, the vet then insisted on multivitamins specially formulated to provide maximum nutrition for miniature species. Next he suggested a liquid wormer that prevented the infestation of unspeakable parasites, and special combs that he promised would improve the texture of Lady's unruly coat. Eugenia couldn't refuse and ended up needing assistance from two of the vet's employees to get all her purchases to the car.

During the drive back to Haggerty, Eugenia sneaked furtive looks at the dog, searching for improvements in Lady's appearance. The wiry hair was shorter but still stuck out at odd angles. And there was nothing that could be done to change the awkward shape of the miniature dachshund, with her long body and short, little legs. Finally, with a sigh, Eugenia decided to be satisfied that the dog was clean.

When they reached Haggerty, Eugenia pulled into one of the parking spaces in front of the new library. She considered leaving Lady in the car while she went inside, but she had seen horror stories on the news about dogs suffocating in hot vehicles. So she picked up the basket and carried it with her into the building.

Eugenia nodded to several patrons and greeted the teenager who was manning the checkout desk. Then she walked around to the computer lab and placed the basket on the floor by her feet. She signed onto the Internet using her library card number and was soon surfing the net in search of a cost-efficient trip to Hawaii. She was just printing off her findings when George Ann Simmons walked up behind her.

"Where in the world did you get that . . . thing?" George Ann asked, pointing at Lady.

The little dog burrowed self-consciously into the padding of her basket. "Her name is Lady, and she's the pedigreed purebred Geneva Mackey left me in her will." Actually Eugenia hadn't been able to make heads or tails out of the registration papers Whit had given her about Lady, but George Ann didn't have to know that.

George Ann assimilated this information then deepened the perpetual frown on her face. "I don't care if she's *royalty*. There's a city ordinance prohibiting pets in public buildings, and that's what the library is—a public building."

Eugenia had never liked being told what to do, but she especially hated being instructed by George Ann. "I've never heard of any such ordinance."

George Ann lifted her nose into the air, giving Eugenia an unenviable view of her long, thin neck. "Well, that just goes to show that you don't know as much as you think you do."

Eugenia's eyes narrowed. "One thing I do know is that even if that ordinance does exist, Lady here is exempt."

"Exempt?" George Ann demanded. "Why would she be exempt?"

"Because she's my seeing-eye dog," Eugenia replied with satisfaction.

"She is not!" George Ann cried.

"Prove it!" Eugenia challenged.

"You're not even blind!" George Ann sputtered.

"Shhhh!" the teenager urged from the checkout desk, causing George Ann to blush crimson.

"Please excuse George Ann," Eugenia whispered to the girl. "She gets a little excited sometimes." Eugenia removed her travel print-outs from the printer tray and picked up the basket. "Okay, Lady, show me the way home." Eugenia held the basket in front of her and, with one last malicious look at George Ann, hurried out of the library.

The prospect of going to her quiet, empty house didn't appeal to her, so instead Eugenia parked her car and walked directly over to the Iversons'. "You've got to get used to Emily and Charles," she told Lady as they entered through the back door without knocking. "I babysit them often, and the sooner you get to be friends, the better."

The kitchen was empty, so Eugenia and Lady moved on into the hallway past Mark's home office and the deserted family room. When she reached the foyer, Eugenia could see that the living and dining rooms were also empty. "Kate?" she called out tentatively.

"We're up here!" Kate called from upstairs. There was the sound of running feet, and seconds later Emily and Charles appeared at the top of the stairs.

"Aunt Kelsey's computer just got delivered," Emily reported. "It's even nicer than Daddy's."

Mark's was a state-of-the-art system owned by the FBI, so Eugenia was startled by Emily's assertion that her aunt's was "nicer."

"Come see!" Charles invited. He turned and ran.

Emily waited at the top of the stairs until Eugenia joined her, then she led the way down the hall. "You brought your little dog," Emily said, peering into the basket. "It smells different."

"She went to the vet today and got a bath and a haircut," Eugenia explained.

"Annabelle's been looking for you," Kate reported when they reached the guest room.

"She knew where I was going," Eugenia replied.

"But she didn't think it would take so long," Kate explained. "And she wants you to buy a cell phone."

"Humph! I wouldn't own a cell phone for anything."

Kelsey looked up from an impressive array of computer equipment that she was unpacking. "Why?"

"Because any day now scientists are going to discover that they give you brain cancer," Eugenia predicted.

Kelsey blinked in surprise as Emily asked, "Can I hold the dog?"

"Sit up there on the bed by your mother and Charles," Eugenia instructed. She waited until Emily was settled then handed her the basket. "Her name is Lady. It's rude to call her 'the dog.' How would you like it if I always called you 'the girl'?"

Emily giggled. "Sorry, Lady." She stroked the dog's ears, and Lady nuzzled against the small hand.

Eugenia turned her attention to the computer. "This is a very nice system," she told Kelsey.

"Yes," Kelsey agreed. "It's so smart, Travis said it barely needs human support."

Eugenia watched as sadness clouded Kelsey's expression and deduced that the absent husband was the cause of the unexpected visit.

"What kind of computer do you have?" Kelsey asked Eugenia politely.

"Oh, I don't have one myself," Eugenia replied. "But we've got four new ones at the library purchased with a federal grant, and I've learned how to use them."

"I'm glad," Kelsey said. "A lot of older people are afraid of computers, but they make life so much easier."

Eugenia took a step closer. "Why do you need all . . . this?" She waved to encompass the complicated system.

"I operate my own business using this computer," Kelsey explained. "It's called For Your Information."

Eugenia was intrigued. "What do you do?"

"I find out things for people."

"What kind of information?"

"All kinds. Genealogical, financial, criminal, historical."

"So you're kind of like an Internet private investigator?" Eugenia asked.

"Something like that," Kelsey acknowledged.

"Maybe I should consider starting my own investigation business," Eugenia said thoughtfully. "I have a certain propensity for detective work."

"She's nosy," Kate put in with a smile.

Eugenia ignored this. "I've helped Mark and the FBI on several cases."

Kelsey seemed surprised and mildly impressed. "Really?"

Eugenia nodded, eyeing the fancy computer. "And I'd be glad to lend you a hand anytime."

"Kelsey is a computer genius and doesn't need help," Kate bragged. "She built her business from nothing and gets so many referrals from satisfied customers that she doesn't even have to advertise."

Kelsey discounted this remark with a wave of her hand. "I don't advertise because I don't want very many clients at one time. It's really just something I do part-time. And I might take you up on the offer of help. I have a new client that's from a town not too far away from here, and if I need any information about the area, you might be able to save me some research time."

"I'd be delighted," Eugenia assured her.

"You have a new client from near Haggerty?" Kate asked, frowning.

"Yes, that's one of the reasons I decided to come here," Kelsey admitted, then looked contrite when she saw the disappointment on Kate's face. "Just *one* of the reasons," Kelsey emphasized quickly. "I did want to visit with Kate too."

Eugenia had more questions for Kelsey, but at that moment Annabelle walked in. "There you are," she said to her sister. Then turning to Kelsey, she added, "I heard Kate had company. Welcome to Haggerty."

Kelsey smiled. "Thanks."

Annabelle's eyes swung over and caught sight of the little dog in Emily's lap. "Eugenia, by now I thought you would have called the exterminator about that thing," she said with a wink at Kate.

"What's an exterminator?" Emily wanted to know.

"Don't pay any attention to Annabelle," Eugenia advised the little girl. Before she could say more, Mark arrived and received an enthusiastic welcome from his children. Eugenia held Lady and her basket out of harm's way while hugs and kisses were being exchanged. Finally Mark deposited both children back on the bed and looked at the basket in Eugenia's arms.

"Who is this?" he asked, reaching out a hand for Lady to smell him.

"Her name is Lady," Eugenia replied as the dog licked Mark in polite acceptance. "She's my inheritance from Geneva Mackey."

"More like a curse if you ask me," Annabelle interjected.

"Which nobody did," Eugenia pointed out crossly.

Mark ignored the sisterly discord and addressed Lady. "It's nice to meet you."

"Kelsey has a local client, and I'm going to use my investigative experience to help her find information for him," Eugenia told Mark.

"Heaven help Kelsey's client," Annabelle murmured, and earned a scowl from her sister.

"You have a local client?" Mark asked Kelsey.

"I do," she confirmed.

"Who is it?" Kate wanted to know.

Kelsey shook her head. "It would be unethical for me to tell you."

Mark looked taken aback by this remark, but before he could comment, Eugenia said, "Oh, I almost forgot." She pulled the pages she had printed at the library from her pocket. "I've worked out an affordable trip to Hawaii for the wedding!"

"Who is getting married in Hawaii?" Mark asked.

"You were *serious* about going to Hawaii?" Annabelle seemed incredulous.

"Mila Edwards and Quin Drummond are getting married in September," Eugenia told Mark. "And of course I'm serious about going to the wedding," she added in Annabelle's direction. "After all, I *was* instrumental in getting them together."

Annabelle rolled her eyes as Kate asked, "So what did you find out?"

"Well, if we drive to Knoxville and fly out of the airport there on a Tuesday or Thursday after six o'clock P.M., we can get a discount on the airline tickets. The best-priced hotel rooms are on the opposite side of the island from Honolulu, but the ad said the accommodations were within driving distance of all the tourist attractions. I figured we could get one room and you young folks can sleep on the floor." Eugenia glanced back at the printouts. "Rental car rates are outrageous, so we'll get the smallest size vehicle and make two trips when we have to go somewhere."

Annabelle laughed out loud. "Gas in Hawaii is so expensive that you'd be better off renting a larger car and making one trip each time—especially if you're going to be staying on the wrong side of the island."

Eugenia nodded. "I guess that might be reasonable." She referred to her printout again. "Then for food I thought we'd pack some of those cereal bars and a jar of peanut butter and jelly swirled together. Once we get to Hawaii, we'll buy a loaf of bread and a bottle of juice and we'll be set!"

Mark was frowning as he said, "I can't imagine putting most of the United States and an entire ocean between myself and my children."

"Bring the kids," Eugenia offered magnanimously. "We can take turns holding them on the plane, and they don't eat much. They won't increase the cost of the trip at all."

"I've been to Hawaii twice, and it's the world's biggest tourist trap," Annabelle said, giving another unsolicited opinion. "If you make the effort to go all the way over there, I suggest that you take a tour to one of the less-traveled islands like Maui."

"How much does that cost?" Eugenia asked.

Annabelle shrugged. "I don't know. Derrick handled our arrangements."

Eugenia frowned at her printout. "It's probably expensive. We'd better stick to the tourist traps."

Kelsey intervened at this point. "If you really want to take a trip to Hawaii, I'd be glad to shop around for you. I get corporate discounts and sometimes luck into really good deals."

"I'd hate for you to waste time shopping for us when you could be earning money," Kate began. She smiled. "But if we go, I would like to avoid eating out of our suitcases."

"And holding your children for hours on various airplanes," Annabelle added.

"There's no guarantee that we'll be able to go," Kate reminded her sister, with a quick glance at Mark. "No matter how good a deal you find. But if you have a little time, maybe you could look around . . ."

"I'll see what I can do," Kelsey promised.

Eugenia took one last, regretful look at the printout in her hand before stuffing it into her pocket. Then she cleared her throat and addressed Mark. "Since you're home early why don't you take Kate out to dinner? I'll be glad to babysit."

Mark and Kate exchanged a warm smile. "I might just take you up on that," he murmured.

"No need for Miss Eugenia to babysit," Kelsey said as she shut down her computer. "I can watch the kids. In fact," she said as she turned to Emily and Charles, "we can make homemade pizza for dinner. Then we'll play hide-and-seek and watch videos."

"Can we, Mama?" Emily begged.

Kate nodded. "If you promise to mind your aunt and go to bed when she tells you."

Eugenia couldn't remember the last time she had felt so completely useless. Probably not since Charles died. "Well, I guess I'll go," she said to no one in particular, and no one responded.

Emily took Kelsey's hand. "What kind of pizza are we going to make?"

Charles grabbed his aunt's free hand. "Can we have pudding too?"

Kelsey laughed. "We'll make whatever kind of pizza you like, and we can definitely have pudding for desert."

"Just make sure they eat the pizza first," Kate cautioned. "I've got to figure out what to wear. How soon do you want to leave?" she asked Mark.

"No rush," he told her.

"Let's go," Annabelle whispered to Eugenia. Then she addressed the others. "See you folks later."

"Bye!" Emily and Charles chorused. Kate waved over her shoulder as she hurried toward the master bedroom.

"Call me if I can help you with that client," Eugenia told Kelsey. Then she allowed Annabelle to propel her down the hallway. Once they were outside, Annabelle invited Eugenia to her house in Albany for dinner.

"No thanks," Eugenia declined.

"You're not mad at me, are you? You know I was kidding about the exterminator." Annabelle reached into the basket and petted Lady's head.

Lady whimpered as Eugenia nodded. "I know. And I appreciate the dinner invitation, but I don't want to drive all the way to Albany just to eat."

"Suit yourself," Annabelle said, moving off toward her car, which was parked by the curb in front of the Iversons' house.

Eugenia waited until her sister drove off, then she looked down at Lady. "I guess it's just you and me and a TV dinner," she told the dog. "A fine couple of old rejects we are."

* * *

Mark insisted that Kate pick the restaurant, so she chose Mark's favorite—a Greek restaurant called Aristotle's. Once they had placed their order, Kate told Mark that her mother had called three times during the day. "She's worried sick about Kelsey."

"I'm sure she is," Mark replied.

"I couldn't even get Kelsey to talk to her."

"Kelsey will talk to your mother when she's ready. For now we'll just have to be patient."

Kate ate a few bites of salad, then said, "And speaking of phone calls, Winston called at noon today."

Mark stiffened. "Really."

"I think he was hoping you'd be home for lunch and answer. That way you'd be forced to talk to him."

"He knows my number at the office," Mark said. "If he wanted to talk to me he could have called there."

Kate shook her head. "He can't call you *directly* because you're having a feud."

Mark frowned. "I'm not feuding with Winston."

"Of course you are," Kate countered as she speared a juicy cherry tomato with her fork. "The two of you haven't spoken since the bowling tournament fiasco."

"I just don't have anything to say to him," Mark insisted stubbornly.

"You used to have *lots* of things to say to him," Kate commented. "Back when you were *friends*."

"Friends respect each other's beliefs."

"Friends also understand that people make mistakes and in the heat of a moment might say something they don't mean."

Mark put down his fork. "I told Winston when he asked me to join his bowling league that I couldn't practice or play on Sunday. He accepted my terms and then got mad when I stuck to them."

"I'm not disagreeing with you, Mark," Kate assured him. "I'm just trying to help you see things from Winston's standpoint. To him you just wouldn't stretch a principle that he doesn't understand in the first place. He thinks you let down the team."

"They may have lost even if I had played with them!" Mark pointed out. "It's foolish of him to cling to this notion that I cost them the county bowling championship."

Kate sighed. "It's also foolish to throw away a friendship over a small disagreement."

"Keeping the Sabbath day holy is a commandment, Kate."

"So is forgiving others."

"Whose side are you on?" Mark asked in obvious exasperation.

She reached across the table to reclaim his hand. "Always yours. That's why I want you to work this out. Good friends are hard to find."

Mark squeezed her hand, then released it and picked up his fork again. "I didn't come here to talk about Winston or to fight with you. Let's enjoy our dinner."

Kate decided that she had pushed him as far as she could, so she concentrated on her meal. After a few minutes Mark said, "I talked to Jack Gamble today."

She looked up, surprised. "You did. Why?"

"Just had a legal question for him. He said to tell you hi. Beth's fine, the baby's teething, and they hope to be home in September."

"Unless the special session is extended."

Mark frowned across the table at his wife. "You knew?"

She laughed. "Beth calls me often."

"Oh." He shrugged sheepishly. "I guess I should have realized that the two of you would keep in touch."

The waitress stopped by to refill their soft drinks, and after she left Kate asked, "What kind of legal question did you have for Jack?"

Mark's response was interrupted by the arrival of the restaurant owner, Mr. Aristotle. "So, was my food okay for you today?" he inquired.

"It was wonderful as usual," Kate assured him.

"Oh, I'm afraid you are just being kind." He stopped a passing waiter. "Bring my friends the Iversons some of our chocolate almond pie—on the house!"

"You don't have to do that," Mark said, trying to decline.

"Of course I do! Now that my friend Mr. Jack Gamble is too important to visit my humble establishment, I have to take good care of the *loyal* customers," Mr. Aristotle teased.

"We were just talking about the Gambles," Kate said with a smile. "They hope to be home in a month, and I'm sure one of the first things they'll do is come here for some chocolate almond pie."

Mr. Aristotle dabbed his eyes with the corner of his apron. "It will be good to see them again. Miss Chloe is almost a lady, and Baby Hank is a year old."

"Hank's teething, so Jack and Beth aren't sleeping," Mark contributed.

Mr. Aristotle laughed. "Good! The sooner Baby Hank gets teeth, the sooner he'll be able to eat my food!" Mr. Aristotle looked around. "Where is that lazy waiter? I'll go get your pie myself."

Before they could respond he had rushed off. "Well," Mark said. "We get free pie."

Kate laughed. "That might not turn out to be such a bargain if Mr. Aristotle brings it personally. He'll probably pull up a chair and join us."

Mark groaned and Kate laughed again as Mr. Aristotle returned with two pieces of pie. He placed them on the table, then pulled up an empty chair from a nearby table. "Now we talk," he pronounced.

After they left the restaurant, Mark suggested they take in a movie, but Kate shook her head. "I'm tired and I know you are, but dinner was nice." She cut her eyes over at him. "In spite of Mr. Aristotle."

They drove slowly back to Haggerty and found the children asleep and Kelsey working at her computer.

"So, how were the kids?" Kate asked.

"They were great," Kelsey replied.

"Trying to find your missing person?" Mark asked, pointing at the computer screen.

"Yep," Kelsey confirmed. "It's turning out to be one of the tougher jobs I've taken."

"You'll find your him or her," Kate said. She frowned. "Or is it he or she?"

"It's a her," Kelsey clarified.

"And if you need professional help, just ask Mark," Kate volunteered generously.

Kelsey smiled up at her brother-in-law. "I'll keep that in mind."

"Finding missing people is not my specialty," Mark warned her. "Now if you need someone to look at old tax returns, I'm your man."

Kelsey laughed. "Thanks."

Kate would have liked to stay, but Kelsey had her hands poised in a ready-to-type position above the keyboard. So Kate led Mark toward the door. "Well, we'll let you get back to work."

"See you in the morning," Kelsey replied, her fingers already striking the keys.

* * *

Eugenia and Lady spent a quiet evening watching television. At ten o'clock, as an installment of local news began, the telephone rang and startled them both.

"Now who in the world could be calling at this hour?" she asked Lady. The dog barked an indignant reply as Eugenia picked up the receiver and said, "Hello?"

"Eugenia?" Whit Owens's voice came through the phone lines. "Sorry to call so late. I hope I didn't wake you."

"Of course not," Eugenia assured him. "You know old people don't need much sleep. Is something wrong?"

"No, I just wanted to see how you were doing with Miss Geneva's little dog."

Eugenia looked over at Lady, curled up snugly in her basket. "Why, we're doing fine."

"Glad to hear it," Whit said. There was a brief pause, then he added, "Do you like pound cake?"

This question caught Eugenia off guard, and she had to consider it for a few seconds. Finally she said, "I'll be honest with you, Whit. I'm very particular about pound cake and rarely taste one I like."

"I started making pound cakes about five years ago," he informed her. "And I think I've perfected my recipe, but I'd like to get your opinion. Maybe I could bring one by and let you try it."

Eugenia was even more surprised by this suggestion. "Well, I guess I could taste-test one of your cakes, Whit," she agreed cautiously. "But I warn you, I won't lie to spare your feelings."

He laughed. "That's what I'm counting on. I'll be in touch," he promised, then disconnected the call.

"Well, what do you think about that, Lady?" Eugenia asked the dog as she hung up her phone.

Lady stood in her basket and barked twice.

"I don't know what to think either," Eugenia said with a sigh. "Now, let's go to bed."

* * *

After Kate had fallen asleep, Mark lay awake thinking about Lyle Tweedy and Erica Helms. Finally he slipped out of bed and walked down to his office. He opened his briefcase and spread out the information on Erica Helms.

Erica's car was found in a satellite parking lot at the airport in Atlanta. It was assumed that Tweedy drove it there after killing her, although no fiber evidence or prints were ever collected from the car to implicate Tweedy. In fact, based on what Mark could tell, there was no evidence at all that linked Tweedy to the murder. He was accused because the MO was similar, and since Tweedy never disputed the charges, that was enough.

Mark jotted down the name of the sheriff in Patton Chapel, then checked his calendar to see when he could work in a field trip. He briefly considered asking Kelsey to see what she could find out about Erica Helms and her death. He could even offer to run that name she was having trouble with through the FBI computer as repayment. But that would be stretching the rules, and he was very careful never to do that. So he abandoned that idea and made a note on his calendar to drive to Patton Chapel the next day.

* * *

On Friday morning, Eugenia harvested squash, tomatoes, and zucchini until it was time to get ready for the monthly meeting of the Junior Service League. When she stepped inside, she was hot and aching from head to toe. "What in the world possessed me to plant such a big garden this year?" she asked Lady. The little dog yelped in commiseration as Eugenia dialed the number for Elmer Stoops's daughter in Houston, Texas, to check on her friend.

"He's about the same," the daughter reported. "I couldn't get him to eat much breakfast."

"Sometimes it helps to put ketchup on it," Eugenia suggested. "And if you read to him out of the Book of Mormon, he's more cooperative. He's especially partial to King Benjamin," she said, then felt embarrassed. Surely Elmer's daughter knew his preferences.

"I'll give the ketchup and King Benjamin a try," the daughter promised. "And I'll call you if there's any improvement."

Eugenia thanked the daughter, then hung up and changed into a dress. "If we don't hurry, we're going to be late for the Junior Service League," she told Lady. "The meetings are too long and the refreshments are awful, but someone usually gets into a fight—so you won't be bored."

When Eugenia arrived at the meeting, all the Junior Service League members made a fuss over Lady, except George Ann, who was apparently still nurturing a grudge over the seeing-eye dog incident in the library, and Annabelle, who insisted that the dachshund was really a rat. The refreshments consisted of stale cookies and weak citrus punch. The main order of business was a parade the league was sponsoring on Memorial Day. George Ann and Cornelia Blackwood got into a disagreement over the parade route, providing the morning's entertainment. Finally a compromise was reached, and the parliamentarian asked Eugenia to take the parade permit application by the police station on her way home.

After the meeting, Annabelle insisted that Eugenia go to lunch with her at Haggerty Station, the old train depot that had been renovated and turned into the town's only restaurant. "You're trying to make up to me for being mean to Lady," Eugenia accused, stroking the little dog's wiry hair.

"Maybe I do feel a little guilty," Annabelle admitted as the restaurant's owner, Nettie, approached them.

"No dogs allowed," Nettie said crossly.

"She's my seeing-eye dog," Eugenia responded in kind. "And if you don't believe me, ask George Ann. I've already been through the whole thing with her. Now seat us before I call the National Association of Handicapped Persons and report you."

Nettie hesitated for a second, then led the way to the back of the restaurant. As she slapped two menus onto a table she said, "You'd better keep that thing in its basket or I'll throw you out, no matter who you call."

Eugenia stuck out her tongue at Nettie's retreating back and picked up a menu. "Since you invited me, I presume you're paying," she said to Annabelle.

"Of course," her sister replied.

Eugenia smiled. "Good, because Lady and I are starving."

When the waitress arrived, Annabelle ordered a chef salad.

Then the girl turned to Eugenia. "And what about you, Miss Eugenia?"

Eugenia frowned at the menu. "I believe I'll have a club sandwich, mozzarella sticks, and a cup of gumbo."

"No onion rings for you today?" the waitress asked.

"I'm trying to cut back," Eugenia explained.

Once the waitress left, Annabelle leaned forward. "Derrick has to attend a meeting in Myrtle Beach for the Albany Horticulture Society, and I'm going with him. We leave tomorrow and don't get back until Sunday night."

Eugenia assumed that Annabelle was providing this information as a preface to asking a favor. "Do you need me to pick up your mail?"

Annabelle shook her head. "I've arranged for it to be held at the post office."

"Water your garden?"

"No, Derrick hired a man to do that while we're gone."

Eugenia frowned. "Then why did you tell me?"

"So you'll know where I am," Annabelle replied in exasperation. "For heaven's sake, Eugenia, sometimes you're so obtuse."

Lady growled from under the table, and Eugenia narrowed her eyes at Annabelle. "I'm not sure what that means, but you'd better be careful about insulting me, or I'll sic my dog on you."

Annabelle laughed. "It sounds like your little dog has a better vocabulary than you do."

Eugenia reached down and patted Lady's scraggly head. "She's very intelligent," she said as the waitress arrived with their food.

Annabelle picked at her salad while Eugenia ate with gusto. She fed little scraps to Lady, who sat politely in her basket. When the waitress brought Annabelle the check, Eugenia asked for a peanut butter pie to go.

"I thought you were cutting back," Annabelle reminded her sister.

"It's not for me," Eugenia explained. "It's for Winston. I figure if I bring him a pie along with the application for our parade permit, he'll be sure to approve it."

"You're trying to bribe a police officer?" Annabelle asked as she handed the waitress her credit card.

"I prefer to call it friendly persuasion," Eugenia amended. "I'll pick up the pie on my way out," she told the waitress. "Thanks for lunch," she added in Annabelle's direction. Then she lifted Lady's basket and headed for the front of the restaurant.

Eugenia walked briskly from Haggerty Station across the town square to the police station. Then, balancing the pie in one hand and Lady's basket in the other, she pushed into the lobby and looked around. There was no one in sight, and the phones were ringing off the walls.

"Winston!" she called, but she got no response. "Arnold?" she tried with the same result. Finally she picked up the phone. "Haggerty Police Department," she said.

"Well, it's about time somebody answered that phone!" the slurred and belligerent voice of Dub Shaw responded. "I've been calling for twenty minutes!" the town drunk (another member of

Eugenia's high school graduating class) continued. "Is that you, Eugenia?"

"It is me, Dub," Eugenia said crisply as she put Lady's basket on the floor by the dispatcher's desk.

"Did I call the wrong number?" Now he sounded more confused than angry. "I was trying to reach Winston Jones at the police station."

"You called the right number, Dub," Eugenia assured him. "Winston's busy at the moment," she said with another look around. "Can I take a message?"

"Well, you surely can!" Some of Dub's previous indignation returned. "You can tell that lazy, no good chief of police that I'm tired of getting my property destroyed. First my tires were slashed, then someone fouled my well. And now they called the power company, pretending to be me, and had my electricity turned off! Everything in my freezer is ruined! That's hundreds of dollars' worth of food, and somebody's going to pay to replace it!"

"Getting your tires slashed shouldn't be too much of a problem since your driver's license is suspended because of all your drunk driving," Eugenia pointed out. "Everyone in Haggerty is on city water, so the fouled well isn't a serious concern either. And if someone tricked the power company into turning off your electricity, I'd say you should be trying to get them, not Winston, to replace the food in your freezer."

"Winston's the police chief, and as a taxpayer I'm entitled to his protection!"

"The last time they printed the back taxes in the paper, I noticed you hadn't paid yours in three years," Eugenia replied. "So I wouldn't count on that argument doing you much good."

When Dub spoke again, his tone had digressed to a pitiful whine. "Winston thinks I'm doing all these things myself after I've had a little too much to drink, but that ain't true, Eugenia. I swear it! Why in the world would I slash my own tires and have my electricity cut off? Even I've never been *that* drunk!"

"Probably kids," Eugenia hypothesized.

"Kids?" Dub sounded doubtful. "Why would kids want to play tricks on me?"

"Maybe they're part of a gang and have to torment old folks to pass the initiation requirements," Eugenia suggested.

"I didn't know we had a gang in Haggerty."

"There are gangs everywhere now," Eugenia informed him with authority. "Just be glad it's not one that requires its members to murder someone before they can join."

There was a brief silence, then Dub said, "You'll tell Winston to get rid of that gang before they decide to kill me, won't you, Eugenia?"

"I certainly will," Eugenia promised. *Just as soon as I can find him,* she thought to herself. "Now you behave, Dub Shaw," she admonished. Then she hung up the phone. It immediately started ringing again. She took a complaint against a couple who allowed their Great Dane to run loose through a subdivision west of town—using neighboring yards as his rest room. Then she gave a couple visiting from Florida directions to the county courthouse in Albany and assured a DirecTV salesman that the citizens of Haggerty did not want to provide prisoners in the city jail with satellite television. After ending that call, she ignored the phone, picked up Lady's basket, and went to find Winston.

He was in his office, sitting at the battered desk with a dazed look on his face. "Hey, Miss Eugenia," he said when he saw her. "I didn't hear you come in."

"Well, I declare, how could you hear a little thing like the door opening when the phone was ringing continuously? Speaking of which, Dub Shaw called and swears he's got someone vandalizing his property."

He nodded. "He calls every day with some new complaint. Crazy old man."

"He may be a drunk, but he's *not* crazy. Someone is playing tricks on him. It's probably kids, but you shouldn't allow it to continue. Besides, if they keep it up, one of those Dobermans Dub keeps is going to bite a vandal, and they'll sue the city for millions."

Winston's look of anxiety deepened. "They can do that?"

"Happens all the time," Eugenia assured him. "You need to go check it out now."

"I know," Winston conceded. "But if I leave here, there's no one to answer the phone."

Eugenia refrained from pointing out that even when he was at the police station, no one was answering the phone. "What about Arnold?"

"He's been handling the night shift."

"Then where's the other officer, Rimson?"

"Answering a call out at Heads Up on Highway 76," Winston explained. "I just can't do this anymore," he added, his despair obvious.

"Do what?"

"Leita's job," he muttered, referring to the dispatcher who had been on sick leave for six weeks after neck surgery.

"I thought Leita was supposed to be back on Monday."

"She was, but her doctor just called and said he's extending her leave for three more weeks. By then this place will be a shambles."

Eugenia looked around at the newspapers, fast food containers, and file folders that littered the room. "It's already a shambles. In three weeks it will be beyond redemption." She put the pie plate on the desk in front of him. "I brought you a treat from Haggerty Station."

Winston barely gave the pie a glance. "Thanks."

Eugenia knew the situation was serious if a pie couldn't cheer Winston up, so she pulled a chair over and sat down, balancing Lady's basket on her lap. "Why don't you call one of those temp agencies in Albany and tell them to send you someone until Leita comes back?"

Winston shook his head. "Can't afford it. We're still paying Leita's salary, and the mayor says the city just can't come up with any more money. I've done the best I can. I've worked late, and my girlfriend's been helping me with the backlogged filing. But she works a full-time job, and I can't let her keep doing that."

"You still dating that woman who runs the new fitness center?" Eugenia asked.

Winston nodded.

"Isn't her name Celeste or Sonata?"

"Ciera," Winston provided.

"Are they staying busy?" Eugenia inquired. He nodded again. "It's a mystery to me how a town the size of Haggerty can support its own fitness center."

Winston shrugged again then answered without enthusiasm. "Exercise is stylish right now. Ciera says she does a steady business."

"Well, anyway, back to your personnel problem," Eugenia said, redirecting the conversation. "What are you going to do?"

"The mayor's suggested that I ask for a volunteer," Winston told her.

"That's not a bad idea," Eugenia said.

"Not bad if I could find someone who'd do it," Winston returned. "Kate would be good, but she has to take care of her kids. I was thinking I might ask Miss Annabelle, since she's got office experience."

Eugenia couldn't stand the thought of Annabelle landing a job at the police station, even a temporary one. "Annabelle's leaving for Myrtle Beach tomorrow," she told Winston in order to eliminate her sister from consideration. "And Kate is out of the question. In addition to her regular duties, she now has her sister Kelsey living with her."

Winston's shoulders slumped in defeat. "So much for that."

With Kelsey staying at Kate's house, Eugenia felt very dispensable, so she said, "I'll do it."

"You?" Winston asked in surprise. "This is a busy place, Miss Eugenia." The phone started ringing, as if to underline his remark. "And with all your committee meetings and your garden coming in— I don't see how you'd have the time."

"It's just three weeks," she reminded him. "I'll miss my meetings, and I'll hire someone to harvest my garden."

Winston's expression was still doubtful, but she could tell the idea was growing on him when he picked up a fork of questionable cleanliness and stuck it into the peanut butter pie.

"Could you start tomorrow?"

Eugenia smiled. "For heaven's sake, I'll start right now."

* * *

Mark forced himself to complete all the pending FBI business before he placed a call to the sheriff's office in Patton Chapel. He was disappointed to learn that the sheriff who had investigated the case had died of a heart attack a few months earlier. However, the deputy, and now acting sheriff, agreed to meet with him. Mark set up a meeting with Deputy Foster Gunnells for three thirty.

The sheriff's office in Patton Chapel was much like the police station in Haggerty—small, understaffed, and outdated. The receptionist directed Mark to the sheriff's office, where he found Deputy Gunnells trying to refill a printer ink cartridge. The deputy seemed embarrassed to be caught at this menial task.

"Mark Iverson," Mark introduced himself as he extended his hand across the desk.

The deputy wiped his hand on his pants before clasping Mark's hand. "With budget restrictions, I have to save money wherever I can."

Mark nodded. "I understand completely. I've refilled my cartridges so many times the printer's half full of BBs."

The deputy relaxed noticeably. "Have a seat." He waved toward a chair in front of the desk. "So you want to talk about Erica Helms."

"Yes."

"Are you reopening the case for some reason?"

"Some questions have arisen, and I want to settle them."

Deputy Gunnells didn't look suspicious of Mark's interest. "I'll be glad to tell you what I can remember about the case. Here's the file." He slid a manila folder across the desk.

Mark picked it up and glanced through it quickly. There was a family picture of a pretty, slightly overweight woman with two cute little kids and a husband who looked tired. "Most of Lyle Tweedy's victims were teenagers," Mark pointed out. "I'm surprised he was interested in Mrs. Helms."

The sheriff shrugged. "She had lots of money. We figure that's what attracted him."

Mark nodded in acknowledgment. "I guess that's possible. The husband and kids were killed in a car accident?"

"Yep," the sheriff confirmed. "Terrible tragedy. Worst thing that's ever happened around here until Mrs. Helms got killed by Lyle Tweedy."

Mark flipped past several black-and-white autopsy pictures and pulled out a fingerprint card. It wasn't the official version. "Where'd you get this?"

"It was in a drawer of Erica's desk. It's part of an Identi-Kit that we distribute to the local schools. We encourage all families to have them."

Mark put the card back in the file. "So how did you like working on a murder case, Deputy Gunnells?"

"Call me Foster," the young man requested. "It was fun for the few days we had it. As soon as we figured out that Lyle Tweedy was our perp, the Feds swooped in and took it away from us."

"FBI?" Mark guessed.

"FBI, GBI, CIA—you name any law enforcement agency you've ever heard of and they were here, grabbing a piece of the action."

"Tough luck," Mark said, although he actually felt that Foster had been fortunate to avoid personal contact with Lyle Tweedy. "How did you determine that Tweedy was responsible for the death of Erica Helms?"

"We had a couple of reports that he was in the vicinity right around the time she went missing, but we didn't make the connection until we found her strangled body."

"Did anyone actually see Mrs. Helms and Tweedy together?"

Foster considered this then shook his head. "No, I don't think so. We figured that he was afraid of being recognized and stayed out of sight."

"He directed her to take the money out of her account, and she did it because she thought they were going away together?"

Foster nodded. "It's so sad that she trusted a creep like that."

Mark involuntarily pictured Tweedy's smiling face. "Tweedy fooled several women."

"True," Foster agreed.

"I'd like to see the pond where the body was discovered. Could you give me directions?"

Foster stood and pulled on his hat. "I can do better than that. I'll take you there."

After they were settled in the sheriff's car and headed down the road, Foster asked, "You like working for the FBI?"

"Most of the time," Mark answered.

"Was it hard to get on with them?"

"It took me years," Mark admitted. "I already had a bachelor's degree in accounting and spoke Spanish fluently when I applied. Before they would accept me, I had to get a law degree as well."

"Wow!" Foster said. "I guess I might as well forget it. All I have is an associate's degree in criminal science from the local junior college."

"There was a time in my life when working for the FBI seemed like all that mattered," Mark told him. "But now—I think I could be just as happy as sheriff of a nice town like Patton Chapel. The main thing is to do a good job wherever you are."

Foster grinned over at him. "Thanks for the advice."

"You're welcome." Mark looked out the window as Foster pulled the car off the road and parked beside a small pond. "So this is it?"

"This is it," Foster confirmed. He turned off the car and climbed out. "We found the body on the other side, weighted down with rocks."

"Tweedy hid the body, which is why it wasn't discovered for several months, right?"

"We may never have found her if we hadn't gotten several complaints about a bad smell coming from the pond," Foster explained. "We figured somebody had dumped a cow carcass or something like that. It's not a deep pond, so the sheriff decided to drain it. He rented a couple of big pumps, and we got started."

"That must have been a nasty job, with the smell and all," Mark commented with sympathy.

Foster scratched his head, apparently thinking. "Now that you mention it, I didn't smell anything when we first started. And when the water got low enough to see into that patch of cattails," Foster pointed out the area, "I was too shocked to notice if it smelled or not."

"So you were here when they found her?" Mark asked.

"Yeah. This woman from some environmental group in Atlanta was putting up a fuss about us draining the pond, so the old sheriff wanted me here in case she tried to take a sledgehammer to the pumps. I had to listen to her spout off about endangered species and natural habitats for two days. But when we found Mrs. Helms, she shut right up. That was one good thing."

In spite of the grim surroundings, Mark had to smile. "Who removed the body?"

"Our local funeral director pulled her out of the sludge on the bottom of the pond, then we sent her to Atlanta for the autopsy."

"Did you know it was Mrs. Helms before you got the autopsy report?"

Foster nodded. "We were pretty sure. We called in her sister who lives nearby, and she identified the jewelry and a few fabric scraps. But we wanted to be sure."

"Of course," Mark agreed. "I guess it was a shock for the community."

"Not as bad as it could have been," Foster replied. "Tweedy was in custody by the time we found the body, so people weren't scared of him. And Mrs. Helms had been a hermit ever since her family died." Foster looked up, apparently concerned that Mark might misunderstand. "Now don't get me wrong. Patton Chapel is a caring community. But it's hard to miss someone you never see."

"Mrs. Helms must have taken the deaths of her family very hard."

"Oh, she did. For a while we were afraid she'd kill herself, but she started going to a psychiatrist in Albany and got a little better."

"Do you think there's any chance that Mrs. Helms did finally give in and commit suicide?"

Foster looked at Mark like he'd lost his mind. "You think she strangled herself, dragged herself out to the pond, tied rocks to herself, and then slid under those cattails?"

Mark chuckled. "I guess that does sound a little far-fetched."

"A little? No wonder it took you so long to get into the FBI," Foster teased, blushing afterward. "Just kidding."

"I know," Mark assured him. "But something doesn't feel quite right about this murder and Lyle Tweedy's involvement," he continued carefully. "I'm trying to figure out what it is."

Foster shrugged. "Seems pretty cut-and-dried to me."

"Well, thanks for your time. I'll look through the file and mail it back—if that's okay."

"Its fine," Foster agreed. "I don't expect to ever need it again."

Mark wasn't so sure, but he said, "And after reviewing the file, if I'd like to talk to anyone . . ."

Foster laughed and headed back up toward the car. "All you got to do is ask, and I'll set you up."

Mark smiled. "Thanks."

"No problem. It can't hurt to have a friend in the FBI."

Mark's smile faded as he climbed into the sheriff's vehicle. The last thing he needed was a small-time sheriff's deputy wanting favors. But as they pulled away from the pond and out onto the road, Mark couldn't shake the feeling that Lyle Tweedy had told him the truth about Erica Helms. And if Tweedy didn't kill her, someone went to a lot of trouble to make it look like he did.

* * *

Eugenia left Winston to eat his pie in peace and carried Lady back to Leita's desk. "Looks like our first step is to organize this mess," she told the dog as she placed the basket in Leita's swivel chair. "You just sit right here."

Eugenia found a box of plastic trash bags in the supply closet and used one to clear away the fast food containers that littered the desk. Then she stacked up the police files in one corner and the official mail in the other. Finally she divided the messages into piles based on urgency. When Winston finished his snack, he walked in and put the pie plate into the bulging garbage bag.

"Are you headed out to see Dub Shaw?" Eugenia asked when she saw that he had his hat in one hand.

"Naw," he replied. "I'll just talk to him the next time he gets hauled in drunk and disorderly. Since you're here to answer the phone, I thought I'd take a ride around town and make sure everything's peaceful."

Eugenia's eyes narrowed. "You wouldn't be planning a stop at the fitness center to see your girlfriend, would you?"

He grinned. "It's my responsibility to make sure things are peaceful there too."

She shook her head in disgust. "Save your social calls for after work. You've got almost a hundred phone messages," she scolded. "Most of them are either unimportant or so old that the poor folks are bound to have gotten their information elsewhere. But several are complaints about vandalism from residents other than Dub Shaw."

Winston scratched his head. "You think we really do have a gang of teenagers causing trouble?"

She shrugged. "That's what the police are supposed to find out. Which is you," she reminded him. Then she picked up a stack of pink message slips and thrust them toward him. "Starting right now. Miss Siesta at the fitness center can wait."

"Ciera," Winston corrected her, with a look that indicated he might regret his decision to accept her voluntary assistance.

The phone rang and Eugenia answered it, then covered the mouthpiece and said, "This is Nettie over at Haggerty Station. She says there's a vagrant hanging around asking for work. She says he looks disreputable. Besides, she doesn't need any help. She told him so, but he won't leave."

"Is she afraid he's going to rob her?" Winston asked.

"I think she's mostly afraid he's going to scare off customers. He's asking everyone who comes in if they have work for him."

Winston nodded and put his hat onto his head. "Tell her I'm on my way."

Eugenia relayed this information to Nettie then hung up the phone and addressed Lady. "Okay, let's see what we can do about the rest of this room."

* * *

Kate tried hard to keep the children quiet during the morning so they wouldn't disturb Kelsey. Apparently she had been successful, since Kelsey didn't get out of bed until noon.

"Good morning," Kate said when they met in the hallway.

Kelsey rubbed her sleepy eyes. "I guess it will be good if I can ever wake up."

"Would you like some breakfast?" Kate asked, checking her watch. "Or how about lunch? There's this fantastic restaurant on the river in Albany that I'm dying to take you to."

Kelsey shook her head. "Sorry, but I can't spare the time. I've already wasted half the day by sleeping in. I'll just fix a bowl of cereal and get to work."

Kate swallowed her disappointment. "Maybe another day."

Kelsey nodded as she walked toward the bathroom. "Maybe."

* * *

Eugenia was filling her third trash bag when Winston returned to the police station. Following behind the chief was the most ragged looking man Eugenia had ever seen. He was tall and very thin. She calculated him to be in his early thirties, although a less experienced eye would probably think him older because of the lines on his face and the gray in his hair.

"Our vagrant, I presume?" she asked Winston. He nodded then proceeded down the hall.

"He doesn't have any identification and won't tell me his name," Winston confirmed. "So I'm going to lock him up until he decides to cooperate." Winston opened the door to the cell block, and Eugenia followed them in.

While Winston unlocked the first cell, the man stared at his feet—the picture of dejection. "Is it against the law to refuse to tell someone your name?" she asked Winston. "It seems to me like it would be a constitutional right to privacy or something."

"It's against the law to loiter, Miss Eugenia," Winston said with a hint of impatience in his voice. "And refusing to cooperate with a law enforcement official can get you thrown in jail." He turned to the man behind him. "This way, buddy."

The man shuffled into the cell without saying a word in his own defense.

"He's probably hungry," Eugenia said, uncomfortable that they were talking about the man as if he weren't there.

"I'll pick him up a Big Mac while I'm out," Winston replied as he closed the cell door.

"You just got back!" she reminded him.

"Yeah, but I didn't have a chance to stop by the fitness center and make sure everything's peaceful there."

Eugenia rolled her eyes then pointed at the prisoner. "What will I do with him while you're gone?"

"Nothing. He can sit in here, and when I get back maybe he'll have decided to tell me his name. Then I can check with surrounding counties for outstanding warrants. If he's clean, he can go."

Eugenia stepped closer to Winston and whispered, "Why don't you just give him a ride to the edge of town?"

"He's not leaving until he cooperates," Winston said firmly. Then he put his hat on his head. "Call me on the radio if you need me."

Eugenia watched Winston disappear through the door then muttered, "The very idea." Remembering the presence of the vagrant, she turned to see him watching her. "I'm sorry about this," she said. "The town of Haggerty is usually more hospitable to guests."

The man gave her a weary smile. "I'd like to introduce myself. My name is Brandon Vance." He extended his hand through the bars.

"Eugenia Atkins," she returned, clasping his hand briefly.

"As William Faulkner would say, you are a tribute to Southern womanhood."

"I've always been rather partial to Mr. Faulkner myself," Eugenia admitted. "Are you familiar with his work?"

"Quite," the man acknowledged. "Until a few months ago, I taught American literature at Georgia Southern College."

Eugenia took a step closer to the cell. "Why don't you teach there anymore?"

"I took a leave of absence to search for my wife."

"She's lost?" Eugenia asked.

"She is the most lost person I know," he agreed. "We had a happy marriage until a couple of years ago when our only child died of leukemia."

Eugenia reached through the bars to pat the back of his grimy hand. "I'm so sorry."

"Thank you," he said, swiping at a tear that coursed down his cheek. "It was a terrible time in my life but not the worst. That came later when my wife withdrew from me and finally demanded a divorce."

"I've heard that oftentimes the loss of a child causes marital problems," Eugenia told him.

"It certainly did in our case. I kept hoping that after some time passed she would be willing to reconsider, but instead she disappeared. She didn't leave a note or anything—"

"And you haven't been able to find her?"

"No. I used up all my assets hiring private investigators. I even sold my house," he said earnestly. "That's why I couldn't give the policeman an address."

"Why didn't you just tell all this to Winston?"

Brandon Vance shrugged. "I may not have anything else, but I do have some pride."

Eugenia studied him through the cell door and realized it wouldn't be long before his pride was also a thing of the past. "What brought you to Haggerty?"

"As a last resort I hired a computer expert who uses the Internet to find people. She said she'd be staying here in Haggerty for a while. I came to see her, but I'm completely broke, so I was hoping I could get a job and clean up a little before I meet her."

Eugenia frowned. "What's her name?"

"Kelsey Pearce."

So this was Kelsey's local client. "Well, I just happen to know Kelsey, and I might be able to arrange for her to come visit you here."

Mr. Vance grasped the bars in front of him with both hands. "I would be forever in your debt."

Eugenia smiled at this dramatic declaration. "I'll see what I can do."

She went out to the front desk and dialed the Iversons' number. When Kate answered, Eugenia asked for Kelsey and explained the situation to her.

"The police station is on the square, right?" Kelsey confirmed.

"You can't miss it," Eugenia assured her.

"I'll borrow Kate's van and be there as soon as I can," Kelsey promised before disconnecting.

Less than ten minutes later, Eugenia returned to the cell block with Kelsey by her side.

"I'm Kelsey Pearce," Kelsey said when she saw the man behind the bars.

He nodded. "I'm Brandon Vance, and I had hoped to meet you under better circumstances."

"I rarely get to meet my clients under any circumstances," Kelsey said, turning to Eugenia. "Please let him out of the cell at once. I can vouch for him."

Eugenia was reluctant. "Winston will be back soon, and once we explain the situation . . ."

"I can't talk to him like this." Kelsey gestured toward the metal barrier with distaste. "And why would Mr. Vance run away if you let him out when he's come here *specifically* to see me?"

Eugenia had to admit that the girl had a point. The phone started ringing, so she made a quick decision. "Okay, I'll let him out, but you'll have to consult in the lobby, where I can keep an eye on him."

Once her terms were agreed to, Eugenia got the key from Winston's desk and opened the cell door. Then she escorted her guests up to the front of the police station. Kelsey and Mr. Vance began their interview, and although Eugenia felt obligated to answer the phone occasionally, she always kept at least one ear on the conversation across the room.

"I have exhausted all my resources," she heard Brandon Vance tell Kelsey. "After I sold my house, I slept in my car, but I had to sell it to pay the last investigator. Since then I've been sleeping in the woods and eating at soup kitchens and hitching rides with strangers."

Kelsey was obviously appalled. "If things are so bad, why didn't you just call me instead of coming here?"

"I felt that I needed to speak to you personally because . . ." He paused, looking down at his hands. "I can't pay your fee. Not immediately." His voice faltered, and Eugenia knew that this admission hurt him deeply.

She was not officially a part of the conversation, but since it was taking place at the police station, where she was a voluntary employee, Eugenia felt free to make a comment. "I declare, Mr. Vance, if you keep sleeping outside and accepting rides from strangers, there's a good chance you'll be killed yourself long before you ever find your wife!"

Kelsey nodded in agreement. "I'm doing what I can to locate your wife. In the meantime, you have to consider your own needs."

Mr. Vance shook his head. "I would never be able to live with myself if I felt I had left a single stone unturned in my quest to find Molly."

"Your loyalty is very commendable," Kelsey told him.

"If a little foolish," Eugenia added from across the room.

With a sharp look toward Eugenia, Kelsey said, "Please go on, Mr. Vance."

"I've come to beg you to continue your search with the assurance that I'll pay you as soon as I can."

"Mr. Vance," Kelsey began.

"Please call me Brandon," he interjected.

"Brandon," Kelsey began again. "I'm not worried about my fee, but I have to tell you that I'm not very optimistic about finding your wife. I've been looking for over two weeks, and I haven't uncovered so much as a trace."

"How can someone just disappear?" he asked, obviously confused and disappointed.

Kelsey shrugged. "It happens—but usually the people who vanish successfully have help from experts in the FBI or CIA. I'll admit I'm surprised that I haven't been able to turn up anything on your ex-wife since she was reported missing." Kelsey paused. When she continued, her voice was gentle. "The day may come when we both have to give up our search."

Mr. Vance closed his eyes briefly then whispered, "Please don't let it be today."

Eugenia could see several emotions play across Kelsey's face. Finally pity won out. "Okay then. If we're not admitting defeat, the first order of business is to get you released from jail." She turned to Eugenia. "What do I need to do to have him discharged?"

Eugenia was at a total loss. "Winston said he had to stay until he gave us a name and address."

"I've told you my name," Brandon reminded her. "But I don't have a permanent address anymore, and I can't get a hotel room here until I get a job."

Eugenia frowned. "Jobs are scarce in Haggerty, Brandon," she said. "Especially for strangers, and we don't have a single hotel. Closest thing is a motel out on Highway 76, and that's going to be inconvenient for you without a car."

"Maybe Kate and Mark would hire him," Kelsey proposed.

"To do what?" Eugenia asked.

"I could do yard work," Brandon contributed. "I had an award-winning garden in Wilsonville."

"If you're willing to do yard work, I could use you myself," Eugenia told him thoughtfully. "I have a huge garden that is producing faster than I can pick it. And now that I'm volunteering here . . ."

"I'd be glad to pick your vegetables," Brandon said with enthusiasm.

"I couldn't pay you much," Eugenia hedged.

"You wouldn't have to pay me anything," Brandon assured her. "Just let me eat some of what I pick and sleep in your backyard."

Eugenia frowned. "You're welcome to eat your meals with me, and there's a shed in back that's big enough for a cot."

Brandon Vance looked hopeful for the first time since he walked into the Haggerty police station. "You won't even know I'm there," he promised.

Eugenia laughed. "Unless you bathe, I'll be able to smell you a mile away."

Brandon's expression changed to one of total embarrassment. "It's been a while since I was able to take a proper bath, and I've been wearing these same clothes for . . ." He shrugged. "I don't even remember how long."

"Well, there's a water spigot in the shed where you can wash up, and some of my late husband's clothes will probably fit you."

"How can I ever thank you?" Brandon asked, his eyes damp.

"You can thank me by taking good care of my garden," Eugenia said. Then she pointed a finger in his direction, giving him a stern look. "But I'll warn you that I have an FBI agent living right next door, so if you've got bad intentions, you'd better take them on to another town."

At this point Winston walked in through the front door carrying a McDonald's sack. "What's going on here, Miss Eugenia?" he asked, eyeing them all with suspicion.

"The mystery is solved," Eugenia told him. "This is Mr. Brandon Vance, previously of Wilsonville and a former professor of American literature at the Georgia Southern College. He's a client of Kelsey's, and that's what brought him to Haggerty."

Winston dropped the sack in front of his prisoner. "So why didn't he just tell me that when I picked him up at Haggerty Station?"

Eugenia glanced at Brandon and said, "Because he's down on his luck and looking for his lost wife and . . ."

"I was embarrassed," Brandon finished for her. "This life as a vagrant is new to me, and when you pressed me with questions that I couldn't answer . . . well, I guess all I can say is that I'm sorry."

Winston sat on the corner of the desk, a frown on his face. "I'll have to make sure there aren't any outstanding warrants on you and call Georgia Southern College to check out your story."

Brandon nodded. "I understand completely."

"And even if everything checks out, you'll still have to leave town since you don't have a job or an address here."

Eugenia cleared her throat. "Actually, he does."

Winston raised an eyebrow. "Since when?"

"Since I hired him a few minutes ago and told him he could sleep in my gardening shed."

Winston looked from Brandon to Eugenia before standing. "I'll go make a few phone calls, then we'll talk some more."

After Winston went into his office, Eugenia answered the phone and eavesdropped on the continuing conversation between Kelsey and Brandon. Finally Winston returned to the lobby.

"Well, your story checks out, Mr. Vance. In fact, the folks at Georgia Southern couldn't say enough good things about you."

The moisture returned to Brandon's eyes. "I'm gratified to hear that."

Winston looked at Eugenia. "But he's still a complete stranger to us. Are you sure you'll feel comfortable with him living in your shed?"

Eugenia nodded. "I'm sure."

With a sigh, Winston picked up his hat and waved it toward Brandon. "Well, then, come on and I'll take you to your new home."

"I've got Kate's van. He can just ride with me," Kelsey offered.

"I'll feel better if I get him settled personally," Winston replied, his tone polite but firm.

Kelsey stood with a shrug. "Whatever."

Eugenia followed them to the door, instructing Brandon about what needed to be picked in the garden and promising to be home soon. "I'll make you a good dinner and find you some clean clothes."

Brandon smiled. "That's something I will certainly be looking forward to."

Eugenia put her hand on Kelsey's arm, delaying her exit. Once Winston and Brandon Vance were out of the front door, she whispered, "The other night you told Kate and Mark that you couldn't disclose the name of your client because it would be unethical. I guess now that I'm helping you with your investigation, I'm sworn to silence too."

Kelsey's eyes widened slightly. "Oh, yes, I'm sure you'll be a lot of help. And it probably would be more ethical not to discuss the case with anyone, including Kate and Mark."

"My lips are sealed," Eugenia promised.

Kelsey nodded then hurried outside to join Winston and Mr. Vance.

Once they were gone, Eugenia addressed Lady, who was just waking up from a nap. "Well, I hope you've gotten your beauty sleep, since we'll be having company for dinner. I was just trying to decide which casserole to defrost."

The little dog barked and Eugenia laughed.

"You're right. Any of them will be delicious."

* * *

When Kelsey returned, Kate was in the backyard watching her children play in their wading pool. Kelsey parked the van in the driveway as Winston pulled his Haggerty police car in behind her. Winston and a man Kate had never seen before climbed out. Kate told the children to stay put while she went to investigate.

"Hello, Winston," she greeted the police chief, her eyes on his passenger. He looked like a homeless person, and Kate couldn't imagine why Winston had brought him here.

"Hey, Kate," Winston returned. "This is Brandon Vance. Vance, this is Mrs. Iverson."

Brandon nodded. "How do you do?"

"Fine, thanks," Kate replied, still mystified by the man's presence.

"Miss Eugenia has hired him to pick the vegetables in her garden," Kelsey explained.

Now Kate was astounded. Miss Eugenia was very particular about who she allowed to *visit* her garden, and Kate had never known her to let anyone *work* in it. "How do you know?" Kate asked her sister. "I thought you were going to the dry cleaners."

"I stopped by the police station to get some information on my missing person case and met Mr. Vance there," she replied.

"If you'll excuse me, I'd like to start earning my keep," Brandon Vance told them. "Nice to meet you, Mrs. Iverson," he added. Then he walked into Miss Eugenia's backyard.

"Why?" was all Kate could think of to say.

"Miss Eugenia's volunteering at the police station until Leita comes back from her sick leave, and she doesn't want her vegetables to rot," Winston said. He moved a little closer to Kate and lowered his voice. "Just between you and me, I think she feels sorry for the guy. He's broke, and she's letting him sleep in her shed."

"He's a little down on his luck," Kelsey added.

Kate looked next door where Brandon Vance was inspecting Miss Eugenia's tomatoes. "Apparently," she agreed.

"Well," Kelsey said briskly. "I've got to get back to work."

"Me too," Winston said. "See you later, Kate."

She watched Kelsey hurry into the house and Winston drive off in his squad car. She walked back to the wading pool where Emily and Charles were splashing each other.

"We need more water," Emily informed her. "Charles splashed it all out."

"It looks like you're doing your share of splashing too," Kate said as she turned on the hose and started the process of refilling the little pool.

The children were splashing happily again when Miss Polly, the Iversons' other neighbor, came over a few minutes later. "Hey, Kate," she greeted. "Have you seen Eugenia? I've been calling her for two days to tell her about a meeting of the Haggerty Beautification Committee, but I never get an answer."

"I just found out that she's volunteering at the police station until Leita gets back from sick leave," Kate replied.

Miss Polly put a hand to her chest. "I don't know why Eugenia would agree to work at the police station! I can't imagine being exposed to the criminal element on a daily basis."

Kate had to laugh at this remark. "The only time the Haggerty jail has a criminal in residence is when Dub Shaw gets locked up for being drunk and disorderly."

Miss Polly considered this for a second then nodded. "I guess you're right. Thanks for the information. I'll stop by and see Eugenia the next time I'm in town."

"Do you want to come swimming with us, Miss Polly?" Emily invited.

Their neighbor laughed. "Heavens no. I don't even know where my bathing suit is." With a wave to Kate, Miss Polly ambled off. Kate stared after her, trying to escape the horrifying mental image of Miss Polly in a bathing suit.

CHAPTER 4

The front door of the police station opened, and Eugenia turned to see the youngest officer on the small police force walk into the station. "Well, Arnold, you're here awfully early for the night shift."

"Hey, Miss Eugenia," the boy said. "I try to come in before my shift starts to help the chief with the phones." Then he frowned in confusion. "What are you doing at Leita's desk?"

"You won't have to worry about the phones anymore. I'm going to fill in for the next three weeks until Leita comes back from sick leave," she told him. Then her eyes zeroed in on his hands. "Arnold! Have you been biting your fingernails again?" she demanded from him. His blush was answer enough. "Look at those cuticles! I do believe they are infected."

Arnold put his hands behind his back. "They're okay."

"No, they most certainly are not 'okay,'" she corrected him. "Once you get germs in your body, they can take root and cause you all sorts of health problems. It's a good thing you came in early. I'll take care of this here and now. Sit down."

Arnold surrendered without a fight. "Yes, ma'am."

Eugenia found a coffee mug and cleaned it with hot water. She made a solution of antibacterial soap and hand lotion. "While you're soaking your left hand in this, I'll work on your right." She pulled an emery board and a pair of clippers from her purse.

Arnold obediently stuck his left hand in the mug and extended his right hand toward Eugenia. She was working diligently over his frequent protests of pain when the door opened again. They both looked up and watched as a man walked in. He was wearing a shiny double-breasted suit, and his longish hair was artlessly styled into a halo of unruly curls around his head. Thinking that he looked like a cross between John Dillinger and Julius Caesar, Eugenia instantly determined that he wasn't from the Haggerty area.

The man took in the scene before him then said, "I was looking for the Haggerty police station, but it looks like I've found a manicurist shop instead."

Eugenia picked up on the sarcastic tone and narrowed her eyes at the stranger as Arnold said, "No, you have the right place. Miss Eugenia is just looking after my cuticles."

Lady stood up in her little basket and growled at the man, further evidence that he was a bad sort. "What can we do for you?" Eugenia asked with impatience.

"My name is Sylvester Muck, and I'm with the state attorney general's office."

Arnold pulled his hand from Eugenia's grasp and held it out to their guest. "Arnold Willis," he provided. "And this is Miss Eugenia Atkins, our temporary dispatcher."

"Who gives manicures on the side," Mr. Muck said, his tone distinctly snide.

Lady growled again.

Then Winston walked in. Eugenia assumed that he had successfully installed Brandon Vance at her house. "What's going on?" he asked.

"This is Mr. Muck from the state attorney general's office," Arnold informed his boss nervously.

Winston frowned at Arnold's left hand. "What is that goo?"

Arnold glanced down at the lotion/soap solution dripping from his fingers and blushed a dangerous shade of red.

"It's a little something I mixed up to treat his infected cuticles," Eugenia replied on behalf of the embarrassed young officer.

"I hate to interrupt your discussion of beauty tips," Mr. Muck said. "But I am here on official business."

Eugenia opened her mouth to set the young man in his place, but Winston spoke first. "If you've got business then spit it out."

Mr. Muck squared his shoulders. "I'm looking for a Brandon Vance. The lady at the diner said you brought him in a little while ago for vagrancy."

Winston looked confused. "The diner?"

"I think he means Haggerty Station," Eugenia provided.

Winston nodded. "Oh."

"Whatever," Mr. Muck said with a dismissive wave of his hand. "I need to speak to your prisoner about a murder case we're investigating."

Winston shot Eugenia a quick look before saying, "We had to release him."

"You released him!?" Mr. Muck asked incredulously. "When there's a bulletin from the state attorney general's office requesting information about his whereabouts?"

Winston frowned at the stacks of unopened mail on Leita's desk. "My dispatcher has been out on sick leave for weeks, and we're way behind on posters and bulletins."

If possible Mr. Muck looked even more astounded. "How can you call yourself a police chief if you don't keep up on wanted posters and bulletins?"

"I check the FBI's Most Wanted list on the Internet every morning," Winston said defensively. "But the other minor ones . . ."

Mr. Muck obviously didn't appreciate the fact that his bulletin fell into the *minor* category. He took a little notebook from his suit coat pocket and jotted down a few notes. Then he said, "You'll be hearing more about this." After shaking his head several times, he put up the notebook and continued. "I presume you at least had the presence of mind to get an address for Mr. Vance."

Winston cracked his knuckles, and Eugenia knew that their visitor had finally pushed too hard. "Do you have a warrant for his arrest?" Winston asked.

Mr. Muck shook his head impatiently. "No."

"Then, if Mr. Vance is willing, I'll be glad to arrange an interview." Winston leaned over the desk and flipped through the desk calendar. "How about tomorrow at two in the afternoon?"

"How about now?" Mr. Muck shot back. "I told you this is a *murder* investigation. Surely that means something even here in Podunkville!"

Winston's lips settled into a tight, straight line, and Eugenia started to fear for Mr. Muck's life.

"What that means here in Podunkville is that if you come to the station tomorrow at two—you can ask him all the questions you want."

"And what am I supposed to do in the meantime?" Mr. Muck demanded.

"Drive to Albany and get yourself a hotel room," Winston suggested.

"I feel I should warn you that failure to cooperate with the state attorney general's office can have serious consequences for you," Mr. Muck informed Winston.

"Well, you've got me shivering in my boots," Winston replied. His tone was pleasant, but his eyes were hard. "And now that I think about it, I'm busy tomorrow. We'll have to set up that meeting with Mr. Vance next week sometime." Winston turned to Arnold and said, "Come into my office where we can work in peace."

Arnold stood and followed his boss out of the room. Seconds later the whole building reverberated with the sound of Winston slamming his office door.

Sylvester Muck, left alone with Eugenia and Lady, seemed unsure of what to do.

"I'm a graduate of the Connecticut School of Law, and I know my rights," he said finally. "I'm entitled to cooperation from the local police."

Eugenia laughed. "Well, today you're learning that what you're *entitled* to and what you *get* are often different."

"I could call my office in Atlanta," he threatened mildly.

"You could," she agreed. "But I wouldn't recommend it. There are hundreds of ways to avoid cooperating, and Winston is a master of all of them."

"Like what?"

Eugenia stroked the tangled hair on Lady's little head. "Well, he could get sick. That's worked well for him in the past."

"You mean just not come into the office?"

"That's exactly what I mean. Or he could decide to take an unscheduled vacation or forget Mr. Vance's address altogether."

Sylvester's shoulders slumped in defeat. "I see. So, my only option is to sit around in an Albany hotel room and wait for him to have pity on me?"

"That is an option," Eugenia acknowledged. "But not your best one."

Sylvester spread his hands in supplication. "What else can I do? The police chief hates me."

"You've gotten off to a bad start here—there's no denying that," Eugenia agreed. "But it's not hopeless. You came in trying to throw your weight around. Now you'll have to eat humble pie."

Sylvester winced. "I don't like the sound of that."

Eugenia pointed at the chair Arnold had been sitting in when Sylvester arrived. "Have a seat, and I'll do what I can to help you."

The man from the state attorney general's office looked suspicious. "Why should you help me?"

"I don't know where the barn is that you were raised in, but people around here are naturally polite and helpful."

Sylvester sat down with obvious reluctance. "So my first mistake was coming in here and demanding the cooperation I'm entitled to?"

Eugenia shook her head. "Your first mistake was choosing to wear that gangster suit."

Mr. Muck looked at his clothing in alarm. "Gangster suit?"

"It might be fine in a big city, but here in Haggerty, trustworthy men wear conservative clothes. During your spare time this evening you might want to visit the JC Penney at the mall and purchase a charcoal gray suit with only three buttons. Ask the sales clerk to pick out a nice white shirt and a tie that actually matches." Eugenia could tell that she had offended the man, but there was no point in stopping now. "Then get a haircut and quit using pomade until you get back to Atlanta."

Sylvester reached up to touch his glossy curls. "Pomade?" Then understanding dawned. "Oh, you mean hair gel."

Eugenia nodded. "It makes you look vain and foolish. Just part your hair on the side and comb it over if you expect to be taken seriously."

Sylvester sighed. "Is that all?"

Eugenia shook her head. "Not by a long shot. Phrase your requests politely, especially when you're talking to the police chief. If you talk down to people, they take offense," she advised. "And don't act like you're in such a rush."

"I'm trying to find a possible murderer," Sylvester said. "I do feel a certain amount of urgency."

Eugenia leaned closer to her Haggerty assimilation project. "You think Mr. Vance knows something about a murder?"

Sylvester shook his head. "I think Mr. Vance *is* the murderer."

Eugenia couldn't restrain a gasp of surprise. "Who do you think he killed?"

"Why, his wife, of course."

Eugenia stared at Sylvester Muck in astonishment. "If Brandon Vance killed his wife, why in the world would he sell everything he has and use the proceeds to hire private investigators to find her?"

"He's very clever," Sylvester admitted. "A college professor."

"I know," Eugenia allowed. "He told us."

"And what better way to look innocent than to search harder than anyone to find her?" Sylvester asked. "And the beauty of it is that if his private investigators do find something—they'll report it to him and he'll have a chance to disappear before the police get wind of it."

"If what you say is true, why doesn't he just disappear anyway and save himself all this humiliation and trouble?"

"Because he wants to keep his life. He wants to go back to teaching at that little college, and he wants people to feel sorry for him. He has a way with women, so you'd better watch out."

Eugenia considered the ease with which Brandon Vance had managed to get himself out of jail, into her shed, and working in her garden. "Why would he want to kill his wife?"

"Insurance money, of course."

"But he can't get that until the police have a body, and if he knows where it is . . ."

"I think he will eventually arrange for that information to come to light in a way that doesn't implicate him. Or he might just wait out the seven years and then have her declared legally dead."

"When he talked about his wife, he sounded like he loved her very much."

"He probably did at one time, but their kid died a couple of years back, and she was a mess afterward. On antidepressant drugs, in and out of psych wards. I talked to a couple of people at the college who said he was about to lose his job over her antics, so he had to divorce her."

"He told me she wanted the divorce."

"That sounds a lot better for him, doesn't it? And she's not around to defend herself."

Eugenia frowned, wondering if Brandon Vance had tried to pull the wool over her old eyes. To Sylvester Muck she said, "I'm sure that your investigation will prove Brandon innocent of any wrongdoing, but I do think it's in our best interest to help you."

Sylvester smiled. "Excellent. So you'll talk to the police chief for me?"

Eugenia heard the door to Winston's office open. "You're about to get a chance to talk to him yourself." She was trying to decide on the best approach when she saw the coffee mug she'd used to treat Arnold's cuticles. "Put your left hand in the mug and give me your right," she told Sylvester.

He looked into the mug and shuddered. "I can't touch that stuff!"

"My cooperation comes at a price," she informed him. "You must obey me quickly and completely."

Sylvester's hand hovered over the mug. "Will it hurt?"

Eugenia laughed. "Heavens, no! It just kills germs and moisturizes."

Sylvester lowered his hand into the mug as Winston and Arnold entered the lobby. Eugenia saw Winston's look of displeasure when he realized that Mr. Muck was still there. Then his eyes moved to the coffee mug.

"I explained to Sylvester that you run a tight ship and don't allow your police officers to go around with ragged cuticles. Since he's planning to stay here for a few days he asked me to give him a manicure just like Arnold's."

Winston seemed suspicious, but some of the hostility left his face.

"He's promised to dress more conservatively and treat his superiors with respect," Eugenia added.

Now Winston looked surprised.

"And he's even volunteered to go through your mail and find all the important bulletins."

At this announcement Winston's expression became hopeful. "Well, that's right friendly of you."

With a covert look at Eugenia, Sylvester said, "Glad to do what I can."

"As soon as I'm through with this manicure, I've got to head home. It's time for Lady to eat." The little dog barked, emphasizing the importance of this. "Sylvester is going shopping for some normal clothes, and we'll both be back here bright and early in the morning."

Winston nodded. "And I'll set up that appointment with Brandon Vance for two o'clock *tomorrow*."

Sylvester smiled. "Thanks." After a brief hesitation, he added, "Sir."

Winston returned to his office and Arnold took Eugenia's place in front of the phone. As they walked out of the police station, Eugenia told Sylvester she'd see him in the morning. "And it would probably be a good idea for you to eat before you come back tomorrow."

Sylvester looked surprised. "Why?"

"Because Haggerty Station is the only restaurant in town and once Nettie finds out that you referred to her restaurant as a *diner* there's not a chance she'll serve you anything edible."

"How will she find that out?"

"News travels at an amazing rate around here," Eugenia said grimly. "If I didn't know better, I'd think the walls have ears."

Sylvester hung his head. "I really got off on the wrong foot here."

Eugenia took pity on him. "Don't worry about Nettie. Once we get you in good with Winston, we'll start to work on her."

Sylvester smiled, then climbed into his fancy, silver sports car and roared off toward Albany.

Eugenia watched him disappear then looked down at Lady, who was sitting primly in her basket. "There's only so much we can do with that boy."

Lady barked and Eugenia laughed as she started toward Maple Lane at a leisurely pace.

* * *

When Mark got home, Kate called the children and Kelsey down to dinner. While they ate, Kate told Mark about Miss Eugenia's new yardman.

"Why does Miss Eugenia need help with her garden?" Mark asked.

"She's volunteered to do Leita's job at the police station for a few weeks and doesn't want her vegetables to rot in the meantime," Kate explained. "And Kelsey said the man is down on his luck, so Miss Eugenia probably used her overproductive garden as an excuse to help him out."

Mark was frowning at his plate when he said, "I admire her Christian charity, but I'm not crazy about the idea of a vagrant living in the toolshed next door."

Kate felt a jolt of alarm. "You think he could be dangerous?"

"He looked harmless to me," Kelsey said as she pushed her food around her plate.

"Most murderers do," Mark replied. "Otherwise they'd never get close enough to their victims to kill them."

"Who killed somebody?" Emily asked.

"Yeah, who?" Charles mimicked.

Kate gave her children a reassuring smile. "Nobody got killed. Hurry and finish your dinner." Then she turned to Mark. "We'll be careful," she promised.

"Please keep the doors locked," Mark requested, "even during the day. And don't let the children play outside alone."

Kate nodded. "I won't let them out of my sight." Then she pointed at Kelsey's plate. "Don't you like chicken casserole?"

"I . . . I'm sure it's fine. I'm just not very hungry." Kelsey pushed back from the table and took her plate to the sink. "Thanks for dinner, Kate. Now if you'll excuse me, I'm going over to Miss Eugenia's."

After Kelsey left, Kate turned to Mark in amazement. "I wonder why she's going over there?"

"Maybe Miss Eugenia is having something good like hot dogs for dinner," Emily suggested. "And Kelsey's going to eat with her."

"Can we go over to Miss Eugenia's and eat hot dogs too?" Charles wanted to know.

"Definitely not," Mark answered. "Now finish your dinner."

Kate gave him a brave smile, then her eyes strayed to the window and she watched Kelsey walk through the door of Miss Eugenia's back porch.

* * *

Eugenia collected an array of Charles's clothes for Brandon and put them in a Wal-Mart sack. Then she added a bar of soap, a towel, and some toothpaste. She was headed out to give it to him when the phone rang. "Hello?" she said into the receiver.

"Miss Eugenia, it's Winston," the police chief said. "I'm a little nervous about you letting that Vance guy sleep in your toolshed."

"Nervous?" Eugenia demanded. "Why? Have you found some kind of evidence against him?"

"No, but I don't like the fact that the state attorney general's office has sent someone to check him out. It would probably be a good idea to tell Mark about him."

"Since I'm working with Kelsey to find Brandon's wife, it would be unethical for me to discuss the case," Eugenia told him. "You, on the other hand, can discuss anything you like with Mark."

There was a brief pause. Winston said, "I'm probably overreacting."

"I declare, Winston Jones, you wouldn't initiate a conversation with Mark to save your life or mine! I don't understand why the two of you can't just forgive and forget about that silly bowling fight."

"It wasn't silly," Winston insisted. "And I'm willing to forgive. It's Mark who won't."

Eugenia sighed in exasperation. "I don't have time for this childishness." With that she hung up the phone and walked outside.

She met Kelsey on the back porch.

"I'm headed out to see Brandon," Eugenia said. She pointed toward a cot leaning against the wall. "Grab that poor excuse for a bed and come with me."

They found Brandon picking green beans. "It's getting dark," Eugenia pointed out. "Why don't you call it a day?"

He stood and rubbed the small of his back. "Maybe I will."

"I brought some clothes for you," she told him. Then anxious to avoid expressions of gratitude, she added, "They're probably moth eaten."

"Thank you," he said simply.

"And Kelsey's got you a cot."

He took the bag of clothes and the folding bed and deposited them inside the shed.

Eugenia put Lady down, and the little dog ran around while they took a quick tour of the garden. "I'm impressed with how much you've already been able to pick," Eugenia praised Brandon.

"I'm impressed with how much you were able to *plant*," Kelsey told Eugenia. "My mother always has a small garden, but I've never seen anything like this."

"Your garden is quite impressive," Brandon agreed. He turned to Kelsey. "Still no luck finding a trace of Molly?"

Kelsey shook her head. "Not a thing—which is strange. Since she didn't take any money from her bank account, she would have to have found some other means of support. But if she's gotten a job, she didn't use her own social security number."

"Maybe she had other money besides what was in the bank," Brandon proposed. "She had gotten really strange about leaving the house, so it's possible that she kept cash at home."

"But where did it come from if she didn't withdraw it from the bank?" Kelsey asked.

He looked frustrated. "The antique jewelry was gone. Maybe she sold it."

"Didn't those pieces belong to her grandmother?"

Brandon nodded.

"Their value was mostly sentimental, so it's unlikely that she's using them as a source of income," Kelsey told him. "Besides, they'd be easy to identify, and none of the pieces have surfaced."

"Maybe she left the country," he proposed. "And that's why you can't find any record of her getting a job."

"I've done several international searches," Kelsey said, pausing, as if reluctant to continue.

"If she has no source of income . . ."

"There are several lines of work that deal strictly in cash," Kelsey told him. "Like drug dealing or prostitution."

He shook his head. "Molly was so sweet and gentle. She would never do anything like that."

Kelsey didn't argue this. "Then she must be living with someone who does have an income and is willing to support her. That's the only thing that makes sense."

"A friend?" Brandon clarified.

"It would have to be a very good friend," Kelsey replied carefully. Brandon's shoulders slumped. "You mean a boyfriend, don't you?" Kelsey nodded. "That would be logical."

"Not for Molly," Brandon responded. "We went to a counselor after our son died, and he encouraged us to have another child, but . . ." Brandon faltered, then seemed to gather his courage and continued. "Molly wouldn't let me touch her. The counselor said her inability to tolerate affection was a result of the emotional trauma."

After a brief pause, Kelsey said, "Maybe it was just you she couldn't accept affection from."

Brandon flinched. "I guess that's possible."

At this point Eugenia decided that he had been tortured enough. "Well, I think we should end our discussion of the case there. Brandon, why don't you go and clean up, then you and Kelsey will eat dinner with me."

"Oh, I couldn't," Brandon started to object.

"Nonsense," Eugenia said. "You're about to starve to death, and I've got more food than I can eat. We'll be doing each other a favor."

"I don't want to be too much of a burden," he said.

"And I'm tired of eating alone," Eugenia told him briskly. "Now hurry and change."

Brandon nodded then walked off toward the shed. Eugenia led Kelsey over to a couple of lawn chairs near the house. They sat listening to the crickets for a few minutes, then Eugenia said, "A man named Sylvester Muck came by the police station this afternoon wanting to talk to Brandon." When Kelsey didn't comment, Eugenia continued. "He thinks that Brandon killed Molly."

"Brandon told me there was an investigation," Kelsey admitted.

"Is it possible that Brandon killed his wife?"

Kelsey shook her head. "No, I'm certain that he didn't."

"Sylvester thinks he did. And he says that by continuing to search for his wife Brandon is trying to make himself look innocent."

Kelsey frowned. "I've been corresponding with him for several weeks and have the reports from the other investigators he hired. Brandon's search has a genuine desperation to it. I can't believe that the whole thing is a ruse."

"Sylvester's going to interview Brandon tomorrow at two," Eugenia informed her. "It might be a good idea for you to attend."

Kelsey nodded as her stomach growled. "Sorry. I guess I'm starving. I haven't been able to keep much in my stomach lately."

"How far along are you?" Eugenia asked.

Kelsey was visibly startled. "What do you mean?"

"I mean, when is the baby due?"

Kelsey sighed. "I'm almost four months pregnant."

"Have you told Kate?"

Kelsey shook her head. "I haven't told anybody."

"You can't keep a secret like that forever."

"I know," Kelsey admitted.

"I notice that your husband didn't come on this little visit to Georgia with you."

"We're having some problems." Kelsey turned her head toward the setting sun, and Eugenia saw that she was fighting back tears. "I know it sounds awful, but I'd like to disappear like Molly Vance. I could get a divorce, move to a new city, and start all over."

"Being a single parent would be very difficult," Eugenia pointed out. "Especially if you were having to work to support yourself."

"I work from home," Kelsey reminded her.

"It's still work and would require time away from the baby. I was never blessed with children of my own," Eugenia said. "But over the years I've helped many young mothers deal with motherhood, and it's not easy."

"It's not *easy* living with a man you don't have anything in common with," Kelsey interjected.

"I guess we can agree that life is hard," Eugenia said. "But it's easier when the responsibilities are shared."

"So you think I should stay with Travis?"

Eugenia nodded. "It's your decision, but that is what I think. For the baby's sake, give your marriage another chance."

Kelsey sighed. "I'll think about it."

At that moment Brandon Vance walked out of the shadows wearing Charles's old clothes, and, for a moment, Eugenia lost her breath. Her mind told her that it couldn't be, but her heart . . .

"They fit pretty well," Brandon said, giving Eugenia the time she needed to recover her sense of reality.

"Yes," she managed. "Yes they do."

Lady ran over and nuzzled Eugenia's ankle. Eugenia reached down and picked her up. "You knew I needed you," she whispered to the dog. To her guests she said, "Let's go in and eat. I've heated up a nice chicken casserole."

"Sounds delicious," Brandon said.

Kelsey picked up a plump tomato from a basket near her feet. "I don't think I can handle the casserole, but maybe some fresh vegetables."

"Goodness knows we've got plenty of those," Eugenia said with a smile.

As they turned toward the house, a nice car pulled into the driveway.

"Who's that?" Kelsey asked, shading her eyes against the setting sun.

Eugenia smiled as Whit Owens climbed out. "I think it's dessert."

* * *

Kate cleaned up the kitchen while Mark supervised the children's baths. They had just finished family prayer when the phone rang. "You get it," Kate said. "I promised the kids we'd play Candyland tonight, so we'll be waiting for you in the kitchen."

Mark walked into the bedroom and picked up the phone. "Hello?"

"I think I might have the wrong number," Jack Gamble said. "I was calling to get the time and weather."

Mark realized that Jack was trying to protect them both in case either of them was ever required to testify about this conversation. "The weather is fair at the moment, but there could be storms ahead. I'm keeping a close eye out."

"I don't like storms. They can be dangerous. Especially when people are far from home."

"Maybe you should work on getting closer."

Mark heard Jack sigh. "It would be easier to control the weather than a room full of politicians."

Mark laughed and said, "The time is 7:48."

"Thanks." Then the line went dead.

"Who was on the phone?" Kate asked when he walked into the kitchen.

"Wrong number," Mark replied, taking a seat at the table.

* * *

Eugenia put Lady in her basket and walked across the backyard to meet Whit at the driveway. "Well, good evening."

"Hey, Eugenia." He reached out and patted the dog. "And how are you, Lady von Beanie Weenie Mackey?"

"I've decided just to call her Lady," Eugenia explained.

"Very sensible," Whit agreed. He handed Eugenia a pound cake with a label proclaiming it to be number 276.

"You number your pound cakes?"

"I made my first one for Enid Smalley when Harold died," he explained. "I wrote a 'one' on it so she wouldn't expect too much. Then it just seemed natural to continue the tradition."

Eugenia glanced down at the cake in her hand. "You've made a lot of cakes since then."

"I enjoy baking," he admitted. "It's relaxing."

"Have you had dinner?"

"Not yet. I'll make a sandwich when I get home."

"Nonsense," Eugenia said, dismissing his idea. "I've heated up a casserole. Would you join us?"

Whit looked genuinely pleased. "Well, I'd be honored."

Eugenia took his arm and led him into the backyard. "Let me introduce my other dinner guests. This is Kate Iverson's sister Kelsey, who is visiting next door, and my new yardman, who will be living in my gardening shed for a couple of weeks."

Whit shook Kelsey's hand then turned toward Brandon, his expression dubious. "A live-in yardman is a surprise, even for a serious gardener like yourself," he said.

"Actually, Brandon is a client of mine," Kelsey explained. "He's a college professor on leave and needed a temporary job near me for a couple of weeks. Miss Eugenia needed her vegetables picked, so it was the perfect solution."

"Kelsey is an Internet private investigator," Eugenia provided. "And she's invited me to assist her on this case."

"How interesting," Whit said. "Do you mind my asking what kind of case?"

"My wife has been missing for over a year," Brandon spoke for himself. "I've hired several people to find her, without success, and Kelsey is my last hope. I've exhausted my financial resources, so when I arrived in Haggerty to offer assistance, the local police chief arrested me for vagrancy. Thus the need for a job and temporary address."

"Winston arrested you?" Whit seemed amazed by this.

Brandon nodded. "Yes, but he had to release me since Miss Eugenia offered me a job harvesting her garden."

Eugenia felt Whit's eyes on her again. "I know news travels fast in Haggerty, but I'm surprised that you learned of Mr. Vance's plight in time to keep Winston from throwing him out of town."

Eugenia laughed. "I volunteered to answer the phone at the police station until Leita comes back from her sick leave, so I was there when Winston brought Brandon in. But I had already decided to hire someone to help with the garden." She waved to encompass the neat rows of vegetables. "I don't think I could have handled all this myself even if I wasn't spending so much time at the police station."

Whit smiled. "The world would be a better place if more people were as civic minded as you are, Eugenia." Then he turned and addressed Kelsey. "I'm glad I was invited to dinner, so I can learn more about your business," he told her. Then his tone became less friendly as he said, "And more about you too, Mr. Vance."

Eugenia stifled a chuckle. She was well past the age of needing protection from a man, but Whit's gallantry was kind of cute. She led her guests through the back porch, which was cluttered with Christmas decorations. "Eventually I'm going to get this stuff put in the attic."

"Waste of time if you ask me," Whit responded. "It'll be Christmas again before you know it, and you'll just have to get it all back down."

"I always thought you were sensible," Eugenia said. "No matter what people say," she added in a teasing tone as they walked into the kitchen. She put Lady's basket in the corner. "I know you're tired," she told the little dog. "You take yourself a nice nap while I feed these folks." Then she said to Whit, "If you want tea, you'll have to make it yourself. When I quit drinking it, I lost the knack for making it."

"Water is fine with me," Whit assured her.

She smiled, liking him even better. "Well, why don't you and Brandon wash and peel some vegetables? Kelsey can help me."

The men walked obediently to the sink and began their assigned task while Lady curled up and fell asleep. Once the table was set, they all took seats and Eugenia offered a blessing on the food. Then she encouraged everyone to eat. "It will hurt my feelings if you don't take at least three helpings," she told Brandon, who looked on the verge of starvation.

"What do you do for a living, Mr. Owens?" Kelsey asked as she nibbled on a slice of tomato.

"I'm a lawyer," Whit replied.

"I might need a lawyer if I have another misunderstanding with the police chief," Brandon said.

"I might need one too," Kelsey said with a glance at Eugenia.

Whit looked up from his meal in surprise. "You're in trouble with Winston too?"

Kelsey allowed herself a small smile. "No, my problems are of a personal nature. What kind of cases do you handle?"

"All kinds," he told them. "And if either of you need my services, I'll provide them at a significant discount since you're friends of Eugenia's."

"Well, if that isn't the nicest thing," Eugenia said, genuinely impressed.

They finished eating, and Eugenia was about to cut Whit's pound cake when Winston and his girlfriend arrived. Winston introduced Ciera to everyone then apologized for dropping in. "I needed to let you know that I'm going to be late in the morning," he said to Eugenia. "And we were passing by, so I thought I'd just run in and tell you in person."

"Well, since you're here anyway, you might as well have some pound cake," she offered.

"I wouldn't care for any," the girlfriend said.

Eugenia studied the woman's thin frame. "You don't eat cake?"

Winston laughed. "She doesn't eat much of anything, but especially not sweets. I'll have a piece, though."

Once Ciera had a glass of ice water and everyone else had cake, Eugenia looked at Winston. "Whit was just offering to represent Brandon if he ever needs a lawyer," she informed the recent arrivals. "Brandon, why don't you tell Whit about how your wife disappeared, so he'll have a head start if he needs to handle any legal work for you?"

Brandon put down the saucer that contained his half-eaten cake and gave a summary of the past few tragic years. He was a good storyteller and everyone listened raptly, even Winston's skinny girlfriend.

"Could you tell where she might have been planning to go by what she packed?" Whit asked after Brandon had finished his sad story.

"No, she took a little of everything," Brandon replied. "Clothes for all kinds of weather, a variety of shoes, personal items, and the sentimental stuff."

"Are you sure that when she left she knew she wasn't coming back?" Winston confirmed.

Brandon nodded. "She took our son's baby pictures and, well, yes, I'm pretty sure."

Ciera put down her glass of ice water and asked, "Was the house a mess, like she left in a hurry?"

Brandon shook his head. "No, everything was very neat."

"Then it sounds like she didn't leave against her will," Whit pointed out gently.

"No," Brandon admitted.

"How did she leave?" Winston asked.

"We don't know," Kelsey answered for him. "Her car was still parked in the driveway, and she didn't make a reservation on any kind of public transportation. I've checked with every airline, car service, rental company, bus station, and travel agent."

"She must be using an assumed identity," Whit guessed.

Kelsey nodded. "Probably." She looked at Brandon.

"Or someone might have picked her up and driven her away," Brandon added miserably.

"Like a kidnapper?" Winston asked in alarm.

Brandon shook his head. "Like a boyfriend."

"Why do you want to find her?" Ciera asked. "If she's gone to all this trouble to disappear and might have a boyfriend—why don't you just leave her alone?"

"I have to know that she's okay," Brandon explained.

"I might be able to give you a few suggestions," Whit offered. "Why don't you come by my office tomorrow around noon and we'll go to Haggerty Station for lunch."

Brandon sent Eugenia a panicked glance.

"Brandon's in the doghouse with Nettie at Haggerty Station too," Eugenia explained. "So there's a good chance she'll refuse to serve him."

Whit frowned at Brandon. "You've been quite busy."

"It wasn't his fault," Eugenia defended her yardman. "You know how crabby Nettie is. Why don't you have Idella pick you up a couple of take-out plates?" she suggested. "That way you and Brandon can eat and talk in the privacy of your office."

Whit shrugged. "Fine with me."

After Winston finished his third piece of cake, he pronounced it the finest he'd ever eaten. Whit accepted his praise then turned to their hostess. "But the opinion I'm waiting on is Eugenia's."

She cleared her throat. "A touch too much salt," she told him honestly. "And it needs another egg."

He didn't seem upset by her criticism. "I'll try that."

Winston stood and pulled Ciera to her feet. "Well, we'd better go."

Kelsey, who was having trouble keeping her eyes open, rose as well. "I'm sure Kate is wondering what happened to me."

"And I need to get a few hours of sleep before the sun comes up," Brandon added.

"Well," Whit said as he stood. "If everyone else is going, I guess I'll head home too."

Eugenia smiled as she walked everyone to the door. Once they stepped out into the warm summer night, she asked Whit, "Why don't you come to Sunday dinner? For years I've eaten with Polly, but she's on a diet, so I'm cooking this Sunday."

"I'd be delighted," Whit accepted quickly. "I'll make another pound cake using your suggestions, and we'll see how it turns out."

Eugenia nodded then turned to Brandon. "You're welcome too," she said, including him in the invitation. "I've already invited Kate and Mark, so Kelsey will be there and the two of you can discuss your case."

"I'll be looking forward to it," Brandon accepted graciously.

"How about me?" Winston asked. "If Mr. Owens is going to make a pound cake better than the one we had tonight, I'd love to try it."

Eugenia nodded grudging approval but was secretly pleased. More really were merrier. "Just don't be late, or we'll eat without you."

Winston settled his police hat on his head. "I'm never late."

"You're not a churchgoer, either, so I'm concerned that 'after church' might not be a term you're familiar with."

"I'll be here at twelve thirty," Winston promised.

Then Ciera surprised everyone by saying, "Can I come too?"

Eugenia frowned. "Winston said you don't eat."

The woman laughed. "Food isn't important to me," she said, pointing out the obvious, then she gave Brandon a shy glance. "But I really enjoyed the discussion tonight and would like to hear more about it on Sunday."

Eugenia watched a blush creep up Ciera's neck and realized that she had been hanging on Brandon's every word all evening. Eugenia stole a look at Winston and wondered if he'd noticed his girlfriend's interest in another man. Then she studied Brandon covertly. He wasn't bad looking now that he was cleaned up. He was too thin for her tastes, but she could see how he might be attractive to a skinny girl like Ciera. "Well, come on then," Eugenia said finally. "But I'll warn you—no one leaves my table hungry."

Ciera nodded her acceptance of the terms and followed Winston to his patrol car. Brandon headed for the gardening shed, and Eugenia said she'd walk Kelsey home.

Kelsey laughed at this. "Why would you do that?"

"To make sure you get there safely."

Kelsey looked over at her sister's house. "You can see the door from here."

"I'd also like to say good night to the children," Eugenia admitted.

"I think I'll go along," Whit said, and both women gave him surprised looks. "I told you I didn't have anything else to do tonight," he reminded them. "And I want to be sure that you get safely home as well," he told Eugenia. "Especially since your eyesight is failing."

"My eyesight?" she repeated.

Whit nodded. "I'm sorry to bring it up. I'm sure it must be a painful subject."

"What subject?" Eugenia asked.

"Why, your impending blindness," he said, and Eugenia burst out laughing.

"You must have been talking to George Ann."

"I saw her at Haggerty Station at lunch today," Whit admitted.

"I'm not going blind," Eugenia assured him. "I just told George Ann that so that I could bring Lady into the library."

"Why would blindness help with that?"

"Because she's my seeing-eye dog!" Eugenia explained.

Kelsey and Whit laughed.

"Eugenia, you're something else," Whit said, wiping his eyes. Then he took her hand and tucked it around his elbow. "But why don't I go ahead and escort you next door just in case."

When they walked in through the Iversons' back door, they found the whole family sitting around the kitchen table playing Candyland. Mark stood to shake Whit's hand, and Kate offered the lawyer some lemonade.

"Thank you for your kind offer, but I've just eaten over at Eugenia's."

Kate sent her neighbor a speculative glance as Emily said, "Do you want to play Candyland with us? Me and Charles are winning."

"Charles and I," Eugenia corrected.

"I think it's time that your mother and I surrender," Mark told his children with a smile. "Bedtime for you two."

Emily and Charles complained in unison until Eugenia said she'd tuck them in. "Will you tell us a story about when you were a little child in the olden days?" Emily asked.

Eugenia glanced at Whit and he winked back. "Of course I will," she promised the children.

"There's no need for you to leave Mr. Owens," Kelsey said as she stood and walked to the door. "I'll put the children to bed."

Eugenia wanted to reject this change of plans, but the children were already out of their chairs and running toward their aunt. So she watched them leave in silence.

"I'll bet she doesn't know any good stories about the olden days," Whit whispered into Eugenia's ear, making her feel better.

"No, they'll have to settle for something silly like Little Red Riding Hood."

Kate looked like she wanted to ask what they were whispering about, but before she could form the question, Polly Kirby walked through the back door. Her friend Lucy accompanied her, and both were wearing jogging suits, running shoes, and sweatbands. Several unkind comments jumped to Eugenia's lips, but she controlled them.

"Well, Polly," Whit said, coming quickly to his feet. "You're looking mighty fine."

Polly blushed several shades of red. "Why, thank you, Whit."

Eugenia was slightly annoyed by this exchange. "What are you doing out so late?" she demanded of her longtime friend and neighbor. "You're usually in bed by this time."

"Not anymore," Polly responded. "Not since Lucy came to stay."

Lucy laughed. "We take a little stroll every morning and every evening. It's good for our hearts and relieves stress."

Eugenia found it hard to believe that Polly Kirby had any stress in her life and doubted that a few turns around the block could undo years of overeating.

"And we're very careful about what we eat," Polly contributed.

"Does it seem to be working?" Kate asked.

"I've lost five pounds," Polly announced proudly.

"And I've lost three," Lucy added.

Eugenia was taken aback. Maybe they were serious after all.

"On that subject," Kate was saying. "We don't want you to have to cook for us while you're dieting, so Miss Eugenia has offered to host the after-church meal at her house on Sunday."

Eugenia expected gratitude from Polly, but instead the plump woman cried out in disappointment. "Oh no! Sunday dinner at my house is a tradition! Lucy and I already made three pies."

"Doesn't baking pies tempt you to break your diet?" Kate asked with obvious concern.

"Life's full of temptations," Lucy pointed out.

"The diet book we're reading says that we must try to keep the social part of eating without succumbing to the high-fat content and unnecessary calories," Polly explained further. "So we have planned a variety of foods for our Sunday dinner. There will be plenty of foods we can eat but others that we'll have to resist."

"Well, you'll have to save that resistance for *next* week," Eugenia said. "I'm having dinner at my house this Sunday."

"Why can't you do *your* dinner next week?" Polly demanded.

"Because I've already invited my new yardman," Eugenia replied. "And Whit here, along with Winston and his skinny girlfriend."

At the mention of Winston's name, Mark's face clouded with irritation. "We've been eating with Miss Polly for years, and I don't see any reason to change that now," he said.

"You just don't want to eat with Winston," Eugenia accused mildly.

"I *don't* want to eat with Winston," Mark admitted. "But we do owe Miss Polly our loyalty."

"I thought you and Winston were friends," Whit remarked in confusion.

"They were until they started bowling together," Eugenia informed him. "The team made it to the county championship, and the final tournament was on a Sunday. Mark refused to participate, since he doesn't consider bowling an appropriate Sabbath day activity. The team lost, and they haven't spoken to each other since."

"There's more to it than that," Mark said to Whit. "But I won't bore you with the details."

"You're entitled to your privacy," Whit returned with a smile. "And, Eugenia, you don't have to feed me on Sunday. I can heat up a can of soup like always."

"The very idea," Eugenia replied. "You've accepted my invitation for Sunday dinner, and I insist that you come. I'm anxious to taste your new and improved pound cake." Eugenia turned to Mark. "But I'm *not* going to uninvite Winston."

"Sounds to me like we got plenty of folks to go around," Lucy pointed out. "Why don't we have two Sunday dinners?"

Polly considered this for a few seconds then nodded. "I guess that would work. Lucy and I will feed Kate and Mark and the children." She turned to Kate's sister. "And Kelsey, of course."

"Thanks," Kelsey returned. "But I need to eat with Miss Eugenia, so I can talk to . . ." She faltered, apparently realizing a little late that she wasn't supposed to admit her association with Brandon Vance. "To her," she finished lamely.

When Eugenia saw the stricken look on Kate's face, she added, "Really Kelsey just wants to talk to my new yardman. He used to be a professor of American literature, and he quotes poetry."

Mark rolled his eyes. "Another reason to eat with Miss Polly."

"And besides, I'll probably need her help," Eugenia continued, although she had never required kitchen assistance a day in her life. She was pleased to see Kate's wounded expression fade. "After all, it's been years since I've cooked a Sunday dinner."

"Well, if you need her," Kate relented generously.

Eugenia reached over and patted Kate's hand in a rare show of affection. "Thank you."

"Come on now, Polly," Lucy said, heading toward the door. "We got to get into bed so we'll be rested and refreshed come morning."

"Good night everyone." Polly followed Lucy outside, and Whit said that he needed to be going too.

He extended his hand toward Eugenia. "I'll walk you home now if you're ready."

Eugenia saw Kate raise an eyebrow but refused to meet her speculative gaze. With a quick wave to the Iversons, she accepted Whit's hand and allowed him to lead her out the door.

* * *

As the door closed behind Miss Eugenia and Whit Owens, Kate mused. "I wonder why Kelsey ate with Miss Eugenia."

Mark came up behind her and wrapped his arms around her waist. "Remember, this is Miss Eugenia we're talking about. Kelsey may not have had a choice."

Kate smiled. "Miss Eugenia *can* be a little overpowering."

Mark leaned down and nuzzled her neck. "Like a hurricane is a little windy."

Kate turned to face him. "I don't mind, really. It's just that I haven't seen much of Kelsey since she got here."

"Your sister needs advice and direction, and those are two things you get plenty of when you spend time with Miss Eugenia. And there's a silver lining for us."

"Which is?"

"If Miss Eugenia is busy advising Kelsey, she won't have time to boss us around. I figure we've earned a break."

Kate laughed then asked, "Did you think that Mr. Owens and Miss Eugenia seemed kind of friendly tonight?"

Mark frowned. "They *are* friends. They were in the same high school graduating class."

"I meant *extra* friendly," Kate clarified.

"Oh." Mark considered this for a few seconds then shook his head. "No, I didn't notice any extra friendliness between them."

"Maybe it was my imagination," Kate said as she started the dishwasher.

"Is there any of that pie left from dinner?" Mark asked.

"Two pieces," Kate told him. "I'll get the pie—you get the plates."

Once they were settled at the table, Kate asked Mark what his plans were for Saturday.

"Well, I need to spend the morning in Patton Chapel."

Kate thought this over then said, "Patton Chapel isn't in our ward boundaries."

"No," he agreed.

"So it's FBI business?"

He nodded.

"Can you tell me about it, or would that be a breach of national security?"

"I rarely deal with anything that affects national security."

She waved this aside with a forkful of pie. "You know what I mean—you have to keep a lot of things confidential."

"Since the people involved in this case are dead, I think it would be okay to tell you. You remember Tuesday night when I had to work late?"

"I remember lots of nights when you've had to work late." She was only half teasing.

"Well on Tuesday afternoon I got a call from the warden at the Georgia Diagnostic and Classification Prison near Atlanta. He said that one of his inmates was being executed that night and wanted to speak to me before he died."

Kate's breath caught in her throat. There was only one person who had been executed in the state of Georgia that week. "You talked to Lyle Tweedy?"

"I did," Mark acknowledged. "It was one of the worst experiences of my life."

"Tell me all about it," Kate begged. "Was he creepy looking?"

"He was very ordinary in appearance, which *was* creepy. It was easy to see why unsuspecting women would trust him."

"Why did he want to talk to you?"

"I'm not sure exactly," Mark admitted. "He said he wanted to set the record straight."

"What record?"

"His list of homicides. He says he didn't kill one of the women he was convicted of murdering. Her name was Erica Helms."

"But you don't believe him?"

"I have no reason to believe him, but the question that keeps coming back to my mind is why would he lie about that? He was convicted of five counts of first degree murder, each with an accompanying death sentence, so one dismissal wouldn't have affected his life span. He might have gotten a temporary stay of execution if he'd brought the discrepancy to the attention of the court—but he didn't."

Kate frowned. "If he didn't kill her, it seems like he would have said something during the trial."

Mark sighed. "It does seem so, but then you have to remember that this guy was *crazy*."

"If he killed her, why would he have you come to the prison on the night of his execution to deny it?"

"To play with my mind," Mark predicted. "Actually, whether or not he killed Erica Helms, the fact that he called me in to hear his little 'un-confession' was almost certainly a mind game. But the thing that bothers me is that if he didn't kill her . . ."

"Then someone else used him to get away with murder," Kate said, finishing the sentence for him.

Mark nodded. "That's why I called Jack Gamble—to get legal advice. He says if I reopen the case, it might cost me my career."

Kate controlled a shudder. "Why?"

"Because if Tweedy was convicted and executed for a crime he didn't commit, the press won't care that he was guilty of other crimes. They'll have a field day."

"And the FBI will take its share of the heat," Kate guessed.

"Yes, and Jack's afraid my head will be the first to roll."

"Just for bringing Tweedy's claim to the FBI's attention?" Kate demanded. "That's not fair!"

Mark shrugged. "No, but he's probably right. Jack advised me to investigate discreetly. He thinks if I can figure out who the real murderer is the FBI will suffer only a glancing blow from the negative press coverage. I proposed that to Dan Davis, and he agreed."

"So it's like a covert operation?"

"No, it's just a regular investigation, but we're keeping it as quiet as possible until we either confirm Tweedy's guilt or have a new suspect."

Kate wasn't happy about the whole thing. "It all sounds kind of shady."

"I guess I should be glad they are letting me look into it at all. I think if I'd told Dan I was going to forget my whole conversation with Tweedy, he wouldn't have objected."

"Nobody wants to be responsible for opening a can of worms," Kate said.

"No," he agreed, rubbing the back of his neck. "If Tweedy was trying to play with my mind, his plan worked. I can't forget about him, and I feel responsible for Erica Helms."

Kate patted his hand. "Erica Helms lived in Patton Chapel? That's why you're going there?"

Mark nodded. "She lived there all her life. She died at age thirty-four. Her husband and two children were killed in a car accident about a year before her death."

This time Kate did shudder. "I don't know how anyone could ever recover from a tragedy like that."

"It was hard on Erica. She kept to herself for a long time after the accident. Then apparently she decided to reach out to another human being, but she chose the wrong man."

"Lyle Tweedy?"

"Or someone else just as bad," Mark confirmed. "She was strangled, then weighted with rocks, and tossed in the pond behind her house. The body was in such bad shape that they had to identify her with dental records and partial prints from what was left of two fingers. And since she'd never been officially fingerprinted, they were lucky she had made a set of her own prints as part of an Identi-Kit."

Kate nodded. "Winston made me do one of those for the kids, just in case . . ." She couldn't put the unthinkable into words, but he nodded his understanding. "I never thought about doing one for you and me, but I guess that would be a good idea."

"The FBI already has our fingerprints."

Kate gave him a narrowed look. "You just don't want to do it, because I said the Identi-Kits were Winston's idea."

He shrugged. "That and the fact that it's unnecessary."

Kate shook her head as she stacked their dishes and took them to the sink. "What will you do in Patton Chapel tomorrow?"

"I'm starting with the acting sheriff, then I'll talk to as many people who knew her as I can," Mark replied. "There were a couple of reports of a strange man fitting Tweedy's description in the area around the time of her death, but no one actually saw them together. If I can find an eyewitness, I should be able to forget about Lyle Tweedy and his last minute accusations."

Kate walked back to the table and put her hands on his cheeks. "This poor woman didn't have a champion while she was alive, but I'm glad she has you now."

Mark smiled as he stood. "Well, that makes one of us." He took her hand, and they walked together toward the stairs. "So you think I'm a champion, huh?"

She nodded, then added, "Don't let it go to your head."

* * *

Eugenia said good-bye to Whit at her back door, then walked through the house to the living room window, where she watched his car pull away from the curb. Once he was gone, she checked on Lady, who was still sleeping peacefully. She finished cleaning up the kitchen and was debating about the wisdom of making a pie for Sunday before she went to bed when the phone rang. Her mother had always told her that phone calls after nine o'clock in the evening always meant bad news. This time her mother was wrong. It was Whit.

"Sorry to call so late," he apologized. "But I wanted to thank you again for dinner."

"My pleasure," Eugenia told him and realized it was true. It had been years since she had done any entertaining, and she had forgotten how pleasant having company could be.

"Did you lock all your doors?" he asked.

"Oh yes," Eugenia assured him. "Mark has gotten me in the habit of that."

"Good. It makes me nervous that you have that man sleeping in your backyard."

Eugenia was surprised and a little thrilled. "Why, Whit, surely you can see that Brandon is completely harmless."

"I don't see that at all," the lawyer countered. "I see him as a stranger whose wife is missing under mysterious circumstances. You need to be very careful."

"I will," Eugenia promised as she rubbed the chill bumps that now dotted her arms. "See you tomorrow."

"I can't wait," he returned. "Good night, Eugenia."

After saying good-bye, she looked up to see Lady watching her. "Well, what do you make of that?" she asked the little dog. Lady barked twice and Eugenia laughed. "I don't know what to think either. Now, let me get you a snack, then we'll go to bed."

CHAPTER 5

On Saturday morning Mark woke up early, intending to leave for Patton Chapel without waking his family. But when he walked into the bedroom after his shower, Kate was gone, and he could smell bacon cooking downstairs.

"A champion needs a good breakfast before he goes into battle," she explained when Mark took his regular chair at the kitchen table.

"This particular champion needs all the help he can get," Mark said as he nibbled a piece of bacon. "What are you and the kids going to do today?"

"We're going to clean house and make a trip to the grocery store, and then I promised we'd play in the park."

"Sounds fun," Mark said a little wistfully.

Kate laughed. "Only compared with what you'll be doing."

Mark finished his breakfast, kissed his wife, and then headed for Patton Chapel.

* * *

Kate let the children sleep until eight o'clock and made use of the time to catch up on laundry. After rousing Charles and Emily, she paused by Kelsey's door, listening for signs that her sister was awake, but all was silent.

"Is Aunt Kelsey going to eat breakfast with us?" Emily whispered.

"I think she's still asleep," Kate replied quietly. "Let's go downstairs and let her rest."

When the children finished eating, Kate gave them some small house-keeping duties, then decided to check and see if Kelsey wanted breakfast before she cleaned the kitchen. She climbed the stairs and noticed that the door to the guest room was open and the room was empty. Kate walked down to the bathroom and saw a line of light shining from under the door. Assuming that Kelsey was taking a shower, Kate turned to go back downstairs. Then the bathroom door opened, and Kelsey staggered out. Her face was deathly pale, and her hair hung in damp clumps against her cheeks.

Kate rushed forward. "Kelsey! What's the matter?"

"I'm so sick," the girl replied weakly. "Help me, please."

Kate put a shoulder under her sister's arm and assisted her to bed. Once Kelsey was tucked under the covers, Kate said, "I think I should take you to the doctor. You might have the flu."

Kelsey smiled. "I wish it was that simple."

Before Kate could reply, Miss Eugenia had appeared at the bedroom door. She was wearing a Sunday dress, and the basket containing her new little dog was hooked over her arm. "Emily sent me up," she said. Then her shrewd eyes took in the situation. "You're sick?" she asked Kelsey. The girl nodded. Miss Eugenia turned to Kate. "Do you have some saltine crackers?"

"Yes," Kate acknowledged.

"That might settle her stomach," Miss Eugenia suggested. "Ginger ale usually helps too. You can pick some up when you go to the grocery store."

"Saltine crackers and ginger ale," Kate repeated dumbly. That was the antinausea remedy Miss Eugenia had recommended when she was suffering from morning sickness during her pregnancy with Charles. Her eyes drifted to her sister. "You're pregnant?"

Kelsey nodded weakly. "Can you believe it? I didn't think my luck could get any worse."

Kate clutched her own barren midsection. Tears stung her eyes, and, for the first time in her life, she felt the urge to slap her sister. "You don't *want* the baby?"

Kelsey shrugged. "I'd like to have children someday, but not now when I'm considering divorce."

Kate took a step toward the bed, angry words on the tip of her tongue. Then Miss Eugenia moved to block her path.

"Kate, why don't you go get those crackers now," she suggested. "Send them up with Emily, and I'll look after Kelsey while you clean that messy kitchen."

Kate knew Miss Eugenia was a deliberately trying to deflect some of her anger away from Kelsey, but still the words stung. "I was waiting to clean up after Kelsey had breakfast," she said defensively.

"Well, I think Kelsey has proven that she can't handle pancakes and bacon this morning, so you can go ahead and get busy."

Kate sent her neighbor a cross look then turned toward the door.

"But since you have extra, why don't you fix me a plate," Miss Eugenia said to Kate's back. "I'll be down to eat as soon as Kelsey feels better."

Kate didn't trust herself to speak. She hurried downstairs and took a package of saltine crackers from the cupboard. After sending them upstairs with Emily, Kate started cleaning with a vengeance—her mind in turmoil. The only thing she really wanted in life, other than what she already had, was another baby. She'd had an emergency hysterectomy after Charles was born, and the thought that her child-bearing years were over was a source of constant grief. Now Kelsey was pregnant with a baby she didn't want. She wiped viciously at a spot on the kitchen counter. Life was so unfair.

Kate was roused from her grim revelry by the ringing of the phone. It was Mark. "Are you in Patton Chapel yet?" she asked.

"I'm not only here," Mark replied. "I've already conducted one interview."

Kate checked the digital clock on the oven. "It's barely eight o'clock."

"The acting sheriff asked me to meet him at a coffee shop. When I got here he told me he had people scheduled to come by every fifteen minutes."

"That was nice of him."

"He's saving me all kinds of time," Mark agreed.

There was a brief silence, then Kate blurted, "Kelsey's pregnant, and she doesn't want the baby."

"How do you know she doesn't want the baby?"

"Because she called it bad luck." Kate's anger toward Kelsey resurfaced.

"Kate," Mark said in a patient tone. "I want you to consider the possibility that the only thing worse than wanting a baby and not being able to have one might be having a baby when you don't really want one—for whatever reason."

Kate's thoughts jumped back to several years before when she'd found out she was pregnant with Emily. Her first husband, Tony, was dead. She was living in a bleak apartment in Chicago—far from her mother and sisters. She had a job she hated, and the future was uncertain. She should have been terrified by the prospect of raising a child alone, but instead she had been thankful that the Lord had given her a part of Tony to keep. "I don't understand how she feels."

"Which is why you shouldn't be too hard on her."

Kate took a deep breath then said, "If she really doesn't want the baby, maybe . . ."

"Kate," Mark interrupted as if he'd read her mind. "Don't get your hopes up. It will be months before the baby is born, and by then she and Travis may be back together."

Kate's shoulders sagged. "It was just an idea."

"Try to be supportive of Kelsey," Mark encouraged. "She's afraid and confused right now. Everything will work out—one way or another."

"Okay," Kate agreed. "Hurry home." She was just hanging up the phone when Miss Eugenia came into the kitchen.

"Is this my breakfast?" Miss Eugenia pointed to the plate Kate had left on the counter.

"Yes," Kate confirmed.

Miss Eugenia brought her plate to the table and put the dog basket on the floor beside her. "Kitchen looks nice and clean."

Kate scowled at her neighbor. "I'm glad it meets your approval. How's Kelsey?"

Miss Eugenia poured a generous amount of syrup on her pancakes. "Resting quietly for the moment."

"Do you think I should arrange for her to see my doctor in Albany?" Kate asked as Miss Eugenia gave the dog a piece of bacon.

"She said she visited an obstetrician just before she left Utah. She isn't scheduled to go again for three weeks, so I'd wait to see if she's still here then."

"Should she call the doctor's office in Utah and tell them that she's sick?"

Miss Eugenia swallowed before saying, "Morning sickness is a normal part of pregnancy. Unless she gets dehydrated, I don't see any reason to call the doctor."

"I just feel so helpless," Kate exclaimed.

"Well you can help *me* by making a few more pancakes. These are delicious."

Kate moved to the stove and reheated the griddle. "I've got to find something that Kelsey can eat besides crackers."

Miss Eugenia pulled an index card out of her pocket and started scribbling. "Some of my potato soup should settle Kelsey's stomach. I'll write down the recipe, and you can get the ingredients while you're at the store."

Kate flipped the pancakes then looked at her watch. "I hate to leave Kelsey alone while I go grocery shopping. How long can you stay?"

"I don't have a particular schedule," Miss Eugenia replied. "I'm going in to the police station for a while, and then I need to get groceries myself, but all of that can wait until after you get back." Looking around, she added, "Where's Mark?"

"Working."

"Humph!" Miss Eugenia scoffed. "It seems like he could at least be at home with his family on Saturdays."

Kate put three fresh pancakes on Miss Eugenia's plate. "It couldn't be helped. I'll go round up the children and head to the store."

"Just leave them here," Miss Eugenia requested. "I'll enjoy their company, and you'll be able to finish more quickly on your own."

Kate considered this for a few seconds then agreed. "I'll just wash up these last few dishes."

"I'll wash my own dishes," Miss Eugenia insisted. "You get on to the store. Kelsey needs that ginger ale," she added as incentive. "Don't forget the ingredients for this potato soup." She put the index card into Kate's hand.

Kate tucked the card in her purse and headed toward the back door. "Tell the kids I'll be home soon."

Miss Eugenia nodded as Kate walked outside and hurried toward her van.

Kate was very familiar with the layout of the local Wal-Mart Super Center and moved through it efficiently, selecting the things from her list and the ingredients for Miss Eugenia's potato soup. She was standing by the dairy section trying to decide what constituted the "block" of cheese listed on the recipe card when Cleo Ledbetter and her son, Earl Jr., walked up.

"Hey, Kate," Cleo said.

"Good morning," Kate returned. Then she saw Earl Jr. and smiled. The six-year-old had been through a series of stages since the Ledbetters had moved to Haggerty. He'd been an astronaut and a cowboy and a policeman and a doctor. Whenever he entered a stage, he always dressed the part. Today he was wearing a miniature football uniform complete with shoulder pads, helmet, and cleats. A stickler for authentic detail, Earl Jr. even had a mouthpiece dangling from the face mask. "What position do you play?" she asked the little boy.

"Quarterback," he responded.

"Wow, that's an important job," Kate told him. Then she turned to Cleo. "So how do you like this stage?"

"It's the worst so far," Cleo told her wearily. "He's nearly torn up all the grass in our backyard with those cleats, and he's covered with bruises from getting sacked."

Kate stepped a little closer to Cleo. "Who sacks him? I mean, does he really have a team?"

Cleo reached out and patted the top of Earl Jr.'s helmet. "Naw. He just throws himself down on the ground." Cleo looked at the two packages of cheese in Kate's hand. "You having a party?"

"No, my sister is visiting from Utah and she's sick," Kate explained. "So I'm making some of Miss Eugenia's potato soup for her, but I can't decide which one of these is a 'block' of cheese."

Cleo studied first the eight-ounce package, then the sixteen-ounce package. "I always say more is better. Buy the big one."

Kate put the larger block into her basket. "Thanks for the advice."

You're welcome," Cleo replied, then she turned to her son. "Come on, Earl Jr. Your daddy's going to be wondering what happened to us." She glanced back at Kate. "We came for a gallon of milk, and we've been here almost an hour."

Kate laughed. "I know exactly what you mean."

After Cleo and Earl Jr. left, Kate completed her shopping and hurried home. Miss Eugenia met her in the driveway, Lady on her arm. "I thought you'd never get here," she said by way of greeting. "Winston's called five times, wondering when I was coming to the police station."

"I'm sorry it took so long," Kate apologized. "Is everything okay?"

"Kelsey's asleep, but you should wake her and let her drink some of that ginger ale," Miss Eugenia instructed as she walked over to her old Buick and settled Lady in the backseat.

Kate watched Miss Eugenia drive away, then squared her shoulders and went up to force-feed Kelsey crackers and ginger ale.

* * *

Eugenia arrived at the police station where she found the phone ringing and Winston pacing. Knowing that Winston would most likely complain about her tardy arrival, she decided to try her luck with the phone. She put Lady on the floor by Leita's desk and picked up the receiver.

"Haggerty police."

Winston stopped pacing and came to hover over her.

"It's Dub Shaw again," she whispered to the police chief. She listened to Dub's ranting for a few minutes then reported to Winston, "He says someone's poisoned his dogs."

Winston cursed under his breath. "I'd better check it out." He pulled his hat on. "I'll be back when I can."

The door barely had time to close behind Winston before it opened again. The new arrival was Sylvester Muck, dressed in a conservative black suit. His hair had been trimmed, and Eugenia couldn't detect a speck of pomade.

"Well, don't you look nice," she said.

The young man blushed. "Thank you." He lifted a Hardee's sack. "I brought sausage biscuits for breakfast. Help yourself."

"I've already eaten," Eugenia told him as she accepted the sack. It was heavy, and a peek inside confirmed that it contained at least six biscuits. "But I'd hate for these to go to waste." She extracted two biscuits and returned the bag to Sylvester. While they ate she asked him how he ended up working for the state's attorney general.

"My father got me the job," Sylvester admitted with obvious embarrassment. "I had good grades and references, but my parents didn't think that would be enough. So my father pulled some strings."

"You didn't want his help?" Eugenia gathered from his tone.

"I wanted to at least try to get a job on my own," Sylvester explained. "And since everybody at the SAG's office knows that I wasn't hired on my own merits, they don't take me seriously. I'm just there."

"That's why solving the case of Mrs. Vance's disappearance is so important to you," Eugenia guessed.

"They gave it to me as busy work," Sylvester acknowledged. "Just a case to review and toss. But if I can solve it . . ."

"You think the people you work with will see you in a different light."

Sylvester smiled. "If they see me at *all* it will be an improvement."

Eugenia laughed then pointed to the stacks of unopened mail. "There are bound to be lots of wanted posters in all that," she predicted. "So you might as well get started."

* * *

Kate watched while Kelsey successfully swallowed two crackers and a sip of ginger ale.

"I feel much better," Kelsey insisted after she finished the second cracker. "I think I'll get up and take a shower."

"Why don't you let the crackers settle for a few minutes first," Kate suggested.

Kelsey shrugged. "Okay."

"Can we get out the play dough?" Emily asked.

"Yes, but keep it on the kitchen table," Kate agreed conditionally. "And don't let Charles eat any."

After the children were gone, there was an awkward silence. Finally Kelsey said, "I know how much you want another baby, and you're probably mad at me for feeling the way I do about being pregnant."

Kate sighed. "I'm not mad. I don't understand how you feel, but I love you and I'll do anything I can to help you."

Kate was surprised to see tears well up in Kelsey's eyes. "Thank you," she said.

Kate sat on the edge of the bed and gathered her sister into her arms. "Everything will be okay. You'll see."

"I haven't told Mom," Kelsey whimpered. "About Travis or the baby or anything. I don't know how to explain it. You see what a bad job I've done telling you."

"Mom will be patient until you figure things out," Kate assured her. "Now you just rest until your stomach has a chance to digest those crackers. Then you can take a shower, and you should feel better." Kate stood and moved toward the door. As she passed Kelsey's computer desk, she saw a name that startled her. She pointed at the printout. "Isn't Brandon Vance Miss Eugenia's yardman?"

If possible, Kelsey turned a shade paler. "Yes."

"And you're doing research for him?"

"Yes."

"The missing person case?"

Kelsey nodded. "His wife is missing, and I'm trying to find her."

Kate wanted to ask more but hated to make Kelsey compromise her ethics. So she decided to drop it for now. "Okay, well you call if you need me."

Kelsey seemed relieved that Kate wasn't going to press the issue. "I will."

* * *

Mark finished interviewing the pastor of the Patton Chapel First Presbyterian Church, where the Helms family had maintained a membership. After the pastor left, Mark turned to acting sheriff Foster Gunnells, who was presiding quietly over the proceedings. "So the Helms family was active in the church without being particularly religious."

Foster nodded. "Sounds about right." He referred to the list in front of him. "Erica's mother refused to come for an interview, so we'll have a little gap before Ken's mother and brother get here."

"Ken was Erica's husband?"

"Yes," Foster confirmed.

"Did you know her? Erica, I mean," Mark asked to fill the silence.

"Everybody knows everybody around here," Foster replied. "Ken was in my graduating class. Erica was one grade behind us."

"So you were friends?"

Foster laughed. "Not really. Erica was part of the popular crowd—cheerleader, homecoming queen—all that."

Mark glanced down at the family picture in his file. The Erica Helms that smiled back at him was a pudgy brunette. "It's hard for me to imagine her as homecoming queen," he told Foster.

"Having children put weight on Erica, but as a teenager she was a real looker," Foster insisted.

"Did you like her?"

"I didn't dislike her," Foster answered carefully. "And she was friendly to everyone."

"But . . ." Mark prompted.

"She wasn't very sincere." Foster seemed to be battling with himself and finally said, "Erica was a user."

Mark was astounded. "A user? You mean drugs?"

Foster waved this aside. "No, not drugs. People. She used people then discarded them when she was through."

Mark considered this for a few seconds then said, "Tell me about your relationship with Erica."

"Didn't have one," Foster replied. "She and Ken went steady pretty much all through school. They had a fight right before the prom, and she asked me to be her date."

Mark had to work hard to keep his mouth from falling open. "You took Erica Helms to your senior prom?"

Foster nodded. "She wasn't Erica Helms then. She was still Erica Purdy."

"And she asked you, not the other way around?"

"Yeah. I was pretty thrilled at first, but I found out later that I was a last resort. By the time Erica had her fight with Ken, everyone else already had dates that had been arranged months before."

Mark leaned forward. "So how was your date?"

"A disaster. Her friends kept coming over to talk or ask her to dance, and they acted like I was invisible. After the prom Erica and Ken made up, and then when she'd pass me in the hall she didn't even look at me."

"Since she didn't need you anymore," Mark guessed.

Foster nodded. "Right."

"How did she get along with other folks in the community?"

"She didn't even try. Erica was a snob. I don't know why, except that she was pretty, because her family didn't have any money. But once she and Ken got married, she developed expensive tastes."

"Nice clothes and cars?" Mark guessed.

"More than that. She went to a hospital in Albany to have her children—like she was too good for our local doctors. And most of their friends were executives from the Honda plant where Ken worked. They were always throwing parties but never invited any of their neighbors."

"So you didn't have much contact with her after she married."

"None really," Foster reported. "I'd see her occasionally, but she didn't speak. That is, until the year her oldest child started school. Her kid's teacher called to arrange a tour of the sheriff's office. All the kindergarten classes study a unit on community helpers in September, and a field trip to the sheriff's office is standard. But by the time the teacher called, I was already booked with tours for the whole week. I had barely hung up the phone with the teacher when Erica called. She remembered me just fine and how we went to the prom together and how we had been friends in high school."

"Did you let her daughter's class come?" Mark asked.

Foster blushed. "I couldn't tell her no. After the day of the tour I didn't see her again until the joint funerals for her family."

"That must have been a terrible time for her."

"Yeah, it was awful. She wouldn't leave the cemetery after the funeral. She kept begging the caretaker not to put her babies in the ground." Mark saw Foster shudder at the memory. "I thought they were going to have to physically drag her away, but finally Dr. Welch, their dentist here in town, talked her into leaving with him."

Mark frowned. "She drove all the way to Albany for doctors, but she had a local dentist?"

"It was the one exception Erica made," Foster said with a ghost of a smile. "She worked for Dr. Welch a couple of days a week, so I guess she figured that made him classy enough. Besides, he was young, and women seemed to find him attractive."

"Is he married?" Mark asked.

"Sort of," Foster replied. Mark raised an eyebrow in his direction. "I mean, he *is* married, but rumor has it that he doesn't take his vows seriously."

Mark made a note to check out Dr. Welch. "I understand that Erica became something of a hermit after the funeral."

"Not something of—the real thing. She rarely left her house. She even had her groceries delivered."

"No more parties."

Foster shook his head. "No parties, no fun, no life."

Before Mark could comment, a man and a woman approached their table. Foster stood and Mark followed suit. "Agent Iverson, I'd like to introduce you to Mrs. Joy Helms and her son Carlton."

Mark shook their hands then invited them to have a seat. "I appreciate you coming to meet with me this morning," Mark told them. "I'm trying to close the file on Erica's death, and I need to ask you a few questions." He turned to Mrs. Helms first. "Were you and Erica close?"

Mark watched as his guests exchanged a quick look, then Carlton Helms answered for his mother. "Ken and Erica were very busy people before the accident and didn't have much time for family gatherings."

Mrs. Helms made a face as Mark asked, "What about after the accident?"

Carlton spoke again. "When Ken and the children died, Erica closed herself off from everyone. We wanted to help her through the grieving process, but she wouldn't let us."

Mrs. Helms leaned forward. "Erica acted like she was the only one who was suffering—the only one who had sustained a loss. I'm not ashamed to say I resented that. Didn't she realize that I had lost my son and my grandchildren?" Mrs. Helms pressed her hands against her chest. "My very *heart?*"

Carlton reached a hand over and patted his mother's shoulder. "It was a hard time for all of us. Erica wasn't at her best, and we understood that."

"Of course I understood, and I was willing to be patient," Mrs. Helms said. "But she never adjusted. She was never able to talk about them or look at their pictures or anything."

"I don't want you to think that Erica didn't try," Carlton said. "She had a psychiatrist, and she met with a grief management group. It's just that nothing seemed to help. She remained withdrawn and, well . . ."

"Crazy," Mrs. Helms provided. "The tragedy drove Erica crazy."

"Were you surprised when she told people she had a boyfriend?"

"I was more than surprised," Mrs. Helms replied. "I think it was a lie. Erica could barely abide someone standing near her. I can't imagine her having a friend of any kind, let alone a *boyfriend*."

Mark said, "Perhaps Erica just found being around your family particularly difficult." What he didn't say was that if Erica managed to visit a psychiatrist and participate in a grief management group— she wasn't avoiding all people.

"I'd like to get my mother home if you don't have any more questions," Carlton Helms said, effectively ending the interview.

Mark nodded then thanked Mrs. Helms and her son for coming. He obtained permission to contact them again if he thought of any more questions.

After they left, Foster sighed. "I didn't know about that grief management group," he told Mark. "I guess you'll be wanting a list of the members."

Mark smiled. Maybe working with an FBI wannabe wasn't so bad. "That would be very helpful."

"I'll get to work on it right now." Foster pulled his cell phone from his uniform pocket and made a call.

Mark used the time to go over his notes. When Foster closed his phone, Mark said, "I wonder what made Erica decide to join a therapy group."

"Maybe she thought it would help to talk to other people who had been through the death of family members."

"I'd like to talk to the psychiatrist, although I doubt he'll tell me anything."

"He's in Albany." Foster pointed to the address on the list he had given Mark. "Visiting his office will be convenient for you."

"But it wasn't convenient for Erica."

"I told you. She didn't use local doctors."

"Except the dentist."

Foster nodded. "Right."

"I think I'd better talk to him too."

"The dentist?" Foster seemed surprised.

"He was her employer for years, and he convinced her to leave the cemetery."

Foster shrugged. "I'll call and see if he can come." The sheriff placed his call and after a short conversation hung up. "Dr. Welch is at the golf course and says if you want to talk to him you'll have to catch him in between holes."

Mark nodded. "I might just do that. Who's our next interview?"

"The receptionist from Dr. Welch's office. Her name is Belva Church."

"Are you talking about me, Foster?" a woman said from behind them.

Mark turned to see a beautiful blond in her late thirties. She had one hand on her hip, and her head was cocked in a coquettish pose.

"Hey, Belva," Foster said, rising to his feet.

"Sit down, Foster," she said as she slipped into the chair next to Mark. "I've only got a few minutes, so talk fast."

"How long did Erica Helms work for Dr. Welch?"

Belva laced her manicured fingers together and considered this. "Let's see. Erica started just a few months after Chuck opened his office here. So I guess she worked with us for eight or nine years."

"She was working to help put her husband through school?"

"At first," Belva confirmed.

"And why did she continue to work after her husband graduated and got a good job in management at the Honda plant?"

Belva glanced over her shoulder then leaned forward, indicating that she was about to divulge something she didn't want anyone else to hear. "There wasn't enough money in the world to satisfy Erica. Maybe it was because she was raised so poor, but she was the biggest cheapskate I ever saw."

Mark couldn't hide his surprise. "I thought she wore nice clothes and drove an expensive car."

"She did," Belva acknowledged. "From what I could tell, they had plenty of money, but she still worked a couple of days a week so she and her family would be eligible for the free dental work."

"It sounds like you didn't care for Erica," Mark commented.

Belva took a deep breath and sat back in her chair. "Erica was okay, but she always had an ulterior motive in everything she did, and that made me nervous."

"You've been with Dr. Welch since he opened his practice here?" Mark asked.

Belva nodded. "From the very beginning."

Mark looked up quickly and read the hidden meaning in her eyes. Belva was in love with the dentist and had been for a long time.

"I understand that Dr. Welch and Erica were particularly good friends," Mark baited, trying to see what he could come up with.

A blush rose in Belva's cheeks. "That's been over for a long time."

Over, maybe, but definitely not forgotten as far as the receptionist was concerned.

"When was the last time you saw Erica?" Mark asked absently, his mind still following the romantic triangle.

"Just a few days before she died," Belva surprised him by saying.

"Where?" Mark asked.

"She came to the dental office to pick up her dental records. She said she was leaving town and wanted to take them with her."

Mark looked over at Foster, and the acting sheriff nodded. This fit with what they knew about the days right before Erica died. "I presume you kept copies of her records, since the sheriff's office used them to identify her body."

"We didn't have to," Belva said with a slight lift of her shoulder. "Erica went to get her records but came back a few minutes later. She said Chuck had convinced her to leave them and let us forward them to her new dentist once she was settled."

"How did she seem when you saw her?" Mark asked. "I mean, did she act happy or excited?"

Belva nodded. "Oh yes, she was downright giddy."

"Did she tell you that she had a boyfriend?"

"Tell me?" Belva echoed. "She wouldn't *stop* talking about him."

"Did she give you his name?"

Belva laughed. "No, but she did say he was handsome and dangerous."

"Dangerous?" Mark repeated. "She used that word?"

"That word exactly," Belva confirmed.

"And you never saw her again?"

Belva's expression became somber. "No." She scooted her chair away from the table. "Is that all? I'm supposed to be at the beauty salon in ten minutes."

Mark and Foster rose to their feet in unison.

"That's all for now," Foster told her.

"Thanks for coming," Mark said.

"See you later," Foster added.

Belva pointed her finger at the acting sheriff. "You'd better make that sooner. It's been over a year since you've had your teeth cleaned. I'll pencil in an appointment and call your office with the date."

Foster's shoulders slumped. "Okay."

After Belva left, Mark regarded the other man. "Your office didn't do a very thorough investigation after Erica's death," he said, trying to keep the words from sounding like an accusation. "You didn't know about the grief management group, and there's nothing in the incident report about Erica's visit to the dental office days before she died."

Foster sighed. "That doesn't mean the old sheriff didn't know about it. Sheriff Rafferty wasn't big on paperwork, so there's probably a lot that he didn't put in the report."

"But you weren't personally involved with the investigation?"

"Oh sure. I did a lot of the legwork for him. He had emphysema. That's what killed him." Foster frowned then added, "Why do you ask?"

"I just wondered if your feelings for Erica might have affected which pieces of information made it into the report. Leaving things out of the report like her therapy group and her improper relationship with the dentist would help to protect her reputation."

Foster had the decency to look ashamed. "She was dead, and I hated to see any more harm done to her, so maybe I did forget to mention a few things. But like I told you, the case got taken away from us early. I figured that the feds checked everything out."

Before Mark could reply, Foster's cell phone rang. He answered it and listened for a few seconds, then hung up and turned to Mark.

"The list of people in the grief management group is waiting for us at the office. We'll swing by and pick it up, then I'll take you to the golf course."

* * *

Dr. Welch turned out to be a nice-looking middle-aged man, who apparently saved all his charm for women. "I'll give you five minutes without a warrant," he told Mark curtly.

"What was your relationship with Erica Helms?"

"I was her employer."

Mark raised an eyebrow. "And?"

"We were friends."

"That's all?"

The dentist nodded.

"I was told that you and Mrs. Helms were involved romantically."

Dr. Welch smiled. "Erica and I had a *close* friendship when she first came to work with me nine years ago. By mutual consent we decided to be just *good* friends a few weeks later."

"So after that decision you never spent time with Erica Helms away from the office?" Mark asked.

"I'll have to take the fifth on that," the dentist replied.

"You can't take the fifth." Mark was annoyed. "You're not testifying."

"Okay, then I just refuse to answer," Dr. Welch said with a smirk. "Time's up."

"It hasn't been five minutes," Foster objected in Mark's behalf.

Dr. Welch swung up into his golf cart. "Time flies when you're having fun." Then he drove away, leaving Mark and Foster staring after him.

* * *

Eugenia spent the remainder of the morning returning case files to the appropriate cabinets while Sylvester opened mail. Lady alternately sniffed garbage cans and napped. By the time Winston returned with sandwiches for lunch, the wanted bulletin board was completely updated and the garbage cans were overflowing with junk mail. Winston passed out sandwiches, and while they ate, Eugenia asked about Dub's dogs.

"It was the darnedest thing I've ever seen," Winston said around a mouthful of all-beef patty, special sauce, lettuce, cheese, pickles, onions, and sesame seed bun. "All four of Dub's dogs were dead—just lying there in the yard."

"What kind of poison did the killer use?" Sylvester asked between bites.

"Not sure," Winston replied. "Called the street and sanitation department to pick up the carcasses. They were going to run them by the funeral home for them to take a few blood samples. They'll send it to Atlanta and hope the lab can determine the type of poison. I suspect antifreeze."

Sylvester nodded. "It's cheap, easily accessible, and deadly if ingested."

"Or it could have been poisoned meat," Winston added as another option.

"But why would anyone want to kill Dub's dogs?" Eugenia asked with a quick look at Lady. "I mean, I know that kids will be kids and that vandalism is almost a right of passage through the teenage years. But there's a big difference between slashing the tires of a broken-down car and killing four dogs with poison."

Winston shook his head. "I don't know. Maybe it was like you said—a gang initiation."

"Or maybe they really are planning to kill Mr. Shaw and wanted the dogs out of the way," Sylvester suggested. Eugenia and Winston both turned to stare at him, but Sylvester wasn't intimidated by their skepticism. "You've got to admit it's a possibility."

"I guess," Eugenia allowed.

Winston sighed. "I'd better arrange for Dub to spend a few days in the county drunk tank. And while he dries out, I'll stay at his house in case he has any unfriendly visitors."

"That sounds like a very good plan," Eugenia said as she slipped Lady a tiny piece of her hamburger.

Sylvester watched this then said, "You know that feeding dogs table scraps is bad for them."

Eugenia was dismayed. "I didn't know that."

"Didn't the vet recommend a special dog food for Lady?"

"Yes," Eugenia admitted reluctantly.

"I thought so. It's especially important for small dogs, who don't eat much, to get plenty of nutrition in every bite."

Eugenia looked down at Lady, who was licking her tiny chops. "I'd feel terrible if I've made her unhealthy by feeding her table scraps."

Sylvester laughed. "She looks very healthy to me, but it's probably a good idea to stick with dog food in the future."

"It seems mean for me to eat in front of Lady."

"Why don't you keep a ziplock bag of dog food in your purse? That way you can give Lady a healthy snack anytime."

Eugenia smiled. "That's a good idea. Maybe you're not such a bad sort after all."

* * *

Kate let Emily and Charles go outside to play on the deck, then propped Miss Eugenia's potato soup recipe card up in front of her and began. She peeled the potatoes, and while they cooked in chicken broth, she grated the cheese and mixed the canned soups with the sour cream. Once the potatoes were "tender," as described on the card, she combined all the ingredients and stirred the soup until it was bubbling hot.

Kate ladled some of the soup into a bowl and placed it, along with some crackers, on the breakfast tray Emily and Charles had given her for Mother's Day. She poured a tall glass of ginger ale and headed upstairs. Kelsey was dressed and sitting at her computer, but she still looked terrible. "You should get back in bed before you faint," Kate warned.

"I can't. I have an appointment at the police station in a little while."

Kate was astounded by this announcement. "You're meeting with Winston?"

Kelsey nodded. "It's about the case I'm working on."

"Oh." Kate thought about the printout with Brandon Vance's name on it. "Well, I've made you some of Miss Eugenia's potato soup. If you eat some before you go, it might give you enough strength to make it to town and back."

Kelsey smiled. "Or it might make me start throwing up again."

Kate shook her head. "Miss Eugenia assures me it will not upset your stomach." She placed the tray in front of her sister. Kelsey picked up the spoon, took a bite, then made a face.

"Sorry, Kate, but the soup is too spicy for me and so thick I can barely swallow it." Kelsey sipped the ginger ale. "This is good, though."

Kate walked over and used her sister's spoon to taste the soup. It was a little strong and very thick. Kate was sorry that the soup wasn't going to provide the hoped-for nourishment for Kelsey, but she didn't actually feel responsible since it wasn't her recipe. "I don't know what Miss Eugenia was thinking. This is awful."

"What's awful?" Miss Eugenia asked from the doorway. As had become her custom, she had Lady in a basket on her arm.

"Your soup," Kelsey said with an amused glance at Kate.

"My soup?" Miss Eugenia demanded. She placed Lady's basket on the floor and charged forward. She picked up the well-used spoon and, after wiping it on the napkin, scooped up some soup and tasted. "Ugh!" she cried. "This *is* awful, but it isn't *my* recipe."

"Of course it is," Kate countered. "I followed it very specifically."

"It has way too much pepper jack cheese in it," Miss Eugenia said. "That's why the taste is so strong."

Kate remembered her decision to go with the larger "block" of cheese. "The recipe didn't specify the size of the block of cheese," Kate defended herself. "I asked Cleo, and she said to buy the bigger one."

Miss Eugenia laughed. "You should have known better than to trust Cleo's judgment. You've seen her house. She always thinks that bigger is better."

Kate frowned. Cleo lived in a replica of Tara from *Gone with the Wind*, built on an average-sized lot a few streets over. She was not known for restraint, and Kate realized, too late, that Cleo was not a good resource for size of cheese or anything else.

"Besides, you cooked the potatoes until they dissolved," Miss Eugenia said, continuing her critique.

"The recipe said until 'tender,'" Kate reminded her neighbor.

"That just means until they aren't hard." Miss Eugenia returned the spoon to the bowl of soup with a scowl. "You'll have to throw this out." She retrieved Lady then said, "I put two baskets of tomatoes on the counter in your kitchen for you to can."

"I've canned every day this week," Kate replied. "As much as I love canning—the abundance of your garden is exhausting me."

"Just be glad Brandon had to quit picking at eleven in order to make his lunch meeting with Whit," Eugenia responded. "Otherwise you'd have *four* baskets."

"You've got to figure out someone else to give all these vegetables to," Kate pleaded.

Eugenia nodded. "At the rate he's harvesting, we'll soon be buried by produce."

"Why doesn't he set up a stand in your front yard and sell what you can't use?" Kate suggested.

"That's not a bad idea," Miss Eugenia allowed. "I'll ask Winston if we have to have a license or something. When's Mark coming home?"

Kate picked up the breakfast tray and started toward the door. "Soon I hope."

"Why don't you call and have him stop by the Wal-Mart on his way in. If he picks up a fresh supply of ingredients you can make another batch of soup so Kelsey doesn't starve to death." With this remark Miss Eugenia turned to the potential starvation victim. "Kelsey, are you ready to go?"

"I am," Kelsey replied with a sly smile in Kate's direction. "I'll be looking forward to trying that soup when I get home."

* * *

Brandon Vance was standing by Eugenia's old Buick when they reached the driveway. "How did your lunch with Whit go?" Eugenia asked as they all climbed into the car.

"Very well," he told her. "I feel more confident knowing that if Mr. Muck is successful in bringing charges against me, I will have competent legal counsel."

"So you're ready for your interview with Sylvester?" Kelsey wanted to know.

"As ready as I'll ever be," he replied.

"Look at it as an opportunity to gather information that might help us find your wife," Kelsey suggested. "It's possible that the state attorney general's office knows something that we don't, and it sounds like this Mr. Muck is inexperienced enough to make a slip."

Eugenia struggled with divided loyalties. Kelsey was Kate's sister and Brandon was her temporary yardman, but she'd grown fond of Sylvester during the hours they'd spent together, and she didn't like the idea of their using his youth against him. "Since you all want to find Brandon's wife, maybe you could work together."

Kelsey gave Eugenia an incredulous look, but Brandon shook his head and muttered, "Sylvester Muck is determined to put me in jail, and if I'm incarcerated, I'll never find Molly."

"We won't let that happen," Kelsey promised with youthful optimism.

"Don't worry," Eugenia added. "I got you out of jail once, and I can do it again if necessary."

CHAPTER 6

Kate went downstairs and poured out the botched soup, then started sterilizing jars for the tomatoes. Mark called to say that he was on his way home from Patton Chapel, and Kate suggested that he stop by the store.

"What do you need me to get?" he asked.

"You'd better pull over on the side of the road," Kate recommended. "It's a very specific list."

After she ended her call with Mark, Kate had the children come inside for lunch. Then she put them down for naps and concentrated on the tomatoes.

When Mark came in with the requested groceries, Kate drafted him into peeling potatoes as she grated the correct-sized block of cheese. While they worked, Mark told her about his interviews.

"Everyone I talked with confirmed the theory that Erica had a boyfriend and that he was probably Lyle Tweedy."

"But you don't sound convinced," Kate said as she pressed the block of cheese against the grater.

"I just can't shake the feeling that it's a setup. It's a little too neat."

"Do you have a suspect?"

He frowned in consideration. "A couple, actually."

Kate put down the cheese and the grater. "Who?"

"Well, Erica had an affair with the dentist she worked for. He's a womanizer and has apparently had relationships with most of the women in Patton Chapel at one time or another. He claims that the affair started right after she went to work for him nine years ago and ended by mutual consent a few weeks later."

"Do you think he's telling the truth?"

Mark shrugged. "I didn't like him, so I don't *want* to believe him. Then there's the dentist's receptionist, Belva. She's a pretty woman who is also in love with the dentist."

Kate frowned. "Does this dentist have a wife?"

Mark finished one potato and picked up another. "Unfortunately."

"So the receptionist or the wife could have killed Erica in a jealous rage."

"It's possible, but I think our killer is a man. The crime requires too much strength for a woman." He concentrated on his potato peeling for a few seconds then said, "And to make things more interesting, the acting sheriff, Foster Gunnells, who was a deputy at the time of the murder, has a history with Erica."

Kate resumed her cheese grating. "Erica was a busy girl."

"Foster found the body," Mark continued. "The old sheriff was sick, so Foster handled all the legwork even though it wasn't officially his case. If Foster wanted to get rid of Erica, he was in a perfect position to do so. Then making it look like Tweedy did the killing would have been child's play."

"If the old sheriff was sick, he wouldn't have been able to supervise Foster closely."

"Right. Since it wasn't Foster's case, if anyone found discrepancies in the records, the old sheriff would be blamed, because the sightings of Lyle Tweedy *were* called into the sheriff's office."

"Did this Foster take the calls?" Kate asked.

Mark shook his head. "No, but then he would have been too smart for that. It would be much better to have someone else receive and record the calls."

"So maybe the deputy prepared a case against Lyle Tweedy and came up with enough circumstantial evidence to have him charged," Kate thought out loud. "But surely he expected Tweedy to deny it."

"Since Tweedy was a mass murderer, who would have believed him? Even circumstantial evidence would be enough, considering the other crimes against him." Mark frowned, thinking hard. "When Foster told me he'd set up all those interviews for me today, I thought he was trying to be helpful. Now I wonder if he wanted to control the scope of my investigation."

Kate shook her head. "You just can't trust anyone anymore."

"Not in my line of work," Mark agreed. "Of course, this is a theory."

"But a good one," Kate told him with a smile. "Now, let's cut up these potatoes and cook them until they're not hard."

With Mark's assistance, Kate had the soup ready by the time the children woke up from their naps. Kate insisted that everyone sit down and try a little of the new batch.

"It's good," Mark said after a couple of bites. "It's a little too warm outside for me to be in a soup mood, but I like it."

Charles was eating his soup happily, but Emily was frowning at her bowl. "It has green specks in it," she complained.

"Just try one bite," Kate requested. "If you don't like it, you don't have to eat any more."

The phone rang at this point, ending further negotiations. Kate wiped her hands on a dish towel before answering it. "Hello." She listened for a few seconds then extended the phone toward Mark. "It's for you."

Mark carried the phone into the hallway where he could carry on a conversation in relative privacy. Kate convinced Emily to try the soup, and they were all eating when Mark returned.

"I've got to go to the church for a while," he told her.

"It's a good thing you had some potato soup to fortify you."

He nodded, but he didn't smile. "It's a very good thing."

* * *

Sylvester's interview with Brandon was over in less than thirty minutes. In Eugenia's opinion, neither party won the confrontation, nor did any new information regarding Molly Vance's whereabouts come to light. Kelsey struggled with nausea throughout the discussion, and by the end Eugenia was worried about her.

"I'm going to run Kelsey and Brandon home," she told Winston. "Then I'll come back and man the phones for the rest of the afternoon."

Winston anchored his hat on his head. "I'll take them."

Eugenia was relieved. "You don't mind?"

"Heck no," he replied. "I'd rather do most anything than be stuck here with these phones—even for a little while."

"Well, go on then," Eugenia told him. "Kelsey's not feeling well."

"While I'm out, I think I'll run by the fitness center and see if Ciera wants to go to dinner with me tonight," Winston said.

"Just don't be gone too long, and remember that you're on duty," Eugenia instructed while helping Kelsey into the squad car. Once Kelsey was settled, she asked, "Would I need a permit or license to sell vegetables in the town of Haggerty?"

Winston considered this for a few seconds then said, "Depends on how much you're planning to sell and for what purpose."

"Well, I've got about a million bushels of vegetables in my backyard. I was going to let Brandon sell some of them to earn a little money."

"Here's what you need to do," Winston said as he opened the driver's door. "To get around paying sales tax and applying for a merchant's license, let Mr. Vance set up his stand here in front of the police station. Then put up a little sign saying that profits will benefit the policemen's retirement fund."

"I can see how that's a good idea for you, and it will keep my vegetables from being wasted, so it's not entirely bad for me either," Eugenia said. "But how does it help Brandon, who, I might add, is the person doing all the work?"

Winston smiled. "The *profit* will be what's left after you pay Mr. Vance a salary."

Eugenia was impressed with Winston's grasp of economics. "Maybe you didn't get this far on your looks alone," she told Winston. She leaned forward and addressed Brandon through Winston's open door. "How does that sound to you?"

"It sounds like a superior idea," the former literature professor replied.

"Well, then, it's settled. Brandon will start selling vegetables here on Monday afternoon." Eugenia saw the sickly pallor of Kelsey's skin and moved back. "Winston, get Kelsey to Kate's house before she faints."

"Yes, ma'am," Winston replied.

She lowered her voice and added, "And thanks for allowing Brandon to set up his vegetable stand in front of the police station. It's a prime location and should maximize his sales."

Winston smiled. "It'll also make it easy for me to keep an eye on him."

Eugenia was still laughing as Winston swung into the car and sped away. She walked back inside and sat down at Leita's desk.

"That Winston," she said to Sylvester as she fished a few pieces of healthy, well-balanced dog food out of the bag in her purse and held it out to Lady. "Are you hungry, girl?" The dog ate directly from Eugenia's palm, answering this question. "He's letting Brandon sell vegetables in front of the police station so he can watch him."

"Sounds smart to me," Sylvester concurred.

Eugenia frowned. "But surely after that interview this afternoon, you and Winston both realize that Brandon could not have killed his wife."

The young man looked up in surprise. "I don't realize that at all."

Eugenia was incensed. "But it's plain to tell that he loved her very much."

"The same passion that inspires love can also inspire murder," Sylvester replied. "Statistics show that most people are killed by someone they know—not by strangers."

Statistics made Sylvester's statement sound pretty well substantiated, and with no official information at her disposal, Eugenia felt at a disadvantage in the argument. "I still don't believe it. Maybe she just ran away."

"She didn't tell anyone she was leaving. She didn't have the electricity turned off or the phone disconnected. She didn't sell her house or clean out her bank accounts. All of that points to murder. And Molly's social circle was so small as to be nonexistent," Sylvester insisted. "She wouldn't have let anyone in her house besides Brandon."

"Of course she would have," Eugenia challenged. "There's not a woman alive who won't open the door for the UPS man if he says he has a delivery. And I believe most women would admit someone dressed like a power company employee if they said there was a problem with the electricity."

Sylvester shrugged. "I guess, but I'm telling you that something wasn't right about Molly Vance's disappearance. I've been to the house, and I had the unmistakable impression that it was made to *look* like she was running away. But it's my professional opinion that Molly Vance never left that house alive."

Eugenia was successful in controlling outright laughter. "Sylvester," Eugenia began patiently. "You're very young, and your professional opinion is still in the early development stages—"

"I know I don't have much experience," Sylvester interrupted. "But I have very good instincts, and something is not right here."

Winston walked back in at this point, looking irritated. "Did Shania turn down your dinner date?" Eugenia asked.

"She wasn't there," Winston replied crossly. "Did anyone call while I was gone?"

Eugenia shook her head. "Amazingly, no. Are you expecting a call?"

"I just thought Ciera might check in with me," he admitted, blushing. Eugenia worried once again that he was more interested in the woman than she was in him.

"I'm sure you'll hear from her soon," Eugenia offered as meager comfort.

Winston shrugged then collapsed into the chair beside Sylvester. "So what did you think of your interview?"

Sylvester sat up a little straighter, obviously pleased that Winston wanted his professional opinion. "I still maintain that Brandon Vance killed his wife and then arranged things to look like she ran away."

"The case you presented against Mr. Vance today is so weak I'm surprised the state attorney general's office is willing to invest any manpower in it."

Now it was Sylvester's turn to blush. "They aren't," he admitted. "They told me to drop the case, but I can't! So I took a week of vacation to pursue it."

Winston laughed. "Then you're not even here officially?"

Sylvester shook his head.

"I could arrest you for misuse of the authority vested in the office of the state's attorney general!" Winston told him.

Sylvester acknowledged this with a little nod. "Yes, sir, you could."

Winston spread his hands in petition. "Why?"

Sylvester glanced at Miss Eugenia then said, "Since I started work at the SAG's office, the most important job I've had is making coffee.

When they gave me an actual case, I was thrilled and determined to solve it. Then they told me to close it quickly, and I realized that they just wanted to be able to say that it had been reviewed by the attorney general's office but didn't really want it investigated."

"Because there really *is* no case," Winston emphasized.

Sylvester looked so sad that Eugenia felt she had to intercede on the boy's behalf. "His father got him the job, and he wanted a chance to prove that he's as qualified as the rest of them."

Sylvester gave her a grateful smile. "I figured this might be the only chance I get."

"I have to admire your determination," Winston said finally. "So I won't arrest you."

Sylvester relaxed visibly. "Thanks."

"But I don't see what I can do to help you."

"All I ask is that you let me hang around here for a while. If we both keep a close eye on Brandon Vance we might catch him in a slip up."

Winston shrugged. "You're welcome to stay as long as you keep helping Miss Eugenia organize the place."

Sylvester stood and held out his hand. "You've got a deal."

* * *

When Kate answered the doorbell she found Miss Eugenia's yardman holding Kelsey in his arms. "That's it," Kate said with determination. "I'm calling my doctor."

"I didn't faint," Kelsey said weakly. "But I was afraid I might so Brandon picked me up. I'll be fine if I can just get into bed for a little while."

Kate watched as Mr. Vance set her sister down. "Do you want me to walk with you up the stairs?" he asked.

"No," Kelsey declined. "I can make it."

Kate took Kelsey's arm and turned toward the stairs. "Thank you, Mr. Vance," she called over her shoulder.

"What's wrong with Aunt Kelsey?" Emily wanted to know as the children followed them upstairs.

"Nothing is wrong," Kate responded, with as much assurance as she could muster.

Emily didn't look convinced. "You said you were going to call your doctor."

"Well, I changed my mind."

"If you take Aunt Kelsey to the doctor, will he give her a shot?" Charles asked, his voice full of dread.

"I don't think so," Kate replied. "But if he does, Aunt Kelsey will be very brave about it." They reached the guest room, and Kate asked her children to go back downstairs.

"Can we watch TV?" Emily asked, obviously trying to turn the situation to her advantage.

Kate nodded. "Yes, but only PBS." She helped Kelsey to the bed then removed her sister's shoes.

Kelsey leaned back against the pillows and said, "I feel better already."

"You do not," Kate accused. "You're just afraid I'll call my doctor."

Kelsey gave her sister a wan smile. "Can I have some more of that ginger ale?"

Kate went downstairs and returned with the breakfast tray.

"Now this looks familiar," Kelsey said as she raised up on one elbow and surveyed the bowl of soup and the glass of ginger ale.

"It's a new batch of potato soup," Kate told her. "I've already made Mark and the kids test it and they said it was good."

Kelsey smiled. "I guess I can give it a try. The worst that will happen is that I'll throw it up."

Kate hated to hover, but she couldn't help herself. She watched Kelsey eat one bite and then another before putting the spoon down. "Can't you eat just a little more?" She wanted to add, "For the baby's sake," but didn't know if this would encourage Kelsey or not.

"Maybe later," Kelsey said in between sips of ginger ale. "But it was good this time."

Kate felt relieved. "I've got plenty more. Just let me know when you want some, and I'll get you a fresh bowl."

Kelsey nodded then turned onto her side and closed her eyes. Kate picked up the tray and walked quietly from the room.

* * *

It was almost dark by the time Eugenia and Sylvester left the police station. She offered to make him a sandwich for dinner, but he said he'd get something in Albany. "What about tomorrow? Are you going to church?"

"I haven't been to church in years," Sylvester replied.

Eugenia frowned. "If you don't go to church, what in the world do you do on Sunday?"

"I usually sleep in and read the paper. Then I eat a late breakfast and watch whatever sport is playing on TV."

Eugenia shook her head in despair. "You poor boy. Why don't you come to the Mormon Church in Albany with me tomorrow?"

"You're a Mormon?" Sylvester looked surprised.

"No, but I've been attending there with Kate and Mark for a couple of years. Services don't start until nine, but I absolutely can't stand to be late, so I'll pick you up at your hotel around eight thirty. Then afterward you can eat a proper Sunday dinner with me."

When Sylvester looked like he was about to decline, Eugenia added, "Brandon Vance is coming too, so it will give you a chance to interrogate him subtly."

Sylvester laughed. "How can I say no to an opportunity like that? I'm staying at the Motel 6 on River Front Road. Room number 209."

"Be standing outside by the lobby door where I can see you," Eugenia told him. "And don't wear that gangster suit."

When Eugenia pulled into her driveway, Brandon Vance came out to meet her. "I got all the ripe tomatoes picked," he told her.

"There will be a lot more ripe by Monday."

"You're right about that," Brandon acknowledged. "Along with plenty of squash, okra, zucchini, and bell peppers."

"Well, that's just more for you to sell at your vegetable stand."

"Do you think Chief Jones was serious about that?"

"I know he was," Eugenia assured Brandon grimly. "I'm going to go in and feed Lady. Would you like me to make you something to eat?"

"No, thank you. Kelsey brought me some potato soup."

Eugenia nodded. "I'm glad to hear she's feeling better." She looked at the Iversons' house. "I was planning to go over and tell the children good night, but Lady's hungry." The little dog barked in agreement.

Brandon followed the direction of her gaze, the longing obvious in his eyes. "Kelsey said they were going to watch a Disney movie."

"Well, I won't disturb them then." Eugenia turned and was halfway to her house when she remembered her manners. "Brandon, would you like to go to church with me tomorrow? Kelsey and the Iversons will be there too."

"Kelsey already invited me, but I think I'll just stay here."

"Let me know if you change your mind. My husband, Charles, had several suits, and I'm sure one of them would fit you." Even in the dim light she could see a blush of embarrassment stain Brandon's face, making her regret her words.

"Thank you, but no."

Remembering that about all Brandon Vance had left was his tattered pride, Eugenia nodded and went into the house to feed Lady.

* * *

It was almost midnight by the time Mark walked through the back door of his house. Kate had left the light over the oven on, and there was a note directing him to grilled cheese sandwiches and potato soup in the refrigerator. He heated his dinner in the microwave then carried it into his office so that he could go over his notes from the Patton Chapel interviews while he ate. Tucked into the back of his notebook was the membership list for Erica Helms's grief management group. Mark frowned as he studied the list. He had intended to call the members that afternoon, but now he'd have to wait until after church on Sunday.

When he was through eating, he turned off the lights in his office and rinsed his dishes in the kitchen sink before climbing the stairs. He stopped by Emily's room long enough to kiss her. Then he walked through the master bedroom to the nursery and, before kissing Charles, untangled the covers the little boy had wrapped around himself.

When Mark climbed into bed, Kate turned toward him and murmured, "It's about time you got home."

"There was a family from Kansas stranded in Albany," he explained wearily. "They were trying to get to Florida, where a cousin is supposed to be getting the father construction work. Their car broke down, and they spent every dime they had getting it fixed. They didn't have food or money for gas, and then their baby got sick. They called the church, and after Sister Park in the family history center learned about their plight, she called me."

Kate propped her head up on her elbow. "So what did you do?"

"I got them a hotel room and some groceries and filled their car with gas. Then I went with the father to take the baby to one of those clinics where you don't need an appointment. The baby's ears were infected, so we got him some medicine. The doctor said he'd be fine in a couple of days."

"They'll be okay, then?"

Mark shrugged. "I think they can make it to the cousin's house in Florida. What happens from there is beyond my control."

"There's so much sadness in the world," she whispered.

"Yes, there is," he agreed.

She reached out and stroked his cheek. "I love you."

He caught her hand and pressed it to his lips. "It's good to be home."

* * *

On Sunday morning Eugenia arose early and did what she could to prepare for her dinner guests. After she was dressed for church and had made a plate of breakfast for Brandon, she explained to Lady that she would be gone for several hours.

"This is the first time we've been separated for so long," she told the little dog. "I hope you are familiar enough with the house that you won't be scared. I've left you plenty of water and some extra food in case you get hungry. But if you just can't stand it another minute, go to the door and bark. I'll tell Brandon that means you want to come outside with him."

Lady barked, and Eugenia caressed her little head. Then with reluctance, she left the house. She saw her yardman sitting under a peach tree in the corner of the yard, wearing a pair of dress pants and a Sunday shirt that had belonged to her husband. She had the oddest desire to hug him. Putting sad memories firmly from her mind, Eugenia crossed the lawn until she reached Brandon.

"You look nice this morning. Did you change your mind about going to church with me?"

He laughed. "No, ma'am. Since you won't let me work in the garden on Sunday, I knew I wouldn't get dirty, so I went ahead and dressed for Sunday dinner."

"Keeping the Sabbath day holy is more than just not working," she enlightened him. "It's setting the day apart—making it special. And I think that wearing nice, clean clothes is a good way for you to do that." She placed the plate in his hands. Anxious to avoid any more blows to his pride, she said, "I made more breakfast than I could eat and was hoping that you would keep this food from going to waste."

He removed the aluminum foil and studied the fried eggs, buttermilk biscuits, and buttery grits that Eugenia had arranged on the plate. "This looks delicious," he said.

"It is," she assured him. "I'll be back around twelve thirty, and I told Lady if she wants to come out, to stand by the back door and bark."

"I'll check on Lady," Brandon promised.

"And if you want orange juice or milk there's plenty in the refrigerator," Eugenia told him as she headed toward her car. "The back door's unlocked." Once she was behind the steering wheel, she murmured a short prayer. "Dear Lord, please don't let him turn out to be a criminal who'll steal me blind while I'm at church." Then she started the car and headed for Albany.

Sylvester was standing in front of the lobby doors at the Motel 6, as he had been instructed, when Eugenia pulled up at eight twenty-five. He climbed into the front seat of her Buick and looked around in amazement. "I saw one of these in a museum one time, but I've never ridden in one."

"A museum—the very idea!" Eugenia cried. "This is a fine, dependable automobile with plenty of good years left in it. Just because I don't have a flashy, little sports car," she sputtered. She saw him smiling and realized that he was teasing her. "You'd better mind your manners, young man."

"I'm sorry," Sylvester said. "I just couldn't resist."

"You're lucky that I have a good sense of humor," she said. "But just don't forget what side your bread is buttered on."

Sylvester arranged his face into an expression of contrition. "Yes, ma'am."

Eugenia narrowed her eyes at him. "A museum. I declare, I don't know what to think about young people today."

When they reached the stake center, Eugenia parked in her usual spot and ushered Sylvester inside. She introduced him to each person they passed and described the meeting schedule. "Mormons have all their meetings in one three-hour block. Regular church is first, then Sunday School, and finally a class where the men and women meet separately. It took a little getting used to, but now I have to admit I see a lot of sense in it. You get all your churchgoing over with at one time and can then enjoy the rest of your day."

Sylvester nodded. "Sounds like a reasonable approach to worship."

Eugenia had just gotten settled on her favorite bench when Kate arrived. Mark walked down from the stand to greet them, and Eugenia introduced Sylvester.

"What is an aide from the state attorney general's office doing in Haggerty?" Mark asked, his curiosity apparent.

"He's just observing things at the police station," Eugenia replied vaguely.

"Like an internship," Sylvester added.

"Are you a member of the Church?" Mark asked.

Sylvester shook his head. "No, I'm not a member of any church, but Miss Eugenia insisted that I come with her today. She promised to feed me afterward."

Eugenia gave her visitor a cross look. "You make it sound like I tied you up and dragged you." She turned to Kate and Mark. "All I did was invite him like any good Christian."

"Well, however you got here, we're glad to have you," Mark told Sylvester with a smile. Then he addressed Charles and Emily. "You two be good and mind Miss Eugenia."

"We will," the children chorused.

Mark returned to his place on the stand while Kate walked up to the organ. "Kate is the organist," Eugenia explained to Sylvester. "And Mark is the bishop of this congregation, which is like being the minister. That's why I have to come to church with them, to watch after their children."

Sylvester nodded as the prelude music filtered through the room. Miss Eugenia distributed Bible story coloring books and crayons to the children then settled back against the wooden bench as the meeting began. During the hymns she shared a book with Sylvester and insisted that he sing. She explained the significance of the sacrament as it was passed, and when the speakers were announced, she told him that each member was occasionally given an opportunity to address the congregation.

"When are they going to pass the collection plate?" Sylvester asked softly.

"They don't," Eugenia whispered back. "But donation slips are in the foyer if you feel inclined to give a little something to the Lord."

Sylvester leaned toward her again and whispered, "You're *sure* you're not a Mormon?"

Eugenia laughed and shook her head.

After church, Eugenia collected Sylvester and drove toward Haggerty. "Usually on Sundays the Iversons and I eat with another neighbor named Polly Kirby. But Polly has a friend visiting and they are on a diet, so I offered to feed everyone at my house this week. Then Polly decided she wanted to test her ability to resist temptation, so she's feeding the Iversons while I host Winston, his girlfriend, Brandon Vance, Kelsey, a lawyer friend of mine, and you."

"It sounds like you got the lion's share of the dinner company."

Eugenia waved her hand. "I can handle it, and I'm glad we're not eating all together. Mark is a trained FBI agent, and if you're with him too long, he'll figure out that you have a professional interest in Brandon Vance."

Sylvester's eyebrows shot up. "I didn't know your neighbor was with the FBI." He considered this then nodded. "But I think you're right. If we spent the afternoon together, he'd probably realize I'm not an intern."

When they got home, Lady was out in the backyard with Brandon. "She did fine until about noon," he explained. "Then she got restless, so I let her out."

"Thank you," Eugenia said as she scooped up the little dog. "Did you miss me?" she asked. By way of reply, Lady licked her owner's wrinkled cheek, and Eugenia was touched. "Well, aren't you the sweetest little thing. Let's get you something to eat before I start working on dinner for our guests."

"Can I help?" Brandon asked.

"Me too?" Sylvester volunteered with a covert wink at Miss Eugenia.

With a barely perceptible nod to let Sylvester know she got his message, she said, "You'd both just be in the way. Why don't you sit out here and enjoy the warm weather. Summer will be over soon, and we should take advantage of it while we can." Before either of them could object, she carried Lady inside and closed the door firmly.

By the time Whit arrived with his pound cake, Eugenia had the pot roast and creamed potatoes on the table. "Get those rolls out of the oven for me, please," she instructed Whit from the stove where she was stirring turnip greens. Whit obeyed without argument.

"They're perfect," he pronounced as he put the pan of rolls on the counter.

"Of course they are," Eugenia said with a smile in his direction. "Now, if you'll slice those fresh tomatoes."

Kelsey walked in clutching a glass of ginger ale. "I don't even know why I bothered to come over," Kelsey confided quietly to Eugenia. "I can't eat anything."

"Not even my potato soup?"

Kelsey shook her head. "Whenever I eat, it's just a matter of time before it comes back up."

"Well, have a seat and at least enjoy our stimulating dinner conversation."

Whit placed the tomatoes on the table while Eugenia put a stick of real butter on a crystal dish. "Brandon! Sylvester!" she called. "Come on in. If Winston doesn't get here soon, we're going to eat without him!"

"I'm here," Winston hollered back from the porch. "Ciera too."

"Make sure you wipe off your feet," Eugenia ordered. "I don't want to spend all day tomorrow mopping floors."

When they gathered around the table, Whit stepped up beside Eugenia and held her chair while she sat down. Then he glided it effortlessly to the table, which, considering her size, was no small feat. Feeling a little breathless, Eugenia asked Winston to say the blessing.

"That is if you can remember how to pray. I'll bet it's been a year since you went to church."

"That's not so!" Winston denied. "I went to the Christmas cantata with Miss Polly in December."

Eugenia sniffed to show her disdain. "Christmas programs don't count. Now bow your head and address the Lord."

Winston stumbled through a few awkward sentences until finally Eugenia interrupted. "For heaven's sake, Winston, just say amen."

Winston muttered, "Amen," and the others around the table added theirs in unison.

"Thank goodness that's over," Winston said, wiping beads of sweat from his forehead with his napkin.

"It wouldn't be such an ordeal if you went to church now and then," Eugenia told him as she handed the pot roast to Whit. "Have some and pass it."

"I went to church today," Sylvester said as he dished several spoonfuls of mashed potatoes onto his plate. "With Miss Eugenia."

Whit looked up from the pot roast. "Then you're a lucky man."

Eugenia laughed. "You make it sound as if you'd like to attend church with me," she said to Whit.

"I'd be delighted to go anywhere with you, Eugenia," Whit told her gallantly.

"Even the Mormon church?" she clarified, enjoying herself immensely.

A confused expression settled on his face. "I thought you were a Methodist."

"I am, but I go to the Mormon church with Kate and Mark to help them with the children. So what do you say?" she teased. "Are you coming with me next week?"

Instead of smiling, Whit reached across the table and took her hand in his. "I'd love to."

Eugenia stared at their hands, momentarily dumfounded. "I declare, Whit," she managed finally. "You're welcome to come to church with me anytime, but I have to warn you—people will talk."

Whit smiled. "People have been talking about me for years, and a rumor that I'm going to *church* would be a major gossip improvement."

"Why would people gossip about you for going to church?" Sylvester asked. "It seems like they'd be glad."

"That just shows how young you are," Eugenia replied. Only Whit laughed. The others were regarding them with various degrees of confusion.

"I've never understood why people want to gossip about anything," Winston contributed. "I don't care what my neighbors are doing." He glanced at Brandon Vance. "Unless it's against the law."

Ciera shrugged a thin shoulder. "I don't get gossip either."

Kelsey nodded weakly in agreement. "At best it's a waste of time."

Brandon Vance cleared his throat. "If our neighbors had been a little more curious about Molly, her disappearance might have been discovered sooner, and I'd have had a better chance of finding her."

Eugenia saw Winston and Sylvester exchange a dubious look, then the meal continued. "Will you pass me those rolls?" Eugenia asked as she focused her attention on Winston's girlfriend. "Ciera, you'd better fill that plate and eat every bite. I warned you that I don't allow finicky eaters at my table."

"Yes, ma'am," the woman mumbled.

"I think that's the first time you've gotten her name right," Winston said, pleased.

"Don't get used to it," Eugenia warned. "It's an odd name, and I'll probably forget again."

"My mother liked to make up names," Ciera furnished, as if this cast great light on the subject.

Eugenia wondered, not for the first time, if the woman was mentally deficient.

"Any news on what killed Mr. Shaw's dogs?" Sylvester asked.

"That's not exactly what I'd call polite dinner conversation," Eugenia reprimanded mildly, turning to Winston. "Well, what killed them?"

Winston shook his head. "I don't have the results yet. Atlanta doesn't get in a hurry when we send them *human* samples. Since our victims this time were canine, it could be weeks."

"Why would anyone want to kill dogs?" Kelsey asked.

Winston shrugged. "We don't know. There's been a lot of vandalism around Haggerty the past few weeks."

"In the course of sorting through all the police reports and filing them, I noticed a pattern with your vandalism cases," Sylvester told Winston.

All eyes turned to him, and Winston asked, "What kind of a pattern?"

"All the victims of the vandalism have at least one conviction for DUI."

Winston leaned forward. "How in the world did you figure that out?"

Sylvester shrugged. "The work was tedious, and to ease the boredom, I started reading the files. After I saw three or four, all with drunk driving records, I started looking for it."

"I didn't realize that we had that much drunk driving in Haggerty, except for Dub Shaw," Eugenia said.

"Because of those bars out on Highway 76, someone drives drunk through Haggerty almost every day," Winston told her. "But we don't catch many of them."

"One of the victims only had one conviction from almost twenty years ago when he was in high school," Sylvester contributed.

"So you're dealing with a vandal with a long memory, who knows how to hold a grudge," Whit said.

"You should check and see if anyone was hurt or killed by any of the victims," Kelsey suggested. "It might be revenge."

Winston nodded. "I'll start on it this afternoon." He turned to Ciera. "If you're not busy, maybe you could help."

Ciera shook her head. "Sorry, but I've got to take a nap. I didn't sleep well last night."

"Speaking of sleeping last night," Eugenia suddenly remembered Winston's plan to stake out Dub Shaw's house. "Did you stay at Dub's place?"

Winston nodded. "Yeah, but the only visitor I had was Ciera, and she came to see me."

Thinking that this might explain Ciera's fatigue, Eugenia asked, "Are you going back tonight?"

"Yeah," Winston confirmed. "I guess I'll try it a couple more nights. Maybe I'll get lucky and catch the guy."

"I'll be glad to help you look for vengeful family members," Sylvester told Winston. "I don't have any plans for this afternoon, and I'm not tired."

"That's because you didn't visit Winston at Dub Shaw's house last night," Eugenia said with a reproachful look at the police chief.

Winston blushed but claimed, "All we did was play Yahtzee!"

Eugenia rolled her eyes then looked around the table. The men had cleaned their plates, Ciera had eaten a few bites, and Kelsey was stabbing her food listlessly. "I guess it's time for dessert. Whit, will you help me do the honors?"

Whit stood and joined her by the counter. Eugenia took a stack of saucers from the cupboard and handed Whit a knife. She watched as he sliced into the cake. "Texture looks good," she said, providing commentary. "No crumbs. That's a promising sign."

Eugenia distributed pieces of the cake to everyone then took a bowl of fresh strawberries and some whipped cream out of the refrigerator. "I'm a pound cake purist myself," she explained as she put them on the table. "But if any of you would like to turn this masterpiece into strawberry shortcake, I won't stop you."

"I'll have some strawberries," Sylvester said promptly. Then he picked up the bowl and put an ample amount of fruit on top of his piece of pound cake. "Will you pass me the whipped cream, please?" he asked Winston.

"I'll trade you for the strawberries," the police chief replied.

Eugenia turned away from this sacrilege and gave her attention to Whit. "Okay, here's the test." She cut a bite of cake and put it reverently into her mouth. She chewed slowly, analyzing, then nodded. "It's perfect."

Whit sighed with obvious relief. "I'm so glad you like it!"

"I *liked* your last cake," Eugenia amended. "This one is incomparable."

Brandon nodded. "A paragon of culinary accomplishment."

Ciera looked up from her dessert. "Huh?"

"He likes the cake," Winston translated for her.

"Oh, yeah, it's good," his girlfriend added, sealing her endorsement.

"And it only took me 277 tries," Whit said with a wink at Eugenia.

"The entire meal was incredible," Brandon complimented.

"There's nothing like fresh vegetables straight from the garden," Whit agreed.

"Well, then tomorrow is your lucky day," Eugenia told him. "Brandon is going to set up a vegetable stand in front of the police station, and he'll be selling more of the delicious tomatoes and turnip greens you ate today. You can all purchase some and have them at home."

"How are you going to pick vegetables and run the stand?" Kelsey asked Brandon.

"I'll harvest in the morning and sell produce in the afternoon," he replied.

"Sounds sensible," Whit said as he stood. "Would anyone else like more cake?"

"Just bring it over here to the table," Eugenia suggested. "I imagine most of us want another piece."

* * *

The food at Miss Polly's house was wonderful, as usual, but without Miss Eugenia, the conversation dragged. So after they'd eaten, Kate and Mark thanked their hostesses and took their children home. Kelsey still wasn't back from Miss Eugenia's, so they put the children down for naps. Then Mark went into his office and started making phone calls while Kate dozed on the couch in the den. When he joined her a while later, she asked, "So are you finished with your phone calls?"

He sat beside her on the couch. "For now, anyway. I reached the leader of Erica's grief management group and five of her fellow members. All of them remembered Erica, but no one could shed any light on her death."

"How many more members were in the group with Erica?" Kate asked, mostly to be polite.

"Two," he replied. "One committed suicide a few months ago, and another's phone is disconnected. I presume she moved, but I'll check it out tomorrow." He sighed. "It seems like I've reached a dead end."

"Then try to forget about it," Kate encouraged. To help him, she changed the subject. "I thought sacrament meeting was good today."

"Yes, it was fine."

"And that young man who came with Miss Eugenia seemed nice."

Mark nodded. "He was all right, but don't you think it's strange that the state attorney general's office has an intern in Haggerty?"

Kate shrugged. "I guess, I don't know."

"I may check on that tomorrow too," Mark said as the back door slammed shut. A few seconds later Kelsey walked by.

Kate jumped from the couch and intercepted her sister in the hallway. "How are you feeling?"

"Terrible," Kelsey replied. "I'm headed up to bed."

Kate stood aside and watched helplessly as her sister climbed the stairs and disappeared into the guest room.

* * *

After the other guests left, Whit stayed to help Eugenia clean up. They had just finished the dishes when there was a knock on the front door. "The only people who come to the front door are Jehovah's Witnesses and Girl Scouts selling cookies," Eugenia told Whit. "I'm tempted to ignore the knocking, but since both Jehovah's Witnesses and Girl Scouts are known for being tenacious, I guess I'd better express my lack of interest personally."

Whit laughed. "You know Mormons are pretty serious proselyters too."

Eugenia wiped her hands on a dishcloth. "Yes, but there aren't any Mormon missionaries in Haggerty—so I know it's not them." She turned to Lady and said, "I'll be right back," then headed toward the entryway.

Whit followed her and was at her side when she opened the door to find George Ann and Cornelia Blackwood, the Baptist preacher's wife, standing on her porch. "It's even worse than I thought," Eugenia muttered to Whit. He laughed again.

Cornelia, who was prone to spontaneous prayer and unsolicited hugs, was apparently too shocked by Whit's unexpected presence to do either. George Ann's eyes were wide with curiosity when she said, "I hope we're not interrupting."

"Not at all," Eugenia assured them. "Whit and several other folks were my guests for Sunday dinner, and he was just helping me clean up."

"I guess I'll be going now." Whit stepped outside. "Thanks for dinner."

"Don't you want to take the rest of your pound cake?" Eugenia asked. "I can wrap it up for you."

Whit shook his head. "No, you keep it." After a wave at the ladies, he descended the steps and walked to his car.

Reluctantly Eugenia returned her attention to Cornelia and George Ann. "To what do I owe this surprise visit?"

Cornelia reached across the threshold and pulled Eugenia into a belated embrace. "Aren't you going to invite us in?"

"I guess." Eugenia disengaged herself from Cornelia's arms and led them into the living room. Once they were seated, she said, "I presume you've both just finished dinner and wouldn't care for anything to eat."

"Actually I'd love some of Whit's pound cake," George Ann requested. "And a cup of coffee, if it's not too much trouble."

Eugenia stood up. "I'll get you some pound cake, but I don't have any coffee made." She saw George Ann and Cornelia exchange a significant look. "How about a nice glass of milk?"

"Just the cake, please," George Ann replied stiffly.

Eugenia nodded. "How about you, Cornelia? Would you like cake too?"

The preacher's wife shook her head. "No, thank you."

Eugenia went into the kitchen and returned a few minutes later with a piece of cake for George Ann.

"Now, what can I do for you?" she asked.

"I heard you had a yardman," George Ann said after daintily patting her mouth with a lace handkerchief.

"You came over here on a Sunday afternoon to ask about my yardman?"

George Ann raised her head, giving Eugenia an unpleasant view of her long neck. "Of course not. I was just making conversation."

"Well, I do have a yardman, just temporarily until I can get my garden harvested. Now what do you really want?"

Cornelia leaned forward. "We've come to tell you about a young couple in town who needs your help."

Eugenia frowned. "Why don't you help them?"

George Ann set her empty saucer aside and said, "You remember Gladys Moss?"

Eugenia rolled her eyes. "Of course I remember Gladys. We were in the same Sunday School class for thirty years, and I was chairman of the luncheon committee for her funeral."

"That's why we've come to you," Cornelia explained. "The female half of the troubled young couple we're talking about is Gladys's granddaughter. Since you and Gladys were friends—"

"And since Gladys was a Methodist," George Ann inserted.

"We feel that you are the person to assist them in righting a wrong," Cornelia continued.

Eugenia put a hand to her temple, which was starting to throb. "I presume the troubled female you're referring to is Rosemary?"

"Yes, Rosemary Moss," Cornelia confirmed.

"And what wrong is it that you want me to right?"

"Well, as you are probably aware, Rosemary has been living in sin with Jackson Clooney for the past year," Cornelia said.

"Closer to a year and a half," George Ann corrected—her eyes downcast in ladylike aversion to the shameful subject matter.

"But we learned that they are planning to elope on Saturday," Cornelia announced cheerfully. "Praise the Lord!"

Eugenia squinted her eyes, more from the pain of her developing headache than concentration on the conversation. "How do you *plan* to elope?" she asked. "I thought the whole point of an elopement was that it didn't require any preparation."

"Both the bride and groom are college students, and neither one of them has time to plan a wedding," Cornelia explained.

"They also don't have any money," George Ann confided. "According to our very reliable sources."

Eugenia controlled a shudder, just imagining what their *sources* reported about her.

"Anyway," Cornelia reclaimed control of the conversation. "It's our understanding that they are eloping because they can't afford a proper wedding."

For the first time since her guests had arrived, Eugenia felt a twinge of interest in the young couple's plight. A romantic at heart, she firmly believed that every bride should have her special day. "So what do you want me to do?"

"Well, organize a wedding for them, of course," George Ann said as if this was plainly evident.

"Not by yourself!" Cornelia was quick to add. "We'll be glad to help you."

"And I'm sure all the members of your *Methodist* Sunday School class will help too," George Ann predicted.

Eugenia noticed the emphasis on *Methodist* and wondered if the whole wedding business was an attempt to draw her back into the protestant fold. "I don't see how I could possibly plan a wedding in six days no matter *who* helps me."

"It doesn't have to be a big wedding," Cornelia pointed out.

George Ann sounded sincere when she said, "I don't believe there's anything you can't do."

"With your knowledge of etiquette and social experience and with your contacts in the community, organizing a little wedding will be a cinch," Cornelia said with confidence.

Eugenia knew she was a fool to fall for this blatant flattery, but she couldn't help herself. "Possible maybe, but not a cinch," Eugenia allowed.

Cornelia seemed to sense that Eugenia was weakening and moved in for the kill. "Do it for Rosemary's eternal soul!" she begged. "Do it for your dead friend Gladys!"

In the face of such zealousness, Eugenia felt she had no choice but to surrender. "I guess I could give it a try."

Cornelia clapped her hands together in celebration. "I knew you'd accept the challenge!"

"I'll talk to Rosemary and offer my assistance," Eugenia consented conditionally. "That's all I can promise."

"I know you'll pull it off," Cornelia encouraged. "Call if you need us to do anything." Cornelia stood and motioned for George Ann to follow her. "I guess we'll be on our way."

Now that they had dumped the wedding in Eugenia's lap, they seemed anxious to leave. "Don't rush off," she said halfheartedly.

"We'd love to stay and chat," Cornelia assured her. "But we've got several other visits to make."

"I *would* like another piece of that pound cake," George Ann said with a longing look at her empty plate. "It was awfully good."

"Whit makes the best pound cake," Eugenia agreed.

George Ann's eyes narrowed. "I had no idea you and Whit were keeping company."

Eugenia laughed. "I guess your sources aren't as efficient as you thought. Whit and I have been seeing quite a lot of each other lately."

"Does he know you're practically a *Mormon?*" George Ann demanded.

"As a matter of fact, the subject of my attending church with the Mormons came up at dinner today, and Whit said he'd like to come with me next week." Eugenia watched with satisfaction as expressions of shock formed on her guests' faces. "Now wait right here, and I'll go wrap you up a piece of that pound cake to take home."

CHAPTER 7

After George Ann and Cornelia left, Eugenia called the number listed for Rosemary Moss in the phone book and arranged for the girl and her boyfriend to come over in an hour. Then she took Lady outside for a walk around the garden. They found Brandon reading a book of poems by Henry Wadsworth Longfellow. "Do you miss teaching?" she asked him.

He closed the book and thought about the question for a minute before answering. "I don't miss quibbling with students over test scores or the never-ending paperwork. I certainly don't miss the evaluations and staff meetings. What I long for is the hours I used to spend wrapped up in beautiful words."

Eugenia nodded. "The real world can be a harsh place."

Brandon stroked the cracked leather cover of the book in his hands. "Most of my life was full of beauty. I had a perfect childhood, married the girl of my dreams, and chose a fulfilling career. Then my son was born, and he brought a whole new dimension of happiness into my life." Brandon's voice quivered. He cleared his throat before continuing. "Then my son died, and I haven't been able to find the beauty since."

"It's still there," Eugenia told him. "The beauty, I mean. It's just that sorrow and misery are hiding it from your view. Keep searching and you'll find it."

He raised tear-filled eyes to hers. "Thank you for understanding."

"I'm not sure I do completely. But I lost my husband a few years ago, and it was a long time before I was able to value life after that. Now I see the beauty again, and it's even more precious to me because it helps to ease the sorrow." Lady nuzzled her ankle, and Eugenia smiled down at the little dog. "I'm not sad," she promised. Then she turned back to Brandon. "There's more pound cake if you'd like some, but you'd better hurry. It's going fast."

Brandon shook his head. "Thanks, but I'm not hungry."

Eugenia decided she'd imposed on his solitude for long enough. "I'm expecting company soon so I'd better go wait on the porch. If you change your mind about the pound cake, the back door is open."

"You are too kind," Brandon said.

"That is too true," Eugenia agreed with a smile as she carried Lady around to the front of the house. Fifteen minutes past the scheduled meeting time, a battered Jeep parked by the curb. Eugenia watched as Rosemary and a shaggy-haired young man emerged from the vehicle. They walked up the sidewalk and came to a stop on the bottom porch step.

"Miss Eugenia, have you met Jackson?" Rosemary asked by way of introduction.

"No, I don't believe I've had the pleasure," Eugenia replied.

"Miss Eugenia Atkins, this is Jackson Clooney." Rosemary turned adoring eyes to her boyfriend. "Jackson, this is Miss Eugenia."

"Hey," Jackson said with a lazy smile.

Eugenia pointed at a pair of empty chairs on her porch and invited them to sit down. "I'm sure you're wondering why I asked you to come over here today."

Rosemary nodded. "Yes, ma'am."

"Your grandmother, Gladys, was a very good friend of mine," she told Rosemary.

The girl nodded again. "Yes, ma'am. I know that."

Eugenia stroked Lady's scruffy coat. "Well, I heard that the two of you were planning to elope on Saturday, but I'd like to do what Gladys would've done if she were alive."

"And what is that?" Jackson's tone was suspicious.

"I'd like to plan a real wedding for you."

"A *real* wedding?" Jackson repeated.

"Like with a white dress and all that?" Rosemary asked a little breathlessly.

"And flowers and a cake and pictures that you can show your children," Eugenia added. "It won't be anything elaborate, but I think we can provide a nice tasteful ceremony at the Methodist church . . ."

"Oh, we can't get married in a church!" Jackson interrupted.

Eugenia frowned. "Why not?"

"Because Jackson is an atheist," Rosemary explained.

Eugenia turned her disapproving gaze to the groom-to-be. "You don't believe in God?" she demanded.

Jackson shrugged. "I'm willing to concede the possibility that there is a superior being of some kind who manages the universe, but I don't advocate organized religion."

"I'm not sure what all that means," Eugenia responded. "But I'll tell you right now that there *is* a God. He is *definitely* managing the universe, and He *does* advocate organized religion—so you might want to reconsider your position." She took a deep breath then continued. "But if you're uncomfortable with getting married in a church, you can have the ceremony in my backyard."

This idea seemed to appeal to Rosemary. "Miss Eugenia has the most incredible flowers," she told Jackson.

Jackson looked around him with a critical eye. "I guess we could have a wedding here." He pulled Rosemary into an embarrassingly passionate embrace and murmured, "Then we'll go on to Gatlinburg for our honeymoon."

Eugenia wasn't sure why a couple who had been living together for over a year *needed* a honeymoon, but she kept this to herself. "Please call and invite your guests this afternoon, and let me know how many to expect so we can plan food."

"Jackson is a vegetarian," Rosemary announced apologetically. "So we wouldn't want you to serve any meat or dairy products."

Eugenia sighed. Nothing could be simple with these two. "Very well," she agreed.

Then Rosemary asked, "Who will marry us?"

"If Jackson doesn't believe in organized religion, I guess that means we can't use a preacher," Eugenia said.

"I have a friend who's a rabbi," Jackson provided. "If he's free, I'm sure he'll do it."

Eugenia frowned. "You don't consider Judaism an *organized* religion?"

"It's more of a culture than a religion," Jackson responded.

Eugenia imagined all the Old Testament prophets turning in their graves and tried not to smile. "Well, talk to your nonreligious rabbi friend, and tell him to be here at seven P.M. on Friday for the rehearsal. On Saturday we'll start the ceremony at ten A.M. before it gets too hot."

"Okay," Rosemary agreed. She took Jackson's hand, and they started down the steps. Just as they reached the sidewalk, she turned and smiled up at Eugenia. "Thanks."

The resentment Eugenia had begun to feel melted away. "You're welcome." She watched them climb back into the old Jeep then carried Lady inside. "Let's go get busy," she told the little dog.

Eugenia's first call was to Polly Kirby—who was given the assignment to provide delicious refreshments for the reception without using meat or dairy products. Then she called Kate and asked if the reception could be held at the Iversons' house.

"We could do the reception outside too, but I'd rather serve the food inside where it's cool. It would take me months to spruce up my house enough, but yours wouldn't require much decoration."

"I'll have to check with Mark, but I'm sure it will be okay," Kate replied. "How many people are you expecting?"

"Oh, just a few," Eugenia assured her on the assumption that the dull and shallow couple she had just met couldn't possibly have many friends.

"I'll let you know what Mark says."

"Remind him of all I've done for him over the years."

Kate laughed. "How could he forget? *You* remind him constantly."

Eugenia said good-bye then made more phone calls, enlisting the help of various Haggerty matrons. Cornelia Blackwood gladly accepted responsibility for the wedding music, and Darnell Mobley at the Haggerty Mortuary promised to have some of his grave preparers deliver fifty white wooden chairs on Friday—with the understanding that a funeral would take precedence. After ending that conversation, she looked down at Lady. "Are you impressed with my organizational skills?"

The little dog barked twice and turned around in an excited circle.

Eugenia laughed and gave Lady fresh water. She was about to heat up some roast for supper when the phone rang. It was Kate calling to tell her that Mark had agreed to host the reception. "That's good," Eugenia replied. "I'll ask Annabelle to pay for the wedding cake, and I'm hoping that Corrine will loan the girl a dress."

"It would be nice if the bride could keep her wedding dress," Kate said thoughtfully. "What about that store in Albany that advertises wedding gowns for ninety-nine dollars."

"Tacky," Eugenia decreed. "I was thinking of a tasteful, cream-colored silk suit I saw at Corrine's."

"Everything at Miss Corrine's is tasteful," Kate agreed. "But nothing is cheap."

"Maybe I can convince Corrine to discount the suit."

"Miss Corrine is pretty soft-hearted."

"I'll get Annabelle to ask. Since she's one of Corrine's best customers, she might be able to get the price of that suit almost within reason," Eugenia calculated.

"Almost," was Kate's parting remark.

Next she called Winston's house.

"I thought you were spending the night at Dub Shaw's," she said when he answered.

"I am," he confirmed. "I'm having my calls forwarded to my cell phone."

"Well, I declare," Eugenia said, truly amazed by the miracle of modern technology. "Have you seen any vandals yet?"

"Not a one. Did you need something?"

Winston seemed anxious to hang up, and Eugenia wondered if he was staking out Dub Shaw's house alone or if he had a skinny fitness fanatic with a made-up name there to keep him company. "What I need is for you to move my piano into the backyard on Friday afternoon."

There was a brief silence, then Winston said, "I don't think I can move it by myself."

Eugenia clenched her teeth in frustration. "Of course you can't move it by yourself! I'm sure Brandon and Sylvester and Arnold would be willing to lend a hand."

"So you think Muck will still be here on Friday?" Winston asked. "I was hoping the little weasel would pack up and go back to Atlanta before the end of the week."

"Don't be too hard on him," Eugenia said reproachfully. "He's been very helpful."

"True," Winston admitted. "He stayed at the station with me this afternoon for almost three hours. We looked through over a hundred files."

"Did you find any victims with reason for revenge?"

"We found a lot of people who might hold a grudge against drunk drivers, and Sylvester said he'd check them out tomorrow."

"See what I mean?" Eugenia exclaimed. "That boy has been a blessing in disguise."

"If he's a blessing, he sure is in disguise," Winston agreed sarcastically. "But he has come in handy."

Remembering the original reason for her call, Eugenia said, "I expect Sylvester will still be here on Friday, but if he leaves before that I'm sure you can round up someone else to help you move the piano. I'd like it in place by three o'clock."

"Yes, ma'am."

"Thank you, Winston," Eugenia said before she hung up. Then, after a few deep breaths to gird up her courage, she called Rosemary.

The girl answered on the fourth ring and said they had just finished calling their guest list. "We've invited 125 people," she announced excitedly.

Eugenia almost swallowed her dentures. "One hundred and twenty-five people?" she repeated to make sure her aging ears hadn't deceived her.

"Give or take a few," Rosemary confirmed. "Jackson has a lot of friends and family around here."

A lot of friends and family that he was perfectly willing to leave out of the marriage process when he was arranging and paying for things, Eugenia thought to herself. "Well, I don't know what to say."

"Is that enough?" Rosemary asked uncertainly. "We wanted to be sure there were lots of people at the wedding to appreciate all your hard work."

Eugenia sighed. "I believe you've already invited plenty of people."

After hanging up, Eugenia turned to Lady. "The nerve," she complained to the dog. "It can't be a church wedding because Jackson is an atheist. We can't have normal food because Jackson is a vegetarian. I declare this wedding would be much better off without Jackson Clooney!"

Lady put her front paws on Eugenia's shin and barked, begging to be picked up. Eugenia scooped the dog up and cuddled her. "In fact, Rosemary would probably be better off without Jackson too, but you can't reason with a woman in love."

Eugenia turned on PBS and watched a documentary on World War II. Just before the sinking of the *Bismarck,* she fell asleep and was awakened a couple of hours later by the ringing of the phone. It was Annabelle.

Eugenia shook her head to clear it then told her sister, "I thought you'd never get home! You've got to come over here right now. I need your help."

"Our flight was delayed, causing us to spend four hours in the airport. I'm hot and tired and just want to get into my own bed. So unless it's a matter of life and death, it will have to wait until tomorrow."

Eugenia thought about Jackson Clooney and the possibility that she might strangle him before Saturday, but she decided that didn't really qualify as a "life and death" emergency. "I guess tomorrow will do," she told Annabelle. "But be here early."

* * *

They let the children nap too long on Sunday afternoon, and Kate had a terrible time getting them back to sleep that night. After reading countless books and singing every song she knew, Kate was finally successful. As she left Emily's room, she knocked on the door to the guest room.

"Come in," Kelsey called.

Kate turned the doorknob and stepped inside. Kelsey was sitting in front of the computer. She was pale and had dark circles under her eyes.

"Checking e-mail," she explained. "There are twenty-five from Travis, and that's just today."

Kate crossed the room and sat on the edge of the unmade bed. "What do they say?"

"Mostly begging me to come home, promising anything if I do," Kelsey reported dully. "He says he's quit riding his bicycle and hasn't been to the organic food store in a week."

"It sounds like he's trying," Kate ventured.

Kelsey made a face at the computer screen. "It's not fair for him to give up all the things he enjoys just to make me happy."

Kate chose her words carefully. "It may not be fair, but that's what love is all about—putting someone else ahead of yourself. After all, Adam gave up the Garden of Eden to be with Eve."

Kelsey smiled. "I'll remember that."

Kate stood and gave her sister a quick hug. "Get back to bed soon. You look terrible."

When Kate reached her bedroom, she found Mark on the bed reading the scriptures with a frown on his face. "Need help understanding a scripture passage?" she teased as she climbed up beside him.

He shook his head. "No, I understand what it says. I wish I didn't. Then I wouldn't need to repent."

Surprised, she asked, "What for?"

"Slothfulness."

Kate laughed. "You may be guilty of some sins, but laziness isn't one of them."

He leaned over and kissed her. "Thanks."

Curious, she looked at his open scriptures. "What are you reading that made you feel slothful?"

"It's not what I'm reading that upset me. It's Miss Eugenia."

Kate waved this aside. "Oh, she's always upsetting me. You'll get over it."

Mark didn't laugh. "She's seventy-six years old and not a baptized member of the Church, but she attends all the meetings and even brought an investigator today."

Kate relaxed against his shoulder. "She is amazing."

He pointed to his scriptures. "I'm reading in Helaman about his sons Lehi and Nephi."

"They were great missionaries," she said, trying hard to control a yawn. It had been a long day.

He traced his finger along the page. "In chapter 5 verse 12, Helaman told them to depend on Christ and 'when the devil shall send forth his mighty winds, yea, his shafts in the whirlwind, yea, when all his hail and his mighty storm shall beat upon you, it shall have no power over you to drag you down to the gulf of misery and endless wo.'" He looked up. "That's how I feel now—miserable and full of woe. I have so many opportunities to tell people about the gospel, but I don't take advantage of them. I want to be more like Lehi and Nephi and Miss Eugenia."

Kate smiled up at him. "I'm sure Miss Eugenia would be pleased to know that you included her in such lofty company." She moved his finger down to the last line of verse 12. "It also says when men use the Savior as their foundation, they *cannot fall.* If you have a desire to be a better missionary, ask for the Lord's help and you'll be successful."

Mark closed his scriptures and put them on the table beside the bed. He gathered his wife into his arms. "That was exactly what I needed to hear."

CHAPTER 8

On Monday morning Annabelle arrived at Eugenia's house early, as commanded, and was welcomed by Lady growling ferociously.

"You've taught her to hate me," Annabelle complained.

"That's ridiculous," Eugenia said, reaching down to pat the little dog. "What do you have in that bag?"

Annabelle pulled a flaky apple fritter from the sack, and Eugenia's mouth started to water. "I stopped at Marsh's Bakery on my way into Haggerty this morning." She looked into the bag. "I got several different kinds. Do you want this?" She held up the fritter. "Or a bear claw or a cream cheese Danish?"

"You eat the apple fritter. I'll take a bear claw," Eugenia said, taking two plates down from the cupboard.

"I got coffee for myself but figured you didn't want any." Annabelle removed the lid that covered her Styrofoam cup.

Eugenia took the bag from her sister and extracted a bear claw. "You should give up coffee too. It will rot your insides." She took a bite of the pastry. "Delicious!"

While they ate, Eugenia told Annabelle all about the wedding. "Oh, Eugenia," Annabelle said finally.

"Don't 'Oh, Eugenia' me. Just say you'll help."

Annabelle looked suspicious. "What will I have to do?"

"I need you to provide the wedding cake."

Annabelle sipped her coffee. "It's pretty late notice, but I'll try."

"Trying isn't good enough. Promise me you'll have a cake here on Saturday morning if you have to make it yourself."

Annabelle laughed. "Okay, I promise."

"And I want Rosemary to have a tasteful, demure dress for the ceremony, so I was thinking I'd send her to Corrine's."

"What's the catch?" Annabelle wanted to know.

"The bride-to-be doesn't have any money."

Annabelle nodded. "Ahhh."

"But I'm hoping Corrine will discount the dress if you ask her to."

Annabelle nodded again. "I'll talk to Corrine."

Eugenia was relieved. "As soon as you have it worked out, let me know so I can send Rosemary over."

Annabelle finished her coffee, threw away most of her apple fritter, and said, "I leave you alone for a few days and look what happens."

Knowing she was guilty as charged, Eugenia couldn't even muster a clever comeback. "I'm glad you're home."

Annabelle patted her sister's hand. "Me too. Let me know if there's anything else you need."

After Annabelle left, Eugenia put away the leftover pastries for later. Then she collected Lady and went in to the police station. An exhausted-looking Arnold was sitting at Leita's desk when she arrived. He stood to relinquish her seat, and she asked, "Are you here by yourself?"

"Yes, ma'am," he confirmed. "Been here since noon yesterday."

Eugenia put Lady's basket down, and once the little dog was happily sniffing, she said, "Well, it's past time for you to leave. I'll handle things here."

"Then there won't be an officer on duty," Arnold said, making a token protest.

"If there's a sudden crime spree, I'll call you," Eugenia promised. "Let me see those cuticles." Arnold held out his hands, and she inspected them and nodded. "My special solution works miracles. You go on home and get to bed."

Winston came in an hour later. "Did you catch any criminals last night at Dub's place?" she asked him.

Winston removed his hat and scratched his head. "No, all I caught was fleas. That house is one of the filthiest I've ever seen. Those teenagers would be doing Dub a favor if they *do* kill him." He looked around wearily. "Where's Arnold?"

"He said he'd been here for almost twenty-four hours, so I sent him home."

Winston nodded as he continued on down the hall to his office.

Eugenia alternately filed paperwork and answered the phone as necessary. Sylvester called and said he'd be late. "I'm interviewing some of the vandal suspects Winston and I identified yesterday," he explained. "I'll be in whenever I get finished."

The next call was from Annabelle. "Things are all arranged with Corrine," she reported. "She's going to discount whatever Rosemary picks out, and I told her to put any overage on my charge account."

Eugenia was pleased. "That was very generous of you. I'll call Rosemary and let her know."

"On a less cheerful note," Annabelle continued. "I stopped back by Marsh's Bakery on the way home and asked if they could do the cake for Saturday. They can't."

Eugenia sighed. "So what are we going to do?"

"Derrick saw an idea in a magazine that uses regular round cakes from a grocery store deli . . ."

"That sounds fine," Eugenia said, cutting her sister off.

"Well, it will definitely be better than nothing," Annabelle agreed. "And that's what Marsh's Bakery can do for us."

After ending the conversation with Annabelle, Eugenia called Rosemary. She tried to approach the subject of the girl's wedding outfit tactfully. "What are you planning to wear on Saturday?" she inquired.

"I have a denim skirt and peasant blouse that Jackson really likes," Rosemary replied.

Eugenia was appalled. *A bride in denim—the very idea!* "Well, the ladies who are helping me with the wedding want you to have a new dress for the ceremony. If you'll go by Miss Corrine's she'll help you pick something out."

"Oh, Miss Eugenia, you're doing so much for me already—I can't expect you to buy me a dress!"

"We want to do it," Eugenia assured her. "Ask Miss Corrine to show you a cream-colored suit that I saw there a week or so ago. I think it would be perfect."

"I don't know how to thank you," Rosemary said sweetly.

"When we see you looking radiant on your wedding day, we'll have our thanks," Eugenia replied. Just as she hung up the phone, Sylvester walked in and sat down in the chair beside Leita's desk.

"So, did you find the vandal?"

He shook his head. "Not even a viable suspect."

"I'm sure you'll find the right person eventually," she comforted.

He shrugged. "I hope so. When is Brandon Vance supposed to get here with your vegetables?"

Eugenia craned her neck to look out the glass door. "He should be here any minute. Why?"

Sylvester gave her a sly smile. "I thought I'd go out and help him."

Eugenia narrowed her eyes in his direction. "You just want another opportunity to interrogate him."

Sylvester wasn't ashamed. "Exactly."

Eugenia saw Brandon walking up the street carrying a huge crate of tomatoes. "Well, here comes your victim now."

Sylvester stood. "Let me go see if I can lend him a hand."

Eugenia laughed. "That's mighty nice of you."

She followed Sylvester outside and, after greeting Brandon, advised the men on how to set up the stand for maximum advantage. "Remember that presentation is very important," she told the men. "Make sure you wipe any dirt off the vegetables before you put them in the baskets." She turned to Sylvester. "Will you go into the station and get Brandon a folding chair? He can't stand up all afternoon."

Sylvester went back inside and returned a couple of minutes later with two chairs. "I thought I'd sit out here and keep you company," he told Brandon.

The temporary yardman shrugged. "How you spend this lovely summer afternoon is entirely up to you."

Eugenia surveyed the setup critically. "I think this will do. Sylvester, if Brandon runs short on any of the vegetables, can you drive to my house and get more?"

"Sure," Sylvester agreed.

"Okay, then." She winked at Brandon. "Now you've got an assistant."

* * *

Mark spent the day trying to catch up on less interesting cases and waiting for a preliminary background check on Foster Gunnells to be sent to him from Atlanta. Marla came to his door at five thirty and waved a sheaf of papers.

"Here's that rush job you requested."

He glanced through it quickly. While the sheriff had never been convicted of a felony, which would have disqualified him for his current job, there were a couple of teenage misdemeanors on his record. Several years before, he had been charged with two counts of harassment, and a restraining order had been awarded to a Miss Erica Purdy.

"Bad news?" Marla guessed.

"Maybe." Mark reached for the phone, and Marla retreated to her office.

Mark called the sheriff's office in Patton Chapel and was told by the dispatcher who answered the phone that Foster Gunnells was unavailable. "Well, tell him that he'd better get available," Mark said with barely controlled fury. "If I don't hear from him within the hour, he'll be sorry." Mark slammed down the phone, angry with himself for trusting Foster Gunnells and for taking his frustration out on the dispatcher. If that little creep turned out to be the copycat murderer, he was going to—

The phone on his desk rang.

"It's that deputy from Patton Chapel," Marla called from her desk.

Mark snatched up the receiver. "Gunnells?" he demanded.

The acting sheriff cleared his throat audibly. "Yes, Mark. What can I do for you?"

"You lied to me," Mark accused. "You said that you only went on one date with Erica."

"That was true," Foster returned.

"You said you didn't have a relationship with her!"

"I didn't."

Mark looked at the papers in front of him. "You were arrested six times for following her around!" he yelled into the phone. "You stalked and harassed her until she called the police *six* times!"

"Actually she called the police more than that, but I was only arrested six times," Foster admitted.

His capitulation took Mark aback. "Why didn't you tell me?"

"It's embarrassing," Foster replied. "I was a stupid teenager obsessed with a beautiful, heartless girl. I try to forget about that time of my life."

"And you didn't feel obligated to remember it when I was questioning you about Erica?"

"No. I wasn't a suspect. I was helping you," Foster said, his voice rising in agitation.

"Well, maybe now you *are* a suspect," Mark told him.

"If that's the case," Foster said, "then any future conversations between you and me will be with my attorney present." Mark heard a soft click followed by the dial tone humming in his ear.

Marla appeared in the doorway of Mark's office. "Do you want me to call him back?"

Mark shook his head. "No, just ask Atlanta to dig deeper on Foster Gunnells."

Discouraged, Mark cleared off his desk and packed his briefcase in preparation to go home. Whether Foster Gunnells was guilty or not, he had been a good source of information, and now Mark had burned that bridge with his accusations. Mark turned off his computer then walked out to Marla's desk.

"I'm going to head home," he told the secretary. "And it's past time for you to leave."

Marla looked up from her keyboard. "I'll leave as soon as I finish this last report."

"Okay, see you in the morning."

Mark was almost to Haggerty when he remembered that he needed to run a check on the woman with the disconnected phone from the grief management group. Using his cell phone, he called his office, hoping to catch Marla before she left.

"FBI," she answered in a businesslike tone.

"Marla, before you leave, will you submit a request for a limited search on a Molly Vance from Wilsonville? Her address and phone number are on a list at the corner of my desk. The phone has been disconnected, and I want to see if she moved or is deceased or what."

"I'll take care of it," Marla promised.

"Thanks." He was about to hang up, then a thought occurred to him. "Would you like to know more about the Mormon Church?" he asked her.

There was a brief pause, then she said, "No, not really. But I appreciate you asking."

He was surprised. "You do?"

"I know how important your church is to you, and I take the fact that you wanted to share it with me as a compliment."

"Well, good," he said. "And if you ever change your mind, all you have to do is ask."

She laughed. "I will."

* * *

At six o'clock Eugenia watched Brandon begin packing up his vegetable stand. Throughout the afternoon they had done a brisk business, requiring Sylvester to make two trips to the garden for more produce. The door opened, and Sylvester stepped inside. He wiped sweat from his forehead as he collapsed into the chair beside Leita's desk.

"Did you trick Brandon into admitting that he murdered his wife, cut her body into little pieces, and fed her to piranhas?" she teased.

Sylvester shook his head wearily. "No, but he did let me bag vegetables for his customers. It seems like I'm never going to solve any crimes. All I do is provide everyone with free labor."

"So you're going to give up your investigation of Brandon?"

He shrugged. "Might as well."

"You should wait until Friday," she suggested. "And instead of spending the mornings at the police station letting Winston take advantage of you, why don't you go to my house under the pretense of helping prepare my backyard for the wedding. That way you can ask Brandon all kinds of questions."

Sylvester gave her a suspicious look. "Are you just trying to use me for free labor too?"

"Of course," she admitted. "But my plan is advantageous for you as well. You'll be able to keep a close eye on Brandon and talk to him in a nonthreatening environment. Who knows what could happen?"

"What would I have to do?"

"I'll have a list for you tomorrow."

Sylvester sighed as he stood. "I guess I can spin my wheels in your garden as well as I can here."

"That's the spirit," Eugenia said with a smile. "Come by my house in the morning, and I'll get you started."

With a discouraged nod, Sylvester left the police station. Eugenia was also preparing to leave when the phone rang. Juggling Lady and her purse in one hand, she grabbed the phone with the other. "Haggerty police," she said breathlessly.

"I'm so glad I caught you!" Whit's voice greeted her. "I was afraid you had already left."

"I should have," Eugenia told him. "But I can't ever seem to find a good stopping point."

He laughed. "I know exactly what you mean. I'm just leaving my office and still have to run to Albany to mail a package FedEx. I thought I'd get something to eat while I'm there and wondered if you'd go along and keep me company."

Eugenia's heart skipped a beat, and she put the phone into the crook of her neck so she could put her hand to her chest. Hoping she wasn't about to have a heart attack, she said, "I've got so much to do on the wedding—I really shouldn't."

"You have to eat." Like the good lawyer he was, Whit used an indisputable fact to convince her. "And we can go somewhere with fast service."

Eugenia put her hand over the phone and addressed Lady in a whisper. "What do you think?"

Lady barked excitedly. Eugenia smiled and uncovered the phone. "Okay, Lady and I accept, but you'd better have plenty of money. I'm not one of those prissy eaters who orders a salad and ice water."

He laughed. "Good. Neither am I."

* * *

When Kate heard Mark's car pull up into the driveway, she sent Emily and Charles to tell Kelsey that dinner was ready. Mark walked in and gave Kate a quick kiss. She studied him closely then asked, "How was your day?"

"Ah, let's see. I wasted most of it on paperwork, forgot to order a report that I really needed, and as the grand finale I alienated the acting sheriff in Patton Chapel by accusing him of murdering Erica Helms."

Kate gave him a hug. "Well, thank goodness you came home early. Given another hour, you might have found a way to destroy the world."

He smiled. "That's looking on the bright side—I think."

"Paperwork is a fact of life, and you can't expect to remember everything."

He nodded. "That's true."

"And don't let the acting sheriff worry you. If he didn't murder Erica, he'll get over it. If he did murder her, you shouldn't care about his feelings."

"You're just a font of wisdom lately," he teased.

"It comes from overexposure to Miss Eugenia," Kate explained, handing Mark a stack of plates. "Could you set the table for me?"

He smiled as he walked over and distributed the plates. "One good thing did happen today. I had a missionary experience on the way home."

Kate looked up from the rolls she was putting into a basket. "Tell me about it."

"I asked Marla if she'd like to know more about the Church."

Kate brought the rolls over to the table. "Does she?"

He shook his head. "No, but she said she took it as a compliment that I asked her."

Kate reached up and stroked his cheek. "Before long you'll be right up there with Lehi and Nephi and Miss Eugenia."

Their eyes met, and her heart beat faster. Then the kids ran in.

"Daddy!" Emily cried. "You're home and it's not even dark yet!"

Both children flung themselves at Mark, and he dropped Kate's hand to pick them up. "What did you do today?" he asked.

"We're having a big party here on Saturday, so Mama made us clean the house," Emily replied. "We worked and worked and worked."

"And played," Charles added honestly.

Mark kissed them both. "I'm glad your mother let you take a few breaks during all that hard work," he said with a smile at Kate.

Kelsey appeared in the kitchen doorway, and Kate rushed to her. "How do you feel?" Kate asked.

"Okay," was the response Kelsey gave as she crossed the room and sat down quickly in a chair beside the table. "Do you have any more of that potato soup?"

Kate nodded, already moving toward the refrigerator. "I'll heat some up. Mark, will you put the chicken fingers on the table?"

Mark served the children while Kate heated soup for Kelsey. Once everything was blessed, they all started eating. "We're going to make s'mores for family night dessert," Emily informed her father. "We got a big Hershey bar and everything."

"Are we going to roast the marshmallows over a fire?" Mark asked.

Charles shook his head mournfully. "Mama said no."

"She said it's too hot," Emily added. "But when you put marshmallows in the microwave, they blow up big and that's pretty fun."

"Yeah," Charles agreed. "That's pretty fun."

"Are you going to come to our family night and make a s'more?" Emily asked Kelsey.

Kate's sister swallowed a spoonful of soup cautiously then shook her head. "No, I'm way behind on my work and need to try and get something done while I'm not throwing up."

When dinner was over, Kelsey excused herself and went upstairs. Kate sent the children into the den to wait while she and Mark cleaned the kitchen. "I wonder why Kelsey avoids being with us," she said as they loaded the dishwasher. "I try not to let it hurt my feelings, but . . ."

"It does anyway?" he guessed.

She nodded. "I can't tell if Kelsey just doesn't want to intrude on our family time or if she really doesn't want to be with us."

"Maybe it's a little of both," Mark suggested gently.

"You think she doesn't like us?"

He shook his head. "She loves us, but it might be depressing for her to be with a happy family when hers is not."

Kate frowned then nodded. "Maybe we could *act* unhappy to make her more comfortable."

Mark laughed. "Or we could just leave her alone and let her come to terms with her life in peace."

Kate made a face at him as she turned on the dishwasher. "I guess that's also an option."

He took her hand and pulled her toward the den. "Come on. Let's get started with family night. I'm looking forward to that s'more."

"You just want to see a marshmallow blow up in the microwave."

"I've been told its pretty fun," he acknowledged as they entered the den.

* * *

Whit and Eugenia ate dinner at a new restaurant on the western side of Albany. "The review in the newspaper said their food is good and service fast," Whit told her as they walked inside.

The hostess who met them objected to Lady's presence. Eugenia was going to try her seeing-eye dog excuse, but before she could, Whit took the girl's arm and told her how lovely she was, how much he'd been looking forward to eating at this friendly restaurant, and how he knew she could look the other way just this once. Completely charmed, the girl forgot all about the rules and said with a smile at Whit, "If you'll follow me."

"Lady is such a good dog no one will even know she's here," Whit promised, and this, at least, was true.

They studied the menu quickly and placed their orders. The waitress was prompt in bringing their drinks and appetizers, but when the main courses were delivered, Eugenia's was poached salmon instead of the prime rib she had ordered.

"The cook must have confused the numbers," the waitress said when the mistake was pointed out. "I can have a prime rib dinner prepared, but it will take a while."

Eugenia examined the fish and determined that it didn't look too bad. "I'll just eat this," she offered, but Whit shook his head.

"No, you ordered a prime rib dinner, and that's what you'll have." He turned to the waitress. "And please tell the cook to hurry. Since it was his mistake, he should give this order priority treatment."

The waitress nodded. "I'll turn it in, but I can't promise that the cook will hurry."

Eugenia could see that Whit wasn't pleased with this response. Anxious to avoid further problems, she said, "This salmon looks fine."

Whit was frowning at her plate. "But it's not what you ordered."

Eugenia leaned forward and lowered her voice. "My sister Annabelle says that if you complain about the food at a restaurant, the cook might spit in it or do other unspeakable things before sending it back out to you."

Whit considered this for a second then signaled for the waitress to return. "I want to speak to the manager," he said in a commanding tone. "Immediately."

The girl didn't seem too concerned about this as she sauntered off in search of the manager.

"Young people these days," Whit said. "Their manners are deplorable."

"Whit," Eugenia began. "I'm sure the cook here won't do anything to my food."

"I can't take the risk," he said grimly.

When the manager arrived, Whit explained the mix-up on the order. Then he said, "We've placed a new order for the prime rib, and I want your guarantee that it will be served promptly and without sabotage."

"We have an excellent kitchen staff," the manager assured him in an aggrieved tone. "I can guarantee . . ."

"There's only one way you can guarantee anything and that is to go back into the kitchen and watch while the meal is being prepared." Whit lowered his voice menacingly. "I'm a lawyer, and I was suing people before you were born. Remember *that* while you're making sure no one does anything disgusting to my friend's dinner."

The manager's Adam's apple bobbed nervously as he nodded. "I'll take care of it, sir." As an afterthought he turned to Eugenia. "And please accept my apologies, ma'am."

Eugenia opened her mouth to tell him it was nothing, but Whit spoke first. "Just get back there and watch that cook."

The prime rib arrived shortly and was delicious. Ignoring Sylvester's dire predictions, Eugenia fed Lady a few little bites of the meat. When they were ready to leave, Whit requested a to-go box and insisted that Eugenia take the salmon as well as her steak scraps.

On the way home Whit asked her what she thought about the restaurant. "I don't eat out much, unless you count Haggerty Station," she prefaced her remarks. "But I thought the food was good and the service timely, if not completely accurate."

"I *do* eat out a lot, and I have basically the same opinion. I'm sorry that I didn't get you home early like I'd promised."

She waved this aside. "It couldn't be helped. And it was quite entertaining the way you sent the manager into the kitchen to watch the cook make my dinner."

"I'm sorry about that too. I hope you weren't embarrassed."

She laughed. "I never get embarrassed, and I particularly liked the part about your suing people before he was born."

"Maybe I got a little carried away," Whit admitted. "But if there was a possibility that the cook was going to ruin your meal on purpose as a protest, I felt like I had to take action. If we don't hold people to high standards, we can't complain when we get mediocrity."

"Well said, counselor," she teased.

"In spite of my questionable behavior, did you have fun?"

She nodded. "Lady and I had a very nice evening."

He smiled. "Good. You're always doing things for other people, and I wanted to do something nice for you. Then I was afraid I spoiled it."

"It's been lovely," she assured him as they pulled up in front of her house.

"Maybe we can make a habit of it," he suggested. "Not of me making a fuss at restaurants, but of going out to eat."

She looked down at Lady, who was sleeping peacefully in her basket, and tried to find the words to explain how she felt. Finally she just said, "Charles was the love of my life."

"I know that, Eugenia," Whit replied softly. "And I'm not trying to take his place. I've got three ex-wives and don't need another one. I just thought we could be friends. Go out to dinner sometimes, maybe to the movies. That sort of thing."

She smiled. "Well, in that case, I'd love to."

Whit came around and opened her door then escorted her to the house.

"You have very nice manners," she praised him.

"It's a vanishing art," he told her.

"Young people these days don't have time for manners."

He laughed. "Sad but true."

"Well, thank you for dinner," she said when they reached the front porch.

"Good night," Whit said, turning back toward the steps. He paused halfway down. "I was a little jealous of Charles in high school for having a steady girl like you."

Eugenia was genuinely surprised. "I thought you liked being a player and leaving broken hearts everywhere you went."

He laughed. "I'll admit I've always had a weakness for beautiful women. Still, I can't help but wonder what would have happened if you'd fallen for me instead of Charles."

"We'd have dated for a few weeks, and then you would have moved on to the next girl," Eugenia guessed.

"Maybe you would have been the one girl I couldn't leave behind. Then I wouldn't have a string of broken marriages."

"Or any children," Eugenia pointed out. "It's no good looking back and playing 'what if.' We make decisions and then we live with them—for better or worse."

He smiled. "You are a wise woman, Eugenia."

"And you just proved your own intelligence by recognizing that." She turned and unlocked her door. "Good night."

* * *

When Mark got to work on Tuesday morning, Marla was already there. "You're here bright and early," he said.

"I was lucky with the traffic," she told him, lifting a stack of papers from her desk. "This was sitting in the fax tray when I got in."

"What is it?" Mark asked as he continued to his office and turned on the lights.

"The preliminary background report on Molly Vance," she replied. "It says she's been missing for over a year."

Mark returned to Marla's desk. "Missing? You mean kidnapped?"

"No, apparently she just packed up and left without telling anyone."

Mark took the report and scanned it. "Divorced, only child died of leukemia two years before. No romantic involvements."

"And no activity in her name since the day she disappeared."

"She's using a different name?"

Marla shrugged. "The real question is why? She was a homemaker for years. After her child died and her marriage fell apart, she became a hermit. Then one day she just packs up and leaves. She doesn't cash a check or rent a car or anything. She's just gone."

Mark frowned "That is weird."

He was still staring at the report when the phone began to ring. Marla answered it and put the call on hold. "It's for you—an Agent Kellum from Jacksonville."

Mark placed the report back on her desk. "Keep digging on this, and let me see whatever you come up with," he requested while walking into his office. "Iverson," he said into the phone receiver.

"Agent Iverson, Tim Kellum from Jacksonville. I'm leaving in a few minutes, headed your way with a convicted drug importer. He's speaking before a Senate committee tomorrow in Washington, and we change planes in Albany. I'm hoping you can help me during the transfer."

"Have you alerted airport security?" Mark asked.

"I have," Agent Kellum confirmed. "And the local police, but I'd like to have another agent on-site just in case."

"You think some of the guy's friends will try to free him?"

Agent Kellum laughed. "More likely some of his enemies will try to kill him."

Mark looked at his watch. "What time do you get here?"

"One thirty P.M., American Flight 7258. Our connecting flight leaves at three forty-five. I'd appreciate it if you'll go on over and make sure the area is secure before we get there."

Mark sighed. "I'll head that way now."

Mark hung up the phone and walked out to Marla's desk. "Leaving so soon?" she teased.

"It looks like I'll be spending most of the day at the airport. If you need me, call my cell phone."

CHAPTER 9

On Tuesday morning Eugenia made a three-page to-do list while she and Lady ate semi-stale pastries from the bag Annabelle had brought them the day before. Then, on the way to the police station, she stopped by Polly's house to see how the food was coming along.

She found both Polly and Lucy in the kitchen making heart-shaped mints in various shades of pink. "These are pretty," Eugenia praised as she picked up rose-colored heart.

"They are also sugar and fat free," Polly informed her. "For guests who are watching what they eat."

Eugenia put the mint back on the tray. "And who don't care about taste," she muttered to herself. "Have you come up with enough finger foods that don't use cheese or meat?"

Polly nodded. "I think so. I don't know what I would have done without Lucy."

"You would have been in a heap of trouble, that's what," Lucy replied.

"How much longer are you going to be able to stay?" Eugenia asked while testing a wedding cookie with caution.

"My son is coming back to get me on Saturday afternoon."

"Please don't talk about Lucy leaving," Polly begged, dabbing her eyes with a lace handkerchief. "I can't stand to even *think* about it."

Lucy walked over and patted her friend's shoulder. "I know, honey. I'm going to miss you too. But we're off to a good start on our diet, and it's time for me to get home."

"How much have you lost?" Eugenia asked, popping another cookie into her mouth.

"Ten pounds," Polly reported.

"Ten pounds?" Eugenia was amazed.

"Some of that was water weight, which you lose at the first of any diet, but I'm very pleased with my results," Polly confirmed. "And Lucy lost eight pounds."

"Well, I'm very proud of you both," Eugenia told them as she picked up a handful of cookies. "I've got a couple more stops to make on the way in to the police station, so I guess I'll go."

After leaving Polly's house, Eugenia proceeded up the block and was surprised to see Dub Shaw coming out of the Piggly Wiggly. "Well, Dub," Eugenia said. "I thought you were staying in Albany for a few days."

"They let me out this morning," he reported. "I stopped by to get a few groceries and had my basket full of Alpo before I remembered that my dogs were gone."

Eugenia glanced down at Lady, and her heart started to pound. "I'm so sorry about your dogs, Dub."

Tears filled his eyes then slipped over his leathery cheeks. "I don't know how I'll stand it out there all alone."

Eugenia had a pretty good idea how he'd stand it. He'd drink himself into a coma. "Dub, instead of going to your lonely, old house, how would you like to perform a public service?"

Dub's tears dried up, and his expression became guarded. "What kind of service?"

"The lobby at the police station needs to be painted. Since you spend about as much time there as anyone, I thought you might like the job."

"How much does it pay?"

"Nothing," she told him. "But you'd get free meals and have lots of pleasant company."

Dub considered the proposal. "It's been a while since I've done any painting."

"It will come back to you," she replied with conviction. "I'll go by the hardware store right now and pick out the paint. You take your groceries home, and I'll have Arnold come get you in a little while."

"I reckon that'll be okay," Dub muttered. He started shuffling down the street.

"Now what do you think about that?" she asked Lady as they walked on to town. "If I can just get Mr. Nattress at the hardware store to donate the paint and other supplies, I'll consider the whole project a complete success."

Mr. Nattress agreed to the donation on the condition that Winston would dress up like Santa and ride on his Nattress Hardware float in the annual Christmas parade. Since she had several months to convince him, Eugenia accepted the deal on Winston's behalf. She picked out a soothing sage green color for the lobby walls and a creamy off-white for the wood trim. Then she headed in to the station.

Arnold was preparing to leave, so she convinced him to go get Dub. "Take him to the hardware store to pick up the paint and other supplies, then drop him off here," she instructed.

Arnold nodded. "Yes, ma'am."

She beamed at him. "You're being such a big help that I might just give you another free manicure."

By the time Winston arrived at the station an hour later, drop cloths and paint cans were scattered around the lobby.

"What's going on?" Winston asked as he took off his hat.

"I figured part of the reason Leita had a relapse is because she couldn't face coming back to this drab, ugly room," Eugenia explained. "So we're painting."

Winston looked at Dub, who was sitting across the room in a folding chair, drinking a Dr Pepper. "I don't see any painting going on."

"Dub is just taking a little break," Eugenia assured the police chief. She lowered her voice and added, "He's grieving for his dogs, and I thought a project would help take his mind off them."

"Who's paying for this?" Winston wanted to know.

"Mr. Nattress at the hardware store donated everything," Eugenia was proud to announce.

"I know there's got to be a catch," Winston replied with suspicion.

"He just wants you to ride on his Christmas float." Eugenia decided to leave the part about dressing up like Santa for later. "You look tired."

"I am tired," he confirmed. "It's a good thing they let him out of the lockup," Winston said with a wave toward Dub. "Because I've spent my last night at his house. The vandals can burn it down for all I care. I've got to get back home where I can rest."

Before Eugenia could comment, the phone rang. It was Rosemary. "I just got back from Miss Corrine's!" she cried excitedly. "And I found the prettiest dress to wear on Saturday."

"Not the cream suit?" Eugenia asked, trying to keep the disappointment from her voice.

"No, ma'am, it's a pale yellow dress, and Miss Corrine said it looks divine on me!"

Knowing that Rosemary's happiness was the most important consideration, Eugenia congratulated her.

"I did have a little favor to ask," Rosemary continued.

Eugenia held her breath. "What?"

"Well, it doesn't seem fair that I'm getting this beautiful dress, and poor Jackson will just be wearing regular clothes . . ."

"I guess that isn't fair," Eugenia agreed. "I'll see what I can do about getting him a tuxedo."

"Oh, thank you," Rosemary gushed. "Saturday is going to be the most special day for us."

"I hope so," Eugenia replied. "Well, I guess I'll see you Friday evening at the wedding rehearsal."

"We'll be there," Rosemary promised. Then she said good-bye.

As soon as Eugenia hung up the phone, it rang again. "How are things at the Haggerty police station?" Whit asked.

Lady ran over and put her paws on Eugenia's leg, barking. Eugenia rubbed the little dog's head. "Lady says hello," she told Whit.

"Please give her my regards," Whit requested.

"I will. Is that why you called—to trade pleasantries with Lady?"

Whit laughed. "No, I called because I've been in a boring deposition all morning, and I knew you could cheer me up," he said. "And to thank you again for going to dinner with me last night. You are very good company."

"I'm sure I enjoyed it as much as you did," she replied.

"And to apologize again for keeping you away from your wedding planning so long," Whit added. "It occurred to me after I got home that I should have offered to help—as a way of making up for the time you wasted on my account."

Eugenia considered this then said, "Actually there is something you can do. The groom needs a tuxedo, and I figure after all your weddings, you've got to know where to get a good one on short notice."

"Give me the young man's name and phone number, and I'll take care of it."

Eugenia recited the information.

"Consider the tuxedo taken care of."

After hanging up the phone, Eugenia lifted Lady onto her lap. "Well now, it's nice to have influential friends, don't you think?"

The little dog barked, and Dub looked up, startled. "I think it's about to storm. I keep hearing thunder."

"It's just my little dog, Lady, barking." Eugenia frowned. "Are you sure that's just Dr Pepper you've been drinking?"

Dub looked offended. "I never drink alcoholic beverages while I'm at the police station." He stood and threw his empty can away then resumed his painting. He'd only been working for a few minutes when a taxi pulled up in front of the police station.

"Well, I declare, what would a taxi cab be doing here in Haggerty?" Eugenia wondered aloud.

Dub peered out the glass door then handed Eugenia his paintbrush. "It's for me. Time to go to my weekly meeting of Alcoholics Anonymous."

Eugenia was surprised. "I didn't know you were a member of AA."

"Yeah, the last time I was in court, the judge made going to the meetings a stipulation for staying out of jail." Dub scratched his head. "I don't know why he wants me to go. Sitting there listening to all those people talk about drinking just makes me thirsty."

Eugenia shook her head in despair. "Hurry on, now. Your taxi is waiting."

* * *

It was five o'clock by the time Mark left the airport. After fighting rush-hour traffic until almost five thirty, he parked his car outside the building where the FBI maintained its Albany Resident Agency. He was frustrated that he'd spent most of the day standing around the airport instead of working on his cases, official and otherwise. But he couldn't consider the assignment a total loss, since he'd given away five pass-along cards and a Book of Mormon.

When he got back to the office, Marla was gone for the day. She had left a note saying she had printed out everything she could find on Molly Vance, and the results were on his desk. Mark leafed through the printout while he accessed his voice mail and listened to the messages that had accumulated during his absence.

He was only paying half attention until he heard a deep voice that identified himself as Dr. Clements, the psychiatrist who had treated Erica Helms. He sat up straight in his chair and dialed the number that the doctor had left. When the receptionist answered, she told him that Dr. Clements could give him a few minutes at six P.M. Mark checked his watch and said, "I'll be there." He tossed the printout into his briefcase, locked up the office, and headed back toward his car.

When Mark arrived at the office building where Dr. Clements had his practice, he parked and walked inside. The receptionist's desk was empty, so he scanned the list of room numbers posted on the wall for Dr. Clements's name. He took the elevator to the third floor, and when the doors opened, he was surprised to find himself standing face-to-face with Dub Shaw.

"Hello, Mr. Shaw," Mark said as he left the elevator and Dub Shaw stepped inside.

"Hey," the town drunk responded briefly before the elevator doors closed, separating them. Mark followed discreet signs that directed him down the hallway to Dr. Clements's office. Along the way he passed the headquarters of the local chapter of Alcoholics Anonymous—which he presumed explained Dub Shaw's presence in the building.

Dr. Clements turned out to be a big, outdoorsy looking man with a firm handshake. Mark liked him on sight. He offered Mark coffee, which he declined, and a seat, which he took.

Once they were settled, the doctor began the conversation by saying, "I'm sure you realize that without a court order there is very little I can tell you."

"Yes, I understand that," Mark acknowledged. "But I'm hoping you can answer a few questions for me without violating your client privilege."

"I'll try." The doctor seemed cooperative, and Mark was encouraged. "What is your interest in Erica?"

"You know that Lyle Tweedy was convicted of killing Erica?"

The doctor nodded. "Yes."

"Were you surprised when you heard that she had developed a relationship with Tweedy?"

He nodded again. "Yes."

Mark studied the doctor, trying to read his eyes. "I talked to some of Erica's family and friends. They said that after the deaths of her husband and children, Erica avoided all contact with people. She even had her groceries delivered. The only social interactions I've been able to find were monthly visits to your office and regular attendance at a weekly grief management group. My profile doesn't depict her as a soul-baring kind of person, and her dedication to the grief group surprises me."

"Erica didn't go to that group by choice," the doctor volunteered. "Attendance was a requirement from me as part of her therapy."

Mark made a note. "Then after months of seclusion, the week before her death, Erica became a social butterfly. She visited the old dental office where she used to work, the bank, and the utility company. During all this contact with people, she divulged that she had a *dangerous* boyfriend and was going away with him."

The doctor showed no surprise. So this wasn't news to him.

"I find that totally out of character for her," Mark continued.

"Yes," the doctor agreed.

Mark could tell that the doctor wanted to help but was restricted by law and ethics. He decided to try a different tactic. "I met with Tweedy for a little while on the night he was executed."

Dr. Clements's expression registered astonishment. "Why?"

"He requested that I come to see him. He said he didn't kill Erica and wanted to set the record straight."

Dr. Clements asked, "Did you believe him?"

Mark shrugged. "Yes and no. But my subsequent investigation has turned up some discrepancies. It's possible that Erica was killed by a copycat murderer."

Dr. Clements steepled his fingers and studied Mark intensely. "I would have loved to talk to Tweedy. He was unique."

"I wish you could have taken my place. It was one of the worst experiences of my life," Mark admitted. "I still have nightmares about it."

Dr. Clements was frowning. "I'm sure you've heard the term *sociopath?*"

"Yes," Mark confirmed. "Is that what Tweedy was?"

Dr. Clements gave him an odd look. "Among other things. You should do some research on the subject. It's quite fascinating." The doctor stood up, indicating that the interview was over.

Mark rose to his feet. "Thank you for your time."

"You're welcome. If you ever get that court order, come back and I'll be able to give you more specific information."

Mark nodded. "I think I'm close to having this all wrapped up, but if I need anything else from you, I'll get a court order first."

Dr. Clements escorted Mark to the elevator and after waving good-bye said, "I hope you have better luck with Erica than I did." Then he turned and walked back to his office.

* * *

When Eugenia got home from the police station on Tuesday night, she walked into the backyard where Brandon was loading up his crates with vegetables to sell the next day. She looked around at the plants, heavy with produce, and shook her head.

"It makes you wonder if you'll ever pick the last of it."

Brandon smiled. "Your bountiful harvest will end. Enjoy it while it lasts."

"I've got a free salmon dinner inside that I'd be glad to share," she offered.

"I've already eaten, but thank you." He glanced toward the setting sun, and Eugenia knew he didn't want to waste the remaining daylight.

"Well, good night then."

* * *

It was almost eight o'clock by the time Mark finally walked into the kitchen that night. Kate gave him a quick hug then started warming his dinner. When she placed it on the table in front of him, he saw that she had been crying.

Forgetting all about the food, he pulled her onto his lap. "Kate, what's the matter?"

She buried her face in his neck. "Oh, Mark. I've done something irrevocable, and now I'm terrified that it was the *wrong* thing."

Mark's heart started to pound. "What did you do, Kate?"

"Kelsey's been so sick," she ranted on a seemingly unrelated topic. "She threw up all afternoon, and I finally had to threaten to call 911 before she'd let me make her an appointment with my doctor for tomorrow morning. Then she started crying and couldn't stop." Kate looked up for emphasis. "I promise she cried for hours. If she hadn't already been dehydrated, she has to be now. She's so miserable and confused, and she's trying to handle this all by herself. I knew she couldn't—"

Mark put his hands on her shoulders. "Kate." He waited until her eyes focused on his. "What did you *do?*"

"I called Travis," she whispered.

Mark sighed. "Oh, Kate."

"I didn't mention the baby. I just told him I thought he should come out here."

"And how did he react?"

"He's flying in on Thursday afternoon," she confessed. "Kelsey's going to kill me! Or worse!"

"Actually, she might thank you." Then Mark qualified his statement by adding, "Someday."

Ignoring this, Kate pulled away from him, wringing her hands. "I don't know how to tell her."

"Pray about it tonight, and ask the Lord to help you find the right time to break the news to Kelsey."

Kate nodded absently then turned toward the hallway that led to the den. "Eat your dinner. I'm going to give the kids their baths and put them to bed."

"I'll be up to help you in a few minutes," Mark promised. He ate quickly and deposited his briefcase on the desk in his home office. He headed upstairs so that Kate wouldn't have to deal with the two rowdy children alone.

It wasn't until later that night, when he held Kate close to him as she slept, that he remembered Dr. Clements's admonition to learn more about sociopathic personalities. After making a mental note to do so first thing the next day, Mark closed his eyes and joined his wife in slumber.

* * *

On Wednesday morning during breakfast, Mark told Kate that he was having trouble focusing on what he was trying to accomplish. "I feel like I'm running around in circles," he told her with his mouth full of cereal. "I usually don't forget things, but lately I have been."

"Like what?" Kate asked.

"I've had a report in my briefcase for two days that I can't remember to review. I need to look up the personality traits of a sociopath on the Internet, but I keep forgetting." He shook his head. "I've got a new case I'm trying to process; I'm trying to figure out who killed Erica Helms and find out why one of the other members of her grief group disappeared; I'm trying to share the gospel. Also, that agent from Jacksonville robbed me of a whole day. It's like I've overloaded my brain." He looked up in desperation. "How can I do so many things at once?"

"It's called multitasking," Kate informed him as she refilled his glass with orange juice. "Women do it all the time."

"Well, I can't function like this," he grumbled. "I have to concentrate on one thing, get it finished, and then move on to the next project."

Kate shook her head. "I see why the Lord won't let men be mothers."

When Mark arrived at the FBI office in Albany, Marla was sitting at her desk. "You've beat me two days in a row," he pointed out. "You're starting to make me feel like a slacker."

She took a deep breath then blurted, "I didn't want to tell you, but my son got into a fight at school, and his punishment is early-morning detention all this week. He has to be at school by seven, so after I drop him off, I just come in to work."

Mark sat down in the chair in front of Marla's desk. "Why wouldn't you want to tell me that?"

She blushed. "I don't want you to think I'm a bad mother."

Mark was confused. "I don't think that. Children get in trouble at school from time to time. Why was he fighting?"

"He said some kids have been picking on him and when he tried to defend himself, he got in trouble right along with them."

Mark nodded. "Zero-tolerance policies don't take fault into account and can be very unfair."

Marla relaxed visibly. "I've been so worried about Skyler lately. We moved after the divorce, and he doesn't really have any friends at the new school. My ex-husband is too involved with his new wife to have much time for our son. Skyler just turned twelve and wants to be a man but has no one to show him how."

As Mark contemplated the problem, a thought came to him. "Does he like camping and hiking and white-water rafting?"

Marla shrugged. "I don't think he's ever done any of those things."

"We have a very good scouting program at church," Mark began, holding up a hand to stave off her inevitable protest. "We have several boys participating who aren't members of the Mormon Church. The meetings are on Wednesday nights, and we follow the Boy Scouts of America guidelines. Our boys go camping at least once a month and attend merit badge seminars and have all kinds of activities. I'm at church every Wednesday night anyway, so if you think Skyler would be interested, I'd be glad to pick him up and introduce him to the other guys."

Mark expected Marla to politely decline his offer, but he wasn't prepared for the tears that sprang to her eyes. "Thank you. I'll ask him and let you know."

A little uncomfortable with her show of emotion, Mark was grateful when the phone rang, giving him an excuse to escape. He was almost to his office when Marla called out that the call was for him. He reached over his desk and picked up the phone. It was his supervisor's secretary. They exchanged a few sentences, then he hung up the phone and returned to Marla's desk.

"I've got to go to Atlanta," he told her.

"Something about your new case?" she asked.

"No, something about an old case that has come back to haunt me."

"Erica Helms?" she guessed.

"Yes. The Patton Chapel sheriff's department has filed a complaint against me, and now I'm being called on the carpet." Mark frowned. "And the secretary said there was some question about the legality of the background checks I've requested—but that must be a mistake."

Marla looked concerned. "If they want you to go to Atlanta, it must be serious."

"It might be," he admitted as he picked up his briefcase. "But I didn't harass Foster Gunnells, and I'm authorized to research anyone associated with an ongoing investigation. So once I explain what really happened, everything should be fine."

"I hope you don't get fired," she said, the dread obvious in her voice.

Mark didn't consider this a likely result of his decision to investigate Erica Helms's death, even if some people within the FBI would have preferred to see his interview with Lyle Tweedy swept under the carpet. "I hope not too."

"Because I really like working for you," she said, blushing.

He smiled. "Thanks." His hand was on the doorknob when he remembered one of the tasks he hadn't had the time to handle. "Do you know what a sociopath is?" he asked Marla.

"I know it's not good," she replied.

"No, it's definitely not good. I have a general idea of what the characteristics are, but if you have time, will you look the term up on the Internet and make me a specific list of the traits? I'd like to go over them when I get back from Atlanta—assuming I don't get fired," he added.

* * *

Kate called her doctor's office and convinced them to work in an appointment for Kelsey on Thursday morning. In the meantime they advised Kate to make sure Kelsey drank plenty of fluids to avoid dehydration. Anxious to share this news, Kate knocked on Kelsey's door.

"Come in," Kelsey called.

Kate opened the door expecting to see Kelsey in bed, but her sister was sitting at the computer. "You have an appointment at my doctor's office at ten o'clock tomorrow morning," she announced.

"Thanks," Kelsey replied. "Although I feel a little better today."

Kate smirked. "That worked once—I won't fall for it again."

Kelsey smiled. "But I really do feel better. In fact, I think I could eat something."

Kate was thrilled. "Like what?"

"Maybe some toast and ginger ale to start with," Kelsey suggested. "We'll see how I do with that and go from there."

"I'll be right back," Kate promised. When she returned with the requested items, Kate stood beside Kelsey and watched her nibble on the toast.

"So far, so good," Kelsey said after she'd eaten an entire piece. "I think I'll let that settle and then try the other one."

"Let me know if you want anything else."

Kelsey nodded, her attention focused back on the computer screen. "I will."

"Any e-mails from Travis?" she asked, testing the waters to see if this was the right moment to admit her interference.

Kelsey shook her head. "Not a single one. Maybe he's finally given up on me." Kelsey's bottom lip trembled a little.

Kate knew she should tell Kelsey that Travis was probably too busy packing for his trip to Haggerty to send e-mails, but she didn't want to upset her sister right after she'd eaten a whole piece of toast. There was still plenty of time, and besides, she just couldn't muster the courage. So she walked to the door and said, "I guess I'd better go wake up the kids. Let me know when you want something else to eat."

"I will," Kelsey promised without taking her eyes off the computer screen.

* * *

Eugenia spent the first half of Wednesday morning alternately making phone calls to her wedding volunteers and moving drop cloths for Dub Shaw. She spent the second half of the morning moving drop cloths and trying to mediate a disagreement between George Ann and Cornelia over whether to use a silver or crystal punch bowl. Finally she gave up on forcing either of them to compromise and told them to use both.

"How can we use both?" George Ann demanded through the police station phone lines.

"Put one in the living room and one in the dining room," Eugenia said wearily. "The guests will consider it a convenience."

"Well, I suppose that will be okay," George Ann relented, to Eugenia's relief. "Of course, Cornelia may not approve. You know how disagreeable she can be."

Eugenia sighed. "I'll handle Cornelia. Just be at Kate's on Friday morning to help set up."

"I'll be there," George Ann replied. "And I'll need a few people to help me polish the silver punch bowl."

Which is why Cornelia wanted to use the crystal one, Eugenia thought to herself. "There should be plenty of volunteers," Eugenia assured George Ann.

After talking to George Ann, she called Cornelia and itemized the many benefits of a dual punch bowl arrangement. "Don't think you're tricking me," Cornelia said finally. "You just don't want to tell George Ann she can't bring that antique punch bowl that her great-great grandmother buried in the backyard during the Civil War."

Eugenia laughed. "You're right. I don't have the energy to fight with George Ann any more today."

"I agree that two punch bowls will work fine, but after the fuss she's made, I refuse to help George Ann polish hers."

"I'll get someone else to help George Ann polish," Eugenia promised. As soon as she hung up the phone, it rang again. "Haggerty police," she said.

"Eugenia? This is Annabelle."

The frustration of the past few hours had taken a toll, and Eugenia responded with a cross, "I know who you are."

"I've been trying to get through for over an hour. I was about to notify the operator."

"What's the operator going to do? Call the police?"

Annabelle chuckled. "I guess you have a point. Anyway, I just wanted to let you know that Derrick and I are driving to Macon tonight. He's giving a lecture at the library up there tomorrow, so we'll spend tonight in a hotel and then drive back after he gives his speech."

This aggravated Eugenia even more. "How can you go off to Macon when you know that I'm trying to give an impromptu wedding? What if I was counting on you to do something for me?"

"That's why I'm calling now," Annabelle said calmly. "So that if there's anything you need, I can take care of it before I leave."

Eugenia couldn't think of any response except, "Oh."

"So, do you?"

"What?"

"Have anything you need me to do?" Annabelle asked.

"Oh, no. Well not at the moment, but something could come up."

"I'll be back tomorrow, and if anything comes up, I'll handle it then," Annabelle said, concluding the conversation. "And try to get to bed early tonight. You're acting more senile than usual."

Eugenia thought of several clever replies after she hung up the phone. "Maybe Annabelle's right," she told Lady. "Do you think I'm senile?"

The front door swung open, and Rosemary Moss waltzed in carrying a plastic clothing bag with *Corrine's* emblazoned across the front.

"Be careful!" Eugenia admonished. "There's wet paint on the door frame."

Rosemary negotiated the doorway cautiously then rushed over to Leita's desk. "They called from Miss Corrine's this morning to say that the alterations were finished on my dress. I just picked it up and wanted you to see it!"

Eugenia smiled. Maybe her day was about to get better. "I declare, I can hardly wait!"

Rosemary pulled up the thick plastic cover and exposed a scrap of yellow silk. "That's a real nice slip, Rosemary," Eugenia said patiently. "But where's your *dress?*"

Rosemary laughed. "Oh, Miss Eugenia, you're so funny."

Eugenia was at a loss. "I am?"

"This *is* my dress!" Rosemary elaborated. "And it fits me like a glove."

"Heaven help us," Eugenia whispered, fingering the flimsy fabric.

The "dress" had tiny spaghetti straps and would hit a tall girl like Rosemary well above the knee.

Rosemary dropped the cover over her dress and turned toward the door. "I've got to go home and wake up Jackson. He's got a big test this afternoon."

Eugenia nodded, adding cloud cover to her prayer list for Saturday. With bright sunlight shining through that thin dress, it would be more like a peep show than a wedding.

* * *

During the three-hour drive to Atlanta, Mark practiced what he would say. He would explain that the call from the prison warden came to his office at work, which indicated that Tweedy was contacting him primarily as an FBI agent. This gave the bureau both jurisdiction and responsibility. After submitting his official report, he told his supervisor that he would be investigating the case discreetly. Although he had suggested that Foster Gunnells in Patton Chapel might be a suspect in the death of Erica Helms, he didn't actually accuse him of murder. Also, requesting background checks on anyone he thought suspicious was well within his authority. So by the time he parked in the deck beside the office building in Atlanta, Mark felt confident that the meeting would go well.

He walked into the building and approached the receptionist's desk. He signed in and told the woman he was there to see his supervisor, Dan Davis. The receptionist checked his badge and asked him to wait in the lobby while she made a call. This was unusual, but Mark tried not to worry about it. He walked over to the panel of windows along the front of the building and watched the Atlanta traffic through the glass. A security guard appeared near the entrance, and Mark had the odd feeling that the man was there to watch him. Finally an agent named Rice, whom Mark had never met, walked up and introduced himself.

"I'm going to take you to the SAC's office," he told Mark. "Follow me."

As Mark fell into step behind Agent Rice, he felt his heart pounding. He had only met the Special Agent in Charge of the Atlanta region a few times and had never been in his office. Nor had he ever had an armed escort while visiting this building. The misunderstanding was apparently worse than he thought.

Neither man spoke as they took an elevator up to the seventh floor. After exiting the elevator, Agent Rice led the way to a door and knocked once before he opened it for Mark. The office looked like most of the others he had seen in various FBI facilities, and Mark felt a calming sense of the familiar. Then he saw Dan sitting on a couch and felt even better.

"Agent Iverson," the SAC said from across the room. "Have a seat." He indicated a chair in front of the desk. Mark looked at Dan, but his supervisor wouldn't meet his gaze.

What was left of Mark's confidence evaporated, and he sat down.

"I presume you know why you have been summoned?" the SAC continued.

Mark nodded. "A couple of weeks ago I got a phone call at the FBI office in Albany—"

The SAC held up a hand. "I read the report you filed. That should have been the end of your involvement unless instructed otherwise. Instead, you've been wasting taxpayer money on useless background checks and harassing people."

"I did not harass Sheriff Gunnells—"

"He said you told him he was a suspect in the death of Erica Helms," the SAC interrupted. "Which is obviously impossible, since Lyle Tweedy was convicted and *executed* for that murder."

Mark detected the SAC's warning tone and proceeded with caution. "But, sir, there were some inconsistencies in that case that were never resolved. Since Tweedy contacted me, I felt that the FBI had both jurisdiction and responsibility—"

"You are not authorized to make that determination," the SAC said, his voice rising in anger. "Only your supervisor can do that, and Dan says he told you specifically to leave the case alone."

Shocked, Mark looked to Dan for support, but his supervisor was staring at the floor. Slowly, understanding dawned. Dan was throwing him to the dogs. Now he had to choose whether to accuse his supervisor of lying or to accept a reprimand that he didn't deserve.

"If it's so dull in Albany that you have time to play around with *solved* cases," the SAC continued, "maybe we should close the office and bring you up here. I can assure you, *we* have better things to do."

Mark tried to ignore this threat and organize his thoughts. "We have plenty to do in Albany too, sir. I've done most of the investigation on this case on my own time—"

The SAC pounced on his words. "So you admit that this investigation was unofficial, off-the-record, or, in other words, *illegal?*"

Mark looked at Dan one last time. When he saw that he wasn't going to get any help from the man he had respected and even considered a friend, Mark cleared his throat. "I filed a report on my conversation with Tweedy and then proceeded with an investigation. I didn't break the law—"

"People have a right to privacy, Agent Iverson," the SAC interjected, obviously determined to keep Mark from completing a sentence. "You can't just go around ordering frivolous background checks. That's the *law.*"

Mark was angered by this ridiculous accusation. "The background checks I ordered weren't frivolous! And two of them were on dead people—"

"I think you're missing the point here," the SAC said, leaning forward in a menacing way. "The FBI has no doubt that Erica Helms was killed by Lyle Tweedy. If you *personally* have questions about that verdict, you're not at liberty to use FBI computers or employees to satisfy your curiosity."

Mark tried to read between the lines. He wasn't exactly being ordered to abandon his investigation—he just couldn't do anything that might make matters worse for the FBI when the press found out about Tweedy's claim of partial innocence. "I understand, sir," Mark answered, hoping he did.

The SAC relaxed against his big, comfortable-looking chair. "I certainly hope you do. You're free to go."

Mark stood, feeling like a child who had just had his hand spanked for something he didn't do.

He started to leave, but as he put his hand on the doorknob, the SAC spoke again. "Agent Iverson, aren't you due for a few days of vacation?"

Mark looked back over his shoulder. Was the SAC encouraging him to complete his investigation of Erica's death, or was he just trying to put some distance between Mark and the FBI in anticipation of negative press coverage? "I guess I could use a few days off, sir," he said slowly.

"I think that might be just what you need," the SAC replied with a grim smile.

Hoping he hadn't misunderstood the man, Mark nodded then opened the door and walked out into the hall. Agent Rice was waiting and walked with Mark all the way to the front entrance.

* * *

By five o'clock the paint fumes were giving Eugenia a headache, so she told Dub to stop for the day. While Dub went to the back to wash out his brushes, Eugenia motioned through the glass door for Sylvester to come inside.

The young man obeyed promptly. "Did you need me?"

Eugenia nodded. "I've got a headache and wondered if you could come in and answer the phone so I can go home."

"Sure," Sylvester agreed, pulling up a chair.

As she instructed him on proper phone procedures, she noticed that he was sunburned and had dirt under his fingernails. She pointed at his hands. "It looks like you worked hard this morning—for a city boy."

"I worked hard for any kind of boy," he corrected. "But actually I kind of enjoyed it. I've never really grown anything or worked in the soil. Brandon knows a lot about plants."

Eugenia noticed that Sylvester was now on a first name basis with his prey and was about to comment on this newfound friendliness when Sylvester added, "It makes me wonder if Brandon poisoned his wife with some weird flower."

Eugenia shook her head. "Oh, Sylvester, you're hopeless."

Dub returned from the back just as Winston walked in the front door. "Glad I caught you," Winston told their voluntary painter. "Darnell at the funeral home says you need to come get your dogs if you want to bury them yourself. Otherwise he'll have to cremate them."

"I'll get them tomorrow," Dub said. "I was thinking about making a little dog cemetery on the corner of my lot over by those sycamore trees."

Eugenia looked over at Lady, curled comfortably in her basket. "Good dogs deserve a decent burial," she said, turning to Winston. "Tomorrow morning when Arnold gets off work, maybe he could take Dub to get the dogs."

Winston nodded. "I'll tell him."

"I sure am going to miss my dogs," Dub continued to no one in particular. "Especially Lou and Sue. They were sisters and so identical that the only way I could tell them apart was by the way they barked." A look of distress crossed Dub's face. "I was going to get Darnell to order me some little grave markers, but since they can't bark for me, how will I know which one is Lou and which one is Sue?"

"I don't see that it makes any difference," Winston said impatiently. "As long as they're both buried."

"Of course it makes a difference," Dub said in an aggrieved tone. "How could Lou rest easy in Sue's grave or vice versa?"

"It's nonsense," Winston said while walking down the hall toward his office.

"Sylvester's going to catch the phone for me so I can go home," Eugenia called after him, and Winston nodded in response. Eugenia leaned down, picked up Lady's basket, and headed for the door. "Try not to worry about your dogs," she told Dub, although she knew the words were a waste of breath. "And Arnold will be by with his truck in the morning to take you to the funeral home."

The warm evening air was refreshing, and by the time Eugenia passed the Iversons' house her headache had disappeared. It had been days since she'd seen the children, and, unable to help herself, she turned up the driveway and walked in through the back door.

"Hellooo!" she called out as she entered the kitchen. "Is anyone home?"

Emily and Charles ran in and gave her enthusiastic hugs. "Where have you been?" Emily asked.

"We missed you," Charles added vehemently. "And Lady too." He reached out to pat the little dog, and Eugenia felt tears prickle her eyes.

"Well, I certainly missed you both."

"Can I hold her?" Emily asked.

Eugenia nodded.

While the dog was being transferred, Eugenia explained her recent neglect. "I've been busy planning a wedding and working at the police station for Chief Jones."

Emily's eyes grew wide. "Do you get to have a badge?"

Eugenia shook her head. "No, but I do get to boss the police officers around."

Emily considered this then said, "That's almost as good."

Kate walked into the kitchen at this point. "Well, hi there," she greeted Eugenia. "We thought you'd forgotten the way to our house."

"She didn't forget," Charles reassured his mother.

"She's been bossing Chief Jones and the other officers," Emily contributed.

Kate raised an eyebrow in Eugenia's direction. "I can't say I'm surprised to hear that." Kate opened the refrigerator and removed a large pot. "Kelsey's feeling a little better today," she reported. "She ate toast for breakfast, and this is her third bowl of potato soup."

Eugenia was pleased. "That soup has never let me down."

Kate heated a small bowl of soup in the microwave then put it on the breakfast tray. "I'll be right back," she promised. She hurried from the room.

"Lady is licking me," Emily said, giggling.

"That means she likes you," Eugenia explained.

"Does she like me too?" Charles wanted to know as he stuck a finger in Lady's mouth.

Eugenia removed his finger. "It's unwise to put your hand in a dog's mouth," she instructed him. "And Lady likes everybody except Annabelle."

The children were laughing when Kate returned. "Would you like some soup?" she offered. Eugenia nodded.

"I think I would. Where's Mark?"

"He had to go to Atlanta today, so I'm not sure what time he'll be home. The kids have already eaten," Kate said as she dished more soup from the pot and put it in the microwave.

"Can we take Lady into the den?" Emily asked.

Eugenia nodded. "If she scratches on the front door, let me know. That means she needs to use the bathroom."

The children left, and Eugenia settled at the table.

"Would you like a sandwich to go with your soup?" Kate asked.

Eugenia waved this offer aside. "Just the soup, thank you."

"Here you go." Kate placed the bowl in front of Eugenia then sat beside her. "You seem to have gotten very attached to Miss Geneva's dog."

"It's funny, but I never think of Lady as Miss Geneva's dog anymore. It's like we've always been together." Eugenia smiled fondly. "She's the perfect companion. She's housebroken, only eats a few tablespoons of dog food each day, doesn't bark much, and she never talks back."

"She *is* the perfect companion," Kate agreed.

Eugenia spread a paper napkin on her lap. "It's good that Kelsey is feeling better."

"Yes," Kate said. "And she's going to the doctor tomorrow morning."

Eugenia took a bite of the soup, analyzed it, and nodded her approval. "That will give you some peace of mind if nothing else."

Kate lowered her voice and confessed. "I called her husband, Travis. He's coming tomorrow afternoon."

Eugenia put down her spoon and gave Kate her full attention. "I take it that Kelsey doesn't know this?"

"Not yet," Kate acknowledged. "I've been trying to tell her, but I can't find the right moment."

Eugenia chuckled. "The *right* moment will likely never come."

"So you think I did the wrong thing?"

Eugenia shook her head. "No, it's not fair of Kelsey to exclude her husband any longer. They need to work things out together—even if they decide to divorce."

Kate sighed. "I'm glad you think so. I've been racked with guilt ever since I made the call. I can't talk to my mother about it, because I promised Kelsey I wouldn't, and, well, now I feel much better."

Eugenia picked up her spoon and resumed eating. "I think what you did was necessary, but that doesn't mean that Kelsey will appreciate your interference. In fact, she'll probably be very angry with you."

Kate's expression fell. "That's what I'm afraid of."

When Eugenia finished her soup, she collected Lady, said good-bye to the children, and walked over to her own house. Brandon and

Sylvester were in the backyard, unloading empty vegetable crates from the back of Sylvester's little sports car.

"So how was business today?" she asked.

"Brisk," Brandon told her with one of his sad smiles. "I gave half of the proceeds up to this point to Chief Jones for the policemen's retirement fund."

Eugenia nodded. "Good."

"And Winston put the money directly into his pocket," Sylvester reported.

"I'm sure he intends to deposit the money," Eugenia said, looking past Sylvester to the backyard. There was something different. She moved closer and saw that she now had two rows of pansies about four feet apart running right through the middle of her yard. "You planted flowers?" she asked, wanting to add *without my permission*.

"Just a few," Brandon admitted.

"The guy at the nursery gave us a good deal, and we split the cost," Sylvester explained.

Eugenia was touched that Brandon would sacrifice some of his meager income, but she still hated the placement of the little flowers. "As much as I appreciate the gesture," she said carefully, "I'm afraid they'll have to be moved. Otherwise people walking across the yard will trample them."

Brandon led her by the elbow to the end of the rows then pointed forward. "It's an aisle," he said. "For the wedding."

Eugenia studied the arrangement from this angle, and, sure enough, the flowers formed a charming little walkway for the bride. At the end of their makeshift aisle was a rose-covered arbor made out of lattice.

"We thought it would be nice for the bride and groom to have something to stand under during the ceremony," Brandon told her shyly.

"Brandon built the whole thing," Sylvester volunteered. "I just handed him nails and helped paint it."

Eugenia walked down the aisle and stood under the lovely archway. "I don't know what to say," she told them. She couldn't remember the last time she had been this surprised and pleased.

"Say you like it," Sylvester suggested.

"Of course I like it," she returned. "I just can't believe that you spent so much time and money on it."

"You've invested a great deal of effort in the wedding," Brandon pointed out. "We wanted to contribute as well."

"And you've done a lot for both of us personally," Sylvester added. "This is an attempt to pay you back."

"Well, you certainly have," Eugenia said. "In fact, after this I'm probably in *your* debt."

Brandon said, "Oh, no! That would be impossible!"

Sylvester just shook his head. "You're too far ahead of us."

Eugenia smiled. "I'm going in to feed Lady. You boys get some rest tonight. You've had a hard day."

As she walked up to her back door, Eugenia swiped at the moisture that had collected in her eyes.

Lady barked as she approached.

"These aren't tears," she assured the dog. "I never cry."

Lady whimpered, and Eugenia patted her scruffy, little head. "I guess I can't fool you, but don't worry—they are happy tears."

Lady stood and turned excited circles in her basket. Eugenia laughed. "I don't know what I'd do without you," she told the dog. "If I ever make it to heaven, I'm going to have to give Miss Geneva Mackey one big hug."

CHAPTER 10

It was six thirty by the time Mark got back to Albany. He expected Marla to be gone, but she was still sitting at her desk. Her son, Sklyer, was sitting beside his mother, playing a hand-held video game. After exchanging a little polite small talk with them, Mark headed toward his office.

Marla followed him and said softly, "I hope you don't mind that I brought Skyler here after I picked him up from school. One of the things the school counselor told me was that he spends too much time at home alone."

"I don't mind at all," Mark told her.

"How did it go in Atlanta?" she asked.

He put his briefcase on the desk. "Not good, but I'm not fired."

He could see her relief as she pointed to a stack of papers on his desk. "That's the information you requested about sociopaths. They're now sometimes referred to as having antisocial personality disorder." She blushed. "But then you probably already knew that."

"No, I didn't. I took a seminar about serial killers a few years ago where sociopaths were discussed, but it wasn't a topic that interested me, so I didn't pay close attention." He picked up the first sheet and reviewed it quickly. "This is about what I expected," he told her, reading from the list. "They are charming and charismatic, glib and persuasive, manipulative and self-serving. They lie easily and well, show a complete lack of remorse for the crimes they commit, and are incapable of love or empathy for others."

"It was a little scary reading about all those criminals," Marla admitted. "Especially since I was alone in the office."

"Having met Lyle Tweedy, I can relate. Whoever coined the phrase 'cold-blooded killer' was probably talking about a sociopath."

"One of the websites I researched warned against stereotyping with sociopaths," Marla told him. "It said that some have additional dangerous characteristics, and some don't exhibit all the common ones. And the worst thing is that they look and seem normal."

Mark nodded, remembering Lyle Tweedy's everyday appearance. "That's true."

"So this is about Lyle Tweedy?"

"Yes, he fits this profile perfectly." Mark opened his briefcase and stuck the printout inside. "Thanks for getting this for me. Now I think it's time for you and Skyler to go home."

Marla nodded. "I'll see you in the morning."

"Actually, you won't," Mark told her. "I'm going to be taking a couple of days off."

She looked alarmed. "Voluntarily?"

He decided not to worry her. "Yes. Kate and I are hosting a wedding reception on Saturday, and she could use some help getting the house ready. I'll be back in the office on Monday."

Marla still seemed concerned, but she smiled. "Okay, well, I'll see you then."

Mark drove straight to the church, where he supervised a youth activity, conducted temple recommend interviews, and edited membership records with the ward clerk. When everyone else was gone, he finally locked up the building and headed toward Haggerty.

He arrived just in time for family prayer, and then Kate said she'd put the kids to bed. "I was going to heat you up some soup for dinner," she told him. "You can do it yourself, or I'll bring it to you when the kids are asleep."

"I've still got work to do, so I think I'll go straight to my office," he replied. "When you get through with the kids, I'd appreciate it if you'd bring me some soup."

He went to his office and spread out all his printouts and background checks so he could study everything at once. When Kate arrived with the soup, she asked, "How was your trip to Atlanta?"

"Bad," he admitted. Then he gave her a summary of his interview with the SAC.

Kate's eyes narrowed. She'd had some experience with the bureau's hierarchy. "I can't believe that Dan Davis is such a coward. But they won't fire you. Mr. Evans won't let them," she said, referring to the SAC from Chicago who had been Mark's boss at one time and who owed them several favors.

"Although I'm disappointed in Dan, I'm not really afraid of losing my job," Mark said. "What terrifies me is the possibility that I won't solve this case and that Lyle Tweedy will haunt me for the rest of my life."

"You're going to keep trying to solve this case? Even after what they said to you in Atlanta?"

Mark nodded. "Throughout our little interview the SAC was sending me mixed signals."

"Mixed in what way?"

"I think he wants me to continue the investigation on my own time, so that if the FBI gets caught in the crossfire, he can sacrifice me."

"That's horrible!" Kate cried.

"Or maybe he just wants to see justice served, but his hands are tied by political considerations."

"I like that better." Kate put her arms around his neck and kissed his cheek. "And if you really intend to solve this case, I think it's time for drastic action."

"Like what?"

She pulled up a chair and sat beside him. "I'm going to help you learn to be a woman."

He raised an eyebrow. "Actually, I'm pretty comfortable with being a man."

"Well then, I'll just teach you to multitask." She looked at all the information spread out on his desk. "First you have to decide which task is the most important and make a list in order of priority."

Mark looked into her intelligent eyes and felt better than he had all day. "What if they're all equally urgent?"

"You just have to pick one. Then you do what you can on it, and when you reach a stopping point, you move on to the next one."

"Stopping point?"

"For instance, if your most important task is to make a cake, you start on it. Then if you need to add eggs but don't have any—that's your stopping point. You delay your cake making and go to the grocery store—which is the next thing on your list."

"It sounds like your list was the problem," Mark teased. "You should have put going to the grocery store first, so you wouldn't have to stop in the middle of making a cake."

"It's just an analogy," Kate said. "Try and work with me here."

"Maybe you could use a different analogy."

Kate shook her head in a "men-are-so-dense" gesture. "This is going to be harder than I thought. Let's say you need information on a case but can't get it yourself. You request it from someone else, and then while you're waiting for them to call you back—you move on to the *next* most important case."

He nodded. "Now I get it."

"Are you making fun of me?" she demanded.

"Yes," he admitted.

"I thought so."

"Instead of teaching me to be a multitasking quasi-woman, maybe you could just kiss me," he suggested, holding his arms out invitingly. "It would probably be as helpful and much more fun."

"Later," she promised. "Now what's your most important task?"

Mark sighed. "I'm not sure. I need to find out who killed Erica Helms, since Lyle Tweedy says he didn't. I need to find out why Molly Vance is missing and learn more about sociopaths—but which task is truly the most important?"

He expected Kate to smile, but instead she frowned. "That's strange."

"It's all definitely strange," he agreed.

"No, I mean Miss Eugenia's yardman is named Brandon Vance, and Kelsey is trying to help him find his missing wife. Could it be the same woman?"

Mark, who did not believe in coincidence, stood up. "Let's go find out."

They knocked on Kelsey's door, and when she called for them to enter, they walked in to find her working at the computer. Mark held out the background check on Molly Vance. Kelsey scanned it then gave it back.

"Have you been hired to find this woman?" Mark asked.

"I can't tell you. It would violate client privilege."

"So Brandon Vance is your client?" Mark pressed.

"I didn't say that."

Mark was irritated. He'd had more luck with a psychiatrist he'd never met than with his own sister-in-law. "Fine, I'll approach this from another direction." He headed toward the door, and, after a quick glance at Kelsey, Kate followed him downstairs. Once they were back in his office, he dialed Miss Eugenia's number.

"Hello?" their neighbor answered.

"Miss Eugenia, this is Mark, and I need to ask you a few questions. It might be important."

"Go ahead."

"It's about Brandon Vance." He thought he heard her sigh but couldn't be sure.

"I'm listening."

"I've been working on a murder case. Erica Helms, from Patton Chapel, was strangled and thrown in a pond to rot."

"I'm sorry," Miss Eugenia replied. "Although I don't see what that has to do with Brandon."

"Patton Chapel is just a few miles from Wilsonville, where Brandon and his wife lived. Molly Vance and Erica Helms were in the same grief management group, and I find it a little strange that one of them is dead and the other is missing."

"Do you think Brandon killed them both?"

This remark surprised Mark. "Do you?"

"Maybe," she admitted.

"I think you'd better explain."

"I'll tell you everything I know." Miss Eugenia then proceeded to fill him in on Brandon's previous career as a college professor, his current destitute status as a result of his futile search for his wife, and the circumstances that led her to hire him as her yardman. "He's convinced that his wife is still alive and may have run off with a boyfriend, but Kelsey thinks she may be dead."

Mark frowned. "And what makes you suspect Brandon Vance?"

"Sylvester."

"Sylvester?" Mark repeated. "The man from the state attorney general's office?"

This time he definitely heard Miss Eugenia sigh. "Yes."

"You said he was here as a police intern."

"Well, his internship started *after* he came to interrogate Brandon. Sylvester was assigned the case, but his office never intended for him to actually investigate it."

"Why?"

"Because Winston says there really is no case—or no evidence anyway."

"But Sylvester believes Brandon Vance killed his own wife?"

"Yes," Miss Eugenia said. "He's been following Brandon's movements and took vacation time to come here and interview him."

"He still has no hard evidence against Vance?"

"Not that I know of, and I've never heard him mention Erica Helms."

"I need to see if we can connect the two cases," Mark thought out loud. "Now is there anything else that you have been keeping from me?"

There was a brief pause. Then Miss Eugenia said, "Nothing that I can think of at the moment."

Mark gritted his teeth. "Please call this guy Sylvester and ask him to come over to my house as soon as possible."

"I'll be glad to," Miss Eugenia agreed helpfully. "And I probably should call Winston too. He did some checking on Brandon when he first came to town and he can tell you about that."

Mark hesitated. He hadn't spoken to Winston in over a month and wasn't anxious to do so. But he had a possible double murder on his hands. After his interview with the SAC that afternoon, he didn't dare use his FBI agent status to induce cooperation from anyone. When he was ready to interrogate the yardman, he would need someone who could exert official pressure. Winston was perfect for that.

Finally he said, "Okay, call Winston."

"So the two cases are related?" Kate asked when he hung up the phone.

"They must be. Winston and Sylvester, somebody from the state attorney general's office, are on their way over. Once they get here, we'll try to figure out how," he told her. "And if I know Miss Eugenia, it won't be long before she arrives."

"Hellooo!" a voice called from the hallway near the kitchen.

"You know her, all right," Kate said with a smile as Miss Eugenia appeared in the doorway.

"I declare, the last thing we need right here before the wedding is a murder investigation."

Mark gave her a bland look. "I'm sure the victims would apologize for the inconvenience if they weren't dead."

"Don't be a smart aleck, Mark," Eugenia admonished. "It's most unbecoming."

Kate was desperately trying to hide a smile as she asked Mark, "Do you want to hold your meeting in here?"

Mark looked around. The room wasn't large, but he wanted to have his computer and all the printouts readily available. "Yes, I think this will be best."

Kate stood. "I'll bring in some more chairs."

"This could turn out to be a long night," Eugenia predicted grimly. "I'll go home and get my coffeemaker. I just hope it still works."

Mark helped Kate bring kitchen chairs into his office. They had just finished when Miss Eugenia returned with Whit Owens, who was carrying her coffeemaker. She poked her head in Mark's office and asked, "Do you mind if Whit stays? He stopped by to tell me about the tuxedo he rented Jackson Clooney for the wedding, and I brought him over in case I can't remember how to make decent coffee."

"You're welcome to stay," Mark said to Whit. "In fact we may need legal advice, as long as you don't repeat anything we discuss."

Miss Eugenia waved this aside with her free hand. "Whit was keeping secrets before you were born."

Whit smiled at Miss Eugenia. "Shall we get started on that coffee?"

They headed toward the kitchen as a knock sounded on the front door.

"I'll get it," Kate volunteered. She left the room and returned a few minutes later with Winston at her side. Mark didn't know what to say to him, so finally Kate addressed Winston. "We really appreciate you coming over so late." She glanced at Mark, but he couldn't make himself second her remark.

"Miss Eugenia said it was important," Winston told Kate.

"I've got potato soup if you're hungry," Kate offered. "And Miss Eugenia and Whit Owens are making coffee."

"I'm not hungry, but I would like a cup of that coffee when it's ready," Winston replied as Kelsey appeared in the doorway.

"I thought you couldn't discuss Brandon Vance," Mark reminded her.

"But I can listen to what you have to say about him," Kelsey returned.

"Only if I say so," Mark pointed out.

Kate looked like she was about to intervene when they heard an engine roar and tires squeal outside.

"What in the world was that?" Winston demanded.

"I think that was Sylvester arriving in his fancy little sports car," Miss Eugenia said as she walked in carrying a tray filled with coffee mugs. "He thinks driving like that makes him look dashing." She shook her head. "Poor boy is always making a spectacle of himself."

Kate went to the front door and a minute later ushered Sylvester Muck into Mark's office. After the introductions were completed, Mark made a point of expressing disapproval that he had been misled on Sunday. "You should have told me the truth about Mr. Muck's reasons for being in Haggerty," he told Miss Eugenia. "If you had, we might have solved both our cases by now."

"I've already apologized for that," Miss Eugenia said briskly. "And if you're so anxious to solve your cases, it seems like you'd be discussing them instead of browbeating helpless old women."

"You're anything but helpless," Mark returned.

Miss Eugenia ignored this remark. "Who wants coffee?" Winston, Whit, and Sylvester all raised their hands, and Miss Eugenia offered them a mug from her tray while Mark addressed the group. He described his meeting with Lyle Tweedy and his subsequent investigation of Erica Helms's murder.

Finally Winston said, "I thought you wanted to talk to me about that Vance guy Miss Eugenia hired to sell her vegetables."

Mark nodded. "I do. I just found out tonight that Vance's missing wife attended the same grief management group as my murder victim. The best estimate of Erica Helms's date of death is September 25. Molly Vance disappeared just a few days later."

"You think they were killed by the same person?" Winston asked.

"I think there's a good chance of that," Mark acknowledged.

"I'll bet Brandon Vance killed them both," Sylvester contributed with enthusiasm.

Miss Eugenia shook her head. "It's hard enough to believe that Brandon killed his wife—but it's ridiculous to think he killed another woman too."

Sylvester stood and paced around the room. "Maybe while he was killing his wife, her friend from the grief management group came by and caught him," he hypothesized.

"Erica Helms didn't have friends," Mark said. "Neither did Molly Vance from what I've been able to determine. It's unlikely that they became grief management buddies."

Sylvester wasn't discouraged. "So let's look at the situation from another angle. They were both lonely recluses—easy marks for a psychopath. Maybe the killer was another member of the group."

Mark nodded. "I considered that. I've talked to the leader of the grief management group and the surviving members. All are women and clear as far as I can tell."

"You're going on the assumption that the killer is a man?" Whit asked.

"Yes," Mark confirmed. "Strangling and transporting a body requires a lot of strength. It's unlikely that a woman could do it."

"If the grief management group is the only connection between the two women, but the killer wasn't a part of it, how did he meet and kill them both?" Winston wanted to know.

Mark shrugged. "I don't know."

"Did you have any murder suspects before you found out about the connection between the two women?" Sylvester asked. "That would be a place to start."

"I did have a couple of suspects," Mark acknowledged. "One is the acting sheriff in Patton Chapel. He found Erica's body and handled the investigation."

Winston smirked. "Pretty convenient if you're trying to cover up a murder."

"And make it look like the victim's death was just one in a string of murders by a serial killer," Mark added.

"Sounds promising," Sylvester agreed. "Who else?"

"The dentist Erica worked for," Mark informed them. "The man has a list of extramarital affairs as long as my arm, and Erica was on it. He was pretty cagey when I interviewed him, and it made me wonder if he had something to hide."

"Someone might have been blackmailing him," Sylvester suggested.

Whit nodded. "I like that theory. People think that murder is about passion—but usually it's about plain old greed."

"You'd better consider the dentist's wife too," Kate said. "If her husband was having all kinds of affairs, maybe she finally got sick of it." She glanced over at Mark. "Remember that in case you're ever tempted."

While Mark was trying to think of a response, Winston said, "Seems like she would have killed the *husband* instead of one of his girlfriends."

"If she kills her husband, she cuts off her source of income," Whit pointed out. "If she kills one of the girlfriends, it sends a warning signal to any other women who might be tempted to fool around with her husband."

"Listen to him," Eugenia encouraged. "That is the voice of experience talking. Whit's had hundreds of girlfriends."

Whit looked embarrassed. "Not hundreds."

Anxious to regain control of the conversation, Mark said, "The dentist's wife would be a long shot, but I do think following the money is a good idea." He turned to Kelsey. "I'd like to hire you to look into the finances of the dentist, Chuck Welch. And while you're at it, make a list of large cash transactions during the past year or so in the Southeast."

"Why?" Winston asked.

"Erica cleaned out her checking and savings accounts before she died, and the money wasn't found with her body," Mark replied.

"So you think whoever killed her took the money?" Sylvester asked.

Mark nodded. "That's what I think."

"That rules out Brandon then," Miss Eugenia spoke up. "He's penniless."

"So he says," Mark replied. "He could be acting poor and have millions stashed in a bank somewhere."

"Why don't you just ask him if he knew Erica Helms?" Kelsey proposed. "That would be more productive than this clandestine discussion."

"If he is the murderer, I don't want to tip him off and give him time to disappear," Mark explained.

"What kind of transaction am I looking for?" Kelsey asked. "A house? Jewelry? Stocks and bonds?"

"Any purchase for around a million dollars," he said, looking around the room. "What would you do if you had that much money?"

"If I'd taken it from someone I murdered, I wouldn't do anything right away," Sylvester told them. "I'd wait a few months to make sure my purchase wasn't associated with the death of the person I killed."

Mark liked this theory. "Good." He turned to Kelsey. "Since Erica's body was discovered in the fall, the murderer might have sat on the money until the first of the year."

"I'll start my search in January," Kelsey replied. "If we don't find anything, I can always go back farther."

"What he did with the money would depend partly on *why* he killed Erica," Mark mused.

"And possibly Molly Vance," Sylvester added.

"He didn't get any money from Molly Vance," Mark said.

Sylvester nodded in agreement. "Which supports my theory that Molly stumbled onto the murderer in the act and was killed to eliminate a witness."

"Unless Mrs. Vance was an accomplice," Winston said.

"I have trouble with that," Mark said. "It's so out of character."

Winston shrugged. "People change."

"And greed does strange things to even the nicest folks," Whit said. "The stories I could tell . . ."

Kelsey was making notes again. "I'll concentrate on *businesses* purchased that have a steady cash flow."

"The murderer may have buried the money in his backyard and then digs up a little at a time to buy his groceries," Winston said.

"He might," Whit acknowledged. "But in my experience, few criminals have that kind of restraint."

"He spent the money." Mark felt certain. "And that's how we'll catch him." Mark looked at Kelsey. "You realize that if Brandon Vance is the murderer, by helping us you could help convict him?"

"I am positive that Brandon did not kill his wife," Kelsey responded. "That's why I'm helping you—to prove it." She stood and moved toward the door. "And you don't have to pay me for my work. It's on the house."

Once she was gone, Mark frowned. "Do you remember those little games we used to get in Cracker Jacks where the balls roll around and you're supposed to get them into the correct holes?"

Kate nodded. "I remember. The first ball was easy, but when you tried to get the others into their holes, the first one would pop out."

"That's how I feel," Mark told her. "Like I have the facts I need, but I can't get them to stay in the right places."

"We're all tired," Kate reminded him. "You might be able to think more clearly after you've had some rest."

"Maybe," Mark murmured.

Sylvester leaned forward. "I'm very familiar with Molly Vance's case. If I look through everything you have on Erica Helms and Lyle Tweedy, I might notice another connection."

Mark nodded. "I'd appreciate that." He started stacking up the printouts. "You're welcome to take all this with you just as long as you promise to bring it back tomorrow."

"I will," Sylvester promised. "Good night everybody."

Kate walked Sylvester to the door, and when she returned to Mark's office, Winston said, "I think we ought to haul Brandon Vance into the police station and grill him."

Mark shook his head. "I don't want to do anything that might jeopardize a future case against him."

Winston rubbed what was left of his hair. "This could all be a big waste of time."

"How so?" Whit asked.

"There's a good chance Lyle Tweedy killed *both* women. And he's already dead," Winston said.

"We don't even know for sure that Molly Vance *is* dead," Mark pointed out with a sigh.

"That's true," Winston conceded.

"It's *possible* that Molly Vance killed Erica then made it look like one of Tweedy's murders," Whit proposed. "With all that money, it wouldn't be hard for her to disappear."

Mark considered this. "Then she took Erica's car to the airport and flew somewhere under an assumed name?"

Winston nodded with enthusiasm. "That works for me."

"That is a ridiculous idea," Miss Eugenia said with disdain. "Brandon's poor, sad wife didn't kill anyone. The only reason that theory 'works for you' is because you think it will get you out of here so you can spend time with your skinny girlfriend."

"A gentleman doesn't keep a lady waiting," Winston teased.

"A lady," Eugenia replied. "The very idea."

Mark sighed. "It's a little far-fetched."

"I feel so sorry for Brandon," Kate put in. "Assuming he's not guilty," she added hastily.

"Yes," Miss Eugenia agreed. "He's already lost his son, and now it looks like his wife is either dead or a murderer."

Mark stood. "Well, let's sleep on what we've discussed, and maybe we'll have fresh ideas tomorrow."

"Or maybe we'll come up with a bunch of new, confusing possibilities," Kate said as she led their guests to the front door.

"That's what I like." Whit gave her a wink. "An optimist."

* * *

On Thursday morning Emily and Charles woke Kate at six thirty. Groggy from lack of sleep, Kate forced herself to get up and fix them breakfast.

"How come you're letting us eat Daddy's cereal?" Emily asked.

"How come?" Charles mimicked his sister.

"Because it's easy, and I'm tired. I stayed up late last night helping Daddy figure out one of his cases."

"Did you figure it out?" Emily asked.

"Not yet," Kate told her.

"Keep trying," Emily encouraged as Mark came into the kitchen.

"You're sharing your cereal," Emily told him with her mouth full.

"Mama said," Charles added.

Mark smiled. "Did you save any for me?"

Emily shook the box of Rice Chex. "Yep."

Kate took the cereal box from her daughter and poured some into a bowl for Mark. "You kids go up and make your beds," she instructed them. "Then change into play clothes and brush your teeth." Once they were gone, Kate asked Mark, "Are things any clearer this morning?"

He shook his head. "No. I still can't see the forest for the trees." He took a bite of cereal. "I guess I'm just not meant to be a multitasker. I'll try dividing the cases into little parts that a mere man can manage."

Kate sighed. "That is probably your best option."

"Kelsey's still in bed?"

Kate nodded. "I peeked into her room, and she was sound asleep. I don't know how late she stayed up after we went to bed, but I thought I'd let her rest until it's time for her to get ready for her doctor's appointment." Kate checked her watch. "And speaking of time—why aren't you dressed for work?"

"I forgot to tell you that one of the weird signals the SAC sent to me was that he thought I should take a couple of days off. So I'm on vacation until Monday."

Kate was astounded. "You're kidding."

"No, I'm serious. It's probably for the best. I won't be able to concentrate on anything else until I settle Erica Helms's case. Why? Don't you want me hanging around the house?"

Kate leaned over and kissed him absently. "You know we love to have you hanging around. I was just surprised. More cereal?" she asked, holding up the box.

"No thanks."

"I'll have some," Kelsey said from the doorway.

"Well, good morning," Kate greeted her. "You look pretty good for a girl who stayed up most of the night."

"I feel pretty good." Kelsey took a seat across the table from Mark. "I checked out Dr. Welch pretty thoroughly and didn't find anything to indicate that he was being blackmailed."

Mark frowned. "No large cash withdrawals?"

Kelsey poured herself a bowl of cereal. "Nope, it looked clean as a whistle."

"How about business purchases in the past few months?"

"I'm still working on that," Kelsey replied.

Mark stood. "Well, let me know if you find something. Now, if you ladies will excuse me, I'll get busy." He kissed Kate's cheek and told her, "I'll be in my office if you need me."

After Mark left, Kate watched Kelsey eat cereal. "You are feeling better," she said when Kelsey finished her second bowl.

"All of a sudden I'm starving."

"Maybe the morning sickness stage is over. Would you like something more substantial, like eggs?" Kate offered.

Kelsey shook her head. "The cereal was fine." Kelsey cleared her throat and asked, "Will you cancel that doctor's appointment? I have so much work to do, and since I'm not sick anymore . . ."

Kate nodded reluctantly. "I'll agree on the condition that you promise to let me know if you get nauseated again."

Kelsey held up her right hand. "I swear!"

Kate rolled her eyes. "Sarcasm is a sure sign you're getting back to normal."

"Hellooo!" Miss Eugenia called from the back door. "Well, look who's up and eating breakfast." She put Lady's basket on the floor, and the little dog jumped out to begin exploring.

"Kelsey feels better," Kate announced proudly.

"I can see that," Miss Eugenia said.

"I've eaten *two* bowls of cereal," Kelsey boasted.

"I offered to make her some eggs, but Kelsey thinks that it might be too soon for that," Kate added.

"I'll take some eggs," Miss Eugenia said. "And bacon if you have it."

Kate searched for an adequate response and couldn't find one, so she stood up and pulled out a frying pan.

Kelsey rinsed her bowl in the sink. "I put out a lot of feelers last night and need to see if I got any bites."

Miss Eugenia looked at her with concern in her eyes. "You're sure Brandon is innocent?"

"I'm sure," Kelsey said firmly.

"Good, then you go on upstairs and get to work."

Kate put the bacon into the microwave to cook and cracked two eggs in the frying pan. While she cooked, she asked Miss Eugenia, "What are your plans for the day?"

"I'm waiting for the funeral home to deliver their chairs, and then I'll head to the police station. Dub Shaw has been painting the lobby, and I need to be there to make sure he doesn't fall off a ladder or succumb to noxious fumes."

"I didn't know Dub Shaw was a painter."

"He's not. Come by the police station if you don't believe me. I just suggested it as a way to keep him from drinking himself to death over his poisoned dogs. He's going to bury them today, and I'm hoping that after that he'll be able to move on. How about you? What do you have planned?"

"Just cleaning house to get ready for the reception."

"Don't go to too much trouble. I'm having a lot of people meet here tomorrow morning to move furniture and arrange things. And to polish George Ann's punch bowl, of course."

"Of course," Kate acknowledged. "Because she insists that we use it but won't polish it herself. I'll be glad when this is over," Kate admitted as she flipped the eggs over. Minutes later she placed Miss Eugenia's breakfast before her.

"Can I have some toast?" the uninvited guest asked. "And some of that mayhaw jelly I brought you last week."

"How about some fresh-squeezed orange juice?" Kate inquired facetiously.

The sarcasm was lost on Miss Eugenia. "The kind in the carton will be fine."

Miss Eugenia was just finishing her third piece of toast when the funeral home van pulled up. "I'd better go supervise, or they'll set the chairs up crooked." She held her toast remnant in one hand and lifted Lady with the other. "Kate, can you get the door for me?"

Kate opened the back door. "At your service," she said, following Miss Eugenia onto the porch.

Miss Eugenia either didn't hear this remark or chose to ignore it. "Since I see that Mark hasn't gone to work yet, maybe you could ask him to come help us with the chairs."

"He's working from home today, but I'll see if he can spare a few minutes."

Kate went inside and found Mark in his office poring over the files on Erica and Molly again. "Find anything?" she asked.

"No—I'm completely frustrated."

"Well, Miss Eugenia needs you to help unload funeral chairs. Maybe if you come outside, you'll clear your mind and gain fresh perspective."

He stood with a sigh. "I guess it's worth a try."

"And even if you don't get new insight, a few minutes with Miss Eugenia will make you long to be locked up in the office looking for a needle in a haystack."

He took Kate's extended hand and followed her into the hallway. She called the children, and they all went outside where Miss Eugenia was overseeing the chair arrangement process. Soon neat white rows lined Miss Eugenia's backyard.

"I love it!" Kate praised when they were finished. "It's completely charming."

Miss Eugenia examined the temporary wedding chapel with a critical eye then nodded. "It will do."

"Here comes Aunt Kelsey," Emily announced, pointing back toward their house.

"Did I mention that she's feeling better?" Kate asked Miss Eugenia.

"Several times," the older woman responded.

Kate turned and watched her sister approach. Kelsey was very pale and clutching her midsection. Alarmed, Kate started forward. "She must have had a relapse!" Kate reached Kelsey just as she collapsed.

"I'm bleeding," Kelsey gasped. Then she passed out.

"Mark!" Kate screamed. "Help me!"

Mark was at her side in seconds. He lifted Kelsey, and they headed toward their van.

"Can you watch the children?" Kate called to Miss Eugenia.

"Of course," their neighbor agreed. "I'll take them with me to the police station."

Kate nodded as she slipped into the van. Her sister groaned, and Kate reached back to stroke her cheek. "It's going to be all right, Kelsey," she promised, then she prayed that it would be.

* * *

Eugenia handed Lady to Emily and the basket to Charles, trying to keep the children from being overly traumatized by Kelsey's emergency trip to the hospital.

Emily rubbed the little dog's head and asked, "Is Aunt Kelsey really bad sick?"

"She's just going to the doctor," Eugenia replied.

"I bet they give her a shot," Charles predicted gloomily.

"Will the shot make her better?" Emily wanted to know.

"If they give her one, I'm sure it will," Eugenia said as she led them toward their house. "Let's go change your clothes before we go to the police station."

Emily fell into step behind Eugenia. "Do we get to boss around Chief Jones like you?"

"No, but I might be able to get you each a badge," Eugenia half promised.

"Wow," Charles said as he trotted to keep up.

Eugenia herded the children inside and soon had them dressed in their Sunday best.

"Why do we have to wear church clothes to the police station?" Emily wanted to know.

"Yeah, why?" Charles echoed.

"Because you never know who might stop by, and I want you to be presentable," Eugenia replied. "Let's go."

At the police station, Eugenia made good on her promise to deputize the children. Once badges were pinned to their chests, she told them, "Now this means that you are honorary police officers for the day, so you have to be very good."

"Can we help paint?" Emily asked, pointing to Dub Shaw, who was balanced precariously on a ladder.

Eugenia shook her head. "No, you might ruin your Sunday clothes. Just sit here and color me a nice picture."

"Sometimes Charles eats the crayons," Emily warned.

Eugenia leveled a stern look at the little boy. "Policemen don't eat crayons."

Charles nodded.

Winston walked in, looked around, and sighed. "First you brought a dog, and then you adopted that little weasel from the state attorney general's office. Next it was Dub—and now," he waved at the Iverson children, "we're a daycare center."

"Don't exaggerate," Eugenia scolded him then lowered her voice. "Mark and Kate had to take Kelsey to the h-o-s-p-i-t-a-l," she said, spelling out their destination to keep from upsetting the children.

It took Winston a few seconds to compile the letters into a word. "Oh!" He was instantly contrite. "Is everything o-k?"

Eugenia shook her head at his hopelessness. "We haven't heard yet, but we're certainly hoping she is *okay*."

Winston pressed his hat back on his head. "They take her to Memorial?"

Eugenia nodded.

"I think I'll run over there and check on them."

"I declare, that's the most sensible thing you've said in ages," Eugenia told him.

Winston made a growling noise under his breath and started toward the door. There he met Sylvester and Brandon, who were coming in.

"Have you heard anything about Kelsey?" Brandon asked in obvious agitation.

"Not yet," Eugenia replied.

"I'm going to see about her right now," Winston added.

"Can I ride along?" Sylvester asked. "I have something I want to tell Mark."

"I'd like to accompany you as well," Brandon requested. Then he added hesitantly, "That is if my presence won't be an imposition."

"Fine by me," Winston said. "Let's go."

CHAPTER 11

Mark sat in a chair in the emergency room waiting area and fought sleep while Kate questioned nurses and made cell phone calls. He was worried about Kelsey—but weeks of stretching himself too thin had taken their toll, and eventually he dozed off. He startled awake when the doors burst open to admit Winston, followed closely by Sylvester Muck and Brandon Vance. Mark suppressed a groan.

"How's Kelsey?" Winston asked.

Kate rushed over and gave the big man a hug. "Thank you all so much for coming," she said. There were tears of appreciation in her eyes, and Mark felt guilty for wishing they had been left in peace. "We don't know anything yet," Kate told the recent arrivals. "Everyone have a seat."

Winston and Brandon sat down in front of the television beside Kate, but Sylvester separated himself from the little group and walked over to Mark. "Can we talk in the hall for a minute?"

"Of course." Mark stood and stretched then said to Kate, "I'll be right outside the door if you need me."

She nodded as he and Sylvester left the waiting room. "Did you find anything in those files you reviewed last night?" Mark asked once they were out of hearing range.

"I'm not sure," Sylvester responded tentatively. "I read through everything several times and made a couple of lists."

"What kind of lists?"

Sylvester started pacing in small semicircles in front of Mark. "I started with things the women had in common besides the grief management group."

"What were they?"

"They used the same dentist, dry cleaner, car mechanic, and insurance agent."

"We've investigated the dentist already, but you checked out the others?"

Sylvester nodded. "They all look clean."

"Not many options for people in small towns," Mark said thoughtfully. "I guess there's bound to be overlap."

"Right," Sylvester confirmed. "So when the list of commonalities didn't lead me anywhere, I made a list of anomalies."

"Things that didn't fit the normal patterns the women had established?" Mark clarified.

"Right. In the case of Molly Vance, there weren't any. She didn't do a single unusual thing before her disappearance."

"But Erica Helms was a different story," Mark said, following Sylvester's line of reasoning.

Sylvester nodded.

"During the week or so before her death, Erica Helms behaved like a totally different person."

Mark was thinking hard. "Go on."

"For over a year she rarely left her house except to visit the psychiatrist and attend the grief management sessions."

"Which she went to only because the psychiatrist made her," Mark interjected.

"Yes, but during the last few days of her life, she went to several places around town. And what makes these public appearances even more odd is that she *initiated* conversations while she was out. She told people she had a boyfriend, although her mother-in-law claimed she couldn't abide human contact, let alone intimacy."

Mark nodded. "True."

"She cleaned out her checking and savings accounts but made no effort to sell her house—worth over $300,000. Why?" Sylvester asked.

Mark shrugged. "Maybe the boyfriend was in a hurry to skip town."

"With that much money on the line? He could have waited another week or so while they sold it at a bargain price."

"You're right," Mark acknowledged. "If the 'boyfriend' was after her money, it doesn't make sense that he wouldn't at least try to sell her house."

"It all has the feel of a setup to me. Way too pat," Sylvester said.

Mark nodded. "I thought the same thing at the very beginning. The question is who set things up?"

"Maybe Molly Vance. She's missing, along with a lot of cash."

Mark considered this. "We threw that idea around briefly last night. Erica was a large woman. It would have been hard for Molly Vance to overpower her, strangle her, and get her into that pond."

"Not if she planned it out," Sylvester said, arguing his case. "She could have sedated Erica, killed her, and used a wheelbarrow to get her to the pond."

"I guess it's possible," Mark agreed. "But why?"

Sylvester sighed. "That's where the theory runs into trouble. I can't see any reason that Molly Vance would kill Erica Helms."

"Money didn't mean anything to Molly," Mark said.

"No, all she wanted was to be left alone with her grief," Sylvester added. "So she had no motive."

Mark frowned. "Unless for some reason—whether rational or not—Molly blamed Erica for her son's death."

"That's a real stretch," Sylvester said.

Mark nodded. "Yes, it is."

Sylvester ran his fingers through his hair, looking tired and discouraged. "But assuming that Tweedy didn't kill Erica Helms . . ."

"Which is a big assumption," Mark pointed out.

"I know—but for the sake of argument."

Mark waved his hand for Sylvester to continue.

"The fact that Molly Vance disappeared at almost the same time Erica died is extremely coincidental. The two events almost have to be related."

"I agree." Mark rubbed his temples. "At least I think I do."

"If this crazy theory is right and if Erica knew that Molly meant her harm, that would explain the Identi-Kit the police found in Erica's house."

Mark frowned, trying to remember something. "Kate said she had gotten one of those for our kids but never thought of doing it for us.

Apparently it's something the local police and sheriff's departments encourage parents to do to help identify kidnapped children."

"That's the way I understand it too," Sylvester concurred. "But I checked the entire house contents list, and there wasn't a fingerprint card listed for her husband or children—only for Erica."

Mark was impressed that Sylvester had scoured the extremely long contents list. "Maybe she did have cards for her children but threw them away after they died."

Sylvester shook his head. "I can guarantee you she didn't do that. She kept *everything* that belonged to her children."

"So you think Erica made the fingerprint card for herself after the children were already dead?"

"Yes."

Marks spread his hands. "Why?"

"The only logical reason I can come up with is to *help* the police identify her body."

"Because she knew Molly was trying to kill her?"

Sylvester nodded. "That's my theory."

Mark was skeptical. "Wouldn't she have gone to the police if she thought she was in mortal danger?"

"Maybe she did. Remember, she and the deputy sheriff weren't on good terms."

"I think Foster was still in love with her. I can't imagine that he would ignore a plea for help. Besides, the old sheriff was still alive then."

"But he was sick, possibly too sick to follow up on phone calls."

"That explains the fingerprint card—but why did Erica go around town telling people she had a boyfriend?"

"Maybe she really had a boyfriend, or maybe the boyfriend was a delusion?" Sylvester suggested. "After all, she was crazy."

"Then what about Molly? How did she manage to disappear?"

Before Sylvester could respond, a doctor came to a stop beside them and introduced himself as Brian Carter. "Are you Kelsey's doctor?" Mark asked.

"I'm the resident on call, and I've been monitoring her," Dr. Carter said. "I've come to give you a report on her condition."

"My wife is Kelsey's sister, and she's anxious to hear about her." Mark motioned for the doctor to follow him into the waiting room.

"Kate, this is Dr. Carter. He's here to give you a report on Kelsey."

Kate crossed the room to stand beside them and asked, "How is she?"

"She's tired but otherwise fine," Dr. Carter assured her.

"And the baby . . ."

The doctor shook his head. "I'm sorry."

Mark put his arm around Kate's shoulders. "When can we take her home?" Kate asked.

"We're going to keep her overnight."

"Can I see her?" Kate pleaded.

"She's sleeping right now, but when she wakes up, the nurse will take you in for a quick visit," the doctor promised.

The doctor left, and Kate turned to the others. "I appreciate you coming to support Kelsey, but there's no point in everyone staying."

"I'll head back and tell Miss Eugenia the news," Winston said.

"And I've got to get the vegetable stand set up," Brandon added.

Sylvester nodded wearily. "Me too."

After they left, Kate checked her watch. "Travis will be arriving soon."

"Do I need to go pick him up at the airport?"

Kate shook her head. "No, he said he'd rent a car and get a hotel room. He'll call to see when I want him to come to the house."

* * *

At noon Eugenia took Dub and the children to Kate's house for lunch. When Dub had finished his soup and sandwich, she sent him back to the police station to resume his painting then put Emily and Charles down for a nap. Once the children were asleep, she turned on the television. The phone rang right in the middle of a particularly lurid segment of *Divorce Court,* and Eugenia answered it absently. "Hello."

"Can I speak to Kate Iverson please?" a voice with a faint western accent requested.

"She's not here. Can I ask who is calling?"

"My name is Travis Pearce . . ."

"Oh, Travis!" Eugenia cried. "I'm Kate's next-door neighbor. Kate and Mark are at the hospital with Kelsey."

"The hospital!" Travis shouted into the phone. "Is Kelsey hurt?"

"I think she's okay," Eugenia hedged. "But, well, I'd better let her explain."

"Can you tell me how to get to the hospital?" Travis asked.

Eugenia considered this request. "Yes," she agreed finally. "That would probably be best." Then she gave him directions to Memorial Hospital in Albany.

* * *

Kate was sitting with Mark on one of the uncomfortable couches in the hospital waiting room when the nurse came to get her. "Your sister is awake and is asking for you," she said.

Kate stood and, after a quick wave to Mark, followed the woman into the cubicle where Kelsey was lying on a bed. Kate waited until the nurse left them alone then climbed up beside her sister. "Oh, Kelsey." She cuddled close, the way they had done as children. "I'm so sorry."

Kelsey buried her face in Kate's neck. "The Lord thought I wouldn't love the baby, so He took it back," she said amid sobs.

"Oh, that's not it," Kate assured her. "Sometimes these things just happen."

Kelsey shook her head, refusing to be comforted. "This might never have happened if I had stayed in Salt Lake and tried to work things out with Travis. I don't deserve to be a mother."

Kate stroked her sister's cheek. "You made some mistakes, but it's not too late."

"It is for my baby," Kelsey returned pitifully.

"Nothing will replace this baby or take away your grief entirely," Kate said carefully. "But hopefully you'll have other children and that will lessen the pain."

"I think Travis has given up on me," Kelsey whispered. "Ever since I left he's been e-mailing constantly, but I haven't gotten a single message since yesterday. What's really strange is that I thought I wanted out of my marriage and my pregnancy. But now that I've lost both—I'm more miserable than before."

Kate was trying decide how to phrase her confession about Travis's imminent arrival when Kelsey continued.

"I felt so threatened by the idea of having a handsome husband."

This odd comment made Kate lose her train of thought. "What?"

"I've always been just okay looking, and since Travis was ordinary too, there was no pressure. But once he got gorgeous, I felt so unattractive."

"I think you're beautiful!" Kate protested. "And I'm sure Travis thinks so too."

Kelsey put a hand to her tangled hair. "The last thing I am right now is beautiful."

"Beauty is in the eye of the beholder," Kate responded, deciding to abandon any attempt at gently breaking the news of her unauthorized phone call. "And speaking of Travis . . ." Before she could say more, the door of the cubicle opened, and the nurse stepped inside.

"You can't be up there," she told Kate. "Only patients are allowed on the beds."

Kate slid off the bed, feeling foolish. "I'm sorry."

The nurse was still looking annoyed as she turned to Kelsey. "There's a man here demanding to see you. He says he's your husband."

"Travis?" Kelsey asked in a strangled voice.

"I called him," Kate blurted. "I couldn't let you go on alone so sick and everything. He flew in today, and I thought he was going to wait at a hotel until we figured out how to approach you about his visit . . ."

Kate's explanation was cut off as Travis burst into the room. "Kelsey!" he cried, crossing the room to gather his wife in his arms.

"Do not get on that bed!" the nurse commanded with a look over at Kate. "I'm trying to maintain a sterile environment here!"

"He *is* her husband," Kate reminded the woman in her best imitation of Miss Eugenia's no-nonsense tone. "So they probably share the same germs, and I think we should give them some privacy." Then she took the nurse firmly by the arm and drew her from the room.

Kate returned to the waiting area and sat with Mark until Travis joined them. His eyes were red, and Kate knew he had been crying.

"Kelsey's asleep," he told them.

"I'm so sorry about the baby," Kate said.

Travis passed a trembling hand in front of his face. "I can't fully appreciate what we've lost, since I didn't find out about the baby until just a few minutes ago."

Kate nodded. "I know."

"I can't believe that Kelsey had to deal with all of this," Travis said, waving to encompass the entire hospital, "alone."

"She didn't have to," Mark reminded him. "She chose to."

Travis considered this, and his shoulders slumped forward. "I've made her so unhappy."

"Marriage is a two-way street," Mark said. "You both have to work together to make each other happy."

Deciding that Travis had received enough lecturing for the moment, Kate asked, "How was Kelsey feeling before she fell asleep?"

"Guilty," he reported. "She kept apologizing for not telling me about the baby and blaming herself for the miscarriage." This seemed to baffle him. "As if she could control nature."

"She acted very glad to see you," Kate ventured.

Travis smiled. "Yes, and that gives me hope."

Mark stood and pulled Kate to her feet. "Well, since you're here to look after Kelsey we'd better head back to Haggerty. I've got a couple of cases at crisis stages, and we're hosting a wedding reception at our house on Saturday."

Travis rose to his feet. "Oh, yes, I can handle things here." He looked at Kate. "I don't know how to thank you—for taking care of Kelsey and for calling me . . ."

Kate gave him a quick hug. "Everything's going to be just fine."

Travis nodded. "I think it is."

"You'll call us if there's any change?" she requested.

He nodded. "I will."

"And when she's discharged, you'll both come and stay at our house until she's strong enough to fly home?" Kate added.

"I'd better not commit to anything until I have a chance to discuss it with Kelsey," Travis replied wisely.

Mark smiled. "You're getting the idea." Then he turned to Kate. "Let's go home."

"I hate to leave Travis alone," Kate told Mark as they walked down the hall. "Maybe we should . . ."

Mark took Kate's hand in his. "Kelsey needs to depend on Travis exclusively for a while."

"When Kelsey called to say she wanted to live with us, I was so honored that she would come to me for help and so hopeful that we could improve our relationship. Then I found out that she came to Haggerty because it was close to Wilsonville, where Brandon Vance lived. Now I have to let her depend on Travis instead of me."

Mark squeezed her hand. "Look on the bright side. At least you helped save your sister's marriage."

Kate sighed. "I guess I'll have to be satisfied with that."

* * *

When Kate and Mark arrived at home, Miss Eugenia and the kids were sitting on the back porch. Sylvester and Whit Owens were there too, and everyone was eating pizza.

"Whit brought dinner," Miss Eugenia told them. "Have some."

"It's really good," Emily added.

Kate declined, saying she wasn't hungry, but Mark picked up a plate and helped himself to a large slice of pepperoni.

"How's Kelsey?" Miss Eugenia asked.

"She's fine," Mark answered to spare Kate the ordeal. "But there won't be a baby at their house anytime soon."

"I see," Miss Eugenia replied with a quick glance at Kate.

"Miss Eugenia gave me a badge," Emily reported, poking out her chest.

"Me too." Charles imitated his sister.

"I can't thank you enough for watching them," Kate told Miss Eugenia.

"It was my pleasure," she replied. "I haven't gotten to spend much time with them lately."

"Why don't we go inside where it's cooler?" Mark suggested around a mouthful of pizza.

Sylvester tipped his head toward Miss Eugenia's backyard. Mark followed the direction of his gesture and saw Brandon Vance working in the garden. "Because we have a better view from here—just in case."

"You still think he might be involved?" Mark asked quietly.

"I haven't been able to rule it out," Sylvester admitted. "But I have a new theory that I'm working on."

Mark swallowed his pizza. "Now you don't think Molly Vance killed Erica?"

Sylvester shook his head. "No, but this new idea's so crazy I can't give you any details until I confirm it," Sylvester replied.

"Why?"

"Because I'm afraid you'll get me an appointment with Erica's psychiatrist in Albany," Sylvester said. "I should know one way or the other by tomorrow."

Mark nodded. "I guess I can be patient for that long. And I'll keep Dr. Clements's number handy, just in case."

* * *

On Friday morning Mark tried to stay out of the way as Miss Eugenia and her army of volunteers transformed the Iversons' home into a reception hall. Kelsey and Travis arrived from the hospital just before noon. Miss Eugenia kept all of Kelsey's well-wishers in the hall while Kate got her sister settled in the guest room. Then Miss Eugenia admitted the visitors one at a time.

Emily and Charles presented their aunt with pictures they had drawn of her feeling better. Winston and Brandon each gave Kelsey a bouquet of flowers. Winston's was purchased at the Piggly Wiggly, while Brandon's was a collection from Miss Eugenia's yard—but Kelsey showed equal appreciation for both. Mark came in last—apologetic but determined.

"I'm so sorry to ask you at a time like this," he began. "But I wonder if you had a chance to check on cash transactions."

"Mark!" Kate was obviously appalled.

"Kelsey is supposed to be resting," Travis agreed.

Kelsey pointed to a printout on her computer desk. "It's right there. I expanded my search to include the sale of property and businesses where there was no mortgage involved," she explained. "Since a *true* cash transaction with a million dollars in a suitcase would be rare—except in Hollywood."

Mark scanned the list then looked up in despair. "There must be thousands of transactions here! It will take weeks to check them all out."

"I'm sorry," Kelsey said, acknowledging the monumental nature of his task. "In order to get the list down to a manageable number, we'd have to narrow the parameters."

"We can't narrow the parameters because we have no idea where the murderer went," he replied, trying not to let her see his disappointment. Holding up the printout, he turned toward the door. "Thanks for doing this, Kelsey. Now I promise to leave you alone and let you get some rest."

Miss Eugenia gave him a stern look as he passed her in the hall. "The very idea," she muttered.

Feeling like the entire world was against him, Mark went into his office.

* * *

At three o'clock the piano movers were assembled in Eugenia's living room. "If you'd like, I can hold doors for you," she offered.

"Thanks anyway," Winston declined for the group. "But I think it would be best if you just step back. We'll get the piano outside, and then you can tell us where to put it."

"You'll be careful with my piano, won't you?" Eugenia pleaded. "It belonged to my mother, you know."

Rather than answer, Winston made a little growling noise in his throat. Deciding that enough had been said on the subject, Eugenia watched silently while the men lifted, pulled, and tugged the heavy, old piano out onto her lawn. Once they had it positioned correctly, she noticed that one of the men she'd assigned to the task wasn't there.

"Where's Sylvester?" she asked.

"Don't know," Winston replied breathlessly. "But the little weasel wouldn't have been much help anyway. That piano must have weighed two tons!"

There was the murmuring roar of general agreement from the other piano movers until the sound of screeching tires and the growl of a souped-up engine interrupted them.

"It sounds like the *little weasel* has finally arrived," Eugenia remarked dryly.

"Yeah, now that we're through moving the piano," Winston said in disgust.

"Mark!" Sylvester came running from the driveway, waving a sheaf of papers. "I've got something to show you."

Mark looked toward his house where ladies were winding tulle around the banisters of the deck. "Can we talk in your kitchen?" he asked Eugenia.

"Of course," she replied. "Just come this way."

Mark motioned to Winston, and Eugenia led them inside. Once she had them settled around her kitchen table, she remained quiet, hoping to blend in with the surroundings so they'd forget about her presence.

Mark addressed Sylvester. "I presume you received confirmation of your new theory."

Sylvester nodded, his eyes shining with excitement. "You're not going to believe this!"

"Give us a try," Winston requested.

"Okay." Sylvester took a deep breath and continued. "We've been going on the assumption that Erica Helms died and that Molly Vance disappeared, but after making my lists I started to wonder if it was the other way around."

Eugenia controlled a gasp and saw the same shock she felt reflected on the faces of Winston and Mark.

Winston shook his head. "You're right. I don't believe it."

Mark was more diplomatic. "How could that be possible? The sheriff's department used fingerprints and dental records to identify the body as Erica Helms."

"Neither Molly nor Erica was ever fingerprinted officially," Sylvester explained. "So the only prints the medical examiner had to work with were from the homemade Identi-Kit found in Erica's house."

Mark nodded. "We've never been able to explain why there was a fingerprint card for Erica but not one for her husband or children."

"Right," Sylvester confirmed. "Then there was the trip Erica made to the dentist's office right before her supposed death. She went into the records room alone, on the pretext of getting her dental charts and x-rays, but then she decided not to take them when she left. Does that make sense?"

"She told the receptionist that the dentist convinced her to leave them," Mark said.

"He didn't," Sylvester countered. "I talked to the good doctor, and he said he didn't even see Erica when she stopped by the office that last time."

"So?" Winston remarked skeptically.

Mark looked up at Sylvester. "You think she switched their records—hers and Molly's."

Sylvester smiled. "I know she did. I checked with the insurance clerk at the dentist's office, and neither woman had dental insurance."

"What difference would that make?" Winston demanded.

"An insurance provider might have copies of x-rays on file that they could use for comparison," Sylvester explained.

"But you said neither woman had insurance," Mark pointed out.

"Right," Sylvester acknowledged. "So I thought I'd hit a dead end. Then the receptionist remembered that Molly Vance had gotten her wisdom teeth removed by an oral surgeon a few years ago." Sylvester paused briefly for dramatic effect. "And *he* had a set of full-mouth x-rays."

"You got a copy from the oral surgeon?" Winston asked.

"And sent them to the medical examiner in Atlanta," Sylvester confirmed. "The body that was fished out of the pond behind Erica Helms's house was Molly Vance."

"Unbelievable," Eugenia whispered from her position by the counter.

"How'd you figure it out?" Winston wanted to know.

"I hate to admit it, but the drunk guy that's painting the police station gave me the idea," Sylvester told them.

Eugenia gave up all pretense of staying out of the conversation. "Dub Shaw?" she demanded.

"Yes," Sylvester confirmed. "You remember the other day when he was talking about how his dogs looked just alike and how he was afraid he was going to bury them in the wrong graves?"

"I remember," Winston said grimly.

"Me too," Eugenia added.

"Well, I couldn't seem to get that off my mind, and then I started looking at my anomaly list."

"Anomaly?" Winston asked.

"Odd occurrences," Mark provided impatiently. "Go on, Sylvester."

Sylvester resumed his explanation. "Molly's life stopped after she disappeared, with no sudden departures from normalcy. But all the odd things Erica Helms did before her 'death' seemed like parts of a setup."

Mark nodded. "Which they were."

"Yes," Sylvester confirmed. "Once I had it all charted, I could see that Erica was our killer, and Molly was buried in the wrong grave."

Winston clapped the little man from the attorney general's office on the back. "Good work. I'm glad we've got that settled."

Mark looked through the kitchen window into Miss Eugenia's backyard. "There's one person who's not going to consider your breakthrough good news."

Sylvester nodded. "I know."

"At least this proves that Brandon is innocent," Eugenia contributed, but Sylvester shook his head.

"I wasn't able to rule out the possibility that Erica had an accomplice—someone to help her move the body and invest the money."

"You think that hypothetical accomplice is Brandon?" Mark asked.

Sylvester shrugged. "I think we need to keep an eye on him until we have all the facts."

"Why don't we get him to take a lie detector test?" Winston suggested.

"Brandon may refuse," Mark said.

"And even if he agrees, the results will be inadmissible as evidence," Sylvester pointed out.

"I know," Winston acknowledged. "But if he passes, you could move him to the bottom of your suspect list."

"And if he fails, I'll know to dig deeper," Sylvester said grimly.

Mark sighed. "When are we going to tell Vance about his wife?"

"There's no time like the present," Sylvester said. "Who wants to go and get him?"

Eugenia stepped forward. "I'll do it." Then without waiting for the men to grant permission, she walked outside and into her garden.

She found Brandon picking squash. He heard her approach and turned to greet her. Something about the look on her face must have warned him of impending doom. He stood, as if preparing himself for the worst.

"I'm afraid I've got bad news," she told him.

His shoulders slumped. "Molly's dead?" he guessed.

Eugenia nodded.

"If you'll come inside with me, Mark and the others will tell you all about it."

* * *

When Brandon Vance walked into the kitchen with Miss Eugenia, his expression was one of resignation and grief. "Either he's innocent, or he's one of the best actors I've ever seen," Mark whispered to Sylvester.

"I agree it's one or the other," Sylvester whispered back.

Mark waited until Miss Eugenia settled Brandon at the table before he said, "Mr. Muck has found new evidence indicating that your wife was killed a year ago. Her body was disguised to look like Erica Helms and then hidden in the pond."

"Why?" Brandon responded dully.

"We don't know yet," Mark answered. "But the body will have to be exhumed for DNA testing, and after that she can be reburied at a site of your choosing."

Brandon nodded. "When will this take place?"

"Monday, if possible," Mark told him.

"I want to be present," Brandon said.

"Of course," Mark agreed. Then he cleared his throat and forced himself to ask, "Would you be willing to take a polygraph test to put an end to any question of your involvement?"

Brandon nodded again. "I'd do most anything to clear my name."

Mark felt relieved. "Good. Chief Jones, could you arrange for the test to be given in Wilsonville?"

"I'll handle it," Winston agreed.

Brandon pushed away from the table and rose to his feet. "I'd like to head back to Wilsonville today. May I call you at the police station to find out the details about my appointment?"

Winston nodded. "That will be fine."

"Then if you'll excuse me, I'll begin my packing."

"I'm terribly sorry for your loss," Mark added as Brandon headed for the door.

The former literature professor nodded. "Thank you."

Everyone was silent for a few seconds after Brandon left. Then Mark said to Winston, "Make sure whoever gives him that test in Wilsonville asks several questions about Erica Helms."

Winston put his hat on and stood. "I will."

Mark turned to Sylvester. "If he passes the polygraph, we'll leave him to his grief."

Sylvester nodded.

"Well, that just about takes care of everything," Mark said, mentally organizing his thoughts for the report he'd be filing with the SAC in Atlanta.

Miss Eugenia stepped up beside the table. "But if Molly Vance is dead—where is Erica Helms?"

"That is a good question," Mark replied.

* * *

When the meeting broke up, they all walked outside. Cornelia, Polly, and George Ann were standing at the foot of Eugenia's porch.

"We've been looking for you," they said in unison when they saw Eugenia.

"You promised to make someone help me clean my punch bowl," George Ann reminded Eugenia in a nasal whine.

"I have a hundred cloth napkins to fold and can't do it by myself," Polly added.

"And I need to be sure the piano isn't going to be moved again before the ceremony, so I can check to be sure it's still in tune," Cornelia contributed.

Eugenia decided to start with the easiest question first. "The piano won't be moved," she told Cornelia. "So go right ahead and check its tune." Then she turned to Polly. "I'll find someone to help you with the napkins." Her eyes settled on Sylvester. "How about you?"

"Sorry," he said, really looking regretful. "I've got to call my office in Atlanta and tell them . . ." He glanced at his audience. "Everything," he finished lamely. "But when I get through, I'd be glad to help."

"I'll do it," Kate offered as she walked up. "Mark too."

Eugenia gave them an appreciative smile and faced her most difficult problem. "Where is your punch bowl?" she asked George Ann.

"In the trunk of my car," was the response. "It's much too heavy for me to carry."

Eugenia turned to Winston. "Will you get George Ann's punch bowl out of the trunk of her car and put it on that utility table back by my gardening shed?"

Winston agreed reluctantly, and while waiting for him to return, Eugenia tried to think of someone she could convince to work with George Ann. It would have to be a stranger, who didn't know George Ann, or someone less than bright, who wouldn't be offended by any of George Ann's inevitable rude comments. Eugenia was about to give up when she saw Winston's girlfriend climb out of a silver sedan. She couldn't remember when she'd been so happy to see anyone.

"Ciera!" she called, and the woman looked up in surprise. "Over here."

Ciera crossed the lawn and stopped beside Eugenia. "I was looking for Winston," she said.

"He's gone to get a punch bowl we're using for the wedding reception tomorrow," Eugenia explained. "And when he gets back, he'll need help polishing it. Would you be able to assist him?"

Eugenia could tell Ciera didn't want to accept the assignment, but finally she nodded. "I guess."

Winston walked up carrying the huge bowl and seemed surprised to see Ciera waiting with Eugenia. "Hey," he said to his girlfriend, a blush rising from his neck to his receding hairline. "What are you doing here?"

"She's about to help you and George Ann polish that punch bowl," Eugenia interrupted. "Take it back there by the shed."

"It's awfully hot out here," Ciera complained, pulling at her little pink T-shirt.

Anxious to avoid a mutiny, Eugenia told Winston to pull the utility table into the shade created by Brandon's rose arbor. "Now, please hurry," she urged. "We need to get everything done before the rehearsal starts."

Winston and Ciera followed George Ann toward the arbor as Cornelia began playing the piano. "It sounds fine!" she hollered across the yard to Eugenia.

Eugenia nodded, thankful that something was going well.

* * *

As Mark folded cloth napkins, his mind drifted back to his brief and unpleasant meeting with Lyle Tweedy.

"What are you thinking about?" Kate asked him.

"Lyle Tweedy."

Kate made a face. "You should try to forget that awful man."

Mark nodded. "It's funny. The man was consummately evil, but by asking me to come and see him, he started a series of events that should eventually result in a murderer being brought to justice— assuming that I can locate Erica Helms."

"If she has any sense at all, she's left the country," Kate told him.

"I'm hoping she isn't that sensible," he admitted.

"How will you go about finding her?"

Mark sighed. "Well, after I turn in my report to the SAC in Atlanta, I'm expecting to get a little support from the FBI."

"Any help would be more than you've had so far," she pointed out. "You're going over Dan's head with your report?"

He smiled. "I thought I would."

"Good."

"Then I'll get a court order and interview Erica's psychiatrist again."

"If Erica is still alive, will he be able to tell you more?"

"Probably not," Mark said. He was reaching for another napkin when his hand froze in midair. He thought about his visit with Dr. Clements. Throughout the conversation Mark had the feeling that the psychiatrist was trying to tell him something, but he couldn't figure out what. Now, he suddenly felt certain that he knew the doctor's hidden message. He turned to his wife. "Kate, I'm sorry to desert you, but I have a phone call to make."

Accustomed to sudden exits, Kate nodded with resignation. "I can finish these myself."

Mark hurried to his office and looked up Dr. Clements's home number. He was formulating a message for the answering machine, but the doctor picked up on the third ring.

"You've been expecting my call," Mark said.

"Yes," Dr. Clements confirmed.

"You knew that Erica was still alive."

"Yes."

Mark was furious with himself for not realizing this sooner. "You required Erica to attend the grief management classes—but nobody made her come to see you. She did that because she *wanted* to." Mark leaned back against his chair. "And she knew that patient-physician confidentiality would prevent you from giving any information about her to the authorities." Mark paused, but when the doctor didn't respond, he asked, "Erica is still a patient of yours, isn't she?"

"I can't answer that question."

Mark took that as a yes. "When I was leaving your office, you encouraged me to learn more about sociopaths," Mark continued, feeling his way. "Is Erica a sociopath?"

"I'm sure you know I can't answer that either," Dr. Clements replied. "But that term would apply to many of my patients."

Mark smiled. Another yes. "Thank you for your time, doctor." He hung up the phone and rushed back up to Kelsey's room. He was pleased to find only Travis standing guard at her door. "I know I promised to leave Kelsey alone," he said when Travis blocked his way. "But I have one more little request."

Travis glanced over his shoulder anxiously. "I don't know about that."

"Come on in, Mark," Kelsey called out. "I'm fine. I don't know why everyone keeps treating me like an invalid."

Mark gave Travis an apologetic look as he hurried into the room. "I've narrowed the parameters," he told Kelsey. "We're looking for the purchase of a business or property that would generate a decent annual income within sixty miles of Albany."

Kelsey's eyebrows shot up. "You *have* narrowed the parameters." She swung her legs over the side of the bed, but Travis objected.

"The doctor said to stay off your feet for twenty-four hours," he reminded her, adding, "please."

"I hate to disobey the doctor's instructions," she said.

Mark struggled to hide his frustration. He was close, he just knew it. "I understand. I'll figure out another way to get the information."

Kelsey frowned and turned to Travis. "It would only take me a minute to create a new printout."

"What about a laptop?" Mark suggested. "You could make your adjustments without getting out of bed."

Kelsey smiled. "That would be perfect."

Mark was already halfway down the hall. "I'll be right back!"

He rushed out the back door in search of Sylvester, who never went anywhere without his laptop. He found the attorney general's representative pacing back and forth between rows of string beans, talking animatedly on his cell phone.

"Sylvester!" Mark called as he approached the young man. "You'll have to hang up for a minute. I need you."

Sylvester held up a finger, requesting a minute.

Mark waited impatiently.

Winston rushed over, wiping silver polish from his hand to a handkerchief. "Where's the fire?"

"This had better be good," Sylvester said, closing his phone and sending Mark an irritated look. "Since you just made me hang up on the attorney general!"

"This *is* good," Mark assured him. "I know where Erica is."

Both men stared back. Sylvester was the first to recover. "Where?" he asked.

"She's still seeing her psychiatrist, so I know she's within driving distance of Albany."

"The psychiatrist told you that?" Sylvester demanded. "That could jeopardize the case!"

"He didn't tell me anything," Mark assured him. "I'm a good guesser."

"That's a relief," Sylvester said.

"Now Kelsey can narrow her search for a large business purchase," Mark continued. "But she can't get out of bed, so I need your laptop."

Sylvester nodded. "It's in my car. I'll get it."

Ten minutes later Kelsey was typing commands into Sylvester's laptop. Finally she pushed a key and leaned back against her pillow. "Now we just have to wait."

"How long will it take?" Mark asked.

"Last time it took several hours, but since the parameters are tighter, I expect the results to be smaller. Maybe an hour," Kelsey estimated. "As soon as something prints, I'll send it out with Travis."

Mark wanted to stay and stare at the printer, but he knew he had imposed on Kelsey and Travis enough. So he led Sylvester and Winston out into the hallway.

"There you are!" Miss Eugenia said when she saw them. "You're all needed in my backyard immediately."

With a sigh, Mark shrugged at his companions, and they followed Miss Eugenia outside.

* * *

Eugenia sent Winston back to his punch bowl polishing and assigned Mark and Sylvester to work with Arnold, wiring white bows to the chairs along the aisle. Once the punch bowl was done, Winston carried it into the house so that George Ann could oversee its placement in the living room. Then Winston returned to Ciera's side, under the shade of the arbor.

"The two of you look mighty natural standing there," Cornelia said as she passed by. "Maybe you will be the guests of honor at our next wedding."

Winston blushed crimson, but Eugenia noticed that Ciera didn't react at all. In fact, the fickle woman turned to Winston and said, "Where's Brandon? I haven't seen him all afternoon."

"I don't know," Winston replied as he lifted Ciera from her feet. "But don't worry—I'm the only man you need."

Ciera seemed uncomfortable with the public embrace, and Eugenia felt sorry for poor Winston. He didn't even have enough sense to realize his girlfriend was halfway gone already.

"Brandon got some bad news today," Eugenia told her. "So he's probably packing to go home."

"What kind of bad news?" Ciera asked.

Winston's voice had lost its playful tone when he said, "His wife is dead."

Ciera's eyes moved toward the gardening shed. "At least he won't have to look for her anymore."

* * *

When Mark told Miss Eugenia they were through wiring bows, she praised their efforts and invited everyone inside for a sandwich to tide them over until the rehearsal dinner. "But please police the area first," she requested.

"I knew that offer was too good to be true," Mark muttered to Sylvester.

While they were picking up ribbon scraps and dismembered flower petals, Travis came running out of the Iversons' house. They all watched as he rushed over to Mark and thrust a piece of computer paper into his hand. "Kelsey said this was important," Travis said.

Mark watched Travis sprint back across the lawn, and then he read the printout. When he got to the portion Kelsey had high-lighted, he blinked, thinking his eyes must be playing tricks on him. After reading it for the third time, he knew it was no mistake. "I have been such a fool." He handed the paper to Sylvester.

Sylvester read Kelsey's report, and they shared a sheepish gaze. "It was staring us in the face all along."

Mark nodded. "We had all the information—we just didn't arrange it right."

"What do you have there?" Winston asked from the arbor as he put Ciera back down on her feet.

Mark walked toward Winston, Sylvester following a few steps behind. "The list Kelsey compiled of all businesses in the Albany area purchased without a mortgage during the past six months."

"You think the murderer is someone on that list?" Winston asked, suddenly interested.

"I think the murderer purchased the Haggerty Fitness Center."

"What?" Winston demanded. "But Ciera owns the fitness center."

"And *Ciera* is an anagram for *Erica*," Sylvester said. "I can't believe I didn't notice that sooner."

Winston seemed completely unable to process the information. "Ciera is Erica Helms?" he repeated stupidly, turning to look at the thin woman he had been dating for months. "You are really Erica?"

"Before asking any questions, you need to read her the Miranda Statement," Mark advised. "And you'll probably want to conduct the interview back at the police station." It was the nicest way Mark could think of to say, "Arrest her."

Winston seemed rooted to Miss Eugenia's lawn. Still staring at his girlfriend, he opened his mouth and shut it again.

"Arnold," Mark suggested finally. "Maybe you could read Mrs. Helms her rights."

As Arnold took a step forward, Erica's hand darted out and grabbed Winston's gun. She pulled it from its holster and pointed at the others. "Everyone stay back," she said calmly.

"There are a lot of us and only one of you," Sylvester challenged. "You can't kill us all."

Erica nodded. "That's true, but I can definitely kill Winston." She shifted her aim slightly so the gun was pointed directly at Winston's head. The police chief's face turned from embarrassed red to deathly white.

"Do as she says," Mark instructed, turning to Miss Eugenia. In what he hoped was a tone that could not be disobeyed, he said, "Walk slowly over to my house and call the county sheriff. Tell Kate I'm fine and that no one is to come outside under any circumstances."

Miss Eugenia looked frightened but nodded slightly and started walking.

"I didn't say she could go anywhere," Erica objected.

"Keep going," Mark urged, pleased that Miss Eugenia didn't falter.

Hoping to distract Erica's attention, Mark addressed Arnold, "Since she won't let you get any closer, I guess you'll have to yell the Miranda Statement from there."

"That's not necessary," she said.

"But it is," Mark insisted. "I have some questions for you, and I want to be sure that your answers can be used against you in a court of law."

"You have the right to remain silent," Arnold began.

"Shut up!" Erica shouted.

"Keep going, Arnold," Mark said. "She can't hold the gun on Winston and shoot you too."

Perspiration was beaded up on Arnold's forehead, but he bravely persevered. "Anything you say can and will be used against you in a court of law. You have the right to legal counsel. If you cannot afford an attorney, one will be appointed for you . . ." When he had finished, he asked, "Do you understand?"

Erica smirked at Mark and nodded. "I understand."

"You don't look anything like the woman in your family picture," Mark said.

"The miracles of diet, exercise, and plastic surgery," Erica replied.

Brandon Vance stepped out of the gardening shed where he'd been since he got the news about his wife. "You killed Molly?" he asked, his voice full of pain.

"I didn't kill anyone," Erica replied. "Molly killed herself. I just cut her body out of the tree in your backyard and put it in my pond."

Brandon shook his head. "I don't believe you. Molly was getting better."

"She wasn't, and you know it," Erica accused. "It had always been a matter of time, ever since your little boy died."

Mark didn't question the truth of what she said. It made perfect sense. So he rearranged the facts of the cases in his mind one last time, then asked, "How did you find her?"

"Molly called and told me she wouldn't be coming to our grief management meetings anymore. I asked her why, and she just hung up. Her voice sounded funny, so I went over there."

"And found her dead?" Mark asked.

"Yes. I'm sure that's why Molly called me. She didn't want *him* to find her." Erica tipped her head toward Brandon.

"But why did you disguise the body so everyone would think you were dead?" Mark wanted to know.

"I wanted to die," Erica said, her voice devoid of emotion. "But I didn't have Molly's courage. Then I realized that if everyone *thought* I was dead—it would be almost the same. I could go away and pretend to be someone else. And maybe, eventually, I'd really turn into a person who doesn't hurt all the time."

Sylvester seemed more skeptical of Erica's story. "How did you cut the body down?"

"I used a ladder," she replied.

"How did you get the body into your car?" Sylvester pressed.

"They still had a wheelchair they used for their little boy when he was sick. I put her in it."

Mark heard Brandon Vance make a sobbing noise but allowed Sylvester to continue. "You took her to your house, changed her into some of your clothes, and put your wedding ring on her finger?"

"Yes." Erica didn't seem upset by the memory. "It took hours."

"Then you weighted her body with rocks and hid her under the cattails at the back of your pond?" Sylvester assumed.

"No," Mark interrupted. "First she got an Identi-Kit from her local sheriff's department and put Molly's prints on the card."

Sylvester nodded. "Of course. That was an important step."

"*Then* she put Molly in the pond." Mark hated the necessity of making this worse for Brandon Vance, but Erica seemed willing to talk, and he wanted to know everything. "Once that was taken care of, Erica went back to Molly's house and packed so it would look like she had left on a trip."

"Actually I did the packing over the course of the next week," Erica said thoughtfully.

"You let me think she was alive all these months!" Brandon cried out in anguish.

"Your grief isn't worse now than it would have been then," Erica told him without an ounce of sympathy. "If anything I gave you a gift—a whole year of hope. There's nothing worse than the finality of death." She looked out at her audience. "Molly would have understood. She would have been glad that her death gave me a little escape from the pain."

"When did you become a vandal?" Sylvester asked, surprising everyone.

Mark turned his startled gaze toward Sylvester. "A vandal?"

Winston roused himself enough to say, "What are you talking about?"

"Be still!" Erica commanded him.

"All the victims of this recent rash of local vandalism had been arrested for driving under the influence of alcohol," Sylvester reminded them. "Mrs. Helms had a particular hatred for drunk drivers. It adds up."

Erica didn't deny the accusation, but her hand began to tremble slightly. "Do you know how many innocent children are killed every year by worthless drunks? They steal babies from mothers and destroy families and ruin lives . . ."

"I suppose that's why you started dating Winston," Sylvester posed, interrupting her diatribe. "To gain access to his DUI records."

"Because of Leita's surgery, Winston was understaffed, so you offered to help with the backed-up filing," Mark elaborated.

Erica glanced at Winston, and Mark thought he detected the slightest amount of regret in her eyes. "I hoped a little revenge would ease the pain."

Winston looked like he had been sucker-punched. "When we met that first time at Heads Up, I wasn't in uniform, so you didn't even know I was the police chief," he finally managed to say.

"Don't be naive," Erica told Winston impatiently. "Of course I knew exactly who you were. Why else would I offer to buy you a drink and then let you come home with me?"

Winston swayed, and Mark almost hoped he'd faint—causing a diversion that might allow them to get the gun away from Erica. "Drunk drivers are a menace to society. No one would argue with you about that." Mark tried to keep his tone reasonable. "But you can't take the law into your own hands. Everyone has rights—even drunks."

"I could have killed them," Erica pointed out. "So they got off easy."

"You vandalized Dub Shaw's property several times and even poisoned his dogs," Mark said. "Why did you punish him more than the others?"

Erica shrugged impatiently. "He saw me coming out of Dr. Clements's office, and I was afraid he'd mention it to someone."

"Were you planning to kill Dub?" Mark asked.

"I hadn't decided for sure yet." Erica squared her shoulders and lifted the gun a little higher. "Now I'm going to leave. Nobody try to stop me."

Winston recovered partially from the multiple emotional blows he'd received during the past few minutes. Mark saw him reach into his left pants pocket, and seconds later Winston had a gun pointed at Erica.

She smiled. "So now it's a standoff."

"Winston has years of experience with a gun," Mark told her. "You'd never survive a shoot-out with him."

She took a step toward the driveway where her car was parked. "I'll take my chances."

"Don't make me do it," Winston pleaded. "Give me the gun."

She shook her head. "I can't." She kept walking, and Winston matched her progress step for step.

"If you don't surrender that weapon, I'll have to shoot you," Winston told her, his voice strained.

"What if I shoot you first?" she taunted, her hand clasping the gun. "It's a big risk to take."

"Ciera, I mean, Erica—please!" Winston sounded close to panic. "You're leaving me no option."

Mark stepped forward. "She won't shoot you, Winston."

"How can you be sure?" the police chief demanded.

"Foster Gunnells, the acting sheriff in Patton Chapel, told me Erica uses people, and I think that's true. She used him, she used Molly Vance—she even used Lyle Tweedy. Now I think she wants to use *you* to put her out of her misery."

Winston looked startled, but Erica didn't flinch.

"Like she said—she doesn't have the courage to do it herself," Mark said softly. "But she can't stand to be alive."

Erica's demeanor changed completely. "If you care for me at all, you'll do it," she said to Winston. "I'm threatening you with a gun, so it will be self-defense."

"Ciera . . ." There were tears in Winston's eyes as he shook his head. "You know I can't. Even if I had to shoot to stop you, I wouldn't shoot to kill."

"I've tried," she wailed. "I really have, but life just isn't worth living without my babies."

As she turned the gun on herself, Mark and Winston both lunged and managed to wrest the gun from her hands before she fired.

"Please," she begged them again. "Just let me die."

"We'll get you help," Mark promised. "It will be better."

She shook her head, weeping pitifully. "It will never be better." Sirens sounded in the distance, and Mark realized that Miss Eugenia must have reached the county sheriff's office. "Nothing can help me," Erica was saying. "I've tried therapy, drugs, and doctors. I even tried being someone else, but the pain never leaves. It is relentless."

A Dougherty County sheriff's department vehicle screeched to a halt in the driveway. A deputy jumped out and ran toward them—his service revolver drawn.

"What's the situation, chief?" he asked Winston.

"We've got it under control," Winston replied, quietly returning his gun to its holster. "This is Erica Helms, and she needs to be taken into custody for her own protection. If you'll take her to the women's facility in Albany, I'll fax them a list of the charges. We've already read her the Miranda Statement."

The deputy stepped forward and grasped Erica firmly by the arm. "Please come with me, ma'am."

She wrenched around and spoke to Mark. "I didn't kill Molly. You can't arrest me."

"You may not be a murderer," Mark told her. "But you have broken the law enough times for us to keep you safely in jail."

Winston stepped away from Erica and turned to Mark, his eyes suspiciously wet. "Will you go with her?" he asked. "And make sure they know she needs to be on a suicide watch?'

Mark nodded. "I'll take care of her."

"Thank you," Winston said. Then with one last look at Erica, he walked to his patrol car and drove away.

CHAPTER 12

Eugenia and Kate watched from the Iversons' kitchen window as the sheriff's deputy handcuffed Ciera and loaded her into his car. They saw Mark pull his cell phone from his pocket and dial. A split second later, the kitchen phone rang.

"Mark?" Kate said into the receiver. Then she stepped down the hall to continue the conversation in privacy.

When she returned Eugenia asked, "What did he say?"

"He's going with Ciera or Erica or whatever her name is to Albany. He said he should be home in time for the rehearsal."

Eugenia nodded. "Good. I'm not sure how dependable this nonreligious rabbi of Jackson's is, and I need to have Mark in reserve."

Kate put a hand to her forehead. "What a mess. I'm glad the kids slept through it."

"Me too," Eugenia agreed. "You'd better go up and give Kelsey the good news that Brandon is innocent—just like she maintained from the start."

Kate smiled. "I'll go tell her."

"You might try to take a short nap yourself," Eugenia suggested. "It's already been a rough day, and we've still got the wedding rehearsal to go."

Kate yawned. "I might just do that. See you at seven."

Eugenia let herself out the Iversons' back door and went home. "Lady!" she called when she walked into the kitchen, but there was no bark in reply. "Let's hope you're with Brandon," she said to herself.

Then she tried to organize her thoughts—wanting to find the right words to express her condolences to her temporary yardman. As she turned back toward the door, her eyes strayed to the quadruple scripture combination on the counter. She picked it up, figuring that the book would provide her with moral support even if Brandon didn't want to hear any verses.

She found Brandon sitting on the cot in the equipment shed, which had been his home for the past few days. Lady was curled up by his feet, asleep. "I hope you don't mind that I allowed Lady to escape from the house for a while."

"I'm glad she didn't have to stay cooped up, and I know she's been good company for you," Eugenia said as Lady roused herself and walked over to join her owner. "I'm so sorry about your wife."

Brandon gave her a sad smile. "Ironically, I thought I had already lost everything of value, but now I see how precious a tiny glimmer of hope can be."

Lady whimpered in sympathy, and Eugenia clutched the scriptures, praying to know which verse might provide Brandon with the most comfort. Then she realized that for someone in Brandon's tragic circumstances, one verse would not be enough. She extended the set of scriptures that Kate and Mark had given her for Christmas toward Brandon. "I know you're not a Christian, but if you love beautiful words, you'll want to read this book."

Brandon opened the front flap and read the inscription. "It was a gift to you."

"Yes," she acknowledged around the lump in her throat. "But the print is so small I can barely read it, and I've been planning to get myself another set anyway."

He closed the book. "Thank you."

Eugenia was comforted by the knowledge that when Brandon left, he wouldn't be completely alone—he'd have the scriptures with him. "I know these last few days have been terrible," she said. "But the way I see it, the worst is over, and you have nowhere to go but up."

He considered this for a few seconds. "That's true."

"So, I guess you'll be leaving us."

"Yes, but I'll make sure the shed is in order, and I'll return your husband's clothing before I go."

Eugenia reached down and picked Lady up. "Don't worry about the shed, and I'd like for you to keep the clothes. I think Charles is pleased that they're being put to good use."

Brandon gave her a quizzical look. "You act as if he still exists."

"I believe that Charles is in heaven waiting for me."

Brandon shook his head. "I wish I could believe that Molly and our son were still . . . somewhere."

Eugenia pointed at the scriptures he held in his hands. "If you read that, you may change your mind about life after death." Then a thought occurred to her. "How will you get home?"

"Because of your munificence, I have enough money for bus fare."

Eugenia knew his earnings from the vegetable stand had been very modest, so a ticket to Wilsonville would likely take it all. "What will you do once you get there? Where will you stay?"

"You needn't be concerned about me," Brandon said sincerely. "Once the residents of Wilsonville are convinced that I didn't kill Molly, I should be able to secure part-time employment until my leave at the college ends. There was a small insurance policy on Molly, and now I can file for the benefits. The money will help me get by until I start earning a salary again."

"I'm sorry your search for Molly didn't turn out like you'd hoped." Eugenia heard voices in the yard and realized that word of Ciera's arrest had spread through town. Knowing she would probably have a steady flow of curiosity seekers dropping by for the rest of the day, and anxious to give Brandon as much privacy as possible, she took a step toward the door. "Don't leave without saying good-bye," she requested.

"I won't," he promised. "And thank you again—for everything."

"You are very welcome," she said. Then, with Lady clutched in her arms, Eugenia left the tranquility of the shed to face her neighbors and their questions.

Polly and Lucy were entertaining a group on the driveway, regaling them with details of the drama. Normally Eugenia would have wanted to involve herself so she could correct any mistakes, but today she didn't have the heart. She put Lady down and started straightening the chairs that had been shifted during the melee. After a few minutes, Kate appeared by her side.

"You decided not to take a nap?"

Kate nodded. "I'm too nervous to sleep."

"And the children?" Eugenia asked.

Kate lined a chair up beside the one Eugenia had just righted. "Travis promised to keep an eye on them."

"I'm glad you came, since I've lost most of my workforce. Mark's gone with Erica, Winston's useless, Brandon's leaving, and Sylvester's back on the phone with the state attorney general's office, bragging about solving this case. And if I don't get Polly away from her audience and inside making finger sandwiches, there won't be anything to eat after the rehearsal."

"There's Kate—she can tell us!" George Ann's strident voice carried from the driveway, and the group of inquisitive spectators started toward Kate and Eugenia.

"Heaven help us," Eugenia muttered.

Kate put a hand over her mouth to hide a smile as George Ann demanded, "Do you think that fitness woman will get the electric chair?"

"Since the state of Georgia doesn't even use the electric chair anymore, I seriously doubt it," Eugenia replied.

"Besides, Erica didn't kill anyone," Kate added.

George Ann was visibly disappointed. "Well, that's not what Polly said."

"Then Polly was mistaken," Eugenia said with conviction. "Now, are you planning to stay and help us get ready for Rosemary's wedding?"

George Ann lifted her head a notch higher and stretched her very white neck. "I would but I have a meeting for the Christian Women Supporting Foreign Missionaries in thirty minutes."

"Then go on to your meeting and take your flock of ninnies with you," Eugenia directed impatiently. "And if a single one of my flowers gets trampled in the process, I won't be responsible for my actions." After Eugenia watched the crowd disperse, she called to Polly, "Do you need me to find someone to help you finish up the refreshments for tonight?"

Polly shook her head. "No, Lucy and I have things under control."

"You'll be able to control things better from inside your kitchen than out here in my yard," Eugenia told her. "And there's no telling what you could accomplish if you quit glancing out your window trying to see what everyone else is doing."

Polly gasped. "Well, Eugenia, I'm sure I don't know what you're talking about."

"I'm sure you don't," Eugenia mumbled. She glanced around, and after assuring herself that things were in order, she turned to Kate. "Thanks for your help. Now go rest." Then she looked down at the little dog. "Come on, Lady. I'll take you inside where it's cool."

* * *

At seven thirty that evening, Eugenia and Lady were sitting on the front row of their makeshift chapel watching the sun set. Kate and Mark were right behind them, trying to entertain Emily and Charles. Polly and Lucy were at the refreshment tables, watching as the rabbi sampled all the finger foods. Annabelle stood under the rose arbor, fanning herself with a funeral program she'd found stuck in one of the white wooden chairs.

"Where are they?" Kate finally asked.

"I don't know," Eugenia replied. "I told them we were starting promptly at seven."

"Why, those young folks are a half hour late already," Lucy exclaimed as she replenished the plate of lemon bars that appeared to be the rabbi's particular favorite.

Polly pulled her handkerchief from the neckline of her floral print dress and dabbed the perspiration that had gathered along her hair-line. "You don't suppose they've had a wreck?"

Eugenia turned and studied the empty street. "I am starting to get a little worried."

"Maybe they heard about all the excitement we had here earlier and were afraid to come," Kate suggested.

Eugenia frowned. "Surely they would have at least called."

Before anyone could respond, they heard a hesitant voice call from the driveway. "Miss Eugenia?"

Eugenia turned around and saw Rosemary wearing a ragged pair of jeans and a skimpy T-shirt. She had hoped the girl would dress up a little for the rehearsal, but she was so glad she had finally arrived that she decided to overlook the thrift-store ensemble.

"Rosemary!" She walked to the end of the aisle where the girl stood. "It's getting late."

"We were afraid you'd had a wreck or something," Polly added.

Eugenia looked around, realizing that the groom was missing. "Where's Jackson?"

"He's waiting in the Jeep," Rosemary replied, twisting her hands together in a nervous gesture.

"Well, tell him to come on." Eugenia was losing her patience. Did the girl think they had nothing better to do than stand around all evening? "We've got to get this underway before the rabbi eats the entire rehearsal dinner." She pointed toward the gentleman in question, who gave them a sheepish smile.

"Um, that's what I've come to talk to you about," Rosemary said with an apprehensive glance at the other guests. "You all went to a lot of trouble, but Jackson and me, well, we've decided to go ahead and elope like we planned. We're just going to drive up to Gatlinburg tonight and get married first thing in the morning. I hope you don't mind."

Eugenia stared at the girl, speechless.

"I know my grandmother would be very grateful for what you've done. It's just that we don't feel this is right for us." She turned to the rabbi. "I'm sorry you came to this practice for nothing."

"No problem," the rabbi said with his mouth full of spinach dip. "The food is great."

Eugenia's tongue was frozen with rage.

"Do you think it would be okay for me to keep the dress?" Rosemary was continuing. "Jackson really loves it."

Eugenia tried again to speak but couldn't make a sound come out of her mouth.

Finally Annabelle walked down the aisle and took over. "Keep the dress, and we wish you good luck with your marriage."

Rosemary glanced at Eugenia—who was still staring at her. "Is Miss Eugenia mad at me?"

Annabelle took the girl by the arm and led her away. "Don't worry about Eugenia. Just enjoy your wedding trip."

Eugenia watched Annabelle load the little traitor into Jackson's muddy Jeep and didn't know who she wanted to strangle most.

Rosemary for her complete lack of consideration? Cornelia and George Ann for getting her into this whole mess to begin with? Or Annabelle for letting the girl off so easy?

Annabelle waited until their taillights disappeared into the fading light, then walked back to join the dejected assembly.

Kate sighed. "Well, I guess that's that."

Polly pulled her handkerchief from the neckline of her dress again, this time to dab at the tears leaking from her eyes. "I can't believe we made all this food for nothing."

"It's a shame, sure enough," Lucy agreed.

Eugenia narrowed her eyes. "We're not going to let everything go to waste," she said, waving to encompass the beautiful scene. "We've got to find someone to throw a wedding for."

"Eugenia!" Miss Polly cried, aghast. "We can't ask someone to get married tomorrow just because we have a wedding planned and no bride or groom."

"I don't mean we should ask someone to get married, but we could ask a married couple to renew their vows." Her eyes shifted to Kate and Mark.

"Don't look at us!" Kate said.

Mark shook his head firmly. "I don't do public displays of affection."

Annabelle laughed. "You'd better think of a better excuse than that. I seem to remember a very public kiss at the Labor Day picnic a few years ago that is now legendary."

Mark blushed. "Labor Day kisses aside, we're not renewing our vows. They're still fresh enough."

"How about Cornelia and Brother Blackwood?" Eugenia proposed.

"They just renewed their vows last year," Polly said. "Don't you remember that huge ceremony?"

"Vaguely," Eugenia admitted. "Well, there's got to be somebody."

"Kelsey and Travis could do it," Polly suggested. "I think it's so romantic that he flew all the way here from Utah just to surprise her."

Kate coughed, and Eugenia smiled. "It's perfect."

"Kelsey just had a miscarriage," Kate interjected.

"Renewing her vows would only require Kelsey to walk a few feet down a short little aisle," Eugenia pointed out. "We could check with her doctor to be sure, but I think by tomorrow morning she should be up to it."

"Who's going to ask them?" Polly wanted to know.

"I will," Eugenia volunteered.

"What if they refuse?" Annabelle asked.

Eugenia's tone was determined when she replied, "I'm not in the mood to take no for an answer."

* * *

After Miss Eugenia left to browbeat Kelsey and Travis into an impromptu second wedding, Kate looked at Mark. "What should we do now?"

Annabelle walked over to the buffet tables. "I say we should eat."

Mark stood up. "Sounds good to me," he told Kate. "If you'll help Emily with her plate, I'll help Charles with his."

Kate nodded, agreeing both to their next course of action and to the division of labor.

They were all settled in the funeral chairs eating finger foods when the back door of the Iversons' house swung open and Miss Eugenia stepped out.

"She's smiling," Annabelle remarked.

"Which means she convinced them," Kate predicted.

"It's all arranged," Miss Eugenia confirmed when she reached them. "Travis insisted that they call and get permission from Kelsey's doctor, but he didn't have any objections. They will be our guests of honor in the morning."

"I'm so glad that we have a new reason to celebrate," Miss Polly said. Then a look of concern crossed her face. "What about the guests Rosemary and Jackson invited?"

"I put Cornelia in charge of calling all the guests and informing them of the change," Eugenia replied.

"Do you think people will still come?" Miss Polly asked.

"It will be a smaller crowd, but Kelsey and Travis will probably prefer that," Miss Eugenia responded.

"And that means more food for us," Mark pointed out.

"I guess you won't need me." The rabbi sounded sad.

"No, I don't believe we will," Eugenia told him. "But it was nice to meet you."

The rabbi stood. "I'll be on my way then. And may I add that I've been to a lot of rehearsal dinners, but this food is some of the best I've ever eaten."

"Why, thank you," Miss Polly said, accepting the compliment with a girlish blush. "You should see what we can do when we're not restricted from using meat and dairy products."

The rabbi gave the food table one last longing look then waved good-bye.

"Well," Miss Polly said after the rabbi was gone. "Things are working out just fine after all."

* * *

That evening Mark volunteered to take care of the kids so Kate could spend some time with Kelsey. Once he had them in bed, he called Dr. Clements at home.

"We found Erica," he said. "She's been taken into custody."

"I know," Dr. Clements replied. "The Albany police station has already called me."

"You've been seeing her all along. That's why she built the fitness center in Haggerty—so she could be near you."

"I can't answer that," Dr. Clements said.

Mark was used to the doctor's code by now. That was a yes. "When you told me to look into the traits of sociopaths, you weren't talking about Lyle Tweedy—you were talking about Erica."

"I have no comment," Dr. Clements replied.

Mark was sure he had been correct again. "Can I ask you a hypothetical question?"

"Of course," the doctor agreed. "That's always safe."

"Okay, suppose you had a patient who had been through a terrible trauma and was, based on your clinical studies, a sociopath. Had she always been one, or did the trauma cause the condition?"

"This hypothetical patient probably always had some sociopathic tendencies—but the tragedy pushed her over the edge."

"Unlike Tweedy, Erica didn't actually kill anyone."

"No, but speaking hypothetically . . ."

"Of course," Mark consented.

"Think of the cold-bloodedness that would be required to cut someone down from a tree, change her into your clothes and jewelry, weight her body with rocks, and put it in a pond. Then to go back to her house and use the utilities for days to establish your own death on a date of your choosing. Then to bide your time until you knew that the body had decomposed beyond recognition before reporting an odor so that the body would be found." The doctor paused for a few seconds then added, "I've worked with professional assassins who didn't have that much detachment."

"A hypothetical patient like this would be institutionalized?"

"Oh, yes," the doctor agreed. "Indefinitely."

"Molly Vance might have chosen the easier route."

"Easier," the doctor agreed. "But not necessarily better. New drugs are discovered every day. Eventually some type of medication might help Erica. Molly Vance removed all hope."

"Well, I've taken up enough of your time. Maybe we'll meet again someday—under better circumstances."

"Good-bye, Agent Iverson," Dr. Clements responded, then he hung up the phone.

* * *

Kate sat beside the bed in the guest room and watched Kelsey sleep. Finally Kelsey opened her eyes and asked, "Have I been asleep long?"

"A couple of hours," Kate replied.

Kelsey looked around. "Did Travis leave?"

Kate laughed. "Wild horses couldn't get him away from you. He's just down the hall taking a shower."

Kelsey smiled. "He's been wonderful about everything. I know I don't deserve his forgiveness, but I'm so glad he wants to work through our problems."

Kate patted her sister's hand. "Me too."

Kelsey pushed up into a sitting position and swung her legs over the side of the bed. "I think I'll get up for a little while so I'll be ready to walk down the aisle in the morning."

"Please don't feel obligated to be our substitute bride," Kate said. "If we have to cancel the wedding, Miss Eugenia will get over it, eventually."

"I want to do it." Kelsey glanced at the door then continued in hushed tones. "I'm hoping that if I pledge my love and commitment in public, it will be more convincing."

"I understand, but promise me that in the morning, if you're not feeling up to the whole ordeal . . ."

"I'll let you know." Kelsey held up her right arm. "I swear."

Before Kate could respond, the door opened, and Travis stepped inside. The expression on his face brightened when he saw Kelsey. "It's good to see you up and moving around."

"I'm feeling much stronger," she said with a reassuring smile. Then she walked back to the bed and sat on the edge.

"Would you like something to eat?" Kate offered. "Miss Polly sent rehearsal dinner leftovers home with me." She turned to Travis. "I can't guarantee that the food is healthy, but it is meat free."

Travis smiled. "I'm sure it will be fine. Kelsey and I have talked about that, and we're going to compromise on what we eat."

Kate nodded her approval. "I think that compromise is the key to a happy marriage—whether you're dealing with food preferences or more serious issues."

"Travis, hurry and get us some of that rehearsal food before Kate launches into a full-blown lecture," Kelsey requested with a wink at her sister.

"And after all I've done for you," Kate said in mock reproach. "Come on, Travis. Let's go get my ungrateful sister something to eat."

When she had her guests fed, Kate went into the master bedroom, where Mark was lying on his back, staring at the ceiling.

"Where are the kids?" she asked.

"Asleep," he replied, patting her side of the bed. "Come keep me company."

She climbed up beside him. "Winston seemed so depressed this afternoon. Do you think we should call him?"

"I already have," Mark surprised her by saying. "It may take some time, but he'll be okay."

"I want to strangle Erica for hurting Winston like that," she said, her fists clenched. "But the crazy thing is that I feel sorry for her too."

Mark nodded. "Erica's been through more than any one person should be expected to bear. She deserves your sympathy."

"Brandon's been through just as much, but he didn't hurt anyone," Kate pointed out.

"Yes, I'd say that Brandon Vance is a prime example of enduring well." Mark put his arm around Kate's shoulders. "You said at the beginning that you didn't think anyone could ever really recover from the loss of their entire family. Obviously Erica didn't recover. She's insane and if I'd realized that sooner, I could have solved this case days ago."

"Don't feel too bad," Kate teased. "After all, you are only a man."

He gave her a quick, hard kiss and said, "So how's Kelsey?"

Kate sighed. "Better. She and Travis are trying to compromise."

"Have they come to terms with the miscarriage?"

Kate considered this and shook her head. "I don't think they're even trying to deal with that yet. Right now they are just concentrating on each other and preparing for their wedding tomorrow."

He gave her shoulders a squeeze and said, "I hope you didn't mind that I declined the opportunity for us to be the vow-renewing couple, but I've already married you twice, and I figure that's enough."

Kate looked into his soft brown eyes. "You confirm your vows to me every day through your actions. I don't need a public declaration."

He cupped her chin with his hand. "Marrying you was the smartest thing I ever did."

"That is so true," she agreed.

* * *

On Saturday the weather was unseasonably mild with significant cloud cover. The ceremony began promptly at ten o'clock. The bride was pale but serene and beautiful. She wore a cream-colored suit from Miss Corrine's that had been delivered personally by the store's owner earlier that morning. In her hands she clutched the bouquet of Eugenia's award-winning roses.

Kelsey walked down the aisle created by two rows of pansies toward her groom, who stood under the flower-encrusted arbor.

Travis beamed with pride and admiration as he watched his wife's graceful approach. When she reached him, he bent down and kissed her tenderly, then they took their positions in front of the small crowd. The bride and groom exchanged vows they had written themselves. Then Lucy's son Tyrone sang "Amazing Grace" while Cornelia Blackwood accompanied him on Eugenia's piano.

"Everything was lovely," Annabelle praised as she and Eugenia walked together toward the Iversons' house for the reception. "I thought the hymn at the end was a particularly nice touch."

"Thank you." Eugenia took credit for the whole event. "However, I won't take responsibility for the music at the reception. I heard that Cornelia's daughter is going to sing."

"Isn't that little girl tone deaf?" Annabelle asked. Eugenia nodded as Whit came up behind them.

"Who's tone deaf?" Whit asked.

"Cornelia's daughter, and she's singing at the reception," Eugenia informed him.

"I wish I had a hearing aid I could turn down," Whit teased.

"Be careful what you ask for," Eugenia warned. "You'll probably be needing one soon."

When they reached the Iversons', Eugenia went to the kitchen to make sure everything was running smoothly there, but Polly sent her right back out. "Lucy and I are in charge of the food," she reminded Eugenia as she escorted her to the door. "Go sit down and visit with the guests. If I need your help—I know where to find you."

Kate saw her standing by the kitchen door and asked, "What's the matter?"

Eugenia shook her head. "Polly just kicked me out of the kitchen."

Kate laughed. "That's a *good* thing. Try to enjoy yourself for a change."

Eugenia fixed herself a plate of food and found Whit sitting with Mark and Annabelle on the back porch. "What are you doing out here?" she asked them. "The whole point of having the reception inside was to make use of air conditioning."

"It's not hot here in the shade," Annabelle replied.

"I suppose," Eugenia said, taking the empty seat beside Whit.

"The weather couldn't be any better if you placed an order," Whit told her.

"Actually, I did," Eugenia admitted. "I asked the Lord to give us cool temperatures, a breeze, and some cloud cover."

"Only Eugenia would dare to give the Lord such a specific request," Annabelle said, shaking her head.

"Only Miss Eugenia and the brother of Jared," Mark added.

"Who?" Whit asked.

Eugenia smiled. "Never mind—it's an inside joke." Then she turned to Annabelle. "And how is the Lord going to know what you want if you don't ask?"

Before Annabelle could respond, Winston walked up onto the deck. He was wearing his uniform, so Eugenia wasn't sure if he was attending the wedding or was there on official business. But she decided to welcome him warmly either way.

"Winston!" She put her plate of food aside and gave him a quick hug. "We're so glad you could make it."

"I'm okay, Miss Eugenia," he replied. "Don't make a fuss."

"I declare," Eugenia said as she returned to her seat. "Since when is telling someone hello making a fuss?"

Winston pulled a chair over next to Mark and announced, "Dub Shaw's house burned to the ground last night."

Eugenia gasped. "And it couldn't have been Erica since . . ."

Winston nodded, sparing her from completing the sentence. "I figure it was started by one of the hundreds of extension cords he had strewn around that place—but it was definitely an accident."

"What will Dub do now?" Annabelle asked.

"He'll be moving into an assisted living facility in Albany on Monday."

Eugenia immediately realized that this was going to create a problem. "So who will finish painting the lobby at the police station?"

Winston shrugged. "I guess I'll have to hire somebody."

"I know you don't have the budget for that, and I feel responsible," Eugenia began, but Whit reached over and patted her hand.

"I'd like to take care of it," he told Winston.

"Why?" the police chief asked.

Whit winked at Eugenia and said, "Public service projects are good for business."

Winston frowned. "You've got more business than you need already. It's time for you to retire."

Whit didn't dispute this. "So my children keep telling me."

Eugenia sighed. "We're getting old."

Winston scooted his chair a couple of inches closer to Mark's. "I've got a few questions about Ciera." He blushed then cleared his throat. "I mean Erica. I wondered if you'd mind answering them."

"I'll try," Mark agreed. "Why don't we go somewhere else, so we won't dampen the mood here." He started to stand, but Eugenia stopped him.

"No!" she commanded. Then in a more gentle tone added, "We're all interested in Winston's questions."

Winston took a deep breath then began. "How did she get the idea to fix things so that it looked like Lyle Tweedy had killed her?"

"I don't know for sure," Mark replied. "But Lyle Tweedy had been front-page news for weeks. She had a body and needed a murderer. He was the obvious choice."

"She must have studied Tweedy and his murders."

Mark nodded. "I'm sure she did. She bought herself time by making it seem that Molly Vance was still alive. During that time she found out what Tweedy looked like and then called the sheriff's office and said that she had seen someone who matched that description around Patton Chapel."

"And since Molly Vance hung herself, her death looked like strangulation," Winston guessed.

"And because Foster Gunnells was in love with Erica, it was easy for her to manipulate him—even after her 'death.' It was a good plan," Mark conceded. "And she would have gotten away with it, except for Lyle Tweedy."

"The Lord works in mysterious ways," Eugenia reminded them as Kate walked out onto the porch. She sat on the arm of Mark's chair, and he put his arm around her to provide back support.

"Hey, Winston," she said.

He tipped his head. "Kate."

"Get yourself something to eat," she encouraged. "Miss Polly has enough meat-free food to feed an army."

Winston shook his head. "Thanks, but I'm not hungry." He turned to Mark. "Haggerty has been invited to participate in the county fall softball league, and the guys were wondering if you'd like to play on our team."

Mark thought for a minute then said, "It would have to be understood from the start that I don't practice or play on Sunday."

Winston nodded. "Understood."

Mark smiled. "Then I'd like to play."

The back door swung open again, and Kelsey emerged. Travis was right behind her.

"Well, here's the lovely bride!" Whit exclaimed gallantly. "And her lucky groom."

Travis pulled his wife into a delicate embrace. "I think she's even more beautiful this time than the first time we got married."

Kelsey blushed with pleasure. "Remind me to make you an appointment to have your eyes checked when we get back to Salt Lake," she teased.

"You shouldn't be standing," Mark said. "Let me get you a chair."

"She can have mine." Winston stood. "I've got to get going." He turned to Mark. "I'll get back in touch with you about the softball league." Then with a wave to the group, the police chief walked down the deck stairs and back to his police car.

Kelsey sat gingerly in the chair Winston had vacated, and Travis stood behind her.

"Poor Winston," Kate said.

Eugenia sighed. "Maybe someday the right girl will come along."

Annabelle turned to Kelsey. "How are you feeling?"

"Much better," Kelsey replied.

"When are you flying home?"

"I'd like to stay until after Molly Vance's funeral." Kelsey looked over her shoulder at Travis. "Which Brandon said will be sometime this week. Can you miss that much work, or do you need to go on home and let me follow later?"

"I'll wait for you," Travis replied.

Kelsey smiled. "Thank you . . ."

"I think it's wonderful for you to go and support Brandon," Eugenia said. "In fact, I might ride along if you don't mind."

"We'd be glad to have you," Kelsey said graciously. "In fact, it will give me an opportunity to talk to you about working for my business."

Eugenia's heart pounded. "You want me to help you with your investigations?"

Kelsey nodded. "I'm great with computers, but I don't deal very well with people. You, on the other hand, are a first-rate interrogator. Some of my cases don't require any personal contact, but for the ones that do, I thought I could pay you a commission."

"I don't know what to say," Eugenia whispered.

"I'll understand if you don't have time," Kelsey said, qualifying her offer.

"I have time," Eugenia assured her. "And I'd love to help you investigate."

Kelsey smiled. "Good. We'll talk more on our drive to Wilsonville, but one of the first things we'll need to do is get you a computer so we can e-mail."

"E-mail?" Eugenia breathed. "On my own computer?"

"Well, For Your Information will purchase the computer," Kelsey corrected. "But it will be set up at your house."

"So I'm official?" Eugenia confirmed.

Kelsey nodded. "You are now an employee of my company."

"Heaven help us," Annabelle said. "As if she wasn't insufferable enough already."

"What do you mean by that?" Eugenia demanded.

"Oh, I almost forgot," Kelsey interjected before a fight could develop. She pulled a piece of paper from her husband's back pocket and handed it to Eugenia. "Here's what I came up with for your trip to Hawaii."

Eugenia reviewed the figures quickly. "It's still expensive," she murmured.

Annabelle gave the numbers a glance. "You'll never be able to do better than that. I recommend that you make your reservations immediately."

The discussion was interrupted at this point by the arrival of Sylvester Muck—wearing his conservative JC Penney suit.

"Well, Sylvester!" Eugenia cried, genuinely pleased to see the young man. "I thought you'd be back in Atlanta by now—receiving all kinds of praise for solving the case of the century."

Sylvester smiled. "Fortunately for me, the century is still young. And I am headed back in a little while, but I wanted to talk to Mark first."

Eugenia raised an eyebrow. "Mark is a popular man today."

"I think you just wanted some of Miss Polly's finger foods," Kate teased.

"That too," Sylvester admitted with a smile. Then he turned to Mark. "The attorney general's office has a deal to offer you."

Mark raised both eyebrows. "A deal?"

"My office wants to take responsibility for sorting out the interrelated cases of Molly Vance, Erica Helms, and Lyle Tweedy."

Mark smiled. "I'll gladly relinquish control," he said.

Sylvester looked a little uncomfortable as he said, "The attorney general also wants credit for solving the case."

"You *did* solve the case," Mark reminded him. "And you were officially assigned to review it. I was officially told to leave it alone."

"So you don't mind?" Sylvester confirmed.

"I'm grateful," Mark assured him.

"Good." Sylvester sounded pleased. Then he turned to Miss Eugenia. "And now for my last item of business. There was a reward for information leading to the discovery of Molly Vance's whereabouts. Brandon and I both agree that Miss Eugenia should receive it."

"Me?" Eugenia was shocked. "Why would I get the reward?"

"Because you offered Brandon a job and kept him in town. You convinced Winston to let me stay at the police station, and you introduced us to Ciera. Without your help, we never would have figured it out."

"Brandon should have the money," Eugenia said. "He needs it."

"He won't take it," Sylvester replied. "He thinks it would be unethical, and I agree. But he said that knowing you were rewarded would give him great tranquility or something like that. You know how crazy he talks."

"I declare," was all Eugenia could say.

"How much is it?" Annabelle wanted to know.

Sylvester handed Eugenia a piece of paper and pointed to a number. "There's the total."

For the first time in her life, Eugenia was afraid she might faint. "Are you sure this isn't a joke?"

Sylvester shook his head. "No, ma'am. There might be some withholding for taxes and stuff, but it will be somewhere around that."

Eugenia put a hand to her chest and said, "Well, folks, start packing your bags. We're all going to Hawaii, and we're going first class!"

* * *

As the reception was winding down, Mark took the children upstairs to change out of their Sunday clothes. The phone rang, and Mark answered it automatically.

"From what I hear, congratulations are in order," Jack Gamble said.

Mark held the phone in the crook of his neck while helping Emily to unbutton her dress. "The case is solved, but the state attorney general's office has taken it over, so I'm completely out of the loop."

"I guess that means you won't share in the glory," Jack commented.

"I don't want any of the glory," Mark assured him.

"We'll be home next week."

"That's good news. I'll tell Kate," Mark replied. "And I'm glad I won't be getting any more wrong numbers."

Jack laughed. "Yeah, they can be such a nuisance."

"Give us a call when you get back home, and we'll all go out to dinner at Aristotle's."

"Now that's an offer I can't refuse. I'll be in touch."

Mark hung up the phone, and Emily asked, "Who was that, Daddy?"

"Just a friend," he said. "Now let's go get Charles. Then we'll lie down on my bed and watch a video."

"Did Mom tell you to make us take a nap?" Emily asked.

Mark gazed into her eyes—so much like her mother's—and knew he couldn't trick her. "Yes."

Emily nodded. "I won't tell Charles, or he'll cry."

"Thanks. And to reward you for your cooperation, I'll let you pick the video," Mark said as they walked together into the master bedroom.

* * *

Eugenia took Lady inside that night after the festivities were over and her yard was returned to somewhat normal. "In all the excitement over my reward money, I forgot to thank Whit for getting Jackson a tuxedo," she told the little dog. "So I think I'll call him."

Lady barked her encouragement as Eugenia picked up the phone. She dialed Whit's number, and after several rings, his answering machine picked up. She replaced the receiver, feeling silly. "He's not home," she said. "It was ridiculous of me to think that a handsome man like Whit would be sitting around on a Saturday night. He's probably got a date."

Lady whimpered, and Eugenia smiled at her.

"Don't worry about me, girl. I'm perfectly happy on my own." Eugenia poured some of the specially formulated dog food from the veterinarian's office into Lady's bowl. "Now let's see what my choices are." She opened the cupboard. "We have chicken noodle soup or chunky beef stew." Neither sounded very appealing, and Eugenia was still trying to make a decision when she heard a knock on the front door. "That's probably Cornelia and George Ann or the Jehovah's Witnesses," she said to Lady. "Based on recent experience, I'm hoping for the Jehovah's Witnesses." She closed the cupboard, picked up the dog, and walked to the front of the house. She opened the door and found Whit Owens standing on her porch.

"Why, Whit, what are you doing knocking on the front door?" she asked. "Don't you know that friends come in through the back?"

He gave her one of his most charming smiles then straightened his tie. "I was taught that when you wanted to impress a lady you're supposed to dress up, go to her front door, and give her a gift." He held up a little jar of blackberry jelly. "I made it myself."

She took the jar and examined it closely. "There's a number one written on the label," she commented. "I suppose that means this is your first batch."

"Yes, since I've perfected pound cake, I decided to branch off into something else for a challenge."

"And you picked jelly?"

He nodded. "Would you taste that and see if it's any good?"

She narrowed her eyes at him. "You know I won't lie to spare your feelings."

He smiled at her. "That's what I'm counting on."

Lady barked, and Eugenia laughed, pushing the door open wide. "Come on in."

HAGGERTY HOSPITALITY

MISS EUGENIA'S POTATO SOUP
1 pint half-and-half
1 can cream of celery soup
1 (8 oz.) carton sour cream
1 block (8-oz.) pepper jack cheese
2 cans chicken broth
1 can cream of onion soup
4 lbs. Idaho potatoes, peeled and cubed

Cook potatoes in chicken broth until tender (not hard). Grate cheese and add it to potatoes (do *not* drain); stir until melted. Add soups, half-and-half, and sour cream. Cook on low temperature, stirring often to prevent sticking. Cook until hot and serve immediately.

LUCY'S SPINACH DIP
1 (10-oz.) pkg. frozen spinach
1 pkg. Knorr vegetable soup mix
1 cup mayonnaise
1 (8-oz.) carton sour cream
1 can water chestnuts (chopped)
2 Tbs. onion, chopped

Mix all ingredients and chill for several hours before serving. Serve with crackers or chips or as a spread for finger sandwiches.

MISS POLLY'S LEMON MERINGUE PIE

1 (9-in.) baked pie shell
1/2 cup lemon juice
4 Tbs. cornstarch
1 lemon rind, grated
1 cup sugar; 6 Tbs. sugar
2 Tbs. butter
1 cup boiling water
4 eggs, separated
1/2 tsp. salt

Lemon filling:
In a double boiler combine cornstarch, 1 cup sugar, and boiling water. Cook, stirring constantly, until mixture thickens. Add salt, lemon juice, and grated rind; continue cooking and stirring until blended. Beat egg yolks until they are light yellow. Pour cooked mixture over egg yolks, stirring constantly. Return mixture to double boiler and cook for 4 minutes. Add butter and blend well. Remove from heat and let the mixture cool. Then pour it into pie shell.

Meringue:
Beat egg whites until very stiff. Gradually add 6 tablespoons of sugar. Beat until it peaks. Spread over lemon mixture completely to the edges. Bake for 15 minutes at 325°F.

MISS POLLY'S WEDDING RECEPTION PUNCH

1 pkg. Kool-Aid lemonade
1-gal. freezer bag
2 cups sugar
1 large can pineapple juice
1 quart water
2 liters ginger ale

Mix Kool-Aid, sugar, and water well. Pour into freezer bag and freeze for at least 48 hours. Ginger ale and pineapple juice should be cold when preparing punch. Remove frozen mixture from freezer 30 minutes before serving. Mash bag until contents are slushy and put it in punch bowl. Add ginger ale and juice. Stir, and serve immediately.

WHIT'S PERFECT POUND CAKE

3 sticks real butter
1 (8-oz.) pkg. cream cheese
3 cups sugar
6 eggs
3 cups cake flour
1/4 tsp. salt
2 tsp. vanilla

Soften cream cheese and butter, then cream. Add sugar and mix well (about 5 minutes). Add eggs 1 at a time, mixing well after each addition. Add salt and vanilla, then add flour 1 cup at a time—mix sparingly (just until blended). Pour into greased and floured pound cake pan, and bake at 350°F for 1 hour and 15 minutes.

MISS POLLY'S LEMON SQUARES

Crust:
1 1/2 cups butter (melted)
3 cups flour
3/4 cup powdered sugar

Mix together and press into the bottom of a jelly roll pan. Bake at 350°F for 20 minutes.

Lemon Filling:
6 eggs
3 cups sugar
1 Tbs. lemon juice
1/2 cup flour
1/2 tsp. baking powder
1/4 tsp. salt

Mix together and pour over the crust. Bake at 350°F for 25 additional minutes. Let cool.

Glaze:
2 2/3 cups powdered sugar
1 cup butter (melted)
3 Tbs. lemon juice

Mix and spread over the top, then cut into squares.

OLD-FASHIONED TEA CAKES

2 sticks butter (softened)
2 cups sugar
4 eggs
2 tsp. baking powder
1/2 tsp. baking soda
1/2 tsp. salt
1 tsp. vanilla
1/4 cup milk
7 cups all-purpose flour

Cream butter and sugar; add eggs 1 at a time. Sift dry ingredients with 1 cup of flour and add. Add milk and remaining flour until dough reaches the proper consistency. Roll out onto floured board and cut into circles. Place on a cookie sheet and bake at 375°F until light brown.

ABOUT THE AUTHOR

BETSY BRANNON GREEN currently lives in Bessemer, Alabama, which is a suburb of Birmingham. She has been married to her husband, Butch, for twenty-five years, and they have eight children. She loves to read—when she can find the time—and watch sporting events—if they involve her children. She is the Young Women president in the Bessemer Ward. Although born in Salt Lake City, Betsy has spent most of her life in the South, and her writing has been strongly influenced by the Southern hospitality she has experienced there. Her first book, *Hearts in Hiding,* was published in 2001, followed by *Never Look Back* (2002), *Until Proven Guilty* (2002), *Don't Close Your Eyes* (2003), *Above Suspicion* (2003), *Foul Play* (2004), and *Silenced* (2004).

If you would like to be updated on Betsy's newest releases or correspond with her, please send an e-mail to info@covenant-lds.com. You may also write to her in care of Covenant Communications, P.O. Box 416, American Fork, UT 84003-0416.